Praise for Andy Remic

"Loud, brash and so in-your-face that it's actually gone right through and is stood behind you, giving you a good kicking when you least expect it."

Graeme's Fantasy Book Review on Biohell

"Hard-hitting, galaxy-spanning, no-holds-barred, old-fashioned action adventure."

The Guardian on War Machine

"If you're looking for something that mixes the sensibilities of Blackadder and an Iron Maiden album cover, with a pinch of vintage 2000 AD thrown in, then look no further... Penetrating insights into the human condition? Not really. Characters pondering their destinies? Hardly. Ballsy, hilariously over-the-top SF entertainment? Absolutely."

Financial Times on Cloneworld

"Remic is a deliberately provocative writer, ripping the heart out of standard space opera and stuffing it back down its own throat. There's even some satire thrown in."

Total Sci-Fi Online on Cloneworld

A NOVEL OF THE ANARCHY
THEME PLANET
ANDY REMIC

SOLARIS

First published 2011 by Solaris
an imprint of Rebellion Publishing Ltd,
Riverside House, Osney Mead,
Oxford, OX1 0ES, UK

www.solarisbooks.com

ISBN: 978 1 907992 10 0

10 9 8 7 6 5 4 3 2 1

A CIP catalogue record for this book is available from the
British Library.

Designed & typeset by Rebellion Publishing

Printed in the UK

Theme Planet *is dedicated to Philip Kindred Dick.*
Dude, you're the reason I started writing SF...
And I wish I had an electric sheep!

And the LORD GOD planted
like, a garden, Eastward in Eden;
and there he put the man dude
whom he had formed. And
out of the ground made the
LORD GOD bro to grow every fizzy tree and weed that is
pleasant to the sight, man,
and all good for food and smoking and stuff;
the tree of life also in the midst of the
garden of the Eden, and the tree of
knowledge, and of the worldshell and, like, good and evil.
Dude.

NEW GENESIS 2: 8-9
The Revised & Rewritten Old Testament
BIBLE II: THE REMIX

PROLOGUE
HIT

CHAINS CLANKED.

Three thousand people sat in bright-eyed anticipation, knuckles white, teeth clenched, gasps gasping. Sunlight defined a glittering broad canvas, as big as the world. A subtle breeze ripe with vegetation caressed the graceful, mechanical ascent. There was a background of excited chatter, a *hum* of anticipation and energy.

Eventually, the climb ended a full *five kilometres* up. The world, the theme park, the *Theme Planet,* spread before the assembled ride freaks, colourful, and awesome, and vast.

To the left, fields of dancing pastel flowers jigged in the wind.

To the right, mountains of obsidian sat like majestic dragon's teeth, quiescent, waiting, glittering.

Ahead, amidst gleaming oiled bodies, jewels sparkled on a turquoise sea crested with foam.

There came a hiatus:

A long moment of peace, and serenity, a pause for thought, a moment to study one's own wisdom in these things; one's own mortality; one's own longevity; one's own connection to God.

Then there came a *bang,* a *clank,* a lurch... and a sudden, violent drop into infinity and oblivion below...

Followed by a three thousand screams as everybody waved their hands in the air.

THE BITTER MOUNTAIN wind ruffled Amba Miskalov's tight jacket. Pine scent filled her nostrils, the rich perfume of the forest. Slowly, she reached behind herself and tied her shoulder-length blonde hair into a pony-tail, then placed ski-goggles over her eyes and checked her twin silenced 9mm Heckler & Koch P7 pistols.

She moved through the red pine forest like a black ghost, halting by her skis. She glanced down the savage slope through mist and gloom, which dropped away into vastness and darkness beyond, more dangerous than any tourist ski-run. It was a scoop out of the mountainside. It was the mountain, mocking humanity with an impossible thrill.

She laid the skis delicately on the snow, and stepped in with tiny *clicks.*

It's time, whispered Zi, her FRIEND, in the back of her mind, and Amba held a hand to her breast where the FRIEND lay absorbed, and *felt* her presence, like an oil cloud muddling her thoughts, a machine spirit reading her mind... before Zi shifted phase, and seemed to fade. In Amba's coat, against her heart, she felt the hard metal of Zi under her skin and her eyes narrowed. No. Zi would not leave; could not. Not now. Not ever.

Especially when it was time for the *kill.*

Amba pushed off, elbows tucked in tight, and gave a small gasp as gravity took her in its fist and threw her down the mountain. In near-darkness she flitted through the snowy forest, trees slamming by to either side in an insane drug-blur, a game of reflex and courage and skill. Amba banked left – right – left, jumped a small embankment and sailed ten feet before touching down lightly and shifting almost imperceptibly right, skimming a tree with inches to spare, cold wind biting her, the forest absorbing her, and a distant owl hooting as if to mark her impossible passage.

Through the dark forest Amba flew, on a course almost pre-programmed in her skull from the previous day's reconnoitre. But here, and now, this was no trial run. This was real, it was painful and pain *giving;* this was life and death.

Skis hissed on snow as the forest breathed around her. Cold air bit tiny triangles of exposed flesh. Adrenaline pumped. And then Amba saw the base flashing towards her, twin high watchtowers and an ominous smooth black wall topped with coils of razor wire.

Amba shifted her stance again, brain calculating fast, Zi allowing her to do her job. Pine branches whipped her. She ducked fast under a low bough that would have removed her head. In a flicker of ghostly white, she saw her target – a mound of banked snow. Her eyes shifted, gauging, and she was satisfied. Satisfied? If it didn't work, she'd be dead, and nothing would matter.

She hit the mound at speed and sailed out over the abyss. Swiftly, she scanned for enemies. Counted eleven on the ground. Heavily armed. Machine gun nests in towers. She drew a P7, and a silenced shot spat through the night, single bullet exploding a watchtower guard's head in a mushroom of brain slop and shattered skull shards. She shifted, and a second shot neutralised the second tower's machine gunner with a hiss and a crack and a dull slap.

Still the guards on the ground had not spotted her; were not aware of her existence. Several were standing round a glowing brazier, warming gloved hands. Several more were patrolling the perimeter, machine guns lowered. Amba, her airborne arc beginning a descent, shifted her weight back and reached down towards her skis, angling herself for the five guards hovering beside the barrel of coals. One looked up, and his mouth opened in shock as Amba detached the binding on her left ski. The sharpened ski flew like an arrow, entering the guard's open mouth, ski-tip exploding from the rear of his head in a tangle of bone and hair. He hit the ground at the same time as Amba, who whirled around, her second ski lifted in gloved hands and slammed like a sword at the four men. The ski hacked left, razor-edge decapitating a man, then right, slicing another from collarbone to hip in a whistling diagonal cut. Shouts echoed, surreal and detached. Cold breath plumed like smoke. Gunshots rattled as if through honey; through a decadent dream.

Stunned, the two remaining guards lifted weapons, stepping forward as realisation gripped their brains in its claws and forced them into stuttering action. Amba dropped the ski blade and leapt, right hand slamming the man on the right in the throat. He staggered back, coughing, as the other guard opened fire and Amba twisted, stepped back, and slammed the weapon down, ploughing bullets into frozen earth; she grabbed his hair and rammed his head into the brazier. The coals sizzled and he screamed and thrashed, but she held him there until he went still. When she eventually let go, she drew twin P7s and focused on the six patrolling guards – three groups of two – who had now noticed her arrival.

Neat, said Zi.

Fuck off and let me work.

Well, you know, if you need a hand...

From you, bitch, I will never need a hand. Just remember why you're here, why we're linked, and keep your damn thoughts to yourself.

The guards were shouting and pointing, and their comrade's hair was on fire, face a mass of bubbling melted flesh as he flopped back limp from the brazier. They growled and opened fire, bullets whining, tracer flashing, kicking up earth and ripping into the gurgling figure whose windpipe Amba had crushed. Amba dropped to one knee and both P7s fired, methodically, systematically, bullets slapping across the killing ground and sending guards sprawling. Two down. Four down, machine gun bullets eating the night sky. Amba rolled right, and the final guards were charging towards her, faces grim under black matt helmets, eyes furious, guns levelled. Machine gun bullets ate across the frozen soil, and several *pinged* from the brazier behind her. Coolly, Amba dropped the spent mags from her weapons and slotted in fresh ammo. A bullet scraped past her arm, slicing the flesh; another grazed her neck, nicking her skin with a lover's bite. And they were there, huge men, heavily muscled, towering over her as she suddenly stood and flipped backwards, landing in a crouch, and two *pops* and a disintegration of lips and teeth and tongues and brain-mush beyond signified the end of the guards. They carried on running, out of sheer weight and momentum, passing Amba on either side before they finally hit the dirt on their destroyed faces.

Amba stood slowly and conducted a quick scan of the courtyard, where cobbles lay rimed in ice. She looked to the far doorway, the edges lit from within, and kicked into a fast sprint, stopping to one side of the portal. She reached out and flung open the heavy oak door, and machine gun fire screamed, opening the night like a zip.

It would seem they spotted you, soothed Zi in her mind, easing in there like cream into coffee, smelling the kill, the promise of the kill, and the need to take possession. The need to take control and... break free. Have some fun.

Focused and unwilling to chat, Amba grunted and rolled across the opening in a quick blur, loosing one shot down the corridor. The guard behind his mounted HMG fell hard and slid across the terracotta tiled floor.

They should give you a medal...

Will you SHUT UP!

Amba appeared silhouetted against the night and drifted along the cold tiles. She reached an intersection and paused, listening, recalling the layout of the facility. She eased up a tight spiral staircase, both P7 pistols before her, but met no more guards. There *were* more, though; there were always more.

She reached the top. Another corridor, dimly lit. At the end, she knew, was her target. She stopped, and looked around the corridor. She shrugged, and strode forwards, and her acute hearing detected the hiss of gas. Still she walked, and the hissing increased and now she spotted the nozzles set in the ceiling, could see a vapour easing free. No doubt some terrible toxin. Some violent and deadly poison.

Amba glanced up with interest, and walked on.

She stopped by the door, which was reinforced with steel. It was large, and heavy, and she took a deep breath and a step back, and front-kicked the door from its hinges and locks with a screeching groan of tortured steel. The door clattered across the room and half-crushed a large oak desk into firewood. Amba stepped inside and stared at the shocked man, seated to one side behind the part-obliterated desk and aiming a pistol at her. He fired and she twitched, a bullet whining past her head. Another shot spun towards her on a column of hot gas, and again Amba shifted so subtly she hardly appeared to move, and the bullet passed between arm and flank, making a dull *thunk* in the rich wood panelling lining the room. Amba dropped, and a small black knife appeared in hand from her boot. The knife whined, sticking in the man's shoulder, and he cried out, fingers twitching spasmodically, forcing him to drop the gun.

Amba walked forward carefully, eyes scanning the room.

"Where is it?"

"I don't know what you're talking about."

Mid-stride, she drew a second knife from an inverted chest-sheath and leapt onto the flattened, armoured door, walking up to stand on the table, towering over the man.

"One more chance."

"I have absolutely no idea..."

"Have it your way," she said, face neutral.

AFTER THE SCREAMS, the whimpers, the pleading and the dying were done, Amba stepped from the smashed doorway carrying a small black case. She wiped a stray droplet of blood from her cheek and pulled free a tiny alloy ECube, which unfolded like a blood-dark flower in her small hand. It had the appearance of something extremely delicate and technologically advanced; in reality, it was very, very *tough* and technologically advanced.

"Maul, I need that airlift."

"Fifteen minutes, Amba," came his friendly bear-rumble. "I'll grab you from the south tower."

Five minutes later she climbed the stairs to the tower, eyeing her recent handiwork. The tower guard was slumped back against the wall, one arm thrown over his head, a bullet hole in one cheek, the back of his skull decorating the rough stones like *Maju* art. He looked strangely at peace, and Amba crouched by him, staring into glassy eyes.

"Was it worth it?" she asked.

Is it ever worth it? mocked Zi. *Come on Amba, time to move. Next, you'll be giving the fucker a bedtime kiss!*

Amba climbed onto the narrow ledge, glancing at the vast drop to the rough earth and cobbles below. She leaned back, clipped the briefcase to her belt, hooked her fingers onto the ice-slippery tiles, swung out over the abyss, legs dangling, and hauled herself onto the steep slope with a grunt. Slowly, stooped, she walked up to the apex and stood, boots planted on the ice, surveying the land around her and the decimated base beneath. Snow-peppered forests spread off in every direction for fifty klicks, and Amba stood like a Queen surveying her Night Realm, head held high, eyes bright. Too bright. Almost as if they glinted with unshed tears.

Her ECube buzzed. "Three minutes," came Maul's rumble. "Did you bring the... General with you?"

"No, I'm... alone," said Amba. "He didn't make it."

"*Shit,* Amba. You were supposed to bring him in alive!"

"He had a different agenda."

"Romero's gonna go *fucking* crazy, man."

"He'll have to go crazy, then, won't he?"

She killed the transmission and breathed deep. Below, eleven corpses decorated the snow and ice-flecked earth. Even from this distance, Amba could see fresh bullet-chips in the stone. No doubt the Earth's Oblivion Investigators, and the Ministers of Joy, would read the battle and understand exactly what she was. And of what she was capable. But then, they'd created her, so they shouldn't fucking complain.

Maul's words came back to her: *Romero's gonna go fucking crazy, man.*

And as the Manta hummed low over distant forest, smashing through the night with rotors thumping and jets burning, so Amba smiled again, and gave a small nod. She would take any punishment without comment. For an Anarchy Android, an engineered human, an engineered *killer* and servant to the Ministers of Joy, this was simply expected.

Androids had no right of appeal.

THE MONOLITH CORPORATION™

<u>Official Advertisement</u>

AUDIO [deep male voice – think Clinty Eastwood]:
*The Monolith Corporation™ in association with Earth's OBLIVION
Government presents,
A THEME PLANET™ Production!*

VIDEO [close up]:
A man dressed in colourless, shapeless clothing. This man is a
bland and colourless *human*. He is bowed with age, face wrinkled
and worn by the ravages of time. The dude is defeated and...
queuing... what he is queuing for is not quite clear, but the old bro
is queuing and the queue is a long one; a very long one – *[camera
pulls back/smooth tracking shot]*. The queue is an incredible and
horizon-bending vast and terrible queue! A queue to make you
sick! A queue to make you slit your wrists!

VIDEO [close-up]:
Watery blue eyes surrounded by wrinkles convey an inner
message of emptiness, frustration and despair. CUT TO: The
old man's feet shuffling forward a step, then pulling back again to
show thousands and thousands of people shuffling forward... all
by a single step.

AUDIO:
A deep and throaty sigh [followed by the deep male voice again,
think Minkles Caine]:
*Are you tired of your life? Your existence? Your age, dude, your fucking AGE?
Are you disgruntled with an eternity of pointless queuing? Like you get
in EVERY damn theme park ever created, bro?*

VIDEO [close-up]:
A nod. Resignation. Disillusionment.

AUDIO:

Are you tired of your... MOLECULES?

VIDEO:

The eyebrows lift, questioning. That old face is now full of dawning wonder, and suddenly filled with intelligence and inspiration and hope. Hope! Open, in fact, to the suggestion of a new and incredibly life-changing experience!

AUDIO:

Well dude, there's no need to be.

VIDEO:

Suddenly, this world-weary example of humanity's disintegration is disassembled, beamed through the glowing atmosphere of Theme Planet™ – and reassembled with a look of total orgasm. The old man's face is filled with *new youth*. Vitality. Eagerness. *Energy, baby, fucking energy!* He looks horny as hell.

AUDIO [song/accompanied by happy jolly music]:

It's better than drugs!
It's better than sex!
It's fun, it's fast, it's neat...
If you haven't been sick, you soon will be!
Zip through a thousand light years on... THE MOLECULE MACHINE™!

VIDEO:

Molecules swirling to form an old man's young smile.

LETTERING IN FLAMES:

Brought to you by Theme Planet™
The Theme Planet Advertising Broadcast Station (ggg)
and THE MONOLITH CORPORATION©

CHAPTER ONE

PUF

DEXTER RAN THROUGH heavy rain, pounding the New Kensington pavement, and it felt good. *Pain,* he realised, *always feels good. It tells you you're still alive. Still breathing. Still fighting. Yeah, right.*

Breathing heavy, with water dripping from his ridged brow and high cheekbones, he glanced right, checking for traffic, crossed the road – stepping in a puddle with a splash – and ducked down Canker's Alley.

Emerging onto a street clogged with QuadDecker buses farting toxins and filth, Dex turned left, jogging under a crescent of plastic trees and finally arriving at Port Square just as the rain stopped and sunlight peeped almost sheepishly from behind iron bruised clouds. Dex looked up, scowling, as steam rose from knurled alloy pavements and Auto-gutters chugged with water, gears thrashing thanks to the sudden flash downpour.

"Great," he muttered, and jogged up the steps to his apartment. His thumbprint opened the door, and he kicked off TekTek trainers in the hall, nose twitching at the smell of frying synbacon and eggy eggs. "Still. The day might improve." *Or not,* mocked his persistent internal mockery.

He climbed more steps, thighs shaking a little after the long run, and peered into the kitchen. His wife Katrina was standing at the ultra aga with a PlakFrak AutoFrying Pan. She glanced over. "Hi, hun. Just in time for breakfast. Get a little wet, did you?" There was a playful gleam in her eye and Dex scrunched his nose.

"You could say that. It's quiet. Too quiet. Have I missed the kids?"

"You're not that lucky," grinned Kat, ladling eggy eggs onto a steel plate. "They're still brushing their teeth. Come on, sit down, before it gets cold."

"I'll just pull on something dry."

Dex was back in less than a minute, and sat opposite Kat, who had a simple plate of cardboard diet toast before her. She picked up the flake and nibbled the corner.

"Why the full fry breks, love?"

Kat shrugged. "Celebrating. Last day at work, and all that. We're going to have *such* a great holiday, hun."

"Is that why you're eating... *that*."

"What?"

"That plastic shit."

"It's good for the waistline, hun."

"You should come running with me," said Dex, sucking up an eggy egg like a long cylinder of phlegm. He winked. "You'll soon drop that puppy blubber."

"Why, you cheeky..."

"Hi Dad!"

"Hi..."

"Dad, Toff says if you use mouthwash it's full of alcohol and you'll be drunk all day at school, but I said she's talking rubbish like the Trashmen of Trashworld because *you're* a PUF policeman and you use mouthwash and you're not drunk all day at the station are you, and you've got a gun, and that wouldn't work if you were a drunk policeman, would it? You'd be shooting everybody all day, wouldn't you, and that's not right for a PUF because killing people is bad no matter what they say in computer games, our teacher told us so."

"Dad, Dad, that's not what I said, what *I said was* if you swallow the mouthwash then it'll rot your guts and..."

Their whirlwind tornadoed out of the opposite door and Dex and Kat stared at one another, then burst out laughing.

"Well, shit," said Dex. "I didn't get time to even *answer,* let alone comment on the conversation."

"I think that was the point."

"Oh, yeah? The old man's viewpoint not count now, does it?"

"I suppose it does," said Kat, her eyes twinkling. She ran a hand through her short, black, spiked hair and continued to nibble card toast. "You okay with this, hun?"

"The holiday?"

"Yeah. The *Theme Planet!*"

"Sure, sure. I mean, we'll have to remortgage the damned apartment..."

"Oh come on, it isn't *that* expensive."

Dex clutched his side. "I know. Argh! I still had to sell that kidney, though..."

Kat laughed, a tinkling of crystal. "You really are a miserly old bastard," she said, standing and moving around the table to him. The table shuffled sideways on little furry feet to accommodate her. She draped her arms over his shoulders from behind, and dropped until her lips touched his ear. "But you're *my* miserly old bastard. And I still love you." She kissed his neck.

"Even after three eggy eggs?" he said.

"Even after three eggy eggs," she said, and nibbled his ear.

"What time are the kids going to school?"

She caught the tone of his voice and laughed. "Hey, you haven't got *that much time,* mister. You'd be late for work..."

"So? It *is* my last day."

"Yes. But you know I'm not a morning kinda girl. We'll save it for tonight." Kat kissed his cheek, and returned to her card toast. "Just think. Four whole weeks! Four weeks of you, me and the kids. Enjoying the sun, the wild theme rides, the rolling beaches, the alien menageries, the crazy funky nightlife..."

Dex pulled a face. "Shit. Now you put it like that... the horror! Do I *really* want to go? I'd rather stay in London shooting bad guys in the face."

Kat threw toast at him, and he ducked, laughing.

"You know what I mean. It'll be a great break. We haven't had a holiday together for..."

"Four years. Toffee was one. She threw up over that snotty businesstyke on the plane; ruined his suit. He tried to invoice us for it. I told him to shove it up his bottom."

Kat barked a laugh. "Oh God, I forgot about that! And *then* you threatened to shoot him!"

"Hmm. So I did. Well, they shouldn't have split up our bloody seating, should they? It was my vomit to endure."

They giggled together for a few moments, remembering the sun and surf, the hot beaches and hotter nightlife. Then Kat gave a small frown, and pursed her lips, eyes looking worried for a moment. "Listen. Dex. Talking of splitting up, I said you'd have a chat with Pegg tonight. Let him bend your ear. Give him some much needed advice."

Dex muffled a groan behind powerful hands, then rubbed wearily at his eyes. "Oh, come on, please tell me you're joking, Katrina. Tonight? Shit. Why *tonight* of all nights? I've... got packing to do."

Kat reached over and punched him in the chest. "Dex, he needs some brother-in-law advice. Come on. You're his friend. Act like a bloody friend! Don't be hiding under the bed covers when the going gets tough."

"Yeah. Well. The problem with Pegg, friend or no friend, is you spend months giving him good solid honest advice; then he ignores it anyway."

"The point is, you gave it to him. It's his to act on. That's what advice is for."

Dex sighed. "Go on. What happened in our private little soap opera?"

"He caught her."

"No shit? Well he'd been following her for long enough. Do we know who the lucky back-stabbing bastard of a whoremonger is?"

"Smark E. Smith."

"Pegg's best mate?" Dex shuddered, then looked hard at Kat. Through gritted teeth, he said, "This is my last day at work. I just want a nice easy day, and a relaxing evening to pack. But that's not going to happen, is it?"

"Does the BearPope shit in the ChurchWoods?"

He gave a tight little smile. "You have such a wonderful way with words, my darling."

They ate in silence for a while, whilst upstairs the children thumped around – as children do.

Eventually, Kat sighed, and tossed her card toast onto her steel plate, where it rattled. "Damn this diet. It's not working, you know? I think you reach a certain age..."

"When your muscles give up and suddenly you're a fat bastard?"

"*No!*" Sharply. "I was going to say, from a woman's perspective, when you've had two kids and the old undercarriage has stretched a little bit."

"That's such a romantic way you have with words, hun," said Dexter, finishing his synbacon and laying his knife and spork down. "Thinking of your saggy old stretched undercarriage makes me all goosebumpy with desire."

Kat threw another piece of toast. Dex ducked – again.

"Will you stop ducking? I can't hit you straight."

"Stop firing bloody bread projectiles then," he grinned.

"Hey, can I help it if you're such a bad target?"

"Must be this slim, agile physique," smiled Dex, good humour returning a little. *One day of crap at the office. One evening of cuckolded moaning. Then... sit back and relax. Ahhhh.* He stood, and his stool shuffled out of the way on little furry feet. "Listen. I gotta shower and go. You know what it's like on your last day; gotta make sure all that paperwork's tied up nice and tight. Make sure the steel docks are clean of bad people. I can do without Jones calling me on the beach to nag about unsigned cases and whoring perps."

"He'd better not." Kat scowled, and the scowl had nothing to do with banter. "Nothing's going to ruin this holiday on Theme Planet," she said, and moved to him again, pressing her small, lithe body in close. He leant down into her kiss, and hugged her tight, and they stayed like that for several minutes until the door burst open...

"Dad, Molly says I'm not allowed to have a Jelly Coat for my birthday because in bright sunlight they turn into sloppy slop, say it's not true, say it's..."

Dex and Kat burst out laughing.

DEX KICKED THE locker at work, and it squeaked open. He changed, slowly, into his PUF uniform. PUF. Police Urban Force. Ten years in, fifteen to go in order to earn that coveted pension, baby, the pension! Along with "a free family trip round the Solar System!!" With double exclamation marks!!

"You okay, man?" growled Jones, slapping him on the shoulder.

Dex glanced back at the stocky black man, who wore an afro which doubled the size of his head. He grinned. "Jones, you big fairy. Of course I'm all right. Last day, then I... *whoosh!* Soar off to the Theme Planet." His right hand imitated a Shuttle taking off for orbit – and beyond.

"Yeah, well, be careful over there, man. You know what they say about those provax aliens."

Dex frowned. "Go on. What *do* they say about those provax aliens?"

"They steal your dreams, man." He saw Dex's cynical scepticism slip into place like a mask. "No, serious Dex. I saw a documentary. On the Twisted Discovery Channel. Straight up."

"Jones, do you realise you're the sort of killdick dickjoy who ruins every good party? You know that? You're the sort of policeman nobody wants to invite."

"I have a disability," said Jones, dark eyes narrowing a little. "I have the urge to tell the truth, no matter in what form I find it."

"Yeah. Well tell it to someone else, mate. I *need* this holiday."
Dex stood, and stretched his back. He rolled his head and his neck
gave a pistol crack. "Man, I'm getting *old*."

"Yeah," said Jones, grinning. "And I just fucking don't fucking
believe I'm older than you, man. I look ten years younger!"

"That's the mileage, mate," said Dex, grinning again. "Come
on. Bad guys won't lock themselves up."

"I wish the shitbags would. It'd make our jobs a whole lot
easier." Jones strapped a D4 shotgun to his back and holstered
twin Kekra quad-barrel machine pistols. "With it being your last
day an' all, Dexter, I thought we'd do the Pussy Patrol. Don't want
you getting shot up before your holidays, now, do we?"

"Very kind of you, Jones. In that case, the donuts are on me."

THE BMW PUF Battlecar hissed across wet concretesteel, huge
tyres carving grooves through toxrain, speed low, Dex and Jones
looking for trouble. It wasn't that there was a *lot* of trouble in
London these days – no more than there'd ever been, anyway.
There'd been the Five Great Food Riots back in '68, and Anti-
Alien Marches which turned nasty in '72. Serial Killers, and indeed
the organised organisation Serial Killers Inc., had been a problem
for a while, where it became fashionable and fucking *chic* to kill
your neighbour – for anything, even trivial stuff like a yakking
dog or catshit on the back black plastilawn. But men like Dex and
Jones with their trusty shotguns soon put an end to that fad. As
Jones used to say, *there's nothing as much fun as shooting a serial
killer in the face. You want to be remembered, Mr Nobody? Well,
be remembered like this.*

The rain came down hard from a hard slate sky, and the hover-
wipers flitted about like angry moths, clearing water from the car's
airscreen-windscreen.

"Stop," said Jones.

"You see something?"

"Over there. The red-brick warehouse."

They were in an old, decrepit, crumbling section of town. The air had a charcoal texture. Water gurgled in leaking iron gutters. Dex squinted, and saw a figure slip through a doorway, wearing a balaclava.

"What's in there?"

Jones punched up the PNC and images spun around into the PUF logo, with a gleaming London bobby holding a traditional electrified truncheon. He aimed the scanner and it gave a *blip*.

"Diamond wholesalers."

"Down *here?*" said Dex. "Are they *mad?*"

"There are probably some tax implications involved."

"Yeah, like a lack of declaration."

Jones grinned. "That's just the way of the world, bro. We both know that shit."

Jones logged in with PUF central and they climbed from the BMW Battlecar and checked D4 shotguns. Then, glancing up and down the street, they splashed through puddles as distant day-lasers wrote sickspam and junkymail against the grey, rain-filled London skies.

You want VVV-Viagra, Big Boy? Telemail 999 696969!

Do you need to get HIGH? Without the PUF PORKERS sniffing out your stash? Our anti-sniff SNIFF SNIFFER SNIFF-STASH SNIFF-BAGS are the bags for stashing your stash!
Dial EASYSNIFFSTASH on your logic cube right now!!

Letters glowed against the clouds selling products nobody wanted to idiots who could afford them. Dex could see the slogans reflected in the dull shine of his shotgun's twin barrels, and he squinted, growling in unease. He'd been the victim of far too much sick sickspam over the years. It made a man want to KILL.

Hello sweet friend, I have unkle in your cuntry who has just received US$57 billion, and needs help transferring funds into his account. For this help you receive US$3 billion *all you need to do is send* YOUR BANK DETAILS *and a skin sample from your inner thigh... and you look very horny and sexy, by the way. Please send photo and I love you long time sweet friend.*

Dex and Jones slammed backs against crumbling brickwork and glanced up and down the street. "No getaway groundcar," said Dex, mouth now a grim line as reality dropped through his brain. Last day. *Last fucking day* and a suspected heist going down like bad shit. Fucking *great*. Just fucking *typical!*

"They'll have something planned."

Dex glanced at the skies. "We going in?"

"With extreme prejudice," said Jones, mouth a grim line, eyes hard, afro wavering. Dex groaned inwardly. When Jones got in a mood like this, in an *I'm the good guy and I'm going to take down the bad guys* mood, well, it was hard to get any sense out of the man, and best just to humour him; let him beat it out of his system. Or at least, beat it out of the bad guys.

"I don't want a slaughterhnouse," said Dex.

"Well, that's up to them guys, ain't it?" said Jones.

Lightning crackled overhead. A God-venom discharge. Jones peered into the portal, signalled to Dex, and headed in. Dex followed, out of the rain, nose twitching at the smell of... fuel. High-octane. *Shuttle* fuel. Shit.

The corridor was long and dark, crumbling and damp. Jones moved slowly through ankle-deep fluid, and it was only when they reached the end of the corridor that Dex realised –with a growing horror – that the fluid through which they stepped was indeed spaceship fuel. Toxic. Deadly. Probably eating their anti-tox toxboots. And very highly flammable.

Dex signalled to Jones, and pointed downwards. An errant spark, and *kaboom!* – Broiled Dexter. Roasted Jones. Not good. Especially considering Dex was due to take his family on holiday tomorrow...

They could hear voices up ahead. And several shouts. There came the *crack* of a pistol and Dex winced.

One spark...

Jones accelerated and Dex went taut, compact, all thoughts of the Theme Planet vanishing like mist under hot sunlight as they reached the end of the fuel-filled corridor and stepped neatly into –

A warehouse.

It was huge, much larger than the exterior had led them to believe. The roof was constructed from corrugated plasti-shields which allowed a dull grey light to filter down like nuclear snowfall. The warehouse was filled with massive H-section struts leading up to the eaves and criss-crossed with large shelves stacked with truk-containers. It was more like a shipping complex than a jewellery wholesalers. But then, as Jones had pointed out, there was probably more tax evasion going down in this backstreet London shit-hole than in any Banker's Convention for Top Level Banking Management. Or maybe *not*.

Dex, back against the wall, surveyed the towering iron shelves filled with truk containers. Again, the stench of fuel was strong; like acid in his nostrils.

Somebody, a woman, screamed.

Jones and Dex charged into action, boots stomping down an alloyconcrete walkway. They rounded the corner to be confronted by a scene which hammered nails of confusion into their skulls. They both stopped dead, D4 shotguns wavering uncertainly. This was not the scene they had expected...

Three people, a man and two women, hung upside down from a beam. They were naked, hands and feet tied tight together, and one woman bled from her mouth, streaks running past her eyes and soaking into her long, blonde, dangling hair, and dripping into a puddle. Their frightened eyes shifted subtly from the two PUF officers who had invaded their torture, and back to the shadows...

Dex reacted first, D4 shifting to the darkness where something, *an outline,* stood perfectly still, camouflaged, only a gentle gleam of eyes watching them without movement.

"What..." said Dex, as Jones stepped past him, levelled his shotgun, and without a sound opened both barrels. *Booms* echoed through the warehouse and Dex blinked, but the figure had flipped out of the way, and from the darkness came three fast *phuts*.

"Down!" screamed Jones, the flat of his hand slamming Dex, and they both hit the ground hard as a line of automatic gunfire cut across the clearing, howling, fire erupting to the backing track of tinkling shell cases. Both men opened their shotguns and more BOOMS smashed through the acid in return fire. Wood splintered. Steel screeched. Concrete crumbled.

For what seemed like hours, there followed a violent exchange of gunfire. Finally, through the smoke and the sound of Dex reloading his D4, Jones grabbed him roughly. "We've got to get out of here."

"But the prisoners..."

"The prisoners are dead."

Dex glanced up. The three *phuts* had been silenced shots. Straight through their skulls.

"We move. Now!" yelled Jones.

Dex said nothing. Trusted his partner's experience and his own screaming instincts. They ran through smoke and gloom as a sudden crackling came to Dex's ears, and behind him the flood of Shuttle fuel ignited. There were cracks and sparks, then a WHOOSH that made every hair on Dex's body stand on end and scream a song of desolation right through to his soul. They sprinted like madmen down a corridor, ignoring the way they'd entered the warehouse. Because...

Dex gave a crooked smile as he felt a wash of heat behind him.

Because hell, *that* was the trap...

They ran hard, boots pounding. Fire roared through the warehouse. Petals uncurled with heat and energy and agony. The warehouse groaned and screamed, and Dex and Jones burst from a second doorway choking on smoke, like unwanted foetal ejections from the glowing vulva of an alien whore.

Dex stood, hands on knees, wheezing.

Jones tracked with his shotgun, face covered by a haze of grey ash, eyes alert.

"What you doing?"

"It's out here."

"What is?" Dex scowled, glancing up.

"The *android*," hissed Jones.

That made Dex stand up tall and finish reloading his shotgun. "Back there? That was a hit?"

"More than that, I reckon," said Jones, voice sour. "Much, much more."

IT WAS ONLY when they were surrounded by an assortment of PUF cars and truks, and five hydroengines tackled the blaze, that Jones finally allowed himself to relax. But even as they sat on the pavement, backs to yet another crumbling brick wall, watching the hydromen fighting the raging blaze and sharing cigarettes, still Jones refused to lower his shotgun. It was as if he were waiting for a follow-up; for payback.

"Go on. What happened?"

"It was when I was in the army," said Jones, voice low. He took a drag on the dregtube. The tip glowed. Jones coughed out blue smoke.

"During Helix?"

"Yeah. Helix. I saw this. Exactly this. Three people, strung up by their feet. The ground doused in high-octane fuel. If she gets interrupted, then *whoosh*. The whole place goes up."

"She?"

"She was an android. An Anarchy Android."

"They're illegal. Especially on Earth."

Jones looked sideways at Dex. "Yeah. Right. How fucking naive do you want to be, compadre?"

"Why a *she*? This could have been a male."

Jones shrugged. "No. They make male androids, sure. But females take KillChips with a higher success rate. It's very, very rare a male becomes an Anarchy Model. Must be in the genetics, or something. The female of the species, more deadly than the male? Damn. Fucking. Right."

Jones smoked some more. Dex considered his words as the hydromen finally killed the fire. The street was a quagmire of foam and black-streaked water. The stench of burnt detritus filled Dex's nostrils like toxic snuff.

It started to rain.

"You think she – *it* – will come back for us?"

Jones shrugged. "No... I don't think so. We're police. They don't want to raise their profiles. Killing police gets a lot of attention, yeah? Too much attention. However, if we'd been burned alive, maybe... well. Fair game, right?" He grinned, then, and slapped Dex on the back. Both men climbed to their feet and stood beneath the ashy rain. It stained them. Dirtied their purity.

"Shit," said Dex. "Just what I need on my last bloody day of work. A triple homicide."

"At least you're going on holiday! I've got more of this to come." Jones's eyes gleamed. "Lots more."

"So they're bad, these..." Dex savoured the words, "Anarchy Androids?"

"As bad as they get," said Jones. "Experts. At torture. Murder. They have no emotions. They have no fear. And they're tougher than a hard-boiled motherfucker. This one we found, out in the jungle on Tashkan during Helix. Well, it took ten of us to drop her. *Ten* of us, Dexter. And she took out a fucking perimeter tank with her bare hands."

Dex holstered his D4 and walked back towards their BMW PUF Battlecar.

He thought about his children. He thought about his family. He thought about losing his family. He thought about how the stakes seemed to get worse and worse, every single day.

Was it worth it?

Was it all *really* worth it?

And he thought, as he occasionally had, about *resignation*.

What would Kat do if some mad-crazed Anarchy Android bitch took his head clean off in the line of duty?

Shit. *Shit.*

Thank God I'm going on holiday, he thought. It would give him space, and time to think. Time to talk. Time to make a decision.

DEX ENTERED THE low-slung dung-bar and the door slammed shut behind him with the sound of a loading shotgun. The bar was military themed, and called *The Full Metal Jacket.* Dex grinned. He fucking *loved* that film. Especially the bit where the Cong Aliens attacked during the Tet5 Offensive, and the retro-panning during the squeezy-boat journey up the Perfume Bottle River in LOS Los Angeles.

Pegg was at the bar, and gave him a vague hand gesture. Dex's grin fell as if he'd been knifed. Pegg was well on his way to the dark side of non-sobriety. Shit. Next thing he'd be telling Dex he was his father...

Dex moved to the bar, where a small, bald barman with a skin ponytail was pulling Japachinese beer into glittering diamond tankards.

"Can I help you, son?" he drawled.

"I'll have a pint of Dublin. Anything for you, Pegg?"

"A half of PissWhiskey."

Dex hopped onto a high stool, which gave the *click* of a landmine priming. *Oh the comedy!* thought Dex. "You out to get drunk, mate?"

Pegg looked up then, and Dex read the pain – the anguish – in his face. Here was a man not just betrayed, but destroyed. Dex's heart fell like a stone down a well, and straight out of his arsehole. Shit. This was going to be a long night.

"Yes."

Dex accepted his black beer and sipped the thick stuff. It went down well. Too well. Like treacle through a toilet pipe. "Kat said you caught Meesha." His voice was gentle. "Want to talk about it?"

"Talk about it? I'll slit the bitch's throat."

"What happened?"

Pegg stared at Dex through bloodshot eyes. "I know you thought I was crazy. Paranoid. Fuck it, even *I* felt paranoid. But just because you're paranoid doesn't mean they're not out to get you, right?"

"Hmm."

"It started off with her working longer and longer hours. Said it was the traffic. But the timings didn't add up. I mean, she was taking three hours to get home and I knew, fucking *knew* it was an hour and a half, max. Then she was leaving for work earlier and earlier, but I was drinking too much anyway by that point, so it took me a few months to notice. Turns out she was leaving for work early so she could *leave* work even earlier; and that's when she was meeting him."

"Who?"

"Smark."

"Your best friend?"

"Yeah. That back-stabbing wife-grabbing cunt."

"Pretty low, that. To do that to your best friend."

"Wait 'til you find out exactly what she *did* do with the hairy bastard! I thought she'd got suddenly more adept at sucking dick. *And* taking it from behind like a begging dog in heat. What a *bitch*."

Dex remained silent. There wasn't much he could say to a remark like that. He knew he was in for a long night of bitterness and hate. And all night he'd have to be careful, have to pick his words with care – because, well, because if they, Peggs and Meesha, ever *made it up* again (which was always a possibility, right? nothing more insane than love or war) then Dex's words would be regurgitated, examined, spun around and re-contextualised. If Dex wasn't careful, at some point further down the line, at a distant spot of illumination towards which he was always travelling like a runaway train in an eternity tunnel... well, one day Dex would become the Bad Man in all this. He'd seen it happen before. Shit, he'd been blamed for worse. And sometimes – sometimes it was just better to keep your big flapping mouth well and truly *shut*.

"She went to the gym for six hours at a time."

"Six hours? Christ. You'd think she'd look like fucking Arnie Neggarschwartz!"

"Well that was one of the giveaways, yeah mate."

Dex scratched his chin. "So things got worse? I assume they did, or we wouldn't be sat here nursing a beer and, er, sharing the fact that your cheating wife is a bitch."

Pegg stared into his whiskey-substitute for a while, lost in thought. When he spoke, he blurted it out like a waterfall of disgorged words, as if eager to excise a cancer from his dark, tortured soul. "I was suspicious. Suspicious for too long, and I kept telling myself I was imagining things, but I let it go and let it go and let it go, her rolling in at four in the morning after being at her cousin's – and that's the worst bit, right? Smark and her, getting it on behind my back, behind her cousin's back. I mean, shit, they're family, right? So I planted a BUG in her handbag, started monitoring her progress. The wily clever cunning bitch was constantly looking out for being followed, she was taking evasive manoeuvres, really weird driving patterns, down back alleys and stuff. I didn't get it at first, until I realised she was parking up down back streets for five minutes, getting out of the car, scouting around to see if somebody was following her. Once, I saw a text she sent. She said she was far too clever to ever get caught. The arse. Not clever enough to delete *that* message, was she? And not clever enough to figure out the BUG. And that was her downfall – thinking everybody else, and *me* in particular, were completely dumb."

Dexter took a long, soothing draught of Dublin. "You caught her, then?"

"Yeah. Last night. Using the BUG. I saw her leave work early and then stop for an hour at a time, maybe two, in Knightsbridge. Obviously meeting somebody. The I had a few night shifts came in, and her nocturnal mobility went crazy. I mean, off the map. Well, off the civilised map. All manner of dark and dingy back woods, plastic parks, places without lights and with low population densities." He stared gloomily into his drink, hands clenched around the diamond tankard, knuckles white. It was then Dex saw... no. It couldn't be.

Blood? On his knuckles?

Dex groaned inwardly. Oh, God. No. Not Pegg. Not Katrina's *brother...*

"I had a night shift last night. But I couldn't take anymore. I followed them on the BUG, down to Green Canary Wharf, you know, the section built on the Thames Sludge. It was quiet. Three AM. When I arrived, I saw her groundcar, all steamed up. I parked, crept over, and there she was on the back seat with Smark. Her dirty whore legs open wide as he pumped away at her. Her face was open in ecstasy – an ecstasy she never bloody showed me, that's for sure."

Dex suppressed the glib joke threatening to slip from his tongue: *You mustn't have been doing it right, mate!*

"What happened next?" Unconsciously, Dex had pushed his drink to one side. His hand slipped to his hip. To his holster. To his Techrim 11mm. Suddenly, his throat was dry. This was beginning to look bad; friend or no friend, brother-in-law or no brother-in-law.

"I took an axe," said Pegg, his voice strangled. "A long-handled axe." He looked up then, a sudden spasmodic jerk. His eyes were red-rimmed, tears glistening like trapped sapphires. "I didn't mean to do it. I didn't *want* to do it!"

"What did you do?"

"She got me in so much fucking *debt* as well, Dexter! I started getting these bills, cred cards, dollar cubes, even bloody clothes catalogues – all in my name. Not only was she humping my best friend, she was going to leave me financially screwed. I know it! Here!" He clenched a fist to his breast. "And even worse. *Even worse.* She was engineering the whole situation; my whole life! Setting me up. Cleaning me out like some scumshit shitbag down in the dregs."

"*What* did you do?"

The Techrim was out. Cool in his hand. Held close against his thigh. A promise. A promise of... *justice*.

"I deserved more than that!" he said, tears coursing down his cheeks now. "I deserved more than being used like that, deserved more than being stabbed in the back. Cheated on for months and months and months. How could she do that to me, Dex? If she wanted somebody else, fine, fuck off and find him... but to keep it going for so long, they were laughing at me Dex, laughing at me even when I banged on the door of the steamed-up landcar..."

Dex's voice was low. "Did you hurt them?"

"She stumbled out into the mud, her stained knickers round her ankles. I lifted the axe up above my head and I swear to you, Dex, I swear I didn't want to do it – but something took hold of my heart, drove splinters of ice through me, pushed me over the precipice of reason and into a deep dark pit of hate..."

Dex pointed the 11mm Techrim at Pegg. His brother-in-law. His wife's brother. His *friend*, dammit, his fucking *friend*. "You know I'm going to take you in, Pegg. I'm sorry. I represent the law. You can't be allowed to do those things."

"Wait a minute!"

Dex was standing, plasticuffs out, and within a heartbeat Pegg's face was on the bar swimming in his own spilt beer and sorrow. Dex cuffed him. Noticed more blood on the cuffs of his shirt. *Shit*.

"Wait, Dex, wait! I didn't *kill them*, oh my god, you really think I killed them?"

Sirens wailed above London. Through the dark. Through the rain. Backup were coming, triggered by the act of Dex using his plasticuffs.

"It's up to the Boys in Blue now, my friend," said Dex, glancing up. Glass smashed distantly. He could hear boots crashing across boards, even through the booming hearty military march playing from the jukebox in the corner, and the slurping sounds of snogging jujunga suckers.

"Wait, no Dex, I dropped the axe, I let them run off laughing through the mud, I *didn't do anything!*"

"What about the blood on your hand and shirt cuff, dickhead?" snapped Dex. Pegg was glaring up at him through watery eyes. Yeah, thought Dex. Tears of self-pity. Dex was hard. His eyes were hard. His lips were grim. If you committed a crime in *his city* then you paid the fucking price.

"I cut myself *shaving!*" wailed Pegg.

"Sure you did."

The PUF squad burst in from three different directions at once, and Dex holstered his Techrim and walked away as they bound Pegg and kicked out his legs. He hit the ground with a grunt, and a MuttBag went over his head, putting out the lights.

Within thirty seconds, he'd left the building.

"You sure about this one?" growled Sergeant Sanders, chewing on his cigar.

"Sue me if I'm wrong," said Dex, face hard as granite.

"Do I HAVE to?"

"Yes."

"What... now?"

"Yes!"

A pause.

"*Really now?* I mean, I haven't finished packing..."

"Now, you flat-footed brain-skewered police-loving bureaucratic fuckwit."

Dex frowned. "A little harsh," he said.

"You deserve it," glared Katrina, and threw a pillow at him.

Dex stood in his pyjamas, a half-packed case on the bed. Kat handed him the comm. Slowly, Dex hit DIAL.

It buzzed.

Don't answer, don't answer, please don't answer, come on, you've just been in the shit, the last thing you really want to do tonight is answer the bloody comm phone...

There was a click.

"Hello?" whined a miserable voice.

"A-ha-ha-ha," said Dex.

"Oh. It's you."

"Yeah. It's me." Dex observed Katrina out the corner of his eye, where she was frowning at him, practically with steam erupting from her ears. She stamped her foot. Actually *stamped it.* He turned his back on her. "Yeah. I, uh, I've called to apologise. About that little misunderstanding tonight."

"Little misunderstanding? Tonight? Where you *had me fucking arrested for murdering my own wife and her lover?*"

"Er," said Dex.

"I told you I cut myself shaving!"

Dex deflated. He admitted it. He felt like a dick.

"I admit it," he said. "I feel like a dick."

"And so you should! All the stuff we've been through, mate! I thought you were my friend. I thought we were like brothers!"

"We are, we are," said Dex. "It's just..."

"Go on."

"I thought you broke the law," he said, quietly. Dex heard Kat give a *huff* behind him and leave the room. That cheered him up a bit. He straightened his shoulders. "Look. I thought you'd chopped her up and buried her in the woods. You did just find her in a compromising, open-legged position..."

"I thought you'd know I could never do anything like that," said Pegg.

"Yeah. Well. I apologise."

"Your PUF boys broke my arm," said Pegg.

"I'm sorry about that, as well. You must have..."

"Fallen down the stairs. Yes. Right." Pegg's voice had become stiff and formal. "Your apology is accepted. I hope you have a good holiday."

"Er. Right. Thank you."

Pegg rung off. Dex sighed and put the comm to one side with a *clack.* He jumped when he realised Kat was standing right behind him. Damn, she could move quietly when she wanted to.

"You're an idiot," she said.

"I know," he said.

"My brother!"

"I know," he said.

"My own flesh and blood!"

"I thought he'd chopped her up, Kat. Come on. You'd have done the same."

"No, I would have discovered the truth!"

"Okay. Okay. I admit it. I'm the Bad Man. Shoot me..."

"I will if you don't get that packing done! We're up at 5AM."

"Has daddy packed yet?" came a shout.

"Can we go out for pizza?"

"Japachinese!"

"Sucky Sushi!"

"Tentacle Soup!"

"Dogmeat Surprise!"

Kat glared at Dex. She punched him on the arm. He didn't complain.

"What a day," he muttered.

"Get packed," she growled, but smiled a little, to show him she forgave him. Just a little bit. "We go to the Theme Planet tomorrow!"

CHAPTER TWO
THEME PLANET

THE SHUTTLE'S ALLOY flanks and black glass gleamed violet and orange under errant sunbeams as the huge, cumbersome vehicle banked ten klicks above the Earth, and tiny jets erupted with hydrogen bursts as the passenger vehicle stabilised. Below, the mammoth ball of blue, scattered with cloud trails and weather cycles, turned with a slow, massive majesty, easing through Her Cycle, a generous host, a caring Mother, the Earth, Mother Earth, Home of Mankind and Cradle of Humanity.

Jets flared. The Shuttle's nose dipped, and it began a carefully orchestrated descent to Earth's specially built Theme Planet Landing Field, a huge building of black alloy and glass, where hundreds stood behind UV screens watching, cameras poised. *Shuttle Watching,* they called it, and the galaxyweb was filled with a million different photos of the same thing from hordes of enthusiasts.

Dexter Colls, Katrina, Molly and Toffee sat in the Waiting Lounge. Huge screens displayed the Shuttle's glowing entry through Earth's atmosphere and Toffee was visibly *vibrating* with excitement, hopping from one foot to the other, jigging and clenching/unclenching her fists. Even Molly, who was keen to find fault and gloom in practically every situation, was reasonably chatty and had a rapturous look on her dark, moody features.

The girls scuttled off to see the Shuttle coming in to land for real, and Dex stretched back, closing his eyes and rubbing his stubbled chin. *But hell, it was nice not to shave for a change. Nice to wear scruffs instead of a uniform. Nice to chill out, baby. To avoid the psychopathic, axe-wielding murderers.*

"You're looking happy with yourself," said Kat.

Dex shrugged and grinned. "I was just thinking how it's incredibly astute of the authorities to search you at customs."

"Meaning?"

"Well, *every single time* we go on holiday, they look at you and think, shit, look at that dodgy rum bitch. She *must* be carrying something illegal. So they search all your luggage and bags whilst me and the girls go and eat cakes. You've got to admit, it's totally hilarious. Must be a genetic thing."

"Rubbish!" she scowled. "What they really think is *you're* the dodgy underhand bastard doing the smuggling, and that you've snuck it into either my case or my loose pants, and they're looking for the evidence prior to busting *your* ass."

"No," said Dex. "No, no. That's not what I see at all."

Kat slapped his arm. "You're a cheeky so-and-so." Then she snuggled up close to him and yawned. "I can't believe how early the alarm went off. I felt like I was going to puke."

"You're so lady-like and sophisticated, my sweet. What you going to chat about next? Toilet habits? Septic tanks? Severed fish heads?"

"Hey, bugger off! Whoever said I was ladylike? Conned you there, didn't I, Dex my sweet?"

He reached down until their lips were nearly touching. "I still love you, chipmunk."

"And so you should. I'm the best fish you'd ever catch on *your* tiny hook."

They kissed for a long time, until Dex snorted a laugh. "Do you remember that time you took The Rabbit on holiday? Showed up on the luggage scanner like... well, like a big pink vibrator."

"Shut up."

"And they took it out of your case, and the damn thing went off like a firework! Sparks and everything! You had every damn idiot in the airport staring at you with flapping lips whilst the uniformed bureaucrats ran around with a sparking, fizzing, burning vibro thinking it was a bomb about to fucking explode!" He laughed.

"Shut up."

"Daddy! What are you talking about?"

"Toffee! We were talking about what a mad little nutcase you're turning into."

"Mummy?"

"Yes, sweetie?"

"What's a mad little nutcase?"

"It's what Daddy married. Now run along and fetch Molly, I'm sure they'll be calling us over to passport control real soon."

As Toffee disappeared, Dex rested his head back and closed his eyes. With his usual cynicism, he said, "Yeah. Right. Well, if we catch that Shuttle on time it'll be a fucking first." But Dex was wrong. The Shuttle was on time. And they boarded, to the *second*, at the time indicated on their glowing holo-tickets.

Theme Planet ran a perfect show.

Theme Planet prided itself in the art of *perfection*.

"DADDY, I CAN see the clouds!"

"No, sweetie, we haven't taken off yet."

"Can I have some Crispo Crisps?"

"No."

"Cokey Cola?"

"No."

"Spunky Spunk Chocolate?"

"Spun... *What*?"

"Spunky Spunk Chocolate, the Spunkiest Chocolate alive! It was all over Kiddy Kid Kid TV yesterday, ask Molly, Molly will tell you, won't you Molly? Tell Daddy about the new Spunky Spunk Chocolate full of Spunky Spunk. It's the next big thing. All the kids in school are eating it."

Dex gritted his teeth and stared hard at Katrina. She gave a tight little smile. "So. You'll be writing *another* letter of complaint to the GGC when we get home, dear?"

"Damn bloody right," he muttered. "Talk about inappropriate. Is it me getting old and grumpy? Or is the world simply tumbling down a toilet into rat-shit?"

"A bit of both, my darling. Look, we're going to the Theme Planet to *relax*. So start by relaxing *now*. Okay?"

"Hmmm," said Dex, and put his Caterpillar Headphones into his ears. He gave a little shiver as the earpieces wriggled into his aural canals, but after the initial discomfort, they began delivering the soothing music of Mozart the Tenth (otherwise known as MozieX).

Time to relax. Time to relax. I know it's time to relax, and I should put back my head and close my eyes and listen to the music. We'll get to the hotel, settle in nicely, have a fine meal and an evening stroll on the beach. Back to the room, kids in bed, open a bottle of Chablis and wriggle under the soft covers for a cuddle and a giggle... just like old times, just like the best times, just like it used to be...

Katrina nudged him. "We're getting ready to take off."

Dex glanced right, and the kids were strapped in their seats, eyes shining. For once, *for once*, they weren't jiggling, complaining or arguing. And that in itself was a minor miracle.

"We're going to fly!" said Toffee, peering out of the Shuttle's window. As the smallest, she sat closest to the porthole.

Molly peered past her. "Look. You can see the moon!"

"We're going past the moon," said Toffee.

"Flying up, up, up into space!" beamed Molly.

"Shush, now, you'll make your father queasy," said Katrina, stroking an errant hair from Molly's forehead. "You know he doesn't like flying."

Dex felt both girls turn their eyes on him. Their joint gaze was more intensive than any psychotic military drill-instructor.

"You're not afraid of *flying*, are you, daddy?" said Molly.

"Haha! Daddy's 'fraid of flying, Daddy's 'fraid of flying..."

"No I'm not," said Dex, closing his eyes and picturing the chopper, out of control, careering round in violent circles, smoke and fire pluming and spitting from cracked engines as screams wailed and people screamed and he wrestled with the controls, face smudged with dirt, a bullet in one shoulder, another in his hip, his lifeblood pumping with every movement across his chilled clammy flesh as the screams of men, and women, and children echoed through his ears, through his head, echoed down long corridors all the way to a fiery frozen Eternity...

"No, I'm not," he breathed.

"Girls, girls, shush, leave your father alone. He's had a bad week."

"Damn right," he muttered, and felt the rumble of engines igniting deep within the bowels of the huge passenger Shuttle. Dex's knuckles tightened that little bit more. He felt an odd *throb* from where the bullet had lodged in his hip. Gone now. Ten years gone. But hot, like it was still there, gnawing his flesh with tiny teeth. Mole Bullets, they called them. Used by happy terrorists the globe over. Once inside you, their teeth emerged and they started a slow burrow towards something deep and meaningful.

The Shuttle lifted smoothly from the blast-pad and Dex peered past his awe-struck daughters as the terminal fell away amongst sheets of vertical rain. There was a *kick* and they accelerated, the nose of the Shuttle lifting now as real power surged through motors and Molly and Toffee giggled, blissfully unaware of the billion micro-gallons of piped Shuttle-fuel bubbling beneath their sweet little backsides.

Dex shivered.

"Some Greebo Champagne, sir?" asked the stewardess.

Dex glanced up. Licked dry lips. "Go on then."

Kat giggled and slapped his arm. "At least look *excited*."

"Oh, I'm excited all right," he said. Then added: *I'm not bloody excited about paying for it all. But then, Dexter Colls, you always were a stingy, tight-fisted old bastard.*

They clinked flutes and sipped Greebo Champagne, and watched London disappear amidst the clouds, then the clouds disappear amidst the swirl of the planet. And gradually, sequentially, the grey and blue turned to black filled with a billion *billion* pin-pricks of stars.

They left Earth behind.

They were on their way to Theme Planet.

"DADDY, CAN I sit on your knee?"

"Mmm?" Dex opened his eyes to see Molly staring at him earnestly. He yawned, and gave a nod. Outside the porthole, stars scrolled past and the *thrum* of the Shuttle's engines was a rhythmic, relaxing constant.

"You okay, Pudding?"

"Don't call me a pudding."

She settled down like a bird trampling its nest. Dex grunted.

"Okay, then. Peanut?"

"I am not," she pouted, close to him, "a peanut."

"What can I do for you, Molly?" He smiled.

"I'd like to discuss our family holiday on the Theme Planet."

Dex nodded, thinking, *gods, but she's growing up fast. It seems like only yesterday I was changing her nappies and using the ultra-modern Suck-o-Suck Poo Sucker & Scraper and Infant Cleansing Apparatus to perform the terrible deed. Now, here she is, eyes all serious, wishing to "discuss" things. Hot damn.*

Dex grinned. "Of course, Miss Molly. I am here to discuss every single element of our wonderful family vacation. Where's your mother?"

"Up ordering our lunch at the bar."

"Hmm. Sure she is."

"Listen Daddy, I've been thinking. I think we should visit *every single* area of the Theme Planet where we're staying, and then, if we've exhausted that area, we should move on to the Red Zone."

"You know we can't go to the Red Zone, sweetie. They won't allow Toffee on any of the rides. She's too young."

"But Daddy!"

"Wait, wait, back-up a minute, Molls. The Blue Zone is designed especially for a family like us. We're staying in the Kool Kid Zone so that *you* and Toffee can have a real fun time. Then there's Adventure Central a short zip tube ride away if I fancy indulging in some adventurous mountain climbing, or something."

"Ooh, yes, I was reading about Adventure Central," said Molly, and Dex caught that gleam in his daughter's eye that *so* reminded him of Katrina. A wicked streak. A sense of danger and wild adventure that had no place belonging to an eight-year-old little lady...

"Now wait a minute," said Dex. "Adventure Central is for adults only. That's the whole point. It's *dangerous*. It's full of adrenaline sport experiences, up in the Skycloud Mountains or on the Death Rapids, or out in the Lost Dunes. It's not a place for children."

"That's cyber-rubbish," said Molly, frowning. "At school, my cousin Vincent's little cousin's brother's friend's dad has been there, and *he* took his little boy who was seven years old and *he* went on the Kid Rapids, and if you think about it, Daddy, they wouldn't even *have* something called the Kid Rapids if it wasn't designed for kids would they? And my cousin Vincent's little cousin's brother's friend's *dad* said there was a place called the Forest of Iron and it had bandits and everything and it led to the Caves of Hades and there was a secret tunnel that leads under the secret sea to the secret island called The Lost Island that everybody at school's been talking about, so please, Daddy, please, please, please will you take me on an expedition to Adventure Central and we can meet bandits and find The Lost Island and everything?"

Dex digested this information. "If everybody at school," he said, carefully, "has been talking about *The Lost Island,* how can it be lost? It means they found it. It's no longer lost. It's been found." He smiled at her. Molly made a *phut* sound and climbed down off his knee.

"That's okay, Dad. If you're too *scared...*"

"Oh, *scared* is it?" he said, and grabbed her round the waist, tickling her ribs. She giggled and started kicking and woke Toffee up, who started crying, just as Katrina arrived carrying two MUGGS of coffee and frowning.

"I leave you three alone for a minute..." she said.

"Daddy said he's taking us to Adventure Central," said Molly, smugly.

"Er, no I did not!"

"You promised!"

"Did I?"

"You did. You did!"

"And I want to go as well," pouted Toffee.

Katrina gave him a withering look. "Well Dex, looks like I'll be sunbathing and admiring all those hunks on the beach *all on my own.*" She grinned, and he took the coffee from her and considered pouring it on her head.

"Yeah. Right."

IT WAS NIGHT. Or at least, night by their body-clocks. The cabin's lights had been dimmed and the Shuttle seats unrolled back into beds. Both Molly and Toffee were covered by Snooze-o blankets and Dex and Katrina were reclining, sharing a bottle of Helix Towers red wine. The Shuttle had been rapidly accelerating for the last ten hours to 0.7LS and they were heading for a JUMP which, Dex knew, would make him want to vomit and feel like he was wearing his internal organs on the outside. Annoyingly, Katrina felt no adverse effects during a JUMP. She used it as another excuse to call Dex a "pussy."

"So then, lover. This time tomorrow, we'll be walking hand in hand down the beach."

"Your reckon?"

"I hope so." She smiled.

"But what about all those hunks you mentioned?"

"Hey, I have my own hunk right here." She stroked his chest and kissed him, and their tongues lingered for a few moments until the flashing lights in the headrests of the seats in front got brighter and brighter and a buzzer started to get progressively louder.

No Snogging, said the flashing sign. Snogging leads to sex. This is a No Sex Shuttle... unless you wish to upgrade to First Class+++, only an extra $£15,000 and have your very own Sex Suite! You know it makes sense.

Dex groaned. "Told off by a fucking headrest. The fucking ignominy."

"That's a long word for a PUF."

"Yeah, laugh it up. I'm not as dumb as you look."

"Cheeky."

"Better believe it."

"So then..." Her hand was still rubbing his chest. "Are we going to visit Pleasure Island whilst we're on TP?"

"You fancy that, do you?"

"Oh yes," said Kat, a sparkle in her green eyes. "There's The Glade of Eternal Delight, the Hanging Gardens of Babylon, a Sex Theme area, The Pleasure Trail..."

"You *have* been doing your research. However, much as I don't wish to spoil your fantasy mental party, you seem to forget we have two psychotic dependents who need psychotically depending on."

"I've looked into that, as well. They have a baby-sitting service. For just this purpose." She winked.

"Interesting."

"You better believe *that*," said Kat, leaning forward.

No Stroking of Chest Hairs, said the flashing sign. Stroking of chest hairs leads to snogging and snogging leads to sex. This is a No Sex Shuttle... unless you wish to upgrade to First Class+++, only an extra $£15,000 and have your very own Sex Suite! You know it makes sense.

The headrest turned red with annoyance when both Dex and Kat burst out laughing.

"DAD! DAD DAD DAD DAD DAD!"

"What? Jesus, kids, can you stop with the bloody shouting?"

"I can see it, it's down there, we're getting close, it's not the time to have a lie-in, Dad, you can see the domes and the hotel cubescrapers and the ginormous roller-coasters and *everything!* Come look, Dad, come on, look!"

Dex looked, rubbing sleep from his eyes. Up and down the Shuttle similar scenes were being re-enacted by excited squawking kids pummelling awake their bleary-eyed parents, who'd known it was far too damn much to hope that they'd get a bit of sleep on the first day of their vacation. Forget Christmas, Juja, Pokaloloa or any other festival which leaves presents beneath a tree precipitating 4AM awakenings by excited young offspring... this was something *else*.

Dex, Molly and Toffee stared out of the Shuttle's porthole as engines screamed in deceleration and the whole world of Theme Planet swung into view, spreading out before them like some massive, mammoth playground – which it surely was. Dex blinked, his eyes funny for a moment, and he realised the Shuttle's porthole was *magnifying* the images for their benefit, thus giving an immediate sense of gratification that hey, hell, they'd picked *the right damn holiday of a lifetime, baby.*

Theme Planet spread out, a tapestry of wonder.

Theme Planet undulated, an image of physical joy.

Green fields rolled, golden beaches gleamed, turquoise oceans lapped, purple mountains sparkled, and amidst the finery and luxury and stunning natural beauty, amidst the perfection of cleanliness and holiness and utter, total perfection, sat the *rides...*

"There's Bubble Guts!" shrieked Molly, pointing. All along the Shuttle other kids were shrieking and hollering as they spied favourite rides seen so many times on TV adverts and filmys. Dex squinted. The entrance to the "ride" was as big as five cubescrapers. It could be seen from *space*.

"What's Bubby Guts?" said Dex.

"Aww *Dad,*" said Molly, giving him *one of those looks.*

Katrina appeared at his shoulder. "You certainly know how to keep up with the times," she said, and nibbled his ear-lobe.

"Careful. Don't want to get spanked by that pedantic head-rest," he said.

"Insane! Insane! Insane!" shrieked Toffee, red in the face.

"You're damn right, you are," muttered Dex.

"No dad, it's the *ride* called *Insane,*" chided Molly, rolling her eyes. "Look!"

Dex looked. It was a five kilometre high rollercoaster with enough loops and curves and flick-backs and twists and turns and jelly-donuts to make the hardiest of hard roller-coaster riders puke his quivering burger into his lap. It dominated the skyline, starting a full five kilometres up in the sky, and dropping into the turquoise ocean where (Molly reliably informed him) it went five kilometres *under the waves.*

Dex stared at his daughter. "Now that *is* insane," he said.

"Can we go on it, Dad, please, please, you can only go on it with your parents, please Dad, please, can we can we can we?"

Dex stared once again at the true monster *mother* bastard *bitch* of all roller-coasters. "The day I go on that ride," he said, voice soft, words carefully clipped, "is the day Hell freezes over, God comes down from his cloud to sign limited editions of *Bible II – The Remix,* and the sun explodes to consume Earth with a comedy Pac-Man MUNCH." He shouted the last word, barking it like a dog.

Molly worked this out. "Aww, come on Dad, Mum, will you tell him?"

"Go on, Dex. Don't be such a stick in the mud."

"Don't worry," said Dex, ruffling Molly's shoulder-length brown hair. "Your mother will take you on it."

Kat threw him a glance like a sock filled with razor-blades.

Again, the Shuttle's engines decelerated with rumbling whines, and as they slowed, and slowed further, and dropped towards the Theme Planet's plush Port Terminal, more shouts echoed up and down the Shuttle's interior.

Criss-Cross! There's Criss-Cross!

Monster Mash! You can see the monsters, look! Look!

Oh, wow, Mum, it's the Power Matrix!

Look, look, it's A-mazing, it's totally amazing!

That's the Survival Jungle!

Over there, Dad, you can see the Movie-Scape...

The Molecule Machine! I can't believe it, I've always wanted to go on the Molecule Machine!

There's Adventure Central! Mum! Auntie Ethel! Uncle Bob! You can see the Museum of Baron Nutcase! And there's our hotel!

I can't wait to eat at Monster's Burger Mush! They say the Slopper is a burger as big as your head!

And so on.

Dex found it quite exhausting. He lay back. Closed his eyes. Folded his arms. And said, "Wake me up when we get there."

It was sooner than he anticipated. The Theme Planet's Landing and Immigration Service was perfect to the point of anal. Which was a good thing for eager, tired travellers; a bad thing for Dexter's snooze-time.

Hundreds of people disgorged from the Shuttle into a series of plush, elegant connecting tunnels, and various families in dodgy sports-gear rushed off with squeaking trolleys as if they'd been injected with a damaging narcotic. Dex frowned as he watched two shell-suit wearing grannies stomp off, each carrying twin walking sticks, as if they were in a race for their lives.

"Come on, Dad!"

"Faster!"

"They'll beat us!"

"There's no point," whined Dex. "Listen to me, I've done this a million times, right. I am well versed in immigration matters, and we're good to wait for a few bloody hours in this first queue alone, I can *absolutely guarantee it*. They have to take fingerprints, blood samples, urine samples, retina scans, faecal-passage scrapes. We have to be assigned genetically modified Personal Drones. Kids, sorry to disappoint, but we're in this queue, and the next one, and the one after that for the best part of the damn *day*. I know bureaucracy. It's a curse, I agree. And Theme Planet, even in all its splendour, can't cure the absolute blight of the low-paid clipboard-wielding official."

"Bah, humbug," said Kat. "Come on girls! Daddy's a rotten egg! He can catch us up on the beach!"

And with that, Dex watched his family stream off like so many other charging idiots, and Dex frowned and got his stubborn head on, and formed his stubborn jaw, and decided he wasn't going to play the idiot's game and wasn't going to show himself up. Oh, no. He was going to walk at a normal pace and be *civilised* and *dignified* about this whole business and to Hell and bloody fire damnation with *getting on the rides first...*

BUT DEX WAS wrong. There were no queues. There were no bureaucrats. There weren't even any clipboards. Everything was automated, and there were beautiful smiling women in smart uniforms handing out welcome flowers to the ladies, welcome bottles of whiskey to the men, and very specific toys to the children. Molly got a Hellhorror PinkPunk doll, and Toffee got a My Little Alien, complete with "realistic slime-puke regurge action." They all stepped through scanners, which blipped and blopped, and then they were through the five-hundred-slot immigration counters, out onto Theme Planet itself...

A heady aroma of flowers and fresh pine wafted in through the Port Terminal's huge reception. There was a bustle of activity, and each family met their Personal Drone when the Personal Drone arrived towing each family's unmolested luggage. No queues. No waiting. No lost bags. No drama, baby.

Kat raised her eyebrows at Dex, as if to say, *there you go, idiot, First Class++++++ service! All with a smile! And no bureaucrats! And no bloody queues!* Queues had been a bone of contention with Dex when it came to booking the Theme Planet holiday in the first place. He'd protested long and hard and longer and even harder, saying he didn't want to spend a King's Ransom on a holiday where you spent most of your time standing aimlessly in queues. And even though the Monolith Corporation's Theme Planet literature proclaimed otherwise, Dex still didn't *believe*.

"Yeah?" he snapped.

"They promised there'd be no queues."

"We'll see," he snarled. "No holiday is *that bloody good*." But he had to admit it, as they were guided towards their *very own personal hover bus,* as provided *for each and every single family on vacation,* he had to grind his damn teeth and actually admit it.

It was starting to look as good as the promise.

As the bus doors opened with a *phizz*, the Personal Drone – which was a small black ball, about the size of a tennis ball and hovering at shoulder height – spun around and glowed softly through various slots.

"Welcome to the Theme Planet," said the Personal Drone. "My name is Lex. I am a GradeB PopBot Pleasure Mechanism with advanced SynthAI and a Machine Intelligence Rating (MIR) score of 2750. I am here to be of constant assistance, and I am indeed your personal servant, Theme Planet guide, childcare facility and even food critic. I have an inbuilt PersonalityChip™ which means every single PopBot PD is unique and can provide endless hours of fun and entertainment. I can even quote Shunkspeare."

"How's it going, Lex?" said Molly, pushing her face in close.

"It's going fine, Molly," said Lex, glowing amber. "I see you have a Hellhorror PinkPunk doll. They're groovy. If you press the button at the base of its spine, it'll do the famous PinkPunk PunkDance."

"Cool!" beamed Molly.

The PopBot rotated to Dex, who growled at it. He didn't like machines. Well, not unless they took bullets and killed bad guys.

"Hello, Dexter."

"Dex to you."

"Hello Dex-to-you. A-ha-ha-ha. Sorry. That is my ComedyCircuit™. It means I have comedy."

"Would you like me to shove this whiskey up your..."

"Dex!"

"Sorry. Sorry."

"Ahh, your entry whiskey, Uncle Scrote's Finest Single Tantalus Malt. A fine dram, if I may be so bold."

"Do you want some?"

"Alas," said Lex, his soothing male voice quavering a little, "I fear it would burn out my circuits and render me useless."

"Really? That's interesting," said Dex, raising an eyebrow.

"Dex," said Katrina, again.

"Okay, my happy little family of Colls, if you'd all like to board the bus, we'll be on our way to your fabulous Hotel Suite. As you are aware, you are staying in the Kool Kid Zone which allows you endless access to the Lolly Pop Forest, Area 51B, the Water Fun Zone, the Gingerbread Mountains, the Dinozens and Create-An-Alien, amongst many, many, many other attractions! How hot would you like your bath water?"

"Sorry?" said Katrina, who had just climbed aboard the hover bus and was watching in fascination as the luggage seemed to be loading itself into the hold.

"Bath water? Temperature? They are running you a Splish-Splash Jacuzzi bath right now, so that you may sink into bubbly delights with some Greebo Champagne the minute you enter the snuggling confines of The Kool Kid Zone Hilton Hotel."

"Hot," said Kat.

Dex chose a seat at random. There was a *click* and a beer appeared in front on him. A chilled *Blue Zone Lager* of finest Japachinese brew. He took a swig. It was perfect. And exactly what he wanted.

As the doors closed, Kat threw a look at him. The kids were giggling as they played on the back seat of the hover bus with some Gigglegum, stretching it between their fingers and toes.

"Well?" she said.

"Damn, but they're good," said Dex, shaking his head.

"I told you," said Kat.

"Okay. Okay. It's not my fault I'm Mr Bloody Cynical, is it? Look at the place where we live. Look at my *damn job*. Look at your tortured brother. Just *look at the world,* mate."

"It's a shame everything back on Earth can't be as precise and efficient as the Theme Planet," said Katrina, sipping an orange sherry – the exact thing she was in the mood for after a long-haul flight. *How did they know that? How the hell could they have even possibly known that?*

"Hmm," said Dex, drinking his lager. "We'll see."

The hover bus hummed away from the Shuttle Port and down rolling lanes between rolling fields. Sunshine shone, and distantly children giggled and soft music played and this new world, this *alien* Theme Planet, seemed like a wonderful, perfect place to be right now.

IT WAS LATER. Much later.

The Kool Kid Zone was... perfect. And the Colls family didn't get a room. They got a *suite* of rooms with every technological advancement, and everything they could ever dream of in a holiday suite, provided as standard. Forget upgrades. The whole of the Kool Kid Zone Hilton was an upgrade.

PopBot Lex entertained the children with an alien holo puppetshow and Gigglegum tricks whilst Dex and Katrina took a long, relaxing bath. She swam over to him (yes, the Jacuzzi was *that big)* and snuggled up close, soaping his chest.

"We're going to have such a good time, aren't we, honey?" she said.

Dex smiled. "You know what? I *have* started to relax. And it's the first time I've ever been on a holiday where everything ran so smoothly; ran like clockwork. I am agog with wonder. I simply cannot believe my eyes."

Kat kissed him, and for long minutes they savoured the kiss, hands stroking one another under the bubbles. Then Kat pulled away.

"You hungry, Mister?"

"Only for you, babe. Come back here. I've got something to give you..."

"Haha, oh, I bet you have. Not now, though, come on, the kids are starving and Lex has recommended a fine Japachinese restaurant just a few minutes away. He's even pre-booked us a table *just in case* we want to take him up on his recommendation. *And* he's persuaded the kids to have a relaxing first day and we'll start on the big rides *tomorrow.* How cool is that? God only knows what he promised them. Drugs, probably."

Dex snorted a laugh. "Hell, that's more like it! The slimy little Lex bastard. I don't trust him." Dex winked. "First chance I get, I'll pour some Cokey Cola down his arse-slot."

Katrina rose from the bubbles and pulled on a silk robe. "Come on, lazy mutt. Out you get. I'm starving. And if you're a good boy..."

"Yes?"

"You can have me for dessert." She winked.

DEXTER STOOD OUTSIDE the entrance to *Insane*. He gazed up. And up. And UP. *Man, that's a big fucking rollercoaster,* he thought to himself. Closely followed by, *there's no way on Earth my little girls will want to go on this when they get up close and personal. Will they? Or did I breed proper little psychopaths?*

He looked down. Molly held one hand. Toffee held the other. They both gazed at him *adoringly.* As if to say: *come on, Dad, don't let us down now, don't let us down* AGAIN. *We want to go on the ride! Pleeeeeeeeeeeeeeeeeease...*

Dex glanced back, over his shoulder, to the viewing area where one-hundred-inch screens zoomed and snapped around with close-ups and pans, and took comedy photographs of screaming punters screaming.

"Great," he muttered.

"Go on!" yelled Katrina. "What are you waiting for, you big girl? Waiter service?"

"Ha-bloody-ha," said Dexter, voice wooden.

"Come on, Dad!"

"This way, Dad!"

"Don't be scared, Dad!"

"It'll be a great laugh, Dad!"

They moved through to the queuing area. *Please let there be a queue. Please let there be a really, really* HUGE FUCKING QUEUE. But for once, there wasn't. For once, Dex had been betrayed by the God of Queues. The bastard. He wanted to stamp his foot in sheer frustration. *You bastard!* He waved a mental fist up at the heavens, scowling. *You bastarding bastard!*

"Look, Dad, there's no queue!" beamed Molly.

"Great," muttered Dex.

"This way dad," said Toffee, tugging his hand.

"Fine," muttered Dex.

"I'll buy the photo!" shouted Katrina, helpfully, from the viewing area.

"Great!" he shouted back. Then muttered: "And I'll buy you a gag."

They walked down various gleaming corridors showing The History of the Rollercoaster, each with a Terrormeter Rating – which started off with 1s and 2s, and finally, just as they were about to board the CAR, revealed that *Insane* had an official Terrormeter Rating of 10.

"Out of a hundred?" asked Dex, hopefully.

"Out of ten, dad!" said Molly, and tugged him into the darkness of the CAR.

*   *   *

CHAINS CLANKED.

Three thousand people sat in bright-eyed anticipation, knuckles white, teeth clenched, gasps gasping. Sunlight defined a glittering broad canvas, as big as the world. A subtle breeze, ripe with vegetation, caressed the graceful, mechanical ascent. There was a background of excited chatter; a *hum* of anticipation, and energy.

Except for Dex. Yes, his knuckles were white. Yes, his teeth were clenched – but that was more from a need to stop himself cursing like a space bum than any real anticipation of the horror to come. *Rollercoasters! Ha! Who invented them? What bloody idiotic idiot invented such a pointless way of achieving "fun"? Eh?*

A breeze whipped Molly's hair, as she peered over the edge of *Insane's* carriage CAR. Like a long metal caterpillar, it clanked and ground its way up the massive incline. And the problem with a massive incline was *not* just the massive descent waiting for you on the other side, indeed, but the *massive* anticipation of the massive descent waiting for you on the other side.

"Ain't this fun, Dad?" beamed Molly. He'd never seen her so happy. Gone was the sullen, dark, moody expression, as if she were some kind of reject from Munsters, Part 6000. No. She had brightened. She had *come alive*. And for that alone, it was worth the price of entry.

The clanking continued.

Metal, killing metal.

Dex breathed deep. They were high now. He tried not to look down. Shit. He failed.

He glanced at Toffee, with her perpetual bright expression of bouncing happiness. Her face was framed by blonde curls; she really was Daddy's Little Girl. Again, Dex's heart melted at the look of sheer exhilaration on her face. The pure *joy*.

Eventually, the climb ended a full *five kilometres* up. The world, the theme park, the *Theme Planet*, spread before the assembled ride freaks: colourful, and awesome, and vast.

To the left, fields of dancing pastel flowers jigged in the wind.

To the right, mountains of obsidian sat like majestic dragon's teeth, quiescent, waiting, glittering.

Ahead, amidst gleaming oiled bodies, jewels sparkled on a turquoise sea crested with foam.

"Aren't we high up, Daddy?" shouted Molly over the buffeting tussle of the wind.

"Mmmmm," said Dex, clinging on in absolute terror.

"Isn't this fun, Dad?" enthused Toffee, her blonde curls whipping about her head.

"Grrrrt," he managed between clenched teeth.

There came a hiatus:

A long moment of peace, and serenity, a pause for thought, a moment to study one's own wisdom in these things; one's own mortality; one's own longevity; one's own connection to God.

Then there came a *bang*, a *clank*, a lurch... and a sudden, violent drop into infinity and oblivion, and Dex screamed and he didn't mind admitting it, he screamed like a girl because *everybody* screamed like a girl as they were caught in the Fist of the Gods and hurled towards the ground at breakneck speed, hitting a loop and careering out of control and hitting a flick-back and Dex felt his spine coming up through his mouth. *Is it fucking safe?* screamed his speed- and dope-addled brain. *Of course it fucking isn't! How can something this bloody insane be bloody safe? But then, it's all in the name you puddle-brained muppet. It's called* Insane *because it IT'S FUCKING INSANE!*

"Waaaaaaaaahh!" went Molly, giggling.

"Braaaaaahhaaaaaaahh!" went Toffee, waving her hands in the air.

"I'm going to be sick," said Dex, clutching his stomach and wondering again how bloody old he was, how bloody grumpy he was, and hadn't he liked shit like this as well when he was younger? Enjoyed the speed? Relished the adrenaline? Thrived on danger? Yeah, right up to the point where you see a dead body, all squashed up and crushed up and broken like a train-wreck doll. Then it didn't seem so much fun anymore...

The *Insane* CAR bucked and rolled, spun and looped the loop-the-loop. It banked and jigged and did all manner of things Dex was pretty sure were impossible under the Laws of Physics. It was a bloody miracle his breakfast stayed in his belly, and that was all Dex could think about. The *churn*.

What was Theme Planet's neat little extended strapline, again? *It's better than drugs! It's better than sex! It's fun, it's fast, it's neat... If you haven't been sick, you soon will be!* Dex grimaced in his rapid descent. Yeah. Well. When he had boots on solid ground again, he was going to find the *manager* of Theme Planet and be sick in his lunch. That'd teach the bastard.

"It's coming!" somebody yelled, and Dex strained to see behind himself; but of course he couldn't, because he was locked in tight and supposed to be looking *forward* and focusing on the *experience*.

"What's coming?" he yelled, and glanced at Toffee, and saw her eyes widen just a fraction in their buffeting, clanking, *clanging*, thrashing, screaming descent.

Oh, no, he thought, and turned his head back as... they hit the sea...

Water splashed up and around filling his world with a deep green watery vision, and it was all around him and he thought, *Oh, my God, they're going to kill us; oh, my God, we're going to drown...*

But of course, they weren't, and it took Dex long, long seconds of struggling violently at his restraining roller-coaster brace to realise that it was all for effect, all for *fun*, baby, and they cruised and dropped, jerked and spanked and flipped and flopped, all within the totally safe confines of a clear tube beneath the ocean.

"Wow," said Molly.

"Wowsers," agreed Toffee.

The *Insane* rollercoaster continued to roll and coast, far beneath the waves.

And even though they were still falling, even though they were still looping-the-loop, now they could see swarms of fishes, colours glittering through the subterranean twilight. Schools of sharks and whales and all manner of other marine life – or whatever Theme Planet alien-breed aquatic equivalent they happened to be – swam and flapped majestically around the still-falling, tumbling, looping rollercoaster.

It's never going to end, realised Dex.

I'm trapped. In Hell. I've been a Bad Man. And it's going toooo laaaassssstt for ever.

There came a solid *clunk*. Dex felt himself jerk forward, then snap back. Tentatively, licking dry lips, he opened his eyes. They were at a disembarkation station, and two thousand nine-hundred and ninety-nine happy customers were disembarking, chattering happily, faces aglow with awe and wonder, laughing and joking, giggling and slapping backs as if... Dex frowned. As if they'd been into battle together, and survived. As if they'd shared some common adversity!

Dex looked around, frowning, to see if anybody else was complaining. They weren't.

So, stubborn as a rampant bull, he looked around for somebody to complain *to*. There was nobody.

Within less than a minute, Dex sat alone in the *Insane* CAR with Molly and Toffee standing on the concrete platform, staring at him.

"Come *on*, Dad," said Molly. "We're the last ones out! Gross!"

"Can we do it again?" beamed Toffee.

Dex clambered out like a monkey with four arms, fighting himself. He was muttering. His eyes had gone hard.

"Didn't you like it, Dad?" asked Molly.

"Yeah. Great. Or something."

"Haha, Dad didn't like it," said Toffee.

Molly grinned with a strain of wisdom that should have had no right crossing an eight-year-old's face. "*I* bet Dad thought we were really going to drown under the sea," said Molly, to Toffee, who sniggered behind her hand. "You know Karen Johnson at school? Well, she came here, and *she* said that *her* dad wet his pants and screamed like a baby! Thought he was going to drown.

Complained to the authorities, and said he was going to the papers and everything. He caused a right stink, and they were banned from the Theme Planet, and shipped off, and kicked out, and sent home, and everybody at school laughed at her when she came in with the photos. They called her a lam0 and a t-plan3t n00b."

"A... a *t-planet noob?*" asked Dex, meekly.

"No, Dad. A *n00b!*"

"Oh. Yes. Silly me. Well. Ahem." He coughed theatrically. "Lead the way." He followed the girls from the tunnel complex, and onto automated walkways that whizzed them back to the surface and *Insane*'s Landing Pad. Katrina was waiting. She was holding something. She had a look of supreme comedy on her pretty features.

"Hey, Dexter..."

"I don't want to see it..."

"You should see it!"

"Let me look!"

"Let me look!"

Mother and daughters spent a few moments laughing at the photo of the three of them, caught at the exact moment the CAR supposedly hit the sea. Dexter Colls did indeed look ridiculous. Not just like a man having a heart-attack, and a man squeezing out a hernia, but also like a man ready to *kill*. Only Dex saw it. In his eyes. The Hunted Animal look. Gleaming. Deadly.

Shit. I know myself too well.

Katrina put her arm around his shoulders and he staggered to a bench under some blue-petalled trees, sinking gratefully into a state of non-movement and non-excitement. "You okay, Big Man?"

"Great. Great! Wonderful."

"Was it that bad?"

"Nah, it was nothing. I think you should have a go." He gave her a nasty sideways glance.

"Ooh, you're tetchy. It was only a ride, Dex."

Dex made a growling sound.

"Come on, Lex is taking us to Area 51B."

"What happens there? They experiment on my internal organs 'cos I'm an alien on this planet?"

"*No*, Dexter. Nothing like that. Come on. All we have to do is watch..."

"Good, 'cos I'm fucking *damned* if you're going to get me on another ride."

"*Tsch*. Language."

Dex gave her a hard stare. "Fuck off," he said, with zero trace of humour.

DEX STARED AT his food with suspicion. Dex always stared at his food with suspicion. He was what Jones generously called "a suspicious eater." Unless he cooked it himself, Dex didn't like to touch it. He was the sort of man who washed pre-washed salad. The sort of man who cut the crusts off bread. The sort of man who didn't like any sort of interference within a one metre circumference of his plate of food – for fear of it being contaminated. He once put an official complaint in at work, citing Health and Safety legislation, because the sinks in the gents' toilets "smelled of fish." He was the sort of man Katrina called a "mardy arse," and the sort Jones referred to as a "pain in the arse." Dex used to grin, and tell them all to "*kiss* his arse."

Katrina cut her fish-steak, and allowed a morsel to melt on her tongue with a piquant delicacy. "Mmm," she said, eyes widening a little. "Delicious! Absolutely fabulous!"

This was Mojojos, the "fine authentic Japachinese restaurant" which had been recommended by Lex, their PD PopBot. The building itself was built in traditional Japachinese white brick and terracotta tile, with – apparently – all materials transported from Earth at very great expense during the old Transport Days, that heady period of Outer-Planet Colonisation.

The interior of Mojojos was cool and dark, with hanging vines and great dark pools filled with the vibrant colours of huge Koi carp – again, transported from Earth and now bred in VATS on the Theme Planet using Ganger technology, which although still in its infancy, was fine for fishpond displays.

Dex pushed his decapus curry around his plate for a while. Kat scowled at him.

"Go on. Eat some."

"I'm just..."

"What?"

"I'm not used to being able to actually finish a whole bloody sentence! You know, without Molly or Toffee kicking their way into the conversation in their size tens."

"I know what you mean." Katrina looked around, in mock fear. "It's way too weird. I just hope they're okay!"

Dex pulled out the KidMonitor and placed it on the table. Molly and Toffee were in the Kiddy Kid Quad of Mojojos, designed "For Kids To Have A Super Time! And Parents To Have A Better One!" Molly was eating pizza, and Toffee was devouring huge "chicken dippers" although what the chicken had been dipped in, Dexter couldn't quite make out on the ten inch plazzy-plasma.

"They're fine, love. Stuffing their faces. As growing girls do," he said.

"Go on, what's wrong with the curry?"

"Nothing... I just, well, obviously I haven't tasted it yet."

"Taste it, damn you!"

"It looks a bit green."

"It's a decapus curry! What colour would you like it to be?"

"Blue?" said Dex, a tad cheekily...

And the waiter was there, removing the plate. "Sir's wish is our command..."

"No, wait," said Dex.

"No, no, please, sir, we will be less than two minutes..."

"Wait!" pleaded Dex as his untouched decapus curry was hurtled away to the kitchens by a man in pink pants.

Katrina stared at him over a forkful of quivering fish steak. He met her gaze. "Idiot," she said.

"I was only joking."

"Yeah, well, they take it seriously around here."

Dex's food was duly returned, blue now, as requested. Grumbling a little, the sort of grumble that wasn't really words, just half-mumbled half-curses, Dex tried an experimental forkful... and his tastebuds seemed to explode. He was hit with richness, flavour, spice and heat. It whirled around his mouth and then his belly, and finally his skull. It was a taste explosion. A sensory hijacking. Indeed, it was the *best* damn curry Dexter Colls had ever, ever experienced.

He looked around at his surroundings with renewed enthusiasm.

"Well?" said Katrina.

"It's brill," he said, with a grin, teeth stained blue.

"Not too hot?"

"No. No, perfect, in fact."

"You mean," Kat feigned mock horror, "we've found some *alien food* you actually like? Ye gods! Wonders will never cease, my handsome, hunky and culinarily-retarded husband."

Dex tucked in. He must have liked it. He stopped talking.

The food was great, the wine superb, and – lulled by a sense of fulfilment and alcohol – Dex didn't even mind when three jajinga chimps came and played guitaviolins by their table. A most hideous screeching noise, to Dex's ears, but for some reason Katrina liked it. *She must be lulled by the romanticism of the whole situation. No point destroying her fantasy, right?*

Later, as Lex led the children back to the hotel and their perfectly climate-controlled rooms, Dex and Katrina walked arm in arm down to the beach. Pretty lights illuminated the walkways in the shapes of various Theme Planet alien constellations. At a low zezub step, they kicked off shoes and walked barefoot in the sand, curling toes, giggling a little, and headed towards the crashing, booming ocean. They stood, holding hands like children, simply staring out at an alien ocean from an alien shore.

"It's just occurred to me," said Dex.

"What's that?"

"I haven't seen a provax yet."

"They keep a low profile in Theme Planet areas. You should have read your in-flight literature. I told you, too. They don't want to get in the way of us *humans* having a good holiday."

"Yeah, but we're on *their* planet."

"And they make plenty of money from us, darling. I've read a lot about the provax; they're not that different from us. We share a similar evolutionary arc. They, too, are descended from apes – or the nearest alien equivalent, hammered out by the same kind of gravity."

"Yeah, well, *The Seeding Theory of Dr Chaos* isn't exactly on my reading list."

They stood in silence for a while. The ocean boomed. Surf rolled up the sand, tickling their toes. It was a long, long moment of perfection.

Dex turned to Katrina. He smiled at her, and felt her face move, shift, a return smile that he couldn't really define in the gloom but could read in the shift of her stance. He knew her too well, he realised.

"I love you," he said.

"I know you do, darling. And I love you back. Love you lots."

"If... if I ever do something bad, or stupid, then I didn't mean it. All right? I love you more than words can say. I'll love you 'til the stars die. I'll love you until the last ounce of breath leaves my body."

She stood on tiptoe, and kissed him, and then held him tight as the ocean sighed and fell around them.

BACK IN THE room, Lex the PopBot had worked a miracle. The children were asleep. Trailing sand, Dex and Katrina moved to the massive bed and stood, holding each other. Slowly, Katrina undressed Dex, her hands teasing on his flesh, running through his chest hair, brushing against his erection. He smiled down at her, and then reached forward to hold her face in his hands. He kissed her, languorously.

Next, with Dex naked, Katrina allowed him to undress her. She stepped from her slinky hydra-skirt (made completely from different colours of suspension-matted oiled water) and they held each other tight in the darkness, naked. In alcoves around the room, sensing the mood, sense candles sprang into light and life. Gentle scents wafted across the space; first, the wide ocean, then pine forests after rain, then the crushed ice of a mountain summit.

"They think of everything," murmured Kat, squeezing her husband.

"They can only add to the experience," he said.

"They certainly can't add to this," she murmured, her hands stroking down his body as she slowly lowered herself to her knees. Dex shuddered, winding his hands through her hair, his eyes closed and his face lifted to the ceiling.

"Didn't realise it was my birthday," he managed.

Pausing, Kat said, "Just as long as you've got those batteries charged..."

"All charged and ready, my love," he sighed.

She stood, and pushed him back onto the bed, which gave a soft hissing sound and contoured itself around him – almost a water-bed, but not quite. "Comfy," he managed.

"It better be strong," said Kat, moving to him, climbing atop him, straddling him. He could smell her want, her lust, her animal need. She oozed sex. *What a wife...*

"You were right," said Dex.

"What's that?" purred Kat.

"This is definitely the best holiday we'll ever have..."

CHAPTER THREE

MISSION

AMBA WALKED DOWN long, bleak corridors formed from tarnished steel. She was naked, her bare feet treading softly, and she looked neither left nor right.

This is humiliating. You should not be treated like this. You are their top killer, their top assassin! Never have you failed your task. Not once has your target escaped. You always get the job done, and done well.

Be quiet, Zi. This is not the time, nor the place.

Amba continued to walk. She passed two heavily-armoured, mounted AI machinegun turrets. They could decimate a human in a heart-beat. Amba ignored their looming menace.

I still think they treat you like scum. Like a prisoner. You deserve more respect. You deserve more... honour! The FRIEND was hard against her heart; a machine threat Amba was oh-so-reluctant to use. The FRIEND was the most savage weapon she'd ever encountered. Simply terrifying.

No, I disagree, Zi. There is no honour in what I do. And they treat me in the way I would expect they treat any dangerous, barely controllable animal. I am not proud of what I do, Zi.

Killing is not something I relish... it's simply a means to an end.

What end?

Amba smiled internally. "Aah, you cannot see that deep, can you?" Her voice seemed unnaturally loud, metallic and abrasive in the hollow reverberating corridor. She felt Zi shrink back, like the toad she was, and Amba found some small gratification in the flash of Zi's bright red fury before her dark sister departed.

Amba felt Zi's mental connection fade like smoke.

Good fucking riddance, she thought.

The corridor ended, leading to a massive chamber – more like the inside of some vast aquatic tank. The floor was corrugated, the walls streaked with rust. High, high above swung several ancient chains, thick enough to moor an Anti-Grav War Frigate.

Amba looked around for a moment, lips pursed, searching for weaponry or a threat of any kind. Warily – Amba was always wary – she strode out towards the centre of the chamber, footsteps echoing. Then she stood, and folded her arms across her breasts, and waited, eyes forward, no expression on her gentle features. And that was the problem, she knew. The way she had been designed. Amba was gently pretty. Not stunningly beautiful – no – that would defeat the object. She was designed to be *typical*. *Average.* A *grey woman.* Engineered normality – on the surface, at least. Until she sprang into action. Until she began the killing...

Amba.

Anarchy Android.

The most lethal lifeform ever created...

There came a *clang,* and across the empty steel tank a wheel spun and a heavy door opened, very much in the manner of a submarine hatch. A figure stepped through. He wore an ankle-length black leather coat, and his hair was long and black, slicked back around neat, powerful features. He strode forwards, and in his right hand he carried a Zippo lighter, and his thumb constantly flicked the lid open, and then closed it; open, then closed.

He stopped several paces from Amba, and stared at her without expression.

She returned his stare, face neutral.

"Welcome home," said the man, finally.

"It is good to be home, Cardinal Romero," said Amba, showing just the right amount of formal respect.

Romero stepped forward then and embraced her, and she held him for a while, thinking how easy it would be to kill him. But then, why would she kill the man who created her? The man who gave her life? To all intents, her living *God?*

"Come with me, Amba. There have been developments."

"You have another mission?"

"Yes. Perhaps your most dangerous yet."

"They are all the same to me, Cardinal. Five or five thousand. It just takes more time."

Romero glanced across at her as they walked, and he marvelled at her normality. At her modesty. At her... average features, average physique. And despite everything, despite her deliberate lack of what were fashionably considered "attractive" qualities in contemporary society, he was aroused by Amba. More than she could have ever believed. *Like a sister,* he thought. *A very special sister.*

Still.

There was a job to do.

They reached the doorway, and stepped through into a warmer environment filled with carpets and glass wall-coverings. A slender robot stood there holding a gown, and Romero gestured. Amba allowed the robot to place the robe over her shoulders, and she stared for just a few moments too long at its polished metal face.

She's still touchy, then, thought Romero. And gave a tight, fleeting smile. That was good. That was information he could use.

They moved past guards and automated AI turrets, down a maze of corridors and through several bullet-lifts which dropped them at dizzying speed further and further below the streets of London.

Eventually, they emerged into a large, plush room. Fountains tinkled, whiskey running through crystal. The walls were decorated in fifty-metre high gold and silver murals. Statues in obsidian were placed at strategic locations, and Amba sensed their hidden high-power weaponry.

"This way."

Romero led her across the vast, garish office, to a genuine oak table around which fifty men could have comfortably sat. Romero took a seat, but Amba remained standing.

"Your tastes grow ever more extravagant," she observed.

"It is a privilege of status."

"Some would call it tacky." Amba gave a smile, but Romero caught the falseness behind the movement. After all, he had designed her. He had engineered her to... perfection.

"You are well, then, Amba? You know, you are my personal favourite of all the Anarchy models. You do *know that*, don't you?"

"I know," said Amba, gently, not looking at him. "What is the mission?"

"So clinical."

"You made me this way."

"So we did."

Romero smiled, reclined, took a cigar from a box and lit it with his golden Zippo. He smoked for a while, watching her. She had left the robe open a touch, and he had a tantalising glimpse of her modest breasts. *Am I that sad? That I lust after the androids I create? Or is it the danger element... even though I created her, even though I designed and coded her genetic structure, she has far surpassed all expectations; has fought and clawed her way to the top of the hierarchy. She has made killing an artform. Even now, she is expecting the random test of her abilities... waiting for it. But then, a creature like Amba sees death and murder in every possible situation...*

They fast-roped from the ceiling, dropped like stones down a well. There were five Anarchy Androids dressed from head-to-foot in black cotton. Each carried a curved black sword and had been trained to the point of extinction with said weapon. They were experts. *Masters.*

They attacked, their movements fluid, from between the statues. Amba somersaulted backwards from a standing position without even tensing her muscles, and swords whistled through the air beneath her; she twisted and kicked off a statue, spinning her trajectory and taking a blade against her arm on its flat side: landing, sliding her arm down the blade to its owner's wrists and breaking them with a swift twist and *crack*. She dropped to one knee, taking the sword from unresisting hands, and rammed the point into the attacking android's groin before standing and front-kicking him from the blade, then reversing it as another leapt from behind and skewering his throat. She stepped left, ripping the blade out sideways in a shower of gore and twirling it expertly as she turned to face the remaining three. They spun their blades slowly, spreading out to surround Amba, and charged as one, and Amba stepped back to the nearest statue, slicing her sword through its protective shell and dropping flat to the floor as the AI's self-preservation took over and all the statues in the room came alive with heavy-calibre machine-gun fire. Bullets screamed through the air, and the three remaining Anarchy Androids were slammed and peppered with bullets, jigging like marionettes with tangled strings.

They hit the ground like roadkill.

Smoke curled through the suddenly silent room.

Slowly, Amba stood, and tossed the sword onto one of the torn, ragged corpses. She walked over to the desk, tilting her head to watch Romero. He was smiling, and still smoking. None of the bullets had gone near him. The AIs were well-programmed like that.

"Predictable," she said, and took a seat across from him, folding her arms.

Romero shrugged. "It's good to see you still have the edge."

"What's the mission?"

"Again, straight to the point. As usual."

"It's what I do. There's no point pretending otherwise."

"Don't you have... *downtime*, Amba? Don't you have any hobbies?"

Amba fixed him with a baleful glare, and a chill ran through Romero. She might be plain. She might be a *grey woman*. But when that stare drilled through your soul, you knew you were dealing with somebody who had side-stepped from the path of humanity. This was no pussycat. This was a psychopath.

"No," she said.

Romero gave a curt nod, and slid a tablet to her. Amba took up what appeared to be a small grey slate, and accessed it with her thumb-print. The grey flickered and displayed an image: an old man, dressed in a smart black suit. The image animated in fits and starts, moving, then freezing, then moving again. To the left, data scrolled in bright green letters.

"He works for the Monolith Corporation."

"Yes. They all do."

"All?"

"Six. Six hits."

Amba gave a nod, and scrolled through the selection of targets on the tablet. Three men. Two women. One teenage, female, and only just sixteen. "No provax?" She gave a wry smile. "You could almost call this race hate."

"No provax," said Romero. "This is political. All six work for Monolith and help with public relations, and the marketing of the Theme Planet, on behalf of the aliens."

"The aliens. I like that." Amba smiled. It was only the *old school* who used the word "alien." Part of humanity's superiority complex – as if they still believed they were the centre of the universe, of an Empire, when in fact they were outclassed in every damn direction, be it genetic or technological.

"Any questions?"

"No."

"You don't want to know what they've done?"

"No."

"Other Anarchy models... well, they want to know. They want to know details. They want justification."

"I don't care." She fixed Romero with that chilling gaze once more, and raised an eyebrow. "Isn't that supposed to be the point? The reason we were made? We're not supposed to care. We're not supposed to crave... humanity."

"Yes, but you always do," said Romero, his voice very, very quiet.

Amba gave a swift shake of her head, and stood. She tucked the hit-list inside her clothing and turned, striding towards the door. She reached the handle, paused, and turned back. Romero was watching her with an expression she could not place.

"You engineered me to kill," she said. And smiled. "So I kill."

Then she was gone, and Romero released his hold on the gun underneath the desk. It was a Techrim 13mm Splinterpistol. They were known, to those in the know, as Android Splitters. And Romero wondered idly if she knew about the gun. *Probably,* he realised. After all, she seemed to know about every other concealed weapon in the room. As she said: it was why they made her. It was what she did.

AMBA LAY ON her bed, in the dark, waiting for her Shuttle time. It was a nameless basic cheap motel room on the outskirts of LLA – one of thousands Amba had stayed in. She did not own a house, felt no affinity nor connection with any property she had ever visited. *Why try to be human?* she'd reasoned. They'd only kill her for it. The government. Oblivion. *Named well,* she smiled, and closed her eyes, concentrating on her breathing.

Outside in a black sedan, two of Romero's killers were watching the apartment. She considered killing them, simply because she did not like being watched – surely her privacy was the one thing she had which they could not *invade,* could not *control.* Her inner thoughts. Her feelings. Her *desires...*

"Other Anarchy models... well, they want to know. They want to know details."

Her reply to Romero had been truthful. She did not want to know. She did not care. One assignment was much like any other assignment. And the minute she started to learn was the minute she started to care. That was a sure-fire way of getting herself *fired*. Ha. Yes. Fired. A bullet fired in the back of her slender skull. Probably from Romero's own Splinterpistol. The coward.

The ceiling cooler hissed and Amba stared at the flickering streamers. She thought back, through long, long years. How many, she really didn't remember. It had been too many, though.

Were you always so cynical? Or did it come after the first few kills? The first five? Ten? Fifty? A hundred? When did it happen? When did the bitterness set in? When did the... death of your longing to join humanity kick you in the guts?

She smiled. Yes. Once she had wanted to be human. Didn't they all? Wanted it so much it burned like a red-hot iron brand in her skull. She had The Dream, and The Dream was a long one, and The Dream was a recurring dream... now a nightmare.

Amba closed her eyes. She prayed, as she always prayed, that she would sleep without dreams, and especially, sleep without The Dream. But it was not to be. God, or the God of Anarchy Androids, was in a bitter, foul mood. He was pissed, pissed at Amber and pissed at her killing. So he would torture her...

Again.

Her eyes closed. She slept.

Amba lived in a small house by the river. It had white walls, and at one corner the brickwork was crumbling and she knew one day she'd have to get round to that damn repair. The windows were very old-Earth, traditional – wooden frames with peeling white paint and single panes of glass. Nothing tech, no plastic-plasty quad-core e-glass thermal glassy glass, oh, no, sir; this was the old type of glass. The stuff that broke and sliced flesh. Nasty shit.

The roof of the house had terracotta tiles, the sort that were kiln-fired. Oldskill. Tradwork. Several were cracked, but such was the roof's construction that no water leaked in. And that was good.

Amba walked up the crushed stone path, her flat shoes crunching, and she breathed the scent from the pine trees surrounding her house. And that was the problem, although not a problem in the dream. Or The Dream.

It was her *house. Ownership. Possession.*

And she revelled in it.

Get to the best bit, bitch, said Zi.

Hey, girl, I knew you'd turn up at the stench of death and corruption! Well done! Welcome to the party.

Hey, fuck you, it's your dream, you invited me.

Zi, nobody would ever invite you. You're worse than plague. More evil than cancer. Go away, somewhere quiet, out in the forest over there. Lie down. And die.

Amba crunched up the path, a gentle incline, and the house came slowly into view, scrolling like a Krunchy Krunch Komputer Game. The white walls. The terracotta roof. And the door. A pale blue door, battered and a little warped, with peeling paint. And it sent shivers down Amba's spine, made her heart skip a beat and lurch up into her mouth like bile. The door. The blue door.

Behind the house, the trees sighed in the wind. Small animals scurried through woodland detritus. The scent of pine was strong, an aromatic wildland perfume. To the right, a river gurgled over rocks. To the left, the forest curved like a scar and rose up the flanks of another pine-clad hill to a circle of stones which sat on the summit, ancient and magical, grey flanks shining.

There was a church up there, as well. Or, more precisely, the remains of a church, with crumbled stone walls, a collapsed rotten roof, and frost-bitten crumbling gravestones. Amba shivered at the thought... and continued up the path towards the door. The blue door.

What's behind the blue door, O little one?

What song will you sing this time?

What dreams will you savour?

Amba reached the top of the path and stopped, panting slightly, drinking in the majesty of the place, and yet... yet filled with the deep fear which always came during The Dream.

Her head moved, shifted, and nothing was real, yet this was more real than real. She focused on the blue door. Behind it was

Heaven and Hell. Her wonder and her nightmare. Something so bad, so evil, so *soul-destroying* she locked it out of her skull every single fucking time, and threw away the key. But with the key fell memory, and so she returned, again and again, to suffer...

Open it, urged Zi, and Amba could sense her inner dark sister's glee.

She did not want to. And as she moved down the path, took hold of the handle, stared at the faded blue peeling paint, she knew – knew in her darkest innermost dark evil place – that she should stop, cease, desist, but she pushed it open anyway... as if there was a switch in her head, a reset switch that could change her, deform her, break her will...

And to Zi's cackle of pleasure, Amba screamed a scream to put out the stars.

Is it so different to be human than android? I mean, we look the same, act the same, are made of the same organic substance, the same flesh and bones; the same raw materials. We eat the same food, shit the same shit. We have the same chemical responses. We both feel love and hate and fear and joy. We respond the same way in most situations. So how can a human have all the rights of life, and yet androids have nothing? We are treated like machines by some, as vermin by others. How does that work? Just because we are created in a laboratory or VAT chamber? Hell, we are genetic cousins...

Don't be naïve, said Zi, crawling into the back of her mind like a slug up the pipe of her spine. *They hate you because you were made better than them. Faster, stronger, more intelligent, more deadly. Humans are frail fucking shells, and they fucking know you're better at everything. They fear you because they want to be you. They hate you, because they are naturally weak, and you are naturally their superior. They will not grant you the gift of recognised life because the early androids committed atrocities that would make even you blush – yes, even with your incredible track record.*

Amba felt herself wither inside, for she knew what Zi said was true.

What shall I do? I cannot carry on like this forever. I cannot kill for Romero and the Oblivion Government indefinitely. At some point, it has to end. At some point, it all must stop; I must stop...

The day you stop is the day you die, said Zi.

And you'd fucking love that, wouldn't you, bitch? snarled Amba. *You'd like to rip out my spine and watch my blood soak into the soil. You'd squat down and piss on my grave, and giggle like a loon as you were doing it.*

Not so, said Zi.

Hah!

Truly. I want you alive, Amba, because if you're not alive, then I'm not alive. If you disintegrate, then I disintegrate. We are symbiotic, my friend; my lover, my sister, my mother. Can you not see that? We are one and the same. Conjoined in mind. Chemically twisted in the flesh...

No, said Amba, *no, that's not the way. Explain it to me, Zi. What are you? Why are you in my head? What brought you here? What brought you to me? What is your end-game? I cannot take your torture any longer... I want you gone, you hear? I want you slaughtered and cast away as ash in the wind. I'll take the fucking FRIEND and toss it into an Infinity Well!*

You don't mean that, said Zi, and Amba heard the hardness in her voice. Like granite. Like lead. Like finely-machined metal designed only to kill.

Yes I do, bitch! I want you gone from my skull!

And who would help you then? snarled Zi, and Amba sensed the sudden rise of her temper, something she had felt a hundred times, a *thousand* times on the battlefield, in dark alleys filled with murder, in bloody crime scenes with the death-drenched FRIEND in her hand. *Who would bail you out when progress became impossible? Who would help you in your moments of weakness, when you break down and squat in the mud in the piss and the shit, and weep your tears of pure unadulterated weakness? Who'd save you then, Amba? Who'd be your backup? Who'd be your saviour?*

YOU ARE NOT MY SAVIOUR! she screamed, then. NOT MY FUCKING SAVIOUR, DO YOU HEAR?

Zi left; and Amba heard her hollow laughter rattling off like dice made from human knuckles on the tin-lid of a pauper's coffin. On the bed, Amba sat up and put her head in her hands.

Am I going crazy?

This is not part of being an android.

This is nothing to do with the Anarchy Models.

Zi, well, Zi is something else...

Again, she considered destroying the FRIEND. It sat on the dresser, small and black and harmless looking. But it was dangerous. *She* was dangerous. Zi was the most dangerous weapon ever created. But it wasn't supposed to *speak* to her; to mock her, taunt her, drive her insane with its challenge. And Zi would never speak of why she was created; what, in fact, was her ultimate purpose.

Amba had once broken into a high-security Oblivion GOV UNIT and hijacked the files on Anarchy. She'd wanted to know... *more.* It had been a quest, not so much about identity, as about *understanding.* She wished to understand herself – at a basic level. At basic concept. At basic construct.

Amba was, to all intents and purposes, human. She had the same genetic core. But her bones were blended with a natural titanium alloy produced by special glands in her throat. Her muscles were harder, stronger, woven with Kevlar. Her internal organs were lined with chitin taken from insect DNA. She was impervious to most toxins, including radiation. And her brain synapses operated at a constant higher rate than a "normal" human creature. Amba was hard. Harder than hard. She was the perfect soldier. The perfect killer. And yet...

Nowhere in the files was there mention of Zi.

Zi, her happy, friendly, bio-encoded FRIEND.

Zi was a weapon. She wasn't supposed to have a... personality.

Zi was a bug in the code. A worm in the apple core. A glitch in the matrix.

And, whether Amba liked it or not, Zi was here to stay...

"Why can't I be human?"

Because you are not.

"Why can I not live a simple human life?"

Because they despise you.

"How can I escape?"

Then she lay on the bed, and she cried, and she dreamt of a time when she would find a man, find the right man, a man to love, and he would kiss her and hold her in the darkness and tell her not to be frightened. Everything would be all right. And they would breakfast in sunlight. They would laugh together at things that were funny, and cry together at things that were sad. They would go for meals at posh restaurants. They would visit the cinema and eat popcorn and hot-dogs, then go out for drinks to discuss the themes in the film. They would visit friends and tell stories and drink wine and laugh long into the night. Then, when they settled down, she would get pregnant and she would have a child...

have a child...

a pretty little girl...

and buy a house...

A house with a pale blue door.

"TWENTY MINUTES, MA'AM."

Amba nodded and shouldered her pack. She looked around the crappy hotel room for the last time. She would never come back to this room – a place she'd called home for three months whilst she completed a series of missions. No. Now, it was time to move on. Now she had a new job. Six hits. On Theme Planet...

And then what?

She smiled, a sour, bitter smile.

And then nothing. Keep on going. Keep moving. Keep on killing. Until *they* killed her.

Amba stepped out the door and it gave a rattling *click* behind her. The corridor was plush, with fake rich-gilt wallpaper and semi-liquid carpets; *fake, like me,* she thought. She walked down the long corridor to the sicklift, which dropped her to ground floor and reception. As she stepped from the sicklift Amba scanned reception, clocking the two men who'd followed her previously – either for Oblivion or... for somebody else. It didn't matter. It was irrelevant. If they made a move, she'd waste them.

Amba moved out into the sunshine. Northside LLA was a heaving termite heap of activity. The roads, both upper and lower levels, were crammed with traffic belching eco-fumes. Snakes of people streamed down footwalks and the whole overpopulated mess was a bustling chaos of bustling hellside.

Amba sighed, licked her lips, subtly checked her pursuers, and stepped into the snakes.

Was sucked into their blood.

Swallowed by their venom.

THE THEME PLANET Shuttle was on time. The Theme Planet Shuttle was always on time. Amba stood at the fifty-foot-high windows watching the huge passenger liner coming in to land, jets belching fire, the throb of the Shuttle's matrix engines pulsing through the floor, through her boots.

Amba finished her coffee, where the cheap beans left a bitter taste, and dropping the cup into a CheeryBin ("Hey-hey-hey! Thank you, ma'am, for not littering! Have a *neeeee*ice day!") headed for the restrooms, signified by door images of a woman and various female alien life-forms. And a red blob.

The restroom was deserted, and Amba moved to a cubicle, hung her pack on the back of the door, dropped her pants and pissed, head to one side, listening. There came a *click*. Heavy boots trod slowly on bathroom tiles.

Amba pulled up her pants and gently lifted her pack. She lowered it to her back, tightening both straps, eyes narrowing. Her nostrils twitched. Whoever was out there was *male*. There came the tiniest of sounds; the sound of something well-oiled, steel, threaded. Like a nut and bolt. Like a silencer being fastened to a pistol...

"Ma'am, this is LLA Shuttleport Security. Can you step out of the cubicle, please?"

"I'm on the toilet, I have bad stomach pains. What seems to be the problem, officer?" she said, flattening herself to one side of the wall.

The door exploded with shards of torn wood as five silenced bullets ate through the cubicle and shattered the porcelain eco-toilet. Amba stepped back into the firing line and front-kicked the door from its hinges. The door slammed into the man, throwing him back with a grunt, and Amba dropped to one knee and peered out. There were four men in black suits, all carrying guns, blinking fast and only just reacting to the kicked door... Amba rolled forward, and as bullets started to *ping* around her, she took the silenced pistol from the hand of the man felled by door, turned, steadied the pistol with both hands – cool, calm – delivered four headshots in quick succession. Blood sprayed the walls and mirrors. Four men hit the ground wetly, their skulls exploded. Pulped brain leaked across the white tiles. Tongues lolled and popped eyeballs turned inwards. Skull shards glistened like teeth.

Amba turned, grabbed the throat of the man stunned by the door, and lifted him up, ramming him back against the vanity mirror wall. The wall cracked under the impact, and the man struggled for a moment in pain, confused, before regaining his composure and looking deep into Amba's eyes.

He glanced left, to his dead comrades.

"It is you," he said.

Amba tilted her head. "Explain."

The man smiled, saliva strung with blood. "Fuck you," he said.

Amba lifted the silenced pistol, and put a bullet through his kneecap. He went rigid for a moment, his breathing becoming heavy and laboured, and he slumped back a little against the broken mirror.

"Explain," she repeated.

"No," he croaked.

"Who do you work for?"

He stared into her eyes, and despite his pain, there was an iron will there. He would not talk. Maybe *could* not talk. He either did not know answers, or he'd been fed braineeze drugs. Amba gave a narrow smile, but there was no smile in her eyes. Shit. Or maybe, *maybe* he was just *tough*. She'd soon see how tough.

She lifted her right hand, extended two slightly hooked fingers towards his eye, and watched as understanding dawned. She would scoop out his eyeball and feed it to him.

"*No...*" he whispered.

"Tell me, fucker," she hissed.

There came a clatter, and a woman appeared with her daughter, who was perhaps ten years old. They were staring, the woman's mouth open in shock, a realisation of horror dawning in her wide brown eyes. But the child stared at Amba in innocence, head tilted slightly to one side as if analysing the android. She was getting a good long look, and it was too much, and it was too bad. Amba's arm snapped up, and at the end of it was –

the gun.

She shot the child first. It was always easier that way. If she'd shot the mother, she would have had to watch the pain of realisation in the child's eyes. So Amba got it done the hard way, but also the easy way. She got it done *the right way.* The young girl seemed to settle down on her haunches with a sigh, a kind of sad deflation, her arms going floppy, a red hole in her forehead above one eye. The mother was turning even at the *phzzt* of the silenced gun. Turning, mouth opening, breathing in sharply to scream –

Amba fired twice, one bullet through the lungs, killing the inhalation with a hiss, second bullet through the woman's mouth, destroying lips, teeth and tongue, then on through the back of her skull. Killing her instantly. Blood spattered the wall in what auteurs called *Picasso Piss.* She was dead before she hit the ground, with shards of teeth and shredded tongue on her blood-drenched chin.

Back to the man. The goon. The heavy. No time. *No time.*

You've no time, said Zi, and Amba knew it. He had his hands raised. He understood. She gritted her teeth. Shot him through his hand and eyeball. He bounced back onto a sink, which began gushing water, then slithered to the floor. The water sounded like rainfall. Beautiful, sultry rainfall.

Amba put another bullet in his skull, then moved through the other attackers, delivering a second BLAM to each. She dropped the gun, washed blood speckles from her hand, and on her way out stopped by the mother. She stared for a moment.

Slowly, drawn by an invisible, unstoppable cord, Amba's head turned to the child. She was pretty. Beautiful, even in death. Her eyes, like her mother's, were large and circular and brown. Amba licked her lips. Shit. *Shit.*

She stepped over corpses and closed the restroom door. Turning, her slender fingers closed over the digital lock and crushed it, twisting. Locking it. Disabling it. Her slender fingers were a lot stronger than they looked. A *lot.*

She queued through passport control, and unusually, her heart was beating fast. After all, this was just another murder, just another killing, right? It was what she did. She did the job, did the job well, did the killing well. End of story. *End of fucking story.*

She boarded the Shuttle. Was shown to her comfy seat. Her face was impassive. And as she settled down, settled back, watched a glass of water placed before her, rested back her head against the comfortable headrest, and watched the surface of the water disturbed *oh, so gently* by the Shuttle's take-off – she thought back, back to the girl, back to the bullet in the skull.

Why me, Mommy? Why did the bad lady shoot me?

Cold, hard eyes staring at her. *Because she had to, darling. Because she had to protect her own anonymity.*

But I wouldn't have said anything, Mommy. I promise! If only she hadn't shot us. If only she hadn't killed us.

Shh, darling. Go to sleep. Go to sleep for... well. Forever.

But why, Mommy? Why?

Hard eyes. Cold eyes. Eyes drilling into her soul. Eyes drilling right down to the core of her existence to find the apple-core was rotten; and she was dead inside. Dead. And lost. And gone.

Because, said Mommy, slowly, her mouth forming words with care, her smashed mouth, her torn mouth with its broken teeth and ripped tongue and bullet-slashed lips, mouth filling with blood even as she spoke, blood which spilled down her chin and stained her flowery blouse, *because she is an android, and androids aren't human; they look human, they sound human, but there's something missing that no genetic engineer can ever create. You see, they're a made thing, a machine organism, and, my sweet, there's no genetic craftsman alive in the Four Galaxies who can build a soul...*

THE SHUTTLE CRUISED smooth, and Amba dreamed about the white house with the terracotta roof. She walked towards the door, the peeling door, the blue door – only now, in her path, stood the young girl she had shot. The bullet hole above the child's eye glistened. She looked pale as moonlight. Dead as a corpse.

What do you want?
I want to understand.
Why?
Because until I understand, I can never be at peace.
What do you want to know?
Why you killed me. Why you killed us. We did you no harm.
I killed you because I had to. To protect my position as...
A killer?
Catch 22.
Round and round we go. Where we'll stop, nobody knows.

AMBA AWOKE WITH a start, and spent a moment reorientating herself. It was rare she slept. The Anarchy models could operate on one hour's sleep every sixty. She gazed out of the Shuttle's porthole at the endless drifts of space. Amba shivered. Here was something far more vast than the desolation of her soul; more empty than her empathy. Here was eternity. Here was cold death.

Amba shivered, and accepted a coffee from a passing drone, which also offered her a thermblanket when it noted her temperature. The drone hovered for a moment, then disappeared. Amba sipped the hot bitter brew, and wrapped herself up tight. She was shivering, and felt far from well. What the hell was the matter with her?

Guilt? mocked Zi, crawling from under her mental rock.

Get fucked.

You need me.

I need you like a hole in the head.

For the hundredth time Amba pictured the little girl she'd killed, and recognised in herself that she *was not right*. Nothing affected her like this. Not murder. Not mass execution. Not genocide. So what was so fucking different now? Where the fuck had this new humanity crawled from?

A queasiness crept over her, and she felt sick. She stumbled down the aisle and into the toilet, which locked behind her and began to play a gentle piano track. She heaved over the sink, vomiting coffee, and then stayed there for a while, shivering, her skin clammy, a sour taste in her mouth and in her soul.

"Damn this place," she muttered. "Damn this mission."

When she awoke, a planet filled the Shuttle's porthole. It was vast. Vast. Theme Planet turned below, in slow motion, majestic, titanic, the oceans painted blue like some wonderful pastel painting, its different continents showing amber and grey and green. Clouds streamed like molten silver. Sunlight painted vast patterns across the oceans. Amba was impressed, and it took a lot to impress the cynical Anarchy Android.

She watched, entranced, as they began to plummet through the atmosphere, and felt a queasy sensation inside. The Shuttle was smooth, with only a little entry vibration, and Amba sipped a snorkel of water and listened to the squeaks of joy from children around her, bouncing in their seats as the Theme Planet's rides steadily came into focus.

"Ladies and gentleman, this is your pilot, Kevin, speaking. During our approach to Theme Planet, you can just make out to your left Adventure Central. I, Kevin, can personally recommend the Museum of Baron Nutcase, which I have wandered around for days at a time. For those with an adventurous streak, and I count myself amongst those people, there's the Skycloud Mountains, especially popular with climbers who want the thrill and danger of high peaks without the danger of falling off and dying... a-ha-ha-ha... there's the Pterodactyl Castle, in which I heartily recommend the *Hunt Your Own T-Rex Supper* quest, and if you squint really tight RIGHT NOW you can see The Canyon of Eternal Torture. See how big it is? See how deep it is? See how many have been impaled *a ha ha ha* only joking youngsters! To your right, the pink, quivering, wobbling island you can make out amongst gently lapping silver waters is *Pleasure Island*, and this one is for the mums and dads, boyfriends and girlfriends, and young lovers of every alien persuasion. I can heartily recommend Sex City where, ahem, every whim and nuance is catered for [sigh] and indeed, walk hand in hand through the Glade of Eternal Delight, the Hanging Gardens of Babylon and around the lapping shores of Virgin's Lake, which is exactly the same shape as a pus... oh, we're coming into land, buckle yourselves down and prepare to visit..." – all the children joined in to shout the words – "the Theme Planet! *It's better than drugs! It's better than sex! It's fun, it's fast, it's neat... If you haven't been sick, you soon will be!* BLEEEUURGGHHHH *hahahahahahahaha!*"

Amba sipped her water. She heard the *crack* and whine as landing gear descended, and then closed her eyes and rested her head back, because she was thinking, reliving memories of a thousand infiltrations and fast SLAM drops and going into battle, machine guns rattling, yammering, bombs exploding, the pattering of shrapnel on the hull of armoured vehicles. She shivered. Shit. And here she was. Back on the ground. Back in the jaws. Ready for the kill. She opened her eyes and shrugged off her humanity like a disintegrating shroud.

Good. That was the way it fucking should be.

Six murders. Six hits.

Then she could go home.

Then they could all go home.

"MADAM, COULD YOU please come with us?"

Amba stopped, holding up the queue of people eager to get through immigration and onto the rides.

"Come on, missus, get out of the way!" said one little girl with green eyes and black hair. Amba stepped smoothly to the side, and one of the guards took her arm in an iron-firm *don't-fuck-with-me* grip.

Amba glanced around. There were five guards, armoured, with black insect-eye helmets. To the right, she saw another ten with machine guns. And there were people – hordes of people, pushing and jostling, eager to get out on the rides, eager to enjoy the Theme Planet, to enjoy their vacation!

"Am I in some kind of trouble, officer?" Amba said, smoothly. "There must have been a mistake."

She moved with the man, who guided her expertly. Amba could have killed him five times by the time they reached the flat grey door, a door that was easy to miss and blended with the wall. Amba tutted to herself. She had let her guard down for an instant, and they'd taken her in a public place. Far too public. No. She would bide her time. Wait.

"This way," he repeated.

She stepped through the door, and something cold touched the back of her neck and zapped her. She was unconscious before she hit the floor.

* * *

AMBA OPENED HER eyes. The walls and floor and ceiling were chrome, polished and gleaming. "That was neat, what you did back on Earth," came a voice, a female voice, and Amba frowned. It rang some distant memory. She placed her hand to her chest, protectively, but Zi was still there, as hard as her heart. She smiled at that. Very funny.

We can do it now, said Zi.

Soon, she soothed, recognising she would need the FRIEND's violence. Intuitively, she realised things were getting... serious.

"I don't know what you're talking about," said Amba.

"Well, your denial is of no consequence."

There came a hissing sound and Amba's eyes flared wide. Gas! So quick? She hadn't anticipated...

Her nostrils twitched. Krakkium cyanide.

She leapt at the wall, hands tearing at the smooth chrome, but was punched back by a massive electric shock which tossed her limp and rolling across the floor.

"Relax," chuckled the voice. "Enjoy the ride."

CHAPTER FOUR
TH3 M1SS1NG

DEX YAWNED AND came round slowly from a deep, necessary sleep. Recharge, he thought. That's what this holiday is. A recharge! The option to get away from it all, get away from the stresses of life in London. To sit back, and relax, and weigh up one's options in life.

Gradually, light oozed through his slumber and, yawning, Dex rolled over and reached out for Katrina, hoping for that soft warm flesh contact that made sleeping with a woman so special. The space next to him was empty. But damn, she was an early riser – even after all the wine and sex? Dex grinned to himself, remembering their previous evening's antics. *God, I'm good,* he thought.

Slowly, he sat up. "Katrina?" No response.

Dex climbed to his feet, back aching a little, knees aching a little, everything aching a little. *I'm getting old,* he thought with just a touch of sourness. *Soon it'll be time to visit the joint-refit doctors!* But he knew, deep down, he never would. Some people visited the *blades* for sheer fun. Vanity obsessives. Others, more restrained, visited only when their human shells – their organic chassis – started to break down, to creak, to show its age like a ground-down, ungreased ball-joint. But Dex, Dex was old school; probably got it from his dad. He hated machines. Hated doctors. Hated scalpels and needles and medical circular saws... he shivered.

Dex padded into the bathroom and peered in the mirror. "Getting old, you old gimmer bastard," he said to his reflection, eyes serious, then cracked his face like an egg and broke into a yolk smile. "Yes, but it's your children that make you feel young again. Right?" Talking of children, why weren't they bouncing up and down on his fat belly?

Dex yawned again, and hit the red button on the mirror console. The mirror shimmered and two tiny openings appeared; from the quivering holes emerged two metal arms, which whirred into life, one holding a toothbrush with paste, which was gently inserted into Dex's mouth to brush at his teeth, the second holding a self-foaming razor, which began its shaving duties. Dex stood, grumbling a little and wondering why he couldn't just do it himself, but Kat insisted he "catch up with the machine times" and "enjoy the technology of today" and, more specifically, that he "stop being a moaning old git of a goat."

As the arms clunked and clattered away, Dex moved to the toilet and relieved himself, eyeing the small fluttering butterfly moppers which cleaned the toilet seat even as he sprinkled. Frowning, he deliberately pissed on the floor. They mopped that up as well. *Oh, to live in such a perfect world! Where the air is always clean, the flowers always beautiful, the people constantly nice to one another. Theme Planet. Theme World. The perfect vacation. The perfect time for fun with the family...*

Dex thought back to London. The guns, the dirt and the killing. Ha! His existence *there* made Theme Planet even *more* surreal. His job in the PUF police made his time *here and now* even more drug-induced; a different world.

Dex stepped into the shower and had a long, leisurely soak. Then he stood as air-blowers dried him, and he stepped out to discover some machine, somewhere, had laid out fresh clothes. He picked up a thin cotton shirt. It smelled distantly of lavender.

"Too fucking perfect," he growled, and dressed in shirt, shorts and sandals.

Dex left the bathroom and moved through the hotel suite, and stopped for a moment in the wide corridor outside the kitchen. Something was wrong. It was quiet. *Too* quiet. Molly and Toffee were *never* that quiet. Even asleep, they argued like torturer and victim.

Dex flip-flopped into the kitchen and put his hands on his hips, looking around. At the dining table were plates of crumbs, and juice cups, half full. The coffee machine was also half full, a tiny red light signalling it was still heated. On the breakfast bar was a cup.

"Kat? Molly? Toffee?"

Dex shrugged, and moved to the empty cup. There was a lipstick mark on it, and dregs nestling in the bottom.

"Must have gone for an early morning swim," he muttered, and moved to the comm.

"And a very good morning, sir. What can reception do for you?"

"Hi, er, this is Dexter Colls in room 237. I wonder, have you seen my wife, Katrina Colls, this morning?"

"Yes sir, I have. They left early. Your two little girls – is it Molly and Toffee, sir? – they were wearing bathing costumes."

"Ah. Right, then. They must have gone to the pool."

"That was my assumption, sir. Would you like me to get somebody to give them a message?"

"No, no, that's okay. I'll pop down in a little while."

He killed the comm and poured himself a coffee. An early morning swim, eh? Well, he had stayed in bed a *rather long time*. Serve him right if they disappeared for an hour without him. Dex added four large sugars to the coffee, and sipped it as he moved across the generous space of the suite's living room. He reached the balcony doors and at a touch, one slid open. Warm air greeted him, and the scent of the sea. Sunlight sparkled silver on distant waves, and Dex stepped out into the beautiful fresh air, drinking in the scenery, the long widening snake of the beach, the turquoise waters, a few watersport fanatics out in boats and on hover-skis.

Dex stood for a while, enjoying the sunshine and the gentle breeze which caressed him, blowing away the cobwebs of too much alcohol and too little sleep. Below, he could hear scattered voices and occasional laughter. And splashes, in the pool. The pool! Dex grinned to himself, and leant over the rail, which gave a warning chime. There, there was the water glittering under sunlight. And there... no. His eyes roved over those present, sunbathing, splashing. Few of them, in all reality. Theme Planet prided itself on vast accommodations; *nobody*, proclaimed Theme Planet literature, *should be forced on top of one another during vacation time!* and Dex heartily agreed.

His eyes roved, but he could not locate Katrina and his girls. He gave a little shrug, went back inside, and arming himself with a lobster ice-cream from the freezer, headed out from the hotel suite.

He padded along quiet corridors. Sunlight gleamed all around from high windows. It was a very relaxing, airy place to be.

Dex reached the lift, stepped inside, and tapped his foot as Ronan the Android sang *Life's Just Another Rollercoasting Coaster*. There was a pleasant *bing-bong* as the lift hit ground level and Dex stepped out into the marble-floored, plant-festooned reception area. It was as big and luxurious as he remembered; no, in fact it appeared *bigger* and *more luxurious* than he remembered. He glanced up at a mirrored ceiling so high it played havoc with his vertigo, and licking ice-cream, headed for the pool area.

It was comfortably hot as he stepped into the sun-trap surrounding the pool. Doors slid closed behind him. Plodding along, licking his ice-cream, Dex's eyes scanned the poolside. He frowned. No Katrina. No Molly. No Toffee. How odd. Maybe Kat had taken the girls to the toilet? Or the shops? The girls were always bloody nagging for a new toy, or some new gadget.

He scanned again, searching the sun-loungers for personal sun towels bearing images of the legendary kids toys, Punky Punk and the Punky Puking Punks, and Bilbo the Badger. There were none to be seen. In fact, there were no sun loungers at all with abandoned towels.

"How odd," he said, out loud this time.

He circled the pool area, and stopped by two young women who were creaming up. "Excuse me. You haven't seen a woman out here with two young girls? I seem to have misplaced my family."

Both women smiled and shook their heads. "Not this morning," said the brunette. "Sorry."

"Thanks."

Dex continued his circuit of the pool area, dropped his unfinished ice-cream into a SuckSuck Basket, and entered the cool interior of the reception. To his right, a man in a cream suit was reading a newspaper. He was heavyset, with dark bushed eyebrows and shades on, despite being indoors.

Dex moved to the reception desk. "Hello. I'm Dexter Colls from 237. I phoned down earlier, and was told my wife and children were by the pool."

"Oh, yes, Mr Colls. Your wife left a message for you. I'll just get it."

Dex felt breath ease from his anxious frame and he relaxed. Of course! They'd got tired of the pool early on, moved somewhere else. But then, hadn't the women at the pool said no family matching his description had even *been* by the poolside? Yes, but in reality the women had just been creaming up. So they hadn't been there long themselves.

The receptionist, a pretty little thing with glossy green hair and a neat black suit, returned carrying a small envelope. Dex broke the seal and removed a small card. On it, in Katrina's small, neat handwriting, it said, **Dexter – got tired of waiting for you. Gone shopping.**

Dex pocketed the card and gave the receptionist a smile and a nod. He moved back to the lift, stepped in, and pressed the button – just as there came a sudden *whoosh* of air and Lex the PopBot hurtled across reception and spun into the lift alongside him.

"Ah, Dexter! There you are!" said the PopBot.

"Have you seen Katrina?" said Dex, as the doors slid shut and the lift continued to play Ronan the Android's happy, chirpy music.

"No," said Lex, the small black ball spinning slowly, "but that shouldn't matter to you."

"Why not?"

"Because I'm going to crack your skull like an egg."

Dex blinked, the words not quite sinking in, and suddenly the PopBot shot across the lift interior. Dex flicked himself to one side as the black ball whined past his face, missing him by a hair's breadth, and Lex bounced from the wall with a deep metallic *thunk,* leaving a massive dent. On the ricochet, Lex slammed back at Dex like an insane return volley in a violent squash game. Dex threw up his arms, twisting, and the PopBot glanced from his limb, leaving a heavy black bruise from wrist to elbow, before whining upwards and smashing into the control panel of the lift. Sparks flew as the lift gave a mighty screech of stressed alloy and tortured components, shuddered and came to a halt.

Dex rolled, came up fast, eyes narrowed and lips drawn back in a snarl over bared teeth. "You little bastard. What have you done with my family?"

The PopBot extricated itself from the smashed instruments and spun for a few moments, tiny lightning arcs scattering across its black casing. Then it shifted to face him, and the slots glowed a deep, disturbing red.

"Just die, like a good boy," said Lex.

"What have you done to my children?"

"Eaten them, you human bastard."

The PopBot hurtled at Dex, and he leapt and caught the ball, which dragged him up with it and slammed into the wall and then the ceiling, where alloy panels rippled and lights seemed to smash and burn all around him. Dex was given a high-intensity electric shock, and flung from the ceiling back across the lift's interior, as Ronan the Android warbled on, happily and blissfully unaware of the fight in the elevator cubicle.

Dex lay for a moment, stunned, then crawled to his knees. Lights and fire smashed through his brain. He spat out a mouthful of blood, and a tooth, and his tongue probed the broken interior of his mouth.

He stood, fast, training and instinct kicking in from years of violence on the streets of London. No weapons, no armour. He knew from experience PopBots were tough little bastards, and it took more than a right hook to damage their alloy cases. His mind worked fast, but not fast enough. Lex the PopBot hummed and spun, and descended from the ceiling to hang, immobile, directly before him.

"Why?" said Dex.

"Because," said the PopBot, infuriatingly.

It darted at him, a deadly circular missile, and Dex threw himself sideways with a speed that surprised even himself. Lex hit the wall, leaving another dent, but Dex was twisting, hand reaching into the cavity of the broken control panel and grabbing the insulated section of a sparking, high-voltage cable...

"Don't..." said Lex, as Dexter swung the thick, steel-woven cable at the PopBot. There came a terrific actinic *zap* which blinded Dex, and the PopBot hurtled into a central support strut. A deafening *clang* followed, and the elevator shuddered. The PopBot hit the ground with a dull heavy *clank*, and lay on the thick carpet, unmoving.

Dex dropped the fizzing cable, panting, and glanced at his injured right arm. The little bastard had taken a strip of skin from wrist to elbow; it was a damn miracle it hadn't shattered his bones!

"Where's my wife?" he said, voice thick, head pounding, and kicked the PopBot. But it was immobile. It was dead. "Shit."

"DO NOT WORRY," came the elevator's automated emergency recording, "THE LIFT IS IMMOBILE FOR YOUR BEST INTERESTS. DO NOT PANIC, DO NOT WORRY, THE LIFT HAS STOPPED, AND YOU WILL SOON BE RESCUED. DO NOT PANIC, DO NOT WORRY, THE HOTEL MANAGEMENT HAVE BEEN INFORMED AND YOU WILL SHORTLY BE RESCUED. ALLOW US TO PLAY RONAN THE ANDROID'S GREATEST HITS FOR YOU WHILE YOU WAIT..."

Dex glanced up at the damaged elevator ceiling. He tensed himself, then leapt, fingers catching the edge of the shattered panel from which he had so recently bounced. He hauled himself up through smashed alloy panels into a tall, cool tower. Dex glanced up at a distant pin-prick of light. Huge cables as thick as his waist hung immobile above him.

"PLEASE COME BACK," said the elevator's automated emergency recording, "YOU HAVE ENTERED A PROHIBITED AREA. HUMANS ARE NOT ALLOWED IN THE PROHIBITED AREA. ALL DAMAGES WILL BE CHARGED TO YOUR ROOM ACCOUNT FOR ENTERING THE PROHIBITED AREA. PLEASE COME BACK…"

Far above, there were various *clangs* and bangs. He could hear voices. Dex picked his way carefully across the roof and noted an emergency ladder in a shallow recess. He started to climb, and within a minute had left the stricken elevator and its dead, blasted PopBot behind.

A cool wind caressed him.

As he climbed, he had a moment to think.

Katrina, and the children, had been taken. Why? And by whom?

What in the name of Hell was going on? Lex, the friendly little holiday rep PopBot, had turned nasty and foul – as so often holiday reps could, admittedly. But they didn't normally try to *kill* the tourists! Had its AI screwed up? Had its programming become corrupt? Was it working alone? Or was it *bigger* than just one menial device…

Dex shook his head, muscles burning with the stress of the ladder ascent. It just didn't make sense. None of it made sense! They were on a bloody holiday! On Theme Planet! A holiday paradise!

No. That just couldn't be it. Katrina and the kids had simply gone out shopping, and this mad little PopBot bastard had burnt a circuit. Gone AWOL from the Logic Department. Got himself a dose of silicon rot, and taken a pop at Dexter; well, he would complain to the management, that's for sure! To the highest authorities!

Dex reached a platform and stopped. There were numbers on the wall and he squinted. Floor 2. His floor. He shuffled around to the elevator doors and glanced down. It wasn't that far, in all reality, but certainly far enough to break a few bones. Or even a skull.

Thankfully, helpful engineers had provided a lever for just such an eventuality. Dex pulled the lever, and it opened the doors with a grinding, staggered mechanical motion. Panting, covered in lift oil, Dex scrambled out through the half-open doors and stood on the plush carpets, feeling disorientated. 237. He turned. *That way...*

He started to run. He wasn't sure why. Why run if it was a simple case of dysfunctional silicon shit?

Dex rounded a corner, reached his hotel suite and slapped his palm on the reader. The door opened and he stepped in – to see a man across the room rifling through a chest of diamond drawers. It was the man from the lobby, the man in the cream suit. He whirled as Dex entered, and Dex froze for a moment, utterly lost. Then the man lifted his hand and at the end of it sprouted...

A gun.

Dex gave a skeletal grin.

"So," he said.

"You're to come with me and not cause any trouble," said the man, eyes hidden behind his sunglasses.

"Oh yeah? I suppose that's why you sent the little bauble to smash my head in?"

The man considered this, then opened fire – but Dex, trained in the scumbag shitpits of London's Arse End, a man who had stayed alive by instinct and training and sheer bloody-mindedness – Dex had read the dude's intentions and was already moving. He leapt across the kitchen counter as bullets whined behind him and dented the cupboards, and dropped into the kitchen behind them. More bullets thumped heavily into the counter, and sparks cascaded above Dex.

"Come out, Dexter Colls. We can do this the easy way, or we can do it the hard way."

Dex said nothing. He knelt up and opened the first draw he came to on slick oiled wheels. Whisks and spoons.

"Come on, Mr Colls. We have your wife and children. If you don't come quietly then they're going to get hurt. Well. Hurt *more.*"

Dex ground his teeth. The third drawer held... knives. He smiled a cold smile. Dex liked knives. He understood knives. He pulled free a handful of diamond-handled blades with a faint rattle, separated them carefully, weighing each one, then eased along the counter, trying his hardest to make no sound. He opened the nearest cupboard, wincing at the tiniest of squeaks, and removed a steel pan.

"I'm going to count to three," said the cream-suited man, "then I'm going to come and get you. And when I come and get you, I won't be a happy man at all. Do you understand me, Mr Colls? Do you understand threats of violence and torture?"

Dex said nothing.

"One."

Dex tensed himself.

"Two."

Dex hurled the pan away from himself and the gun yammered. Dex was up, his arm whipped forward, and a long heavy blade sailed through the air. It slammed into the man's throat, slightly off-centre. Blood spewed out. The man gasped, gun falling from loose fingers, and he went down on one knee. His hand came up and touched the blade gingerly. Blood pumped over his fingers, down his cream suit. He dropped to his other knee and Dex stood, leaping over the kitchen counter, glancing right to check the door, then moving to the man and glancing down at him, another knife in his fist, grim despair on his face.

"Where's my wife?" said Dexter.

The man smiled. Dex back-handed him across the face, knocking him onto his side, where he rolled, gurgling for a moment. His sunglasses had been knocked free and his eyes were orange; and very, very bright.

So then. A provax. One of the aliens that ran Theme Planet. One of the "men" in charge. *Great.*

The man – the *provax*, Dex corrected – was stretching slowly for his gun as milky blood oozed from the wound. Dex strode and scooped up the weapon, eyeing the archaic markings on the dull black metal. Almost human. Almost.

He pointed the gun at the provax.

"Talk."

Wheezing, the provax sat up, back against a comfort chair, and again probed the knife. "You... you bast... ard," he managed.

"Where's my family?"

The man started to chuckle, milk blood bubbling around the wound. His hands dropped to his sides, and gritting his teeth Dex knelt down on the rich carpet beside him and took hold of the embedded knife.

He glanced around. This was too weird. Too surreal. The perfect hotel suite on the perfect holiday planet. Coffee cups still littering the worktop. Kids' toys on the settee. Discarded cardigans. Bullet dents in the alloy kitchen cupboards. Sunlight streaming through balcony doors.

Distantly, the sea roared.

Too weird. *Too fucking weird by a long shot.*

"As you said, I'm going to count to three. Then..."

"It won't work. I don't know where they are."

"Well." Dex considered this. "I'm going to torture you anyway."

He pushed the knife in a little bit more, and the man in the cream suit started to thrash, gurgling, his hands hitting limply at Dex. Dex moved his face in close to the man. "Tell me where they are, cunt, or it's going to take you a fucking long time to die."

The man started shaking, and Dex glowered at him, spittle on his lips and a furious anger in his mind. What was going on? What the fuck was happening to the world? And that was the problem, wasn't it? – this wasn't his world. This was an alien world. And for some reason, the fuckers had turned on him! On his family!

He realised with a start that the provax was laughing. His bright orange eyes glazed over, more blood pumped out, and he went slack in Dex's hands. Dex threw him down roughly and stood, fists clenching, shaking with fury. He lifted the gun again and stared at it. What now? Call the police? Call his own people?

He moved to the comm and lifted the handset, then stopped. He stared at it, and slowly put it back in its cradle.

Paranoia. Where they all in on it?

Of course they were all fucking in on it! The receptionist. Lex the friendly happy PopBot. The hotel. Who else? How far did it go? But worse, what did they want?

Dex moved through to the bedroom and pulled on long pants and boots.

He had to get out of the hotel. Had to get to a *legitimate* police station. They'd respect him because he was Earth PUF – urban force. They had a *reputation*. They'd help him. After all, and he gave a sour grin at this; he was one of their own. Right?

He came out of the bedroom. The air seemed fuzzy. Dex didn't feel very well. He kept thinking of Molly and Toffee. The last time he touched them. The last time he held them. His mind whirled in a maelstrom of crazy thought. *I'm going to find my wife and children. And then I'm going to hurt somebody for this. For this injustice. For this sacrilege.*

Dex moved towards the door, but it opened even as he approached. There was a woman. Slim, dressed all in black, shades. She registered confusion when she saw Dex, and her hand snapped up carrying a gun... Dex responded automatically, reflex, his own confiscated weapon darting up and his finger squeezing the trigger before the brain even engaged. The gun *cracked*, the bullet *whined*. It hit the woman in the chest, and a blood splatter exploded against the wall; she staggered back several steps, and her gun fired, the bullet hitting the ceiling with a tiny *puff* of plaster. Her mouth opened, and she panted, and staggered back to the wall in the corridor, hit it with a wet slap, and slid down leaving a white smear. Dex ran to her, mind torn, half filled with apology, half glad he'd shot her. She'd been gunning for him. She was part of this thing. This... abduction.

Dex took the woman's gun and put it in his pocket. He pulled off her shades to see bright, bright blue eyes that burned into him, feverishly, full of tears, full of hate. She was breathing fast. Her chest was a destroyed mess.

"Tell me where my wife is," said Dex, softly. The woman reached up, her fingers shaking, milky blood on her lips. Dex took her fingers. She licked her lips. Her breath came in short, pained gasps.

"She is... gone," said the woman. The provax. Feyprov. Female. A damn site more deadly than the male...

"Please, tell me where my little girls are," said Dex.

The woman's panting suddenly halted, as if a switch had been thrown. Her free hand came up fast with a long slender dagger and Dex flinched, twisting, his arm deflecting the blade, which cut him deeply through skin and muscle. He yelped, pulled his hand from her fingers, and before he could stop himself put a bullet between her eyes. She lolled to the side like a broken mannequin.

Dex stood and stared down at her corpse.

"Stupid," he growled.

He pocketed the gun, and strode down the corridor, past the elevator and towards the steps. He took them two at a time, heart pounding, barging through regulation fire doors with his mind swirling. Who had taken Katrina and the girls? And why? Was it something to do with his work back in London? Or maybe some twisted, fucked-up terrorist organisation out to punish tourists? Shit. *Shit.*

Dex crossed the reception area, saw the receptionist watching him. He burst through the glass doors and out into the sunshine. There was a taxi rank of HumCars to his right, bobbing gently on their leashes, and Dex moved to the nearest one. He climbed in.

A short man in a cotton shirt turned and grinned. "Where to, buster?"

"The police station."

"Having problems?"

"Yeah. You could say. It's turning into a real shit day."

The HumCar pulled out onto the quiet street, and they hummed along under the tall, wavering trees, which offered pleasant shade.

The pavements featured occasional tourists, ambling along, sometimes with buckets and spades. Dex stared out the back window, checking they weren't being followed.

"You okay, buster? You seem a bit twitchy."

"I'm far from fucking okay," snapped Dex.

"Hey, okay, okay! I just work here, man!"

They came to a highway and blasted along, overtaking other HumCars and regular vehicles like trucks and tankers. High walls of rock hid the surroundings, but in the distance, overhead, Dex spied the glinting rails of massive rollercoasters, rolling and twisting through the air. They even zoomed under a chunky water ride, and the HumCar's wipers kicked in to clear the overspray.

"You here with your family?"

"Yeah," said Dex.

"You have something stolen?"

"You could say that."

After a few minutes they turned from the highway, and Dex watched as they headed inland. The trees grew more and more clustered, until the rock walls gave way and they were in the midst of a deep forest. The thick green conifers were occasionally broken by the fanned branches of a tree with glossy blue leaves.

Dex stared out of the window, and a frown slowly formed – reflected in the glass. To the right, in the distance, there were logging trucks. And then they passed a long, low industrial estate, containing hundreds of thick black pipes which, with a blink, Dex realised were ride tracks. The HumCar turned right into the compound and suddenly screeched to a halt, tyres chewing gravel.

Dex was thrown forward, then back, and came up to face –

A gun.

"This is getting tiresome," he muttered.

"Sometimes, you just need to learn how to play dead."

"What did we do wrong?" said Dex softly, looking into the man's eyes. He wasn't a prov, this one. Oh no. He was human. A back-stabbing human who'd sold out his own fucking species for the aliens...

"I just work here," said the taxi driver. "Now get out. I don't want to ruin my seats."

Dex fired through the back of the leather, and the bullet entered the taxi driver's stomach low down, clawing through his bowel. He tensed, looking as if he were going to shoot, but slowly the gun slipped from his fingers and his eyes rolled up. Blood came out of his mouth and he slumped sideways, head banging off the glass.

Dex sat for long, long moments, staring out of the car's side-window.

Outside, trees swayed in the gentle breeze rolling in from the ocean.

So then. The PopBot, the receptionist, the man in the cream suit, the woman in the corridor, the taxi driver.

Crazy. He'd been stitched up tighter than a fat man in a wetsuit.

Now what? What to do?

The police? Yes. There was *no way* the police could be so corrupt. This had to be the work of some kind of gang which had infiltrated the hotel. They'd taken Kat and the girls, and Dex was supposed to either pay a ransom, or go on TV weeping and begging the Theme Planet government – indeed, the Monolith Corporation – to meet whatever demands the terrorists had in mind. He had to get to the police. *Had* to. Out here, he was operating alone; no backup. And he couldn't fight this sort of organisation alone... he had the heart, just not the guns.

Dex climbed out of the HumCar and stood, listening. Trees whispered. That was all.

He dragged the body of the taxi driver from the vehicle and across the dirt, grunting at the man's dead weight. "Too many Porky Paul burgers, buddy," he muttered, and dumped him in the dust behind a rack of old, burned ride tracks.

Burned? Odd. I thought Theme Planet was *perfect*...

Back to the HumCar, and using the taxi-driver's jacket, he soaked up the worst of the blood. Looking in the boot he found blankets, and draped them over the car seat. After all, he didn't want to march into a police station covered in dead man's skull chunks.

Shit. *Shit.* He stood there, and shook his head.

Madness. Total madness.

He climbed in, wound down the window, and started the smooth, quiet engine. *No noise pollution on Theme Planet!* he mused, dancing along the edges of a building hysteria. He spun the car, wriggling a little at the bullet hole and charred leather in the back of his seat which dug into him like poking fingers.

Grimly, he headed back to the highway.

DEX PARKED THE car and stared up at the neat, white police HQ. It looked so pristine, so smart, so noble. A pinnacle of law enforcement. Not that there were many crimes on Theme Planet. Monolith prided itself on its tiny, tiny crime figures. Criminals were dealt with most harshly.

Dex walked up the wide marble steps, past a proliferation of police officers, his bad nerves disappearing, confidence returning. If anybody would help him, these people would help him. *He* was police, *they* were police. They were his kind of people. They were brothers in adversity. They were brothers in the solving of crimes!

Officers filed past him on the steps, dutifully ignoring him. To these officers in their smart black uniforms, he was simply another tourist. But he would soon get some attention. Soon illustrate the gravity of the situation.

He stepped through the doors, into the heaving complex of the police precinct...

Into an ants' nest of insane activity...

And the world came alive, with screeching sirens and bright flashing lights directed into his eyes, blinding him instantly. Reflexively, Dex's arms came up, shielding his eyes from the harsh intensity. He heard the cocking of many weapons; a field of hardware. An arsenal.

"On the ground, motherfucker!" somebody screamed.

"Get down!"

"Down, dickhead!"

Slowly, Dex fell to his knees. "It's okay," he said. "I'm a police officer. From London, Earth. I'm police."

"Two pistols," he heard somebody say.

"Room 237," came another voice.

Then something hit him across the back of the head, and the world went black.

WATER SPLASHED HIS face, and he groaned. His head was thumping. His mouth was dry and tasted of vomit. He opened his eyes. He was in a bare grey room, seated on a steel chair before a steel table, his hands tied tight behind him. Spaghetti Cuffs, no doubt. LiveWire. Very dangerous shit.

Dex breathed deeply, and tried to focus. Two men came into view. One wore a black suit, one a cream suit.

"Well, well," said cream suit. He carried a small DigPad, and he placed it on the steel table with a *clack*. "You've been a busy boy, haven't you, Dexter Colls?"

Dex leaned forward and spat blood on the floor. He coughed, and looked up, into the man's eyes. And he was a man – not a provax. He was human. That was good. Very good. They should be able to connect. Dex turned to the man in the black suit, who had his eyes hidden behind shades – because the daylight hurt him, hurt his bright bright eyes. He was a provax, brought up on a dark world, a nocturne world. That was why he was so pale. Earthmen called them vampires; the provax hated it.

"My name is Rogen," said the provax in the black suit. "Tell us what you've done with them and this will go easier for you."

"Done with... with who?"

"Don't play the smart fucking arse with us," said the man in the cream suit. Dex saw his small, neat name badge. It read: JIM.

"If you mean my wife, Katrina, and my little girls, Molly and Toffee, then they've been kidnapped. Taken! And then I was attacked, first in the lift by that..."

Rogen held up his hand. "Destroying a PopBot is an offence, Mr Colls," he said, "under the Trade and Tourism Laws. You do understand that, don't you?"

Dex took a deep breath. "Listen, you two apes. And listen good. I am Dexter Colls, Precinct 881, London. You can call my Commanding Officer there, Jackson. He will vouch for me. I have over twenty years on the PUF."

"Oh, he vouched for you all right," said Jim, perching himself on the edge of the desk. "But then, murder *is* murder – no matter if you're Police Urban or just little people. Isn't that right, Rogan?"

"Damn right, Jim."

They exchanged a long glance. Dex frowned. He wasn't sure what that glance meant, and he was good at reading people – hell, he'd had decades of experience.

He licked his lips, and his brain hurt. This was crazy. Insane! And panic thumped him with iron fists as he thought about his wife and children. He had to find them. Help them. Rescue them! Instead, he was here, with these crazy fuckers who were intent on framing him for the very crime he wished to solve.

"Listen," said Dex, leaning forward.

"No, you listen, sonny boy," snapped Jim, eyes angry now and glaring down at Dex. "You fucking tourists, you come out here to Theme Planet and you think you're above the law! If you're not getting pissed and causing fights with each other or the locals because of race hate, or your basic human superiority complex, then you're shagging on the beaches or trying to deviate the bloody ride drives. You're like a virus on the face of this planet. If I were the provax, I'd kick the lot of you out."

Dex closed his mouth with a clack at this vehement outburst. He glanced at Rogen, who was grinning.

"But – you don't often come here and commit *murders*," he said. "Tell us where you buried the bodies and we'll go easy on you."

"I told you what happened, and this is a bad fucking joke!" growled Dex, face harsh, eyes falling down into hate. "They've been kidnapped, you dumb plod, taken – so what makes you so adamant it was me?"

"We have evidence," said Rogen, smoothly, and pulled up a chair, reversing it and sitting with a panel of steel between himself and Dexter. "Lots of evidence. An orgy of evidence. So, let's begin again."

"Bullshit," snapped Dex. "You have nothing!"

"What we *do* have," said Rogen, voice still calm and controlled, "is the Theme Planet Travel and Tourism Torture Laws."

"Torture Laws?" said Dex, going cold. He could see himself reflected in Rogen's shades. He did not have a good look.

"It's part of Quad-Gal Statute with regards aliens, in this case *you*, visiting the land of a protected species, that's *us*. Yes, we invite you here; yes, we take your money; but you *are* expected to behave. You should have read your in-flight literature, Mr Colls. It explains about our Torture Tubes, way down below the ground. Down where the rollercoasters go to die." He smiled, and coughed, and stood up. "We have certain, if not God-given rights, then certainly *Gov*-given rights." He coughed again, and nodded to Jim. "I'm going to give you a few moments to think about your situation. When I come back in, I strongly recommend you have some information for me about the whereabouts of your family."

Rogen left the room. Jim remained standing, staring at Dex.

Dex ran his hands through his short brown hair and groaned. *This couldn't be happening! The bastards should be out there looking for his little girls! They should be doing their jobs, like all good police! Instead, he was locked up here, being threatened with torture...*

Jim moved close. He seemed to be scanning the room. Dex tensed. What was this? More 'good cop, bad cop'?

"Listen carefully. Your life depends on it," said Jim, without looking at Dex.

"Go on."

"Follow my lead."

"Follow your..."

The door opened, and Rogen returned, carrying a cup of coffee, steam curling from the surface like mist from a lake. Jim turned in one swift movement, drawing his holstered police issue Makarov and firing a single shot. There was a dull *crack* as the bullet smashed through Rogen's shades and entered his skull between the eyes, exiting in a mushroom shower of brainslop which splattered up the grey walls of the holding cell.

There was a moment, a hiatus in time which lasted an infinity, like stars unspooling from a galaxy reel.

Rogen staggered back, hit the wall, and collapsed suddenly in an untidy heap.

Dex, mouth open, stared at the body. Jim leapt to the dead provax policeman, reached inside his dark jacket, took out a gun. The first thought that flitted through Dex's mind was *hell, I'm being framed. How much harder can my day get?* But then Jim crossed to him, pulled free a small knife and cut through the wires. Dex rubbed his wrists. Jim stood to one side, staring at the provax corpse.

"Here." He handed Dex the dead alien's gun.

Dex turned the small pistol over and over in his hands. He'd never seen this type of Makarov before.

"It's prov issue. Don't be fooled by its size, this fucker will bring down an Air Tank."

"What's happening?" said Dex.

"Just follow my lead. If we get out of here alive, I'll explain. Just now, you're my prisoner, and we're going to walk out the front doors. Understand?"

"Yes."

Jim moved to the door, Dex close behind. Jim took hold of Dex's wrists, which he crossed as if bound, and they stepped out into the busy precinct.

The floor heaved like a disturbed anthill, a ceaseless flow of police personnel, both in and out of uniform. As Jim led Dex through the throng, moving slow with the tide of bodies beneath high arches of white marble, Dex glanced around nervously. Most police were provax, but he caught sight of the occasional human. It was the eyes, always the eyes which gave them away.

"Over here," said Jim. They were halfway to the precinct doors. They tried to quicken their pace, but it was impossible.

Dex felt like he was swimming with sharks. Or, at least, piranhas.

His mind screamed with a million questions. Where were his family? Why was this policeman helping him? In fact, why had he killed a fellow officer? Not exactly normal police procedure!

They were ten metres from the door when somebody screamed. Alarms screeched from wall-mounted PopBots. Jim pushed Dex forward and they started to run.

"There!" somebody yelled.

Dex heard a blast, felt a *whoosh* of superheated air and the woman next to him was picked up and tossed violently across the precinct, her body horizontal, spinning, slamming into other police and mowing them down. Dex ducked, and Jim, ahead of him, turned and started firing with the Makarov.

Policemen were smashed from their feet in a ballet of collapsing bodies. Dex ran for the door, head down, cursing as more people around him were hurled from their feet or, even worse, exploded, showering the precinct with blood – red and milk. *They're fucking firing on their own!* screamed his mind. *What the fuck's going on? Since when do your own people become expendable?*

He leapt through the scanners and hit the doors with his back, spinning through as they opened, and then stood on the high marble steps, stunned for a moment by the sunshine. In the distance, on a three-klick-high rollercoaster, people put their arms in the air and screamed in joy and pleasure on the long descent. Dex could hear the rumble of wheels on track, even from this distance.

Jim burst out behind him. His cream suit was stained with blood, and his eyes were hard, hard like Dex had seen in the war. During Helix. During the Bad Times.

He shivered.

"This way," growled Jim.

Dex ran down the steps, needing little urging, and there was a traffic cop's parked hover bike. The cop was standing five feet away, smart uniform, goldfish-bowl helmet with blue and white stripes, flashing red light atop the helmet. Even as they ran, Jim's gun came up. Dex wanted to cry, "No!" because this man was an innocent, a victim, a human-fucking-being, but the gun gave a blast and Dex felt the suck of rushing wind, and the traffic policeman's head was blown clean off, to roll clattering down the street, like a penalty football, rattling and bouncing and spraying red blood. Human blood.

The woman who'd been speaking to the cop ran, face behind her hands, screaming.

Jim levelled his gun, but Dex shoulder-charged him and the blast howled off into the sky, over towards a cluster of whirling, whizzing machines containing screaming, laughing tourists.

"No!" he snarled.

Jim stared at him for a moment, then shrugged. "Get on the bike."

Jim leapt on, and Dex climbed on behind him, frowning at his submissive role. But he had to admit, between clenched teeth, that he was being rescued. By a psycho cop-killer, oh, yes, but rescued he was.

Now, a platoon of police were piling out of the precinct. They scattered onto the steps like fire-ants from a burning nest. Jim kicked the hover bike from its leash and they leapt up into the sky, nearly vertical. Dex felt immediately, violently sick as Theme Planet was tossed away and the islands and towering rides and posh hotels and sandy snaking beaches all grew quickly small; became toys scattered in a sandbox.

Dex held on tight, as if fearful of falling, but the BMW had fieldgrips which made sure he didn't topple from the bike and die in a mangled heap of man and rollercoaster far below. Still, he clung to Jim like a drowning man to an Olympic swimmer, mouth opening and closing at the sheer insane acceleration of this powerful bike.

They soared across Theme Planet, taking in the sights and sounds from a God's-eye-view.

"Shit," muttered Jim, and Dex felt his body tense. He glanced behind. Three hover bikes were in pursuit, and the body language of the traffic cops said *grim*. Jim – and Dex by association – were cop-killers. Not a good thing to be.

Suddenly the bike dropped, and Dex felt his stomach crawl up his oesophagus and claw its way past his teeth. Every atom of his being screamed at this abuse of physics. Beneath him, the engine throbbed like a missile – which was, in fact, what it was.

They slammed towards the ocean, the three bikes in pursuit. Fumes left tracer across the sky. Roars from the abused engine bounced around the heavens over Theme Planet. Dex watched helplessly as they jigged right and veered towards high gleaming rails of a vast, high rollercoaster. The cars passed, holding people with open mouths and wide eyes, staring at them as they dropped and hammered through an O of curling track. Dex ducked involuntarily and the people in the CARS screamed for a different reason...

Behind, the three cop bikes spread out, tearing past the ride.

Jim dropped them towards the sea once more, turning inland and skimming low over the beach. The three cop bikes followed, unshakeable. Then their guns began to fire, blatting and clacking. The bike rocked as the shells came close, superheating the air and scorching Dex's legs. Jim dropped them towards the sand and they smashed through a collection of wooden deckchairs. Splinters spun off behind them, accompanied by colourful streamers of torn fabric.

Jim turned. "Shoot them!" he screamed, and Dex remembered the gun in his hand. He leaned back, sighted through the slipstream of hazy hot air, and fired off two shots, three, four, five. The bikes jigged in evasive action, but he must have hit something, because one cop bike suddenly lifted its nose and, faster than Dex could blink, looped-the-loop, ploughed into the beach, and exploded. Black smoke billowed up in a thick pillar. Tourists ran up the beach screaming, dripping sun-tan cream and coral dust.

"Good shooting," yelled Jim.

Dex felt sick.

Through the cloud of smoke screamed the two remaining bikes. Jim veered left, inland, and at mere inches above road level, headed for Tengall, the nearest city. Dex felt even more cold inside.

The cop bikes followed. They fired again, blats slamming past Dex's head. Dex lined up his gun to fire, but Jim slammed right and they veered down a narrow alley riddled with steel fire escapes and criss-crossing bridges. They hummed and spun past walkways, which hissed in his ears as they passed. The cops followed, dodging with equal success until Jim jockeyed the bike right, screamed, "Hang on!" and jerked the arse-end of the vehicle into a steel bridge. Sparks scattered behind them like a shower of industrial fireworks, and both bikes came through them – into the path of another bridge. The lead bike saw the obstacle and swept up, over it, but his bulk obscured the obstacle from his companion, who came to a halt with a heavy *clang* which reverberated up and down the valley. It would take five police with shovels to put their friend in a bodybag.

One more, thought Dex, but felt sicker than sick. There was no pleasure in this. No joy. The whole thing was horseshit. The whole journey was *wrong*... They were police. They didn't deserve to die.

But then, neither did his family...

They shot from the alley like a bullet from a gun, veering left and entering a maze of moving traffic. Still at ground level, it was obvious Jim hoped to throw off their final pursuer by ploughing him into a car or truck. But he was good. As good a pilot as Jim, at least.

They slammed along the highway, weaving, dodging, and the police bike gained on them. Dex glanced back, could see the shades on the provax, the grim line of his mouth, the trace of sweat on his upper lip. This was one determined son-of-a-bitch. He was no longer hunting for arrest. This was personal; this was execution. And the sad thing was, Dex *understood*. And he *agreed*. But he couldn't let it happen. Because to die now was to let Kat and the girls down. And they'd have to bury him first...

They came to a wide, high bridge over a mammoth gleaming river, which fed the sea. Large green seagulls cawed and circled, and the banks of the river were thriving with yachts and pleasure cruisers. People were sunbathing, partying. Sunlight sparkled off crystal. Dex imagined he could hear the clink of ice cubes in bourbon.

They slammed along the highway, and Dex glanced right. A large pleasure-liner with three massive black funnels was creeping along the river, obviously on its way out for a slow romantic crawl around the islands. Alarms started sounding on the bridge, and the traffic stopped. Instead of slowing, Jim powered the bike along and lifted it a little, skimming over the rooftops of the groundcars. On the liner, Dex could see high towers with personnel controlling the bridge. Sunlight glittered on car glass. The throb of the cruiser's engines echoed across the water.

The bridge was rising, and they skimmed over its parting, rising decks, the traffic cop close behind now, a gun in his hand. His face was thunder. His bike vibrated hard and Dex squinted, realising it was damaged. Fuel spilled from a hole in the rear flank. One of his bullets must have cut through the alloy. The rider seemed unaware, or uncaring... shots followed them, and Jim veered right, between tight rungs of steel – and then they were out, roaring over the river, gulls circling above them, screeching in protest, or in hunger.

Dex squeezed Jim's shoulder. "Go right!" he yelled. "Head over the ship!"

Jim nodded, and dropped the bike towards the pleasure-liner. It honked, a long, low tone which Dex took to be a warning. They dropped further, banking right, and headed straight over the first massive funnel – and Dex glanced down, could see the glow of engines, or whatever method the ship used for propulsion. A heat blast hit them, shaking the bike as if it were a live thing, an uncontrollable bucking bull. The engine screamed – and then they were past, over the funnel, over the glow, and the cop in close pursuit realised his peril a split-second too late...

Close enough to nearly touch, there came a sudden *glow* of ignition from the rear of his bike. Fire raced up the trail of leaking fuel and Dex, watching, saw the realisation twist the cop's face as his bike –

Detonated.

A ball of fire expanded fast, uncurling, glowing bright. The bike and rider were gone instantly, either vaporised, or...

"Shit – faster!" screamed Dex as he realised what had happened.

The burning bike had risen, burning, then what remained dropped down into the pleasure liner's engines...

The whole river shook as if experiencing some massive underground quake. And then the huge cruiser seemed to glow from within, a bright, bright orange, brighter than a provax's eyes, and there was a stream of quick-fire detonations and Dex fancied he heard screams, and the ship seemed to fold up into a V as a terrible explosion tore the core of the ship apart. Fireballs and shrapnel screamed out, and Dex clung onto the bike, which was buffeted violently as it fled, shrapnel whizzing past it.

The pleasure-liner screamed, a dying behemoth, and everything seemed to happen in slow motion. Fire raged along the decks, eating the tourists. The arms of the V grew tighter as the ship folded itself further in half, accompanied by a terrifying rending and tearing of steel. Then the whole thing seemed to jump a little, out of the water, as more deep detonations rocked it, and then it slid slowly down into the river, waters surging and gurgling as more wailing tourists leapt from the tilting bow and stern...

They flew off up the river, bike whining. It had been damaged sometime during the chase.

"We lost them," shouted back Jim.

Dex nodded.

They cruised, and were soon out of the city and away from the tourist districts.

A cool breeze caressed Dex.

And he shivered, deep down to his core.

Jim touched down by the side of the river. Orange trees wavered overhead and Dex shuddered in the breeze. What had happened to his life? What happened to his world?

"Why did you help me?"

Jim dismounted from the hover bike and stretched. His eyes were dark, face hooded. "You should never have come here. They should have told you."

"Told me what?"

"You're PUF, right? Police Urban Force?"

"Yeah? So?"

"You shouldn't have come here," said Jim. "Shit. You slipped through the net."

"I don't understand!" snapped Dex, spittle on his lips.

"That doesn't matter. Here – take the bike. Go back to the hotel, pack your bags and get the fuck off Theme Planet. Then, and only then, might there be a chance your wife and children will live." He shivered. "They might send them back to you. If you're lucky."

"They'll be waiting for me. At the hotel."

"No. Trust me."

"I can't go back like a fucking puppy with its tail between its legs. I have to find Kat! I have to find Molly and Toffee!"

Jim stared hard at Dex. "Listen. That's your bravado, your ego, your damn machismo speaking. This is not about you. It's about them. Now, you mustn't go down that path," he said, gently. "You shouldn't be here. To save them, you must leave."

"What did I do wrong?" said Dex, feeling small, feeling like a pawn in a very big game. He turned towards the bike. He could hear Jim breathing, slow and cool.

He opened his mouth again, to speak, but something struck the back of his skull and the lights went out.

CHAPTER FIVE
BROKEN

AMBA LAY STILL. Gradually, she shut down her systems. One, by one, by one, by one.

Clever, said Zi.

Do they understand?

No, said Zi. *Some people never understand.*

"WHAT HAPPENED?"

"I'm not sure. Get her over here, on the bench. Gods, she's heavier than she looks. Solid."

"Stop fucking yammering. Check her pulse."

"Shit! She's dead!"

"Impossible, we gave her a blast, yes, but..."

"Remember the man? With the beard? Dodgy heart?"

"Call the medics! Quick! MEDICS!"

"I CAN'T BELIEVE it. Somebody's going to get a kicking over this one."

"Have you checked her documents?"

"Yeah. They check out. I have an idea."

"And idea which doesn't involve us all getting locked up?"

"Yes. Only the three of us know, right?"

"Mm-*hmm*."

"We can junk her. Nobody will find her down there."

"What about her family...?"

"Well, she was travelling alone. Here, now, as far as the Port Authorities are concerned, she disembarked, was accepted through immigration, headed out into Theme Planet and simply... disappeared. A missing person. We do get them occasionally, you know. Despite all the failsafes. Despite all the drones and the skycams."

"Good. Burns, go and sort out the immigration docs. Make sure you tweak the times. You good for that?"

"Consider it done."

"And remember – all of you. We never fucking heard of Amba Miskalov. Right? Not just your jobs, but your *lives* depend on it. Monolith won't allow fuck-ups like this in its organisation."

MOVEMENT. OR, THE sense of movement. She was on a stretcher, although it was hard to ascertain because so many bodily functions were shut down. She still had natural internal gyroscopes, though, and she knew they were heading... *down.*

Down, under the rides, under the islands, under the machines.

Beneath Theme Planet.

She could hear voices, muffled, as if heard from the bottom of a metal well. They continued to move, and she had only a vague sense of time. She had activated her coma call. Play dead. Fool the enemy. Rise like a phoenix from the ashes and execute every motherfucker in her path. It was – almost – a last resort tactic. They'd used some new tech on her; the coldness at the back of her neck remained. What the hell had that been? More importantly, did they realise she was *android?* And even more importantly, did they realise she was an Anarchy Model? Bad shit. Hardcore shit. Military shit.

Doubt nagged her. They'd taken her out easy. Way too easy. It was as if they'd known. Were primed. Waiting for her?

That's a possibility, said Zi.

I'm well aware of it. Hang around, babe, I think I might need a FRIEND soon...

And she meant it. Because, when Amba reversed her fake death, when she restarted her android body and the heart started to pump and brain started to fly, for a while she would be groggy, and slow, and weak, and it would hurt – hurt like a motherfucker. Hurt like falling into a star. She would need Zi then. Need the expertise of her FRIEND...

They'd stopped. It took her a while to realise.

More voices drifted through, now. There were many voices. All male. They echoed around her and she shivered, in her cocoon of unreality; in her death sleep. She felt hands on her, and she knew what she felt were delayed experiences, like echoes of the real thing. She felt something wet slide across her cold dead lips and she grimaced internally. She had an idea what was going on. Had an idea what those bastards could be doing...

Where had they taken her?

Downwards, into basements or sewers, or into the machine workings under Theme Planet. The bowels of the rides. The city under the city, the country under the country, where all the provax – the real provax – lived. In the dark. The shade. The shadows. The cool.

Under the shell.

Under the crust.

Under the fake topside tourist shithole.

Amba smiled, deep inside her mind.

A world within a world, a globe within a shell.

She felt hands over her body. They removed her clothes. They probed her. Touched her. She felt a deep throb of *anger* within.

Do it, said Zi.

Yes, Amba said. And there was a *click*. And it was done. Her heart gave a spasm, fluttered, and restarted. Sluggishly, blood started to pump through her veins. Her eyes fluttered, but the men standing around her, where she lay on a wheeled trolley stretcher, were more interested in her naked flesh, her firm body, than in the fluttering of her eyelashes.

Slowly, life returned. Her cheeks flushed red. Her heart set up a steady beat. And the metallic voices grew louder, gained clarity, and Amba remained motionless, listening, sucking in breath, allowing her android body to fully awake, to recharge, before she leapt into action...

"I bet she was a good fuck when she was alive," came one voice.

"Yeah, look at her breasts. Fabulous. Not too large, not too small..."

"Too small for me. I like a good handful, mate."

"Ha, you *are* a good handful, mate!"

Laughter.

"Come on, Janko, we haven't got all night. What you kissing her for, anyway? She's fucking *dead!*"

"Hey, I like to get into the groove, baby. Get the full experience. And stop saying she's dead, you're putting me off."

"If it's putting you off, you shouldn't be here, dumb fuck."

Amba became suddenly aware of the tongue in her mouth, and the fingers inside her vagina, working at her, working her hard. The cold throb of anger became a lead ball of fury, but she controlled herself with infinite effort, controlled herself as the slick worm of a tongue roved around inside her face. The FRIEND. Damn! Where was the FRIEND?

"Did you figure it out yet?"

"Naw. It's some alien piece of shit. Look." There came a *click*, but no detonation. Amba smiled again, at that. There'd be a fucking detonation all right, real soon, right here in this dark damp stinking room on the fetid underbelly of the con that was Theme Planet.

Her senses were returning fast. Accelerating. It *was* dark and damp, and smelled of old engine oil, mould, and fungus; her nostrils twitched as the man's tongue continued to probe. Then he withdrew his tongue, and she could sense him gazing down at her. So far, she'd identified eight men in the room – but there could be more.

So be it.

Amba gave a sigh, and opened her eyes.

The man's mouth dropped open like a drawbridge with the chains cut, eyes going wide for a moment as Amber did two things. First, her vagina clamped his fingers so tight they broke with audible *cracks*, like the snapping of dry timber. Second, her right hand came up and two of her fingers invaded *his* flesh without permission. Straight through his eyeballs, popping them with soft squishes.

The man screamed, and Amba brought one foot back and kicked him across the room, where he crashed into the wall, both popped eyes dangling on his cheeks like deflated balloons. His companions turned, following his trajectory, and stood there, stunned, mouths open, staring at his face and wobbling eyes.

Amba swung her legs from the trolley and stood smoothly, watching as the men slowly returned their gazes to her naked form. One grinned, an old provax with grey eyes and gold capped teeth. "Hey, we're sure going to have a party now, guys," he said, gesturing slightly with his head.

"You bet," smiled Amba. She stepped forward and punched him in the throat, swayed back from a wild whirring counter-punch and stamped right, breaking a man's knee backwards. Her elbow shot up, breaking his jaw and lifting him from the ground, and then they were on her. She punched a third man in the belly, fingers extending to push through his flesh, hook his bowel, and pull it out in a blue-grey stream through the hole. She dodged more blows, moving like a dancer, grabbed a fourth man by the hair, kicked a fifth in the face, her toes slamming his nose and pushing a knife of cartilage up into his brain. She kicked off from his falling body, twisting around, snapping the neck of the man whose hair she was still holding. An iron bar slammed at her, and she took the blow on her arm, twisting, allowing the bar to slide across her skin as she dropped to one knee, punched the attacker in the groin like a pile-driver, and took the bar. It whacked left, then right, cracking two skulls, and the final man standing went into a fast-forward reverse, hands up as she strode towards him. "No," he said, "no!" The iron bar slammed down, breaking his fingers and driving straight down between his eyes, leaving his skull in a V-shape with brains oozing out around the rusted iron. He dropped without further sound.

Awww, Amba! complained Zi.

"What?" she hissed, as she located the FRIEND.

You left none for me.

Later, Zi. That was too easy. Trust me, it'll get harder. You'll get your turn.

I wanted some fun NOW...

Later, soothed Amba.

Amba found her clothes and dressed, slotting the FRIEND slowly into her chest. Feeling fully whole with Zi inside her, she checked the bodies of her would-be abusers, finding the one whom she'd left alive, with military precision and a torturer's finesse.

He was sat, back to the wall, popped eyeballs on his cheeks, whimpering, half-in and half-out of consciousness. She moved to him, seated herself cross-legged before him, and he jerked as if stung, coming out of his well of self-pity and stretching out his hands towards her.

"No, don't kill me," he said.

"Janko. We have some talking to do."

"It was them! They made me do it! I'm sorry, I'm sorry!"

"Shut up and listen, and I might let you live."

Janko clamped his teeth shut. Fear gnawed him like rats in his belly. He was blind now; likely he would never see again. And this strange, deadly woman – who had been wheeled down to them as a cadaver – had shown she was far from dead. In fact... his brow furrowed. No. It couldn't be. They'd introduced them, at the end of the war; at the end of the Helix War. A sneaky fucking human manoeuvre. Androids. Androids with the ability to play dead – an infiltration device.

"You can help me," said Amba, voice soft now, almost caring. "I am looking for somebody. You will tell me everything you know."

"You're one of them, aren't you?"

"One of what?"

"The androids. They can play dead. I've seen it."

Amba considered this, then reached forward, took one of his eyeballs, and ripped it free with a squelch. Janko screamed and keeled sideways, cradling his face, sobbing, spit and snot drooling from mouth and nose.

Amba waited for a couple of minutes, then again reached forward and helped Janko to sit up. "You're obviously ex-military," she said. "Good. That saves us some time. I'll explain it to you. I'm not just an android; I'm an Anarchy Model. Do you understand?"

"Yes," whispered Janko through his snot and drool.

Amba placed a finger delicately against her lips, leaving a tiny trace of blood. "I'm looking for Dr Jmes Kooky, Professor of Ride Enjoyment at Theme Planet Central University. Now. I want to know everything you know."

DR JMES KOOKY, Professor of Ride Enjoyment at Theme Planet Central University, sat in his office staring at the six students before him with unadulterated distaste, loathing and despair. The fact that it was actually the students who, through their student fees, paid his salary, seemed of little consequence to Jmes. From his elitist, experienced and some would say narcissistic point of view, Jmes had fashioned a world view in which he was the *core*, he was the *centre,* he was in fact the most important organic entity to ever walk the planets of the Four Galaxies. Everybody else was just gravy. In Jmes's world, Jmes ruled. And in Jmes's office, students were some kind of primordial slime sent to him to simply facilitate one function – annoyance. After all, what other service did a student provide? They were lazy, useless, pointless specimens who stayed in bed all day, drank and shagged and did their utmost to do very little. It was rare Jmes came across a student who was actually worthy of his attention, and indeed these "worthy" specimens tended to be brunette, voluptuous, and with a "thing" for older gentlemen.

On this bright, sunny day, with beams of sunlight cutting through dust motes and the distant lazy sounds of the Theme Planet rides rumbling on the horizon to the accompaniment of thousands – nay, *millions* – of delighted screams, Jmes focused on his little group and said, "Take out your EPads," whilst absently rubbing at the grey bristles of his beard.

The six students complied, and Jmes caught one young brunette, a new student to the campus, eyeing him shyly from behind her EPad, tongue licking her dry lips, big baby-blue eyes shifting coquettishly from his rotund physique and back to her work. Jmes appraised her, and with a deft flick of his eyes, checked for her name on his list. Karenta. That was a sweet name. Jmes flicked his eyes back to her, and she was looking at him again, EPen poised. She had masses of curled hair and fabulous breasts. *Fabulous* breasts.

Forcing his mind back to the present, he said, "Okay, today we're going to be looking at ride design ergonomics. As you know, Monolith Ride Systems design every single ride on Theme Planet, and of course their paramount design concern is that of safety. Safety of passengers, safety of ride controllers, and indeed – where alien organisms are used as part of a ride system – safety of the ride organism itself."

He eyes swept his class. The punk with the pink Mohican was dozing into his EPad. The fat girl on the left was picking her nose with the end of her EPen. The spotty teen on the right was fumbling with his cock through his pants, no doubt either: a) rearranging his tackle after an impromptu and unasked-for erection due to the benefit of the nearby Karenta's mostly visible bosom (it was a naively sexy plastic see-through dress), or b) rearranging his tackle due to a cheap shot at covert masturbation due to the benefit of the nearby Karenta's mostly visible bosom. Dr Jmes made a clicking sound of annoyance.

"Is everything okay, Jmes?" asked Karenta, blinking at him with those big baby-blues.

Jmes flapped his mouth a little, so surprised was he at being addressed thus. After all, he was a doctor with a PhD in Ride Enjoyment, and indeed, an appointed Professor specialising in research into the fields of Ride Enjoyment. One addressed him as "Doctor." Or "Professor." Or even "Sir" or "God" would suffice. Jmes was not used to such a slack ignorance with his mode of address, and during various avenues of study had in fact chastised many a student of all age groups on the topic. The fact that this had led to a group of students within his own cohort naming themselves "Dr Narcissist's Lonely Hearts Club Band" did nothing to deter him, trouble him, or force him to desist in his course. Even when one boy called him "Old Permanent Doctor Cunt" – to his face – there was barely a tremble in his lip, although the drugged-up little bastard's subsequent savage beating never made the student newspaper, *Anarchy News* – "For The True Anarchist! (Whilst Not Disturbing Your Studies.)"

"Erm," said Jmes, unable to stop himself before his anally retentive affliction kicked in, "*actually*, you must address me as Doctor, Professor, or simply Sir. Although I prefer Professor. Because I didn't achieve this position without considerable effort, you know, young lady."

Karenta gave a small laugh, politely, behind her hand, and said with a confidence he would never have given her credit for, "Oh, come now, Jmes, we really shouldn't stand on such formality here, in such a small group, should we? I thought when I enrolled last week we'd be like one big happy smiling family."

Jmes spluttered, and felt a red flush riot through his cheeks. When he'd first spotted her, she hadn't seemed dazzlingly beautiful, not what Jmes would called a student "stunner" who all the Professors would seek to be the first to take to the little den at the back of the university campus – fondly known as "Shag Corner" – but now her confidence did something to Jmes. It brought out a blossoming in her character, an attractiveness that had been hitherto hidden behind shaded layers. Jmes didn't want to be so crass as to use the analogy of an onion, but that was what Karenta was when it came to her beauty. Her attractiveness was built up in layers, and Professor Jmes Kooky looked very much forward to peeling back her layers. Beginning with her clothes.

The tutorial continued, and Jmes outlined various functions of Ride Enjoyment – both physical and psychological, and how as a ride designer – or "TP Engineer," to give the guys and gals on the shop floor their complete professional titles – was so much more than simply building units on a production line. The Engineers were a class of their own on Theme Planet, with their own guild and hierarchy and police and prison systems. Whereas some cultures worshipped precious metals, or sex (he threw a glance at Karenta when he said the word, and was thrilled to see her staring straight at him), the whole provax culture – and indeed, Theme Planet's religion – was based around the perfection of the *ride*. Enjoyment, excitement, pleasure, these were things that provax lusted after, and had indeed been the social building blocks which led to the creation of the Theme Planet in the first place.

"I'm confused," said Karenta, at one point.

"About?"

"On Earth, the humans say the provax have no emotions. They call them *fish*, because to humans the provax seem to display very little love or hate, fear or loathing. If that was the case, if they were so emotionless, why would they seek enjoyment, excitement and pleasure?"

"This is a commonly-held misconception," said Jmes, resting his chin on his steepled fingers and trying his very hardest to project an air of cultured sophistication and sexy-older-man magnetism. "Provax do not have a *lack* of emotions, it's just their emotions work in a different way, and to many layman humans, seem diluted. Provax do feel emotions like humans, and in moments of very great stress or love, appear very human indeed. However, they react differently to humans – they are, after all, an *alien species*. Yes, many look physically similar, and share the same style of internal organs – were hammered into life on very similar worlds, evolved in very similar fashions (notwithstanding the echoes and theories surrounding molecular and evolutionary seeding from some ancient and yet-undiscovered alien culture) but provax and humans are very, very different. At a base level. Genetically, and physically."

Karenta nodded and made several notes, dark curls falling down over her EPad. Jmes watched her, and felt a deep stirring within.

IT WAS EVENING. Outside, the sun was sinking in a stunning violet blaze of fire. Rides still clanked and rattled, an eternal theme park aural soundtrack; riders screamed and laughed, and holidaymakers enjoyed the pleasures and thrills of the Theme Planet.

Jmes stood at the window, looking down at the university grounds, with their mock stone and fountains, flowerbeds and manicured lawns. At the centre of the campus was a five–kilometre-high vertical drop rollercoaster called the SPLAT, and it was a test of nerve for every first-year undergraduate to drink ten pints, eat a kebab then do three runs on SPLAT. Presumably to see if a) they made a splat, or b) they produced a splat. Whatever, the rails gleamed in the light of the dying sun, and high up, a solitary five-man CAR was cresting the summit. It paused, glinting, and then plummeted towards the university and its manicured lawns, screams wailing out over the campus.

Jmes turned back to his study.

The tutorial had gone on far longer than expected, with a two-hour break in the middle. It had gone on for so long, with Karenta bringing up so many interesting concepts and questions, that the punk's Mohican had started to flop, the spotty kid's spots had all popped, and even the fat girl seemed miraculously to lose some weight without a never-ending supply of Fatto Fat Burgers. Thankfully, Professor Jmes called an end to the torturously long session, and with his back turned, invited the students to scuttle off to whatever little hellholes of student digs they inhabited, replete with crappy little cooking facilities, dirty needles and unprotected sex.

The door clacked shut.

Jmes turned back, expecting an empty room, but Karenta had remained. She was smiling at him and here, now, she appeared much less innocent and naive. In fact, she seemed suddenly older than her years.

"Haven't you got a home to go to?" asked Jmes, feeling a thrill run through him as he realised why she'd remained. There could only be one reason – especially after he had punished them so hard with such a long, gruelling tutorial session (even though his reputation *was* for long and gruelling tutorial sessions; they didn't call him Old Iron Bastard for no reason, a nickname he secretly relished). No. There could only be one reason. For unlawful carnal knowledge. He smiled encouragingly.

"I have," said Karenta, looking shyly at the ground. "I just thought, you know, that we could continue the session."

There was something about the way she said *session* that made Professor Jmes hard. Harder than hard. Here was a ripe and succulent little fruit he intended on plucking. Not just plucking, but biting, sucking and fucking, if he had his way with her.

She moved closer. Outside, the light was fading fast in a dying shower, like a slow-exploding sun. Her face caught the sunlight and seemed to glow, perfect, her hair highlighted with violet, plastic dress with strategic transparent panels gleaming.

"You know," said Jmes, stepping closer and inhaling her scent, "that a Professor like me, somebody as important as me, somebody so academically tuned, somebody so high up on the university ladder – well, to have a friend like *me* means you'll go a long way in this education business."

"I know," said Karenta, and her voice was husky.

Jmes shuffled even closer.

"If you treat an old Professor like me in the right way, I can certainly guarantee you a wonderful future. I can guarantee you extra *help*, shall we say, and high grades, and sparkling success."

"I understand," said Karenta.

Jmes placed a hand on her hip. She swayed a little, and pressed in close to him. He felt his breath coming in short sharp bursts, and his cock was so hard it was ready to burst free from his neatly pressed suit trousers.

"You're a gorgeous creature," he said.

"Haven't you a wife and child at home?" said Karenta.

"Er. Yes. But..."

"But nothing," said Karenta, taking a small step back and punching him in the stomach.

Professor Jmes heard the "whoosh" of air expelled from his own body before he felt the pain, and was indeed already doubled up and foetal on the carpet before he even understood what had happened. He lay for a while, and for a period of time – it could have been seconds or minutes, or it could have stretched into hours – he simply lay, and waited, and prayed for the pain to go away. It was like nothing he'd ever felt before, that blow; and he'd been shot by rubber donkey-bullets during the protest marches in his student years. No. This was worse. Far worse. Or maybe he'd simply gone soft in his mellowing older years?

He watched, barely able to see for the tears in his eyes and gasps in his throat, as Karenta crossed to his study door. She glanced back at him, then locked the door and switched off the light.

She moved back to him, and taking a bright table lamp, stood it on the floor where it shone in his eyes. She sat down, cross-legged on the carpet, and simply waited.

After a while, Professor Jmes started to regain his composure. He thought of the 9mm Glock Tock in his desk drawer, still unused, still in its cellophane wrapper. He'd never had need of it. Not until now.

"You crazy bitch," he said, finally, words coming out between gasps and wheezes. "What did you do that for?"

Karenta stared at him, and said nothing.

"I'm sorry if you don't find the fact that I have a wife and child at home palatable, but this is the way the fucking world works. Don't you get it? You do me a favour, and I'll give you good essay grades. It's the way it's always been..."

"Really?" said Karenta, raising an eyebrow. She reached up, peeled back her curls and tossed the wig to one side. It gave a *buzz* and folded down, over and into itself, until it was the size of a packet of gum.

Jmes gradually, painfully, pushed himself into a sitting position, his face red from pain and humiliation. "I'll... I'll... wait. Why the digiwig? Who are you?"

"I have been sent to talk to you," said Karenta, and she smiled, but Jmes saw something in that smile he didn't like. He surged forward, and Karenta grabbed his face in one hand and shoved him back down, savagely. Now the smile was gone. Her eyes pierced him, eyes that he'd thought of as beautiful, big and fluttering; now they were narrowed, focused, as if she were a machine with a job to do.

"Wait," Jmes said, weakly. "Did... did Romero send you?"

Amba tilted her head at that. She considered him. "You know Romero?" she said.

"Oh, yes, we go back a long way." Slowly, Jmes settled himself down for more comfort. He rubbed at his bristles. She could see his mind working, ticking away. "Which means, if he sent you, you're... *one of them.*" He stopped. He looked up at her. There was pity in his eyes. Pity, and... superiority. She'd soon change that.

"What do you mean by 'one of them'?" said Amba, voice level, voice controlled, but something tugging at the back of her brain, like a mental tick.

Jmes gave a bitter laugh, and spread his hands. "Shit. I'm fucking dead, aren't I? If you're here, then that's it. Bullet in the brain. But tell me – how much is he paying you? I'll double it. Triple it. I'll give you a new contract – to go back to Romero and shove your fist up his arse."

"Fine words for an academic," said Amba, and pulled out her FRIEND. The small weapon sat in her hand, dull and black and menacing.

Shall I do it now?

Not yet. Wait a moment...

Professor Jmes paled, and lost his cocky assuredness. His eyes were fixed on the FRIEND; Amba wasn't sure if he knew *exactly* what it was, or simply thought it was a weapon, an odd-looking gun capable of blowing off his head in a splatter of skull chunks.

"Will you take my commission? To kill Romero?" Jmes was licking his lips, and his eyes were wandering frantically. Looking for a weapon. A means of escape. *Anything...*

"You think I'm shit," she said. "Don't you?"

"No. I think you're an android. Not human."

"I have thoughts. Feelings."

"Not real," said Jmes.

"I'm not here to discuss this." Amba leant forward slightly, and touched the FRIEND to Jmes's head. "I'm looking for a woman. She's called Lady Goo Goo, a Researcher for Ride Organics and Alien Testing. I know you know her. I know you were friends. I've read your file."

"She's gone into hiding after an attempt on her life," said Jmes, slowly, looking beyond the FRIEND touching his skull, beyond, deep into Amba's eyes. "I don't know where."

"Want to bet your life on that?"

"Wait. Don't kill me. I don't know it, I swear..."

Amba shrugged. "One last chance."

Jmes shook his head. "If I tell you, will you let me go?" His voice was a dry croak.

"Too late," said Amba, and fired.

THE FRIEND WHISTLED, and Zi cheered, and a memory bullet shot from the barrel and entered Professor Jmes's forehead. It broke through the skull and wormed into his brain, and Jmes gasped and blood spurted from the wound and he was punched backwards against his desk, one leg kicking out and knocking over the lamp. The bullet slowed, and turned, mapping Jmes's brain from the inside, then turning, it drilled through brain matter towards the dorsolateral prefrontal cortex. The bullet stopped, still spinning, and began to scan, relaying information back to Zi. After maybe a minute, in which Professor Jmes was twitching spastically on the floor, the bullet shifted again, drilling through to the parietal lobe.

Outside his skull, Amba Miskalov watched impassively from her seated position on the floor. Occasionally, a pulse of blood would leak from the bullet's entry wound, and she held the FRIEND loosely, and hummed to herself, considering his words – the words of this clever man, this academic man, this professor man...

You're one of them... an android. Not human.

I have thoughts. Feelings.

Not real.

Amba thought back, to the airport, and the little girl she'd killed. The girl, and her mother. Innocent. Simply in the wrong place at the wrong time – when a cursed Anarchy Android went to work.

Why me, Mommy? Why did the bad lady shoot me?

Because she had to, darling. Because she had to protect her own anonymity.

But I wouldn't have said anything, Mommy. I promise! If only she hadn't shot us. If only she hadn't killed us.

Amba pictured that little girl. The perfection of her skin. Glowing hair. Pretty lips. Just like the girl she would love to have, to feel growing inside her, nurtured and protected in her womb. The child she would always want. The child she could never have. Because of what sat in the white house. Because of what hid behind the pale blue door.

Jmes said she wasn't human. And he was right.

"You fuckers," growled Amba, and cleared her mind. She could feel the FRIEND's bullet was nearly done, and she prepared herself for the *sting* of information. She steadied herself. Felt it coming, like a rush, like a tidal wave, a sensory overload flowing and gushing into her mind, into the channels of her brain designed for the purpose – and she was swimming, floating in this man's life, and Zi was there holding her hand, and Zi was naked and beautiful and black – not the black of a different race, but a metallic black, like her skin was infused with the steel and alloy of the *FRIEND*...

Let me, said Zi, and Amba allowed her access and entry and total, utter control, for if she'd tried it herself then her brain would have twisted in upon itself with the sheer scope of thoughts and emotions, of an entire life within her own life, a mind within a mind fighting to be free.

Zi searched and channelled and worked.

And Zi smiled at her, and her teeth were glossy black, her tongue black, her eyes black, glowing, shining with the light of an alien place. Zi squeezed Amba's hand, reassuring the Anarchy Android.

You're safe, that hand said.

Safe with me...

AMBA OPENED HER eyes with a start. She shivered, as if somebody had walked over her grave. Everything, the world and life and evolution, was a blur. Gradually it cleared, and Amba shook her head. She coughed once and stared at Jmes.

He was swaying a little, where he sat, slumped against his desk. He seemed conscious but dazed, which was probable, for he had a bullet in the brain. As Amba watched, another trickle of blood slowly rolled from the bullet's entry wound and down the professor's forehead. Then, like slow-mo filmy in reverse, a circle of steel appeared at the dark hole, filling it. There was a tiny grating sound, of metal on bone, and the bullet reversed from its path, from its worming exploration, and Jmes lifted a hand and, with a tiny *squelch*, removed the bullet from his own skull.

He looked down dully at the tiny sliver of steel in his hand. His mouth worked spasmodically, jaws opening and closing, before he finally looked up at Amba and cocked his head to one side, eyes full of questions, pain haunting his features.

"You know?" he said, finally.

"I know. Lady Goo Goo is currently in hiding, under protection at Monolith's FireIce Mountain High-Security Military Facility."

"You'll never get to her," said Jmes.

"We'll see."

"I won't say anything."

"Huh?" Amba had turned away, scanning the darkened room. Outside, the sun had fully dropped below the horizon. Still the permanent party of the Theme Planet went on. People were laughing and cheering.

"I won't say anything. If you let me live."

Amba stood. Fireworks erupted in the sky, sparkling streamers as wide and high as cubescrapers, roaring into the heavens and filling the world with stars. Silver and gold petals glittered. Firework horns sheared off and faded into nothing.

There was a deep darkness after the display.

Amba lifted her FRIEND and fired, point blank, into Professor Jmes Kooky's face. This time it was a *real* bullet, and it detonated his brain and skull across the side of his desk.

"Nobody gets to live," said Amba, and holstering the FRIEND in her chest, turned and left the room.

CHAPTER SIX
LABYRINTH

DEX STOOD UNDER the shade of turquoise trees, leaning against a slick, glossy trunk, watching the hotel. Everything appeared normal. There were no heavy-handed tourist police, no forensics, which was incredible because, technically, both kidnap and murder had happened under that very roof. Dex had worked PUF for years, he knew the protocols, and the whole damn place should have been shut down and crawling with forensics. But then, this was a *tourist*-fuelled world. He'd read reports about Theme Planet. Once, a provax terrorist organisation called The Sons of Reality demanded that humans were not allowed on their theme park world due to atrocities committed during the Helix War. They had waged a war via planted IEDs which left various holes in various landscapes, and derailed a fair number of high-speed theme rides. Monolith Corporation's first response had not been in Dex's eyes the logical one – which was to communicate with the terrorist group. Instead, Monolith had deployed a veritable army of quick-response drones with the sole purpose of doing quick "cover-up" jobs, the ability to sniff out IED traces from a thousand klicks, then deliver to the perpetrators swift bloody retribution.

Dex rubbed at his tired eyes, and then the back of his neck where he'd been *stung* by Jim. The bastard.

He'd awoken a few streets away, lying on a bench in the sun, mouth tasting of metal.

What to do, what to do?

Had Jim been right? Get his gear and clear off TP? Was that the only thing he *could* do?

And what the hell was wrong with Police Urban Force officers visiting the damn planet in the first place? Dex had never heard of anything in news or papes with a negative spin on PUF visiting the theme world. Why would it matter? Who would care?

Questions upon questions upon questions, each one leading further into a labyrinth of questions. But the simple, glowing fact still remained – should Dex trust Jim and get the shit off the planet? Or should he try and get things done himself? Dex grinned, and it was a nasty grin, a bad grin, the grin of a man teetering on the knife-blade of insanity. After all – you could only push somebody so fucking far. And Dex's whole world had turned to rat-shit. He could trust nobody. Fuck everybody. Everybody was a potential enemy. Dex wouldn't get caught with his pants round his ankles.

He rubbed at his eyes. Shit. The only way Kat and Molly and Toffee were leaving Theme Planet was if Dex put in the groundwork.

Okay.

Backtrack.

Jim wanted him to leave, and had happily turned on his own. Did he really work for the police? For Monolith? Or was he part of the same organisation as had kidnapped his family? Had he helped Dex in order to help himself? But why would he do that?

Dex's eyes narrowed. He, himself, was trouble. The Earth government knew he was on Theme Planet, and he was PUF, which meant Big People. Important people. People it was certainly harder to make disappear.

Okay. Assume, then, that Jim was helping him *for a reason*. But not the same reason Dex really thought.

Back up further.

Dex could trust *nobody*.

It had been suggested he pack his stuff and leave Theme Planet voluntarily. Which meant this had the sanction of Monolith – who else could clean up the hotel and allow him to waltz in, gather his shit, and leave? If that *was* the case, then he had to play the game for a little bit...

Okay. Play the game... see what happens.

He crossed the road and mounted the steps, wincing a little as he waited for the sniper's bullet. But no. To kill him in broad daylight on the steps of the hotel – too risky. Anybody could see. They had back-pedalled themselves, now, and were treating him differently. His would not be a death on the street, or a clumsy bomb in a car. Amateurs had done their best to fuck it all up, and Jim had been called in to correct the situation. Dex was sure of it.

He crossed reception. He smiled at the receptionist, now a lady with bright green provax eyes, and Dex stopped at the lift. It had been repaired. Gods, that was fast! But then, Monolith were experts at the cover-up, ever since The Sons of Reality started blowing the tracks on rollercoasters.

He got in the lift, feeling strange. The last time he'd been in the lift he'd been battling for his life with a cross-wired PopBot. The doors closed with a *bing* and Dex studied the panels carefully, searching for a dent, a mark, a scorch from live wires, anything. But he could spy no evidence whatsoever. He started to consider the possibility that he'd gone crazy, and was currently paddling upstream through a mire of his own insanity, when the doors opened and he caught the *whiff* of fresh paint. Dex licked his lips. Not going mad after all.

He moved to his room, and it had been repaired, tidied, the corpse removed. Great stuff. Even the doors of the dented kitchen cupboards had been replaced. Even the bullet holes had been filled and painted. Dex crossed, frowning, and touched the wall. The paint was dry.

"Those fuckers."

He moved to his room, dragged out his small case (he always had his own small case, so that when his wife inevitably overloaded their family case to five times the baggage weight allowance, he could justifiably allow her to pay the extra charges herself; she called him an old skinflint bastard; he called her a wilfully decadent baggage stuffer). He filled it with a few clothes and anything he thought might be of use. His police issue gun was gone, no doubt taken by Jim, or some other Monolith spook. Dex went back to the kitchen, removed various hefty chopping blades from their diamond block, and wrapped them in clothing inside his case. But what he really needed was a pistol. No, a machine gun. No, a fucking *rocket launcher!*

Plan. Plan. What to do?

He had to appear to be playing ball, then disappear off the grid. But then what?

Jim. It had to link back to Jim. Jim, the *human* policeman. The bastard knew what was happening. He knew where Dex's wife and children were. So, it would just be a matter of gentle persuasion. Right?

Dex stared down at the blade.

He changed, pulling on muted green cargo pants and black boots. His wife always, *always,* mocked him about his insistence on taking his boots on holiday. *Why in the name of arse,* she would say, usually brandishing a chopping knife in his direction, *would you want boots on the beach? Sex on the beach, I'll grant you, but bloody big fat stomping army boots? Have you got a screw loose? A joker missing from the pack?* But Dex would grind his teeth and thrust out his lower jaw and absolutely adamantly take his damn and bloody boots. They were a part of him. Comfortable. As much a part of Dexter Colls as his chest hair. And that's what you got for years on the streets of London, walking the beat and beating the crims.

Dex pulled on a long-sleeved dark top without any fashion insignia, something he'd brought along for the chilly nights (or so he reasoned) but now something which would be an aid to night-time subterfuge. Over this, despite the heat outside, he pulled on a brightly coloured orange and pink Hawaiian comedy shirt, the type of item he usually wore to PUF officer stag night drinking sessions.

He moved to the bathroom mirror and looked at himself. His eyes bore dark rings, his brow was creased with stress, and there was no smile in his eyes. As he turned, he caught a glimpse of a small framed photograph of Molly and Toffee, and his heart leapt. It depicted both girls, their arms draped over one another, laughing. Katrina took it everywhere with her. Dex lifted it, slid off the back and removed the photograph. As he watched, slowly the photo dissolved into another image, of the girls in costumes on a sunny beach in Clearwater, Florida. This was Kodak Multi-Paper, and could display up to a thousand images. Katrina kept just three on it: the second image dissolved and became the four of them, sat around a table for Molly's seventh birthday. There was a cake in the shape of a princess (with black hair, moody eyes, black fingernails and mosh boots – a kind of *anti*-princess) and sparklers sparkled and they were all laughing. Good times. The best of times. Happy times. Dex folded the paper and tucked it inside his shirt. His face went grim and he straightened, looking at the door. He touched the hilt of the knife in his belt, under his brightly coloured vomit shirt.

Time to go to work, he thought.

THE TRIP TO the Shuttle Port was an uneventful one. In the taxi (an automated one this time; Dex didn't relish the prospect of killing *another* taxi driver) he was deposited at the loading ramps, and he moved through into the first waiting lounge, taking his time, eyeing up everybody he passed. There were thousands of people checking into desks, which were moving swiftly, fluidly. Theme Planet prided itself on not fucking its customers about. Their bureaucracy was a well-oiled machine; their organisation second to none.

Dex found a ticket office, and booked a one-way flight to Earth. He charged it to his Bastards Inc. credit card. This was a credit card company that at least acknowledged their position in the universe. "Leave it to us," ran their marketing motto, "and we'll do the best to let you fuck yourself up!" It was a novel approach to advertising – Tell It How It Is. Dex had to admit it, he admired their balls.

"Is there a reason for your unexpected departure? And is there any reason Mrs Colls and the children aren't accompanying you back to Earth?" asked the Shuttle Booking staffer.

"Yes. My father's ill, back on Earth. I'm rushing back to help look after him. We didn't see the point of upsetting the children; they may as well enjoy the rest of their vacation."

The provax's bright eyes fixed on him for a few moments, and Dex thought he caught a hint of... disbelief? Then she smiled a dazzling smile with ruby lips and ivory teeth, and handed him the ticket.

"Have a safe journey, Mr Colls. And the whole of Theme Planet will be thinking of your predicament. Hope your father gets well soon."

"Thank you," he said, thinking *it'd take a fucking miracle. He's been under the fucking soil for twenty years.*

Dex moved into the toilets and, when locked safely in a cubicle, removed the rest of the knives. Another went down his pants, and one down the back of each boot. Happy now the luggage was empty, he returned and checked in his luggage, surrendering his passport in the process. *Fuck it,* he thought. *I won't be needing that anymore, anyway. I'm either leaving Theme Planet illegally, with Kat and the girls in tow... or I'm leaving in a fucking bodybag.*

Dex moved to the fast food hub, and hung around for a while, observing the bustle. Many security guards passed him, their machine guns and RPGs gleaming with the gleam of the fanatically polished. But not one guard looked at him. No glances. No glint of recognition in feverish eyes. Did that mean his description hadn't been circulated? Or were they just damn fine actors?

No. They're playing it low-key now, thought Dex. But he knew. At some point, a hit was going to come. When did they plan it? And he smiled. Of course. The minute he got back to Earth, the minute he left the Shuttle Port in London. That way, he was Earth's fucking problem. Just another dead pig.

Well, this piggy's going kicking and screaming all the way to the bank. Or at least, the morgue.

This little piggy's going to fuck up *the whole damn show*.

Porky Pauper's Huge Fat Burger stand was a bustling powerhouse of activity. Huge industrial conveyor belts of burgers were manned by what appeared, to Dex, to be hundreds of spotty teenage burger-eating rejects. He grinned. He fucking hated Porky Pauper's, but he could see his hole.

After all, he didn't dare go any further through security. Not with his personal arsenal of knives...

Dex sidled closer to Porky Pauper's Huge Fat Burger stand, then moved to the menu, casting what looked like a detailed eye over the burgers. FAT BURGER, DOUBLE FAT BURGER, FATTY FAT BURGER, MEGA FATTY FAT FUCK BURGER, WHOPPING FAT FUCKING FAT FATTY CRAPPY FAT FAT BURGER... the list went on and on.

One of the staff passed him, a young man (human) of perhaps only nineteen years. He wore a badge which read Benjamin Leadhead. He headed for the toilets, and Dex followed him, straight in, towards the cubicle, and Benjamin Leadhead was just loosening his fat belt around the fat waist of his sweaty fat joggers, when he turned to shut the cubicle door and realised somebody else was standing there.

"What the..."

Dex's fist hit him square on the nose, and Leadhead stumbled back, sitting on the toilet and adopting a state of unconsciousness. "Sorry, mate," muttered Dex, taking the apron and cap (depicting a WHOPPING FAT FUCKING FAT FATTY CRAPPY FAT FAT BURGER, with all its sauce and drippings) and closed the door. Going into the next stall, he stood on the toilet, reached over – grunting as he stretched – and flicked shut the lock, with a tiny *bleep*.

Dex pulled on the apron – which was a little too big, but hell, nobody would notice – and placed the cap on his head. It stunk of fatty fat burgers. Whistling, Dex left the toilets and headed for Porky Pauper's Huge Fat Burger stand, where he walked confidently through the STAFF ONLY door and down the aisle of busy burger workers. Nobody challenged him, too busy were the Porky Pauper's Huge Fat Burger staff at their jobs, and he walked all the way past the huge conveyor until he reached the back door. This led out into a series of corridors, all grey and anonymous. Dex smiled. Now, he was in the Shuttle Port's innards.

He moved with care, trusting his sense of direction and heading down. After a while he heard the clanking of machinery, and homed in on the noise, still wearing his Porky Pauper's Huge Fat Burger outfit as a disguise.

Luggage conveyors, he thought.

Exit.

THEY WERE SEATED *around the table. Toffee hadn't been born, and Molly was only two, her face the innocent face of an angel. She was currently tucking into a bowl of "mash," with a little butter, and for which she had invented her favourite name.*

"Go on," *urged Dex,* "say Molly."

"Molla" *grinned Molly, face covered in mashed potato.*

"What are you eating, Molly?"

"Is good," *said Molly.*

"What is it?"

"Mash unyinyin."

Dex and Kat laughed in pleasure, as if their genius daughter had just been awarded the Nobel Peace Prize.

"Mash unyinyin?" *continued Dex.*

"Is good! Mash unyinyin! Mash unyinyin mash unyinyin mashunyinyin!" *Getting excited, Molly started mashing her spoon into the mash unyinyin and laughing as it exploded everywhere, covering Kat's silky black dress and Dexter's PUF uniform. He grimaced; then grinned again.*

"You little monster!"

"NO! DADDA MONSTA!"

Kat raised her eyebrows, as if to say, well, you bloody trained her! You bloody started it! You can deal with the lunatic child, you mad, bad, Daddy unyinyin!

"MASH UNYINYIN," MUTTERED Dex. He could smell fresh air. Where had that come from? That perfect moment? That illustration of a simple time, a simple life which had once been his and had been stolen away in the blink of an eye when his back was turned?

Somebody's going to pay, he thought.

And if they've been harmed?

The whole fucking planet will pay.

He continued towards the clanking sounds, eyes narrowed, hand on the knife in his belt. It was simple, solid, reassuring. Not as good as a Kekra quad-barrel machine pistol, he'd be the first to admit, but a damn sight better than fucking nothing.

He came to a simple steel door, and peered around the frame. The sunshine was bright, his view of the runway restricted by concrete buildings. The clanking was loud now, and he could see a wide rubber conveyor, travelling in loops and delivering luggage into an untidy pile on the concrete. There was nobody about. *So much for fucking Shuttle Port security, hey?* Dex could have had a riot rooting through people's luggage and stealing shit, or planting bombs. *Nice.*

He looked around for cameras. There were none – or none he could see.

He back-tracked and tried a side door, peering into a long, low cupboard holding a veritable orgy of cleaning utensils, along with various industrial vacuum and polishing machines. There were cleaning drones, immobile and dark, parked in recharging sockets. They looked suspiciously to Dex like inactive killing machines, just waiting to slip out blades and begin an onslaught of carnage. But they weren't. Or at least, weren't *yet*.

Dex removed his burgerman disguise and his colourful Hawaiian shirt, folded them neatly, and stashed them at the back of a shelf behind some boxes. Now, dressed in cargo pants, boots and a long-sleeved dark top, he stood out less. He closed the door, moved back to the luggage conveyor, breathing in the fresh warm air and for the first time, *really* feeling like he was free. Free. Free of being watched, free of spies and shackles.

He walked around the building, keeping close to the wall but moving with a casual, steady gait. No sneaking. That was the quickest way to rouse suspicion. The sunlight was bright, but Dex had lost his shades somewhere in the past twenty four hours.

Dex followed the various contours of the huge building and its annexes, and as he rounded another corner he came to a mesh fence, which he scaled with ease. He landed lightly on the other side, and followed the wall once more. Around another corner, and he saw a field of parked groundcars, sunlight gleaming from polished bodywork and gleaming glass.

A ride. Perfect.

Dex found the nearest car, a sleek Honda, and was amazed to find the door open. He stepped into it, sank into the seat, had a look around the ignition for something he could interfere with, and on a whim hit the starter. The engine fired immediately, purring with a gentle hum.

No security. No security at all!

Dex grinned to himself. Why was he so surprised? There was damn near *no crime*. In which case, why the hell had there been so many cops? The station had been crawling worse than an anthill full of sugar! What the hell were they all doing, these upholders of the law? Prevention? Training? Or something more sinister?

He eased the Honda backwards, then purred along the wide road. It was racetrack smooth.

Damn. Even the roads were perfect.

Dex was staring to *hate* this place.

* * *

THE BLOCKY, ANGULAR building across the road from the police station was a Spoofatex Restaurant, selling the best in "Authentic Galactically Spoofafied Cuisine." Dex had crept around the back, stood on the AI garbage cans (which moaned and griped constantly about their stinking, humming contents), leapt and caught the bottom of a roof inspection ladder, then hauled himself up onto the flat roof, where his boots left imprints in the soft tar. Creeping behind the lip, he kept himself low and peered over the rim at the police station, watching the marble steps up which he had travelled (although *that* little incident felt like a lifetime ago) and down which he had sprinted.

How long did he have? Before they realised he was missing?

Dex chewed his lower lip, spied an old plastic bucket, and dragged it over to the edge of the roof. He settled on the filthy container, chin on hand, the sun beating down on him like an alien hammer against an anvil. His dark eyes watched the doors like a predator weighing up its prey, waiting for Jim to emerge, his mind twisting and turning things over and over, picturing first the face of Katrina, sweet Katrina, her spiky black hair, elegant features, port-red lips; then Molly, dark eyes, dark hair, sombre expression, always ready with a negative comment but hey, that's just the way she was, as dark as Dexter had been when he was younger; then Toffee, bright as a bowl of summer petals, her laughter infectious, a permanent smile creasing pretty young features. How the ladies in the everythingmarket used to stop him, and fondle her hair, and scratch under her chin and make cooing noises because she was so pretty, so *delightful*.

Dex craved a cigarette, the first in a long, *long* time.

"Shit," he muttered, and his impatience was an alien in his chest, beating to get out. His disappointment was a discovered love letter from another man. His frustration was a premature ejaculation.

"Damn you all," he growled, and glanced up at the sun, at an alien sun, and yet it felt so normal, felt like Earth. Part of the con, he realised. Part of the sick trick. No wonder Theme Planet did so fucking well. It was the perfect location; exotic, but not too exotic. Foreign, but not too foreign. Ideal for wannabe adventurers who really *didn't want* an adventure. It's fake, he realised. The whole fucking place, the whole fucking thing is FAKE. Fake experiences, fake rides, fake thrills, fake adventures. Even on Adventure Central, the climbs up the Skycloud Mountains, the rides down the Death Rapids, exploration in the Lost Dunes, searching for treasure in the Caves of Hades... all constructed adventures, all manufactured experiences. None of it was real. None of it was *genuine*. Not like this. Here. Now.

Dex watched the police station. There was absolutely no indication there had been a violent shoot-out on the marble steps involving Theme Planet's finest law enforcers. Dex narrowed his eyes, once again suspicious. Everything was just too neat, too perfect, too damn *clean*.

As Dex waited, fuming gently, he analysed himself. A few bruises and a spinning mind seemed his only injuries. And his knuckles. They hurt like a motherfucker. They always did.

The sun crawled across the sky. In the distance, children squealed in pleasure and wheels rumbled on tracks. The fake pleasure of the Theme Planet really started to grate on Dex's nerves. It was all created. All fake. All false. An ersatz *world*.

A groundcar pulled up, and five provax police piled out, running up the steps. They left the motor running, modest fumes *phutting* from gleaming exhaust pipes.

"There's something *so wrong* here," he muttered, and wondered about talking to himself. Kat always told him off for his little guilty pleasure, but the more time he spent trawling the streets of London looking for crimes to solve, bad guys to put down, evils to cure, wrongs to right, the worse and worse he got. Only now, *now* he would have preferred London a thousand times over, preferred the dark violent corners of the Concrete Grove, rejoiced in the dirt and grime and human effluence in Downtown Bury, sang with celebration to the High Gods for only a moment of fighting in

Dirtside Ringside – when compared to the plastic grass and fake pleasure of Theme Planet. "It's bad here," he realised. "As fake as plastic steak. As false as *Bible II – The Remix*."

There.

Jim had stepped out from the shade of the building, and was glancing up and down the street. He seemed wary – and quite rightly. If Dex had his way, he'd shove a fucking battleaxe up Jim the policeman's arsehole, sideways, and with multiple prejudice.

Jim stood for a few moments, then lit a cigarette. Even from this distance Dex could see the glow of the tip, and he imagined he could smell the smoke. *Bastard*, he thought, now even having *more* reason to hate the man. *That son of a bitch's bitch*. Dex wondered if he could take a cigarette from a dying man's mouth...

And now Dex knew something was corrupt. The last time Jim was at the police station, he'd been sprinting and shooting fellow policemen. And here he was, cool as cucumber, on the scene of a recent massacre?

Yeah right.

Seemingly satisfied that no Dexter Colls was going to leap out and machine gun him, Jim walked down the steps and started along the street. He stopped by a battered old brown Ford – somewhat at contrast to the sleek hydrogen groundcars of Theme Planet – opened the door, and looked up and down the street again. *He knows*, poked Dex's paranoia. *He fucking knows what you're thinking, knows what you're planning*. But of course he didn't. As far as Jim was concerned, Dex was being a good boy and getting on the next Shuttle bound for Earth. In Jim's world of tough hotshot cops, fuckers did what they were told, and if they didn't, Jim shot them. He was old-school; Dex could tell. He'd met men like Jim a thousand times over – and they weren't necessarily a bad thing. After all, they got the job done, and got the job done good.

DEX LANDED ON the paved car park, boots thudding, and ran to his groundcar. He wheelspun from the car park, hammered down the road, then slowed as he saw the brown Ford up ahead. He dropped back further and allowed a few cars to interject between himself and the car he was tailing. Having worked PUF in London for years, Dex was proficient in following suspects, but as he so rightly recognised, Jim *was* police, and police were the best in the business not just at following, but at recognising, in turn, that they were being tailed. Dex kept a good distance, and they headed inland, away from the tourist resort to the north of the Kool Kid Zone.

The sun was still gleaming in the sky, and Dex felt incredibly tired as he followed Jim. He was filled with self-doubt and a constant, niggling fear. The what-ifs which could poison a man's brain.

No, he told himself. *You have to stay focused, buddy. You have to see the job through and get the job done, no matter what the cost. And this Jim bastard? Well, he's going to become a casualty of war.*

Jim did nothing suspicious, nothing to make Dex think he knew he was being followed. But Dex knew he would check; all police did, simply as a matter of course. After all, in this day and age, there was always some dangerous motherfucker wanting you dead. Dex knew that better than most. London was a rough town, one of the worst. A living, breathing beast, a dark beast, which sucked people in and only allowed them to escape in pieces.

They turned from the interstate after twenty minutes of driving, and Dex allowed Jim to escape into a gated housing estate complex. There was no way he could successfully tail him in such close confines. He had to cruise, so as not to be discovered. It was much better this way.

Dex waited five minutes to give Jim time, then as another car entered he nipped through the gates behind it – a woman driver, an elderly lady who drove as if her car carried a gyroscope triggered nuclear bomb, with greatest, anally-retentive trepidation.

Once inside the housing compound, Dex eased the Honda around the sweeping streets between colourful trees, with red, yellow, blue and green trunks as well as leaves, and between bushes of what smelled like lavender and rose. The whole place was alive with sensory information. *Ha. The benefits of being Theme Planet police. But it's still fucking fake!*

It took him ten minutes to find Jim's car, and then he settled down up the street in the shade of various multi-coloured, sighing trees. Opening his window, again Dex craved a smoke. Just to soothe his nerves. Just for old time's sake. After all, any minute now he could get a sniper's round in the back of the skull...

If they wanted him offworld that bad.

If they wanted him *quiet*.

Dex eased back the Honda's seat and tried his best to relax. He imagined Jim entering the house after a hard day's work, placing his gun on the side, kissing his wife on the cheek as she emerged from the kitchen with an apron covered in flour. "Hi honey," she'd say. "Hard day at work?" He'd frown a little, and then mutter, "No, nothing unusual. Fucked over an Earth policeman called Dex Colls, but hey, that's just the way of the world, isn't it?" Then his kids would come galloping down the stairs and he'd swing them into the air, kissing their scented hair, smiling in response to their laughter...

Dex awoke. Something had changed. He wiped away a tear, and focused on the brown Ford. Jim was standing outside in casual clothes (well, casual for a piggy-pig-pig, thought Dex, bitterly) and his wife stepped out. She had long, curled black hair, and the two boys that emerged shared her dark colouring. Jim ruffled one boy's hair as he passed and climbed into the back of the Ford, and for some reason, despite his earlier fantasy, despite his earlier imaginative rambling, this clamped Dex's heart worse than any electric-shock therapy, and *squeezed* it, and filled him with bitterness and bile. This was no longer some fantasy, this was real, and Jim had his own family and that was just *bad*, so bad, worse than anything Dex had ever felt. "Man, where's your fucking empathy?" he thought. "Where's your fucking humanity? How could you do this to me, how could you treat me like this? I'm the same as you, I'm the fucking *same*, Jimboy."

The Ford reversed off the drive, and headed down the street like something out of the old Earth filmys. Dex followed at a casual distance, wondering idly where they were headed, but not really caring. The worst of the burn had eased off, and the sun was finally sinking. It was cooling down, shadows lengthening as they hit the highway and flashed past signs for DINOZENS, KIDDY'S COASTER OVERLOAD and LOLLY POP FOREST.

Surely not now, thought Dex. Not rollercoasters, *now*...

They finally reached the DINOZENS turnoff, and Dex followed the Ford up a wide twenty-lane sliproad and through colourful avenues, until they reached a car park which stretched off for as far as the eye could see. Jim parked up and his family climbed out of the car. The young boys were bouncing excitedly.

The car park wasn't the only thing that stretched off for as far as the eye could see. So did... the *dinozens*.

Dex sat, and stared up, and stared up, and gawped like a drooling village idiot. They were big. Hell yes, they were BIG.

"What, in the name of *fuck,* are those?" he mumbled, and climbed out of his groundcar. He glanced around warily, but received no undue attention. He stared at the beasts. There were perhaps fifty of them that he could see, each as big as a forty-storey towerblock or cubescraper. They were all manner of shapes and sizes, some reptilian with great jagged heads covered with armoured plates and tusks and scales that gleamed violet in the dying rays of the sun. Their eyes glowed; several breathed fire. And it was with a *blink* they reminded Dex of *dinosaurs*. Of course, he groaned inwardly. Dinozens. Dinosaurs. Aliens. Alien *dinosaurs*...

They were a deformed mimicry of Earth's ancient fossils, even bigger than Earth dinosaurs, even wilder of eye and sharper of tooth and fang and tusk and claw. They roamed around this section of the KOOL KID ZONE with great ponderousness, swinging their huge heads, some sharp, some armoured, some shaggy like a wild thing, moving and turning, shifting and watching with baleful reptilian eyes.

Dex realised Jim and his bouncing family were getting away, and he followed at a wary distance. Now all he needed were a few spare moments with Jim. That was all it would take, Dex knew. He gave a sour grin. Oh yes. The hand had been dealt, Dex treated like a fucking loon. Not any longer. Now, Dex was wiser than wise, harder that hard, streetcool and tuned in to the *game*, fucker.

He made the gates, passed through the turnstiles (there were no charges here, not like other theme parks where charges applied at *every damn step of the way, sucker* – pay for travel, pay to park, pay for entry, pay to piss, pay to eat, pay to fucking *breathe* in some of those money-grabbing bastard establishments – and those were the ones Dex could mention and remember and spit and moan about). He took a map. DINOZENS was zoned, with different breeds of dinozen occupying different areas, some with very high fences and warning notices. Dex narrowed his eyes, only giving the map a cursory glance. It couldn't be *that* dangerous; after all, it was for the kids, right? And anyway, he was more intent on seeing where Jim and his wife and kids went.

There. Down a wide, leafy walkway.

"You back-stabbing traitor," muttered Dex, and hurried after them. So, they were out for an evening's entertainment. Enjoy the Theme Planet on which they lived and worked, and on which so many poor dumb schmucks had to *pay* a fortune just to visit for two or three weeks.

I'll show you some entertainment, thought Dex.

They moved past various pens, Jim's boys cooing and warbling in wonder. Then a gift was offered to Dex on a big golden platter, probably sprinkled with God-nectar and dipped in Whiskey-ambrosia. Jim's wife took the two boys into a toilet block, cleverly disguised as a dinozen backside – thus making its overt purpose artful, in-theme and conspicuous.

Dex looked around, and started to move quickly. It was evening, and there were only a few people about, despite each and every park or zone or yard being open 24/7. Yes, people sometimes visited for evening jaunts, as Jim was showing, but on the whole it was a damn sight quieter than during the bustling day.

Dex paused, as a sixty-foot creature with feet as big as cars plodded past, then he moved with extreme caution to stand behind Jim. He palmed the knife, and stuck it against Jim's back.

"Don't even move, motherfucker, or I'll make your wife a widow and your kids instant orphans."

Jim half turned. He was tensed harder than an archer's bowstring. "I thought you got the Shuttle."

"No, dickhead. I didn't get the Shuttle. Now, don't move. I'm going to take your gun."

Expertly, Dex eased his hand around Jim's waist, removed the gun, prodded the gun in Jim's back, and slid the knife into his belt.

"Let's move," he said. "Up ahead. Don't look back. If you do *anything*, I'll fucking drill you. Nod once if you understand."

Jim nodded, and they started to walk, past the stomping feet of a big green dinozen and then veering right, down a narrow walkway, then left, down another. They passed between heavy screens of bushes, until Dex was sure they'd cleared Jim's family.

"You're insane," said Jim, slowly.

"Shut up unless I ask you a fucking question."

"You should have gone back to Earth," said Jim, shaking his head.

"Over there. Through those trees. *Move!*"

They headed off the path, into what appeared to be a sparsely populated conifer woodland. The ground was soft and spongy, filled with a riot of colours. Each tree was a spread fan of rich, thick needles, some green, some orange, displaying wild and wonderful patterns. Above the canopy, the eerie shapes of the dinozens loomed and wandered ponderously in and out of view.

They moved deeper into the woodland – into a *fake* woodland. It was quiet here. The trees sighed occasionally, or gave a gentle pattering of needlefall on the sumptuous carpet.

"Stop." Dex's voice seemed unnecessarily loud and brash.

They stopped. Jim turned to face Dex, and his face was curled into a snarl. "What are you doing, you crazy bastard?"

"Saving the situation," growled Dex, jabbing the gun towards Jim's face. "So shut the fuck up, listen, and answer my questions, or I swear by all that's holy I'm going to kill you where you stand."

Jim paled.

"Don't do that, Dexter. I was only doing what's best for you. You know that, right?"

"I know *shit*, you back-stabbing motherfucker. Now answer me this. Where are my wife and children?"

"I don't know."

"Where are my family?"

"I don't *know*, Dexter."

"So help me, if you say that one more time you get a bullet in the skull."

"Dex, you don't understand."

"No, you cunt, *you* don't understand. I've been Urban Force for long enough now, I know the rules, I know how the game is played – by both sides. Monolith are in on this, Monolith are responsible for taking my family – for God only knows what purpose. But I want them back, and I'm willing to kill the entire fucking planet to get what I want."

"No," said Jim.

"Where are they?"

"This is nothing to do with Monolith," said Jim, and his face was shadowed, painted by brushstrokes of violet from the dying sun. He looked suddenly very, very dangerous. Demonic.

"Oh, yeah? Who is it, then, my mother?"

"No, Dexter, this has come from on high. From Oblivion Government. From the very people who rule Earth."

Dex paused, shock registering on his face. "What?" he said.

"I warned you, Dex. You shouldn't be here. You should have been told. You're an illegal here. You're not wanted." He smiled, and it was a grim but knowing smile. The smile bit Dex like a knife between his ribs.

"What do you mean, I'm an *illegal*?"

"Somebody really should have told you, Dex. You're PUF. London Squad." He shook his head sadly. "You're not welcome, mate."

"And *Oblivion* give you an open passport to shoot the shit out of your own policemen over here? That brings a new meaning to interstellar legal cooperation, don't you think?"

"Ah, that. The escape? Is that what's bothering you? A lot of it was staged, Dexter."

"Staged?" Dex hated the stupidity, simplicity and naivety of his own questions.

"Robots. Animatronics. Fast filmy exploding realtime makeup for gunshot wounds." He winked. "We're good with stuff like that. No policemen were harmed in the making of this feature, and all that shit."

"That fucking traffic cop who melted into the pleasure liner wasn't staged; and the damned boat going down and killing thousands of people wasn't staged, either."

"That was... unfortunate." But by the look on his face, Dex could see Jim cared nothing for the innocents. He was hard, and he was brutal, and now given the opportunity he'd slot Dexter hardtime bullet-time.

"Where are my family?" Dex's voice was soft.

"No fucking idea."

Dex lowered the gun, and fired a single shot into Jim's kneecap. Jim screamed, his scream swallowed by the surrounding conifers as bone shards exploded from the back of his leg, and blood drenched the springy heather behind him.

Jim rolled on his side, clutching his bent, twisted leg, face torn into a cracked platter of agony.

"Now, my friend, you're going to limp for the rest of your life," said Dex, and lined up the gun again. "The next shot guarantees you'll be a cripple."

"Wait man," panted Jim. "Stop, stop," he held out a hand stained with blood. "I can't tell you. Monolith will kill me."

"I thought you said it was Earth Government, fuckface?"

"They're working together," said Jim, panting, spittle foaming on his lips. "They want you off Theme Planet. They want you off *bad*."

Dex's brain wrestled with itself. He needed to know where his family was, but he also wanted to know why this policeman claimed the two most powerful organisations in the QuadGal had supposedly turned against him... bullshit, he realised, shaking his head. It had to be bullshit.

"Last chance," he said, kneeling, and putting the gun to Jim's other knee. "Where's my family?"

"Dex, please, they'll kill me if I tell you," he hissed, eyes wide with fear.

"I'll kill you if you don't."

"They're on The Lost Island," panted Jim, eyes squeezing shut in pain as he rolled onto his back, wheezing, blood pumping between his fingers. "Please don't kill me!"

Dex stood, and glared down the gun at Jim. Here, and now, an ocean of rage and resentment and frustration surfaced. His finger tightened on the trigger. He could do it. Kill the bastard, right here, right now...

A screeching of distressed timber filled Dex's head, seemed to fill the entire world. Dex looked up as the entire forest canopy came rushing towards him, crashing down, entire fifty-foot trees breaking and snapping like dry tinder, like children's toy sticks, as *something* came stomping into the forest and knocked the woodland aside like skittles.

Dex gawped for a moment, blinking rapidly, confusion his mistress, as through the violet light stomped a *dinozen* easily a hundred feet high. It lifted its head and gave a massive, mammoth trumpeting cry which shook the ground. It reared up, its huge, armoured, spiked trunk swinging lazily like a pendulum, and its flat-plated feet, each one as big as a house, came down with a colossal THUMP, which shook the trees out of the earth and sent Dex toppling backwards. The trunk swung towards him, and he swallowed, watching the deadly barbs like sharpened razors. They cut through trunks with a smashing, crashing, screaming sound of tortured wood, of tearing timber, and Dex leapt, flattening himself into the heather as what felt like a *skyscraper* ploughed overhead and destroyed another hundred trees.

Jim disappeared in a swathe of shredded wood, like a man swallowed by quicksand.

Dex leapt up, and started to run. "Holy mother of God," he breathed, and sprinted for all he was worth, Jim and the murder of Jim clean forgotten in a whirlwind of panic. The great beast's head lowered, and its tiny yellow eyes focused on the running man.

Again, the dinozen trumpeted, shaking its great head, and began to charge after him with a clumsy, lumbering gait, which was nevertheless a jog faster than Dex's sprint.

Dex skidded, leaping behind a tree, and aimed the stolen gun at the great beast's face. He began shooting – five bullets, ten – and the beast roared now, flicking its great shaggy head from left to right and back, as if blatting away annoying flies. It could certainly feel the bullets, but that was a long way from being dropped like a bastard.

"Son of a bitch," muttered Dex, and stood, and with a brutal clarity headed for the theme park area, and the women and children beyond. If, as he suspected, these creatures were machines, controlled machines or even AIs, they would have inhibitors built-in. After all, Monolith couldn't have the bastards running riot all over the Theme Planet, killing tourists! That would make bad economic sense.

Dex sprinted for all he was worth, Jim gone and forgotten and hopefully *dead*, and pine needles scattered and branches snapped and cracked, and all around him it rained bark and twigs. To his left there came a terrific *thump* as a fifty-foot trunk hit the ground only a few inches away. Dex shied away, his trajectory changing. His arms pumped, gun forgotten. He knew, deep down, his only salvation from this creature were the tourists...

Through the gloom of the forest ahead there came another scream, blood-curdling and bestial. Dex froze right through to his core, as if the dinozen had reached forward and ripped out his spine. Realisation struck him a hammer blow. They were coordinating, trying to cut him off! His face went hard, forming into a narrow brittle mask. So. They were being controlled. Who by? Earth's Oblivion Government? Monolith? It had to be. Nobody else had such authority on Theme Planet...

Dex veered left, ducking under branches. He heard hooves on the forest floor, pacing him to his right, and behind him the huge lumbering beast was still cracking and breaking trees, but slowing now, as if it had been called off. It was too big, Dex realised. Too frightening. They wanted the smaller, more inconspicuous dinozens to take over...

Dex gave an evil grin.

And you know what that means, kiddies?

Bring in the predators!

A creature burst from the undergrowth before him, and Dex flipped left, gun cracking in his hand, bullets thumping up fur and into flesh with spurts of blood. Whatever the *thing* was – part bear, part dinosaur, part lion, a cocktail of fur and armoured bone plates – it sailed past him as he continued to fire, bullets eating into the creature's body as teeth flashed and gnashed and snarled, straining to get at him, and he hit the ground rolling, gun still pumping. Then he stopped, and smoke was in the air, and he climbed to his feet and stared down at the creature. It was panting hard, fur matted in blood. Pale blue malevolent eyes watched him with hatred. He took a step closer, and it snarled like an injured lion.

"Goodnight, fucker," he said, and put a bullet between its eyes.

Breathless, his chest hurting, muscles burning, his mind screaming, he orientated himself. Deep in the forest there were three sounds of huge lumbering beasts, all in different directions and cutting off escape routes. *The bastards are forcing me into a narrow channel,* he realised, mind working fast. *They want me away from the tourists. Away, so then they can kill me and bury me in a shallow grave. The bastards. The utter bastards.*

So? What did you expect? To find your family and live happily ever after?

Damn. Fucking. Right.

Dex crouched suddenly, and reversed into the centre of a thick bush. The scent of pine resin was all around him, thick and cloying. He closed his eyes, and tuned himself into the forest. The gun was cold and hard in his hand, an alien thing, a part of a different culture, a different world. *All I want to do is take my family home,* he realised. *But no. They're going to make me fight. Well, I'll give them a fight they'll remember...*

Something paced into the clearing from the right. It was like a panther, but its body was an oiled green. Its eyes were bright and old and reptilian, and its jaws were open, panting softly. A tongue flickered out, red and forked. Dex watched the creature, analysing it carefully. It moved with all the grace of a big cat, fluid, muscles rolling easily and powerfully beneath thick skin. It dropped its nose to the ground, seeking his scent. *Aah*, thought Dex. *Aaah.*

He readied his gun. He was going to come out fighting!

And then he saw the second oiled green cat; it slunk into the clearing, circling its comrade. Both of them, Dex realised with a start, weren't *sniffing* the ground, they were *tasting* it, with their flickering forked tongues. A sibilant hissing came to him. Shivers ran up and down his spine. *What are they?* his mind screamed at him.

"We're danjos," said a soft voice, right by Dex's ear, the words tickling him with proximity; and very, very slowly, he turned, to look straight into the eyes of the third oil-skinned beast. It was so close they could kiss, and Dex's nostrils twitched at the scent of its sleek hard body. He became suddenly, painfully aware of the creature's sheer *mass*. Its bulged with muscle, with power, and exuded a force that far outweighed Dex's meagre human form; his shell.

The other two creatures had stopped their search, their *bluff*, he realised, and orientated on Dex's hiding position.

But he didn't dare shift his gaze from that ancient reptilian stare, sat so close...

As close as lovers.

Because to do so, to move, to act, to fight, would be to die...

CHAPTER SEVEN
INTERNAL EXILE

AMBA MISKALOV STOOD in the shadows of the Spikefist Mountain Range, boots planted firmly on pale rock as she shaded her eyes and studied the distant mountain. The FireIce Mountain High-Security Military Facility was clearly visible, two-thirds of the way up the towering rockface of the largest mountain dominating the range. There was an open-sided hangar, like a rectangular maw in the bulk of the mountain. All it was missing were teeth.

Looks impenetrable, said Zi in her mind, her words like the cool kiss of an iced lover.

Nothing's impenetrable.

You'd don't have the equipment.

I have you.

Zi chuckled then, and Amba got a momentary glimpse of the woman inside the FRIEND, the *spirit/ghost/demon* not just inside the FRIEND, but inside Amba's own body, in her mind, in her fucking *soul*.

Yes, Amba. You will always have me. Until you die. Until we both die.

Why do you think Romero wants her dead? Why do you think Oblivion want her dead?

Our role is not to question why, Amba. Zi actually sounded shocked. Amba had never before asked such a question. For some reason, this amused Amba immensely.

What are you smiling for?

You, dickhead. Getting all noble with me, when we both know what I do – hell, what we do is about as low as it goes. We're the scum at the bottom of the barrel, Zi. We're the dregs, my friend.

I disagree.

Why so?

We are the elite. We do the things nobody else would ever dream... or be physically able to do.

Bullshit. I'm an android, Zi. I'm an android, and I'm hated by the humans because I look like them, act like them, but they think I'm inferior because they created me, they fucking played at God and I was the abortion. I'm hated by other androids because that's just the way with androids, isn't it? We hate each other, as if we're all competing for the same gulp of air, the same slice of life, and we're afraid it'll suddenly turn into a scrum and so we're always looking over our shoulders, always keeping our eyes on the ball. Who knows when the order will come from Oblivion to have us all put down? Not murdered, you understand, but like in an old filmy: "retired." As if we're so much old useless scum, detritus, something not real, not living, not breathing, but a machine to be decommissioned. Well, I'm no machine, Zi, and I'm getting tired of being treated like a second-class citizen by every motherfucker who discovers I'm an android.

So what's the answer?

I'm sick of doing another man's work.

So you want to retire yourself?

If by "retire" you mean murder myself, then no. But if by "retire" you mean turn against my masters, rend and slay, then find a cave somewhere to sit and live out my life in a simple, honest existence – then maybe.

Zi remained silent. She was considering.

Don't worry, Zi. I know you report back to Romero. I'm going to get this job done. Then I'll decide what to do.

Amba, I'm shocked you think so little of me! I promise you, I am not a puppet of Romero, Oblivion, or any other organisation; I am here... for you. I am here to help you. Here to help you achieve what you want.

Yeah. Right.

I am hurt you do not believe me.

Explain yourself, then. What the fuck are you, Zi? Where did you come from? Where did the FRIEND come from? Why me? Why choose me? Why help me? I never asked for your help, and I can get by just fine on my own.

There was a long pause, and Amba moved across the rocky ground to the hover bike she'd stolen ten hours earlier. It had been a long, uncomfortable ride through the night, under cold stars and spirals of fusing hydrogen sculpting patterns in the sky. But now she was here. The sun was up, and it was warming her android skin. It felt good. All of a sudden, it felt good to be alive.

I cannot explain it, said Zi, and her voice was soft, a gentle tickling in Amba's mind. *What I can say, though, is that you are barking up the wrong tree, my dangerously fragile human machine. Have you ever stopped to consider that maybe I'm not here just for your benefit? Maybe I'm here for myself, as well.*

What, by killing on my behalf, by doing the things you do – that helps you?

Yes.

Why, Zi, what are you?

"LAY DOWN YOUR WEAPONS AND PUT YOUR HANDS IN THE AIR!" commanded the loudhailer of the police drone, which swept around the rocky outcropping with flashing green and yellow lights, and hovered, nose down, in an aggressive attack position. Amba breathed out slowly, eyes fixed on the twin mini-guns that had her in their sights. She smiled, lifted her hands in the air, then whipped out the FRIEND, selected and fired quicker than a striking cobra...

The police drone was roughly the size of a groundcar, and early morning sunlight gleamed from its alloy panels. Little eddies of dust swirled under its hover jets, and a heat haze shimmered to the left from hot exhaust ports. Despite there being no human – or android – occupant, the drone was considered AI, considered *alive*. This was often a point of bitterness for Amba; after all, an AI – openly a machine – had more rights than an android. This police drone had more right to exist than a living, breathing, organic created human.

The FRIEND went BLAM even as the drone realised, a picosecond too late, that this meat creature wasn't in fact subserviently doing what it was told (as most creatures *did* when faced by the terrible barrels of twin mini-guns) and there came a rattling as the weapons started to spin up... but by then, it was too late.

For such a small weapon, the FRIEND had an almighty kick. The police drone was picked up and tossed across the desert, but it wasn't a simple blast of energy, this was what was known in the industry as a *cube blast*, something physicists still claimed was impossible and attempted to disprove. Maybe it *was* impossible. But the FRIEND still delivered one...

When the drone had spun for thirty feet, it was suddenly thrust up into the air and folded down and in upon itself, over and over, with rhythmical crunches of crushing alloy, then thumped down to the ground in a quivering, gleaming, raw-metal block.

A silence resonated, and Amba gave a sideways look at the FRIEND, then placed it back in her chest. She walked across the rock, eyes scanning left and right to check there weren't other drones in the vicinity.

It must have followed you, said Zi. *When you stole the hover bike.*

Hmm. Yeah. You fucked that up pretty bad, didn't you?

You wanted him quiet in the quickest possible way, yes? You didn't want to attract any attention from the damned Military Facility, yes? Well, he got put down and out of the game.

You said "him."

So?

It was a machine.

Oh don't start that again, Amba...

Amba crouched by the compacted police drone. Inside, there was a buzzing noise, and metallic scraping – as of metal spinning against metal. Amba stood, and stretched in the early morning sunshine. She yawned, and moved back to the hover bike.

"Time to go to work," she said.

How are we going in?

That's the easy bit.

Through the front door?

Yeah.

THE HOVER BIKE cruised across rock and sand, the hover jets sending out a swirl in the machine's wake. Amba, hair tousled from the wind, focused on the perimeter fence at ground level, and the fifty towers which lay scattered across the valley, each mounted with a heavy, automatic, AI pulse laser. She slowed the bike as she approached the fence, eyes flickering up to the walls of sheer rock beyond – the mountain, and the high rectangular mouth of the facility entrance. All along the fence, in a variety of languages, sensory field warnings made the message clear and simple:

KEEP OUT OR YOU WILL DIE.

Amba slowed the hover bike at the foot of a tower, and lowered it to the ground. She sensed the AI pulse laser watching her from above.

Amba climbed from the bike, staggered theatrically, and went down on one knee, hand slapping out to break her fall.

"YOU MUST VACATE THIS LOCATION AT ONCE," boomed a suitably metallic robot voice. "OR YOU SHALL BE SHOT!"

Amba fell to her other knee, and held up a hand to the tower. "It's okay, I'm okay, just give me a minute..."

"YOU WILL GET BACK ON YOUR HOVER BIKE AND LEAVE IMMEDIATELY – OR YOU WILL BE SHOT. I WILL SHOOT YOU. I AM NOT JOKING ABOUT THIS SCENARIO. I REPEAT, YOU WILL BE SHOT. SHOT DEAD. BY ME. IN THE HEAD. WITH A LASER."

Amba vomited on the floor, then flopped to her side and lay still.

The AI pulse laser shuffled forward to the edge of the guard tower and peered down past its wide, flat barrel containing metal eyes.

"ARE YOU ALL RIGHT, HUMAN MEAT?"

Amba remained motionless.

The AI pulse laser considered its options for a while, and then sent a buzz back to the guard tower control block at the foot of the mountain. A few minutes later, a JEEP snorted into life and throttled across the rough rocky ground, tyres thudding and bouncing over rocks, its engine growling, thick black fumes spitting from its exhaust. Aboard, there was a Battle SIM in full desert camouflage combats, heavy armour, and carrying an MP7000. The SIM was a big man, with a helmet and a face that screamed *Sonny, there just ain't no comedy in war.* SIMs were universally renowned for having a serious lack of a sense of humour – so bad, in fact, that many a comedy stand-up routine on Earth poked fun at SIMs and their anal retention, saying they didn't just lack a funny bone, they did in fact have *negative* comedy appreciation. Obviously, serious SIMs found these comedy routines seriously non-funny, and took every opportunity to shoot up, massacre and generally exterminate comedians at every opportunity. They considered it fair payback.

The JEEP slammed to a stop, and the Battle SIM fought for a while, rocking the vehicle as he tried to extricate his slabbed bulk from the narrow seat. Finally, he managed to work his way free (*ho ho*! the comedians would have joked, *too many tins of beans and sausage for that FAT BLOB SIM!*) and then he stomped over to the fence and the nearest section of fence looking out over Amba's prostrate form. Although there was no door in the thick cable mesh, the Battle SIM punched digits into a mobile door bar, reached out and opened a section of the fence – which became a door under his control. Doors could be summoned at any point in the fence; it was the premier unique selling point for the military fence company.

The SIM peered out, looking carefully to left and right in what would have been a comedy exaggeration if he hadn't meant it in all complete seriousness, a seriousness backed up by an MP7000 and an itchy trigger-finger.

Happy there was no ambush, the SIM stepped out onto the rocky ground, boots kicking up little squirts of dust. He strode over to Amba and, reaching out with the long barrel of the MP7000, poked her in the head.

"You. Human. Get up."

Amba did not move.

"Human. You not allowed here. This is a secure area. Gov will have the human smashed and locked up if the human stays here or tries any kind of infiltration. The human must listen carefully. The human must get on hover bike and leave."

Amba groaned, and rolled onto her back. Her eyelids flickered. The Battle SIM was stepping from one armoured boot to the other. He cursed, shouldered his MP7000 and reached down, easily lifting Amba into his chunky battle-arms, and walked back to the JEEP, carefully closing and evaporating the door in the thick cable fence behind him. His heavy boots thudded on rock. He was staring straight ahead, armour-plated face showing no emotion.

Amba gave a little whimper. "Thank you," she murmured.

The Battle SIM stopped by the JEEP. He stared down at Amba. He frowned. "The human is not to get any ideas, Battle SIMs are not fond of humans and likely to shoot them into a pulp. I am only helping the human because I have orders to help useless pathetic wounded humans under some kind of treaty arrangement with Monolith Corporation, and if it was left to me, then the human would be left out in the desert to bake in sun and get killed and get eaten by any passing snake predator. So the human is not to make any noise. The human is not to make any movements. I will take the human into the Base

Cave and the human can recover enough to FUCK OFF. I hope the human understands all this."

"Uh huh," moaned Amba, throwing back one arm unconsciously, which slapped at the Battle SIM's armoured face – not hard, but enough to widen his scowl. He dumped her in the back of the JEEP, squeezed his body into the driver's seat with several grunts, and started the engine with a rattle and plume of black smoke.

Amba opened one eye as they bounced along, the fence and AI guns disappearing, the Battle SIM bumping and farting up front. He was moaning. Something about the terrible effects of B&S on his digestion. Amba did not understand.

You did well, said Zi.

Yes.

You outsmarted the so-called bloody smart guns! So much for AI. It's fucking overrated, if you ask me.

Yeah. Well. They'll be waiting for me on my way out.

But you'll be moving fast, then, said Zi.

Yeah. Moving fast.

The JEEP growled, and suddenly the rock face seemed to *shift* in perspective and Amba spied a wide tunnel that had not been there previously, either by accident or design – and knowing Theme Planet, definitely by design. The JEEP zoomed into the rocky enclosure and the sunlight was extinguished like a snuffed-out candle. Darkness and shadows fell over Amba's face. Cold air surrounded her, and she could smell damp, fungus, and gun-oil. An armoury? More SIMs?

They zoomed through the cold and the dark, and the JEEP was wrenched to a halt by a heavy application of brakes. Amba sat up, looked quickly around – there was a steel-walled guard house of some kind, filled with computer equipment and blinking lights. Then she nimbly leapt from the JEEP and scanned for more enemies...

There were none.

She focused on the Battle SIM, who was staring at her with a particular kind of loathing. "The human has moved," he said, and started rocking, trying to get out of the JEEP. The whole vehicle creaked and squeaked on ancient leaf suspension.

"Whoa, fat boy, just wait there for a minute," she said, holding out a finger.

The SIM stopped his rocking, and scowled at her. "You *dare* to call a Battle SIM 'fat boy'?"

"Yeah, that and more, dickhead."

"You *dare* to call a Battle SIM 'dickhead'?"

"You really are a dumb fuck, aren't you, SIM?"

"You *dare* to call a Battle SIM 'dumb fuck'?"

"Wait, wait, wait a minute." Amba held out all her fingers. "With your limited intellect I fear this argument could go on for way too long. So let's cut to the chase."

As the SIM's lips formed around the words and his brow creased in concentration, Amba leapt at him, her right fist cracking his face three, four, five times with blows that would have felled a lesser man. Indeed, would have dropped a Justice SIM.

Slowly, the Battle SIM lifted his head and glared up at her. His eyes were red-rimmed, small, piggy, evil. Blood was trickling from the corner of his mouth and his nose, from under the armoured plates. It had been said Amba's punch was as hefty as a kicking horse. She'd never put it to a direct test, but here, and now, she realised it wasn't quite hard enough. Not for this brute.

Shoot him, urged Zi.

I can't... the sensors will pick up the discharge. She gestured up to the corners of the chamber, and several narrow steel poles. Energy scanners.

Well, they'll know you're here soon enough anyway...

The Battle SIM surged from the JEEP with an almighty grunt, and there came a massive CRACK as his fat arse split the vehicle in two. Steam spat and fizzled from a broken cooling system, and bits of automotive metal tinkled to the ground. The SIM surged free, and looked suddenly behind him, realisation crashing across his stupid, armoured face.

"Did I do just that?" he rumbled.

"Your fat arse did," said Amba, and a second later both boots struck the SIM's face. But he was surprisingly fast, he was bulky, stocky, powerful; yes with an overhanging gut of beer and B&S, but he *was* a Battle SIM, and he *was* a tough motherfucker. He caught her legs, and flung her across the cave.

Amba flew, and rolled lightly, coming up in a crouch. Poised. A natural predator. Natural fighter.

The Battle SIM began a charge to the steel hut, but Amba interjected herself between the two and the SIM stopped. He eyed her warily, and scratched at his chin. Then he reached around, pulled free his MP7000, and aimed the weapon.

"I wouldn't do that," said Amba, smiling.

"Ha! The human say I have fat arse! The human make deroga... docraga... dickorrogaragotory... fuck it, *bad* comments about me. I not stand for it! I not take it! I shoot human in face and face consequences later, if there are consequences, because stupid human meat should not be here in this military compound in the first place..." He paused. He seemed to remember where he was, what his job was, and what the problem was. It was a big problem. A problem he needed to sort out. Probably with extreme prejudice.

The SIM opened fire...

Only he didn't, because at some point during their combat connection, Amba had activated the twin-switch auto-disassemble function of the MP7000. With a tiny series of *whirrs*, the MP7000 started to deconstruct itself into three hundred and seventy nine discrete parts, guaranteed to make any squaddie sweat, which fell from the Battle SIM's hands like a tumbling metal waterfall.

The Battle SIM stared in disbelief at the weapon parts, then at his hands, then up at Amba with an ever-widening scowl of understanding. "You bugger, you. Human meat bugger! Well, here's something for you, human, when I get my hands on you, I'm going to flip you over and *give you* a bugger! It'll take me five whole damn hours to put gun back together again! I is not amused!"

With a determined step and determined glint in his eye, the SIM advanced. Amba raised her fists.

"This is going to hurt, fat boy," she said.

"*STOP* calling me fat, human effluence!" snapped the SIM, reaching her and taking a wide swing that Amba shifted away from. Another punch whirred past her, and another. Five, six, seven, eight punches – all aimed at taking her head off, all dodged with ease and, seemingly, a minimum of effort.

"You need to be better than that," said Amba, and gave him a cracking right hook that sent him stumbling to one side.

The Battle SIM glared at her. "The human is little shit," he said.

Amba hit him again, and again. He smashed a left cross, but she moved easily from the SIM's cumbersome path. She hit him with a combination of blows, increasing her power with incremental steps, until the SIM was staggering around, waving his arms around his head and trying to ward off her blows as if she were a cloud of stinging insects. She stopped, and he lowered his hands, and Amba ducked a little, came in close and delivered a crippling uppercut that, although it didn't lift him from his feet (the SIM was *way* too heavy for that), at least uncompressed his spine, pointed his chin at the cave's roof, and sat him back on his backside with an "ooof."

Amba lowered her hands, and pulled out the FRIEND. Her eyes flickered around the chamber. Still, there were no alarms. She had triggered no sensors. Despite the infiltration, the fight, the noise, nobody had come rushing to the Battle SIM's aid.

They trust the AI guns, said Zi.

Maybe...

"The human is a cheat," said the SIM, scowling, his eyes focused on the FRIEND in Amba's hands. "But then, I understand now, the human not playing fair, because the human isn't a *real* human, the human is one of those super-duper snazzy made-in-a-VAT humans, ain't that right?"

The SIM looked at Amba with his tiny piggy eyes, and Amba clamped her mouth shut. She narrowed her eyes, also. So. He'd realised...

"Androids are not made in vats," said Amba, voice soft.

"Ooh, touch a nerve, did I?" said the SIM. "And you call *me* touchy about my B&S overhang! Well, at least I not *hated* by the humans, well not much, except bastard comedians – damn them all to hell and buggery – but at least I not a *slave* like you. You're not legal, fucking *android,* and you and I know they kill you on sight. So do your worst, because even if it take me a hundred years to die, screaming and bloody on a bloody battlefield, my eyes in my lap and my balls in my boots, even if it take me a *thousand* years to die, at least I not suffer the disrespect you suffer. At least I not despised by those who create me. You is like a plague, android, a pestilence hated by all. You are dirty. Right down to your clockwork soul."

Amba stepped forward, touched the weapon to the SIM's forehead as if injecting a bolt into cattle, and pulled the trigger. There came a dull BLAM and the SIM slid slowly sideways. Amba grinned a sickly grin, and looked around once more, FRIEND in her hand, mind settling to calm.

Good shot, said Zi. *You put that aggressive moaning whining warmongering milporn bastard out of his misery, hey? And don't listen to him slagging off androids, after all, he's a fucking Battle SIM, by all the gods, how the hell could he ever know what he was talking about? Right?*

No, said Amba, and she seemed to shrink for a moment. *He was right.*

What bullshit is this? snarled Zi.

He's right. I am hated. By everybody. Hated, like a rat. Like a leper. Hated and unclean and infectious.

Awww, bullshit, Amba. Come on, let's find this Lady Goo Goo bitch and spread her body parts around the room. That'll make you feel better! Just like in the good old days when you'd go on a Double Kill, a Triple Kill, a fucking RAMPAGE! You're unstoppable, Amba, you are the fucking best, and the only reason you are hated is because you are feared! You're the top of the food chain, my girl, and you should be damn happy you're there. Because...

Yeah?

If you're not top of the food chain, then you're just meat.

Amba said nothing, simply staring at the dead SIM. His blood was leaking out onto the rocks and he looked, strangely, at peace. Even his armoured face plates did nothing to ruin the look of serenity on his features. He was at peace. At last. At peace...

Don't get any fucking ideas, growled Zi.

Not yet, pulsed Amba, but in the back of her mind, in the tiny dark cave where nobody was allowed, not even the intrusive dark angel Zi, back in that dark private recess she thought to herself –

But soon.

THE BLAST HAD tripped silent alarms.

Amba knelt in a narrow stone corridor, one hand touching the wall to steady herself as, below her, the world fell away into a vast deep chamber, like the inside of a volcano. Below, the world glowed a distant, molten red, and heat streamed past her face.

How do you know? said Zi.

I can feel it.

And she could. She could *feel* the alarms had been tripped. She wondered if anybody had stumbled across the body of the Battle SIM back in the groundcar compound. He needed a proper burial...

There it was again. Regret. Sorrow. Just like the little girl in the sparkly LLA restroom...

Amba could feel the alarm through her hands, through her feet, smell it in the air, taste it in the warm volcanic breeze. She moved a little closer to the edge of the drop, where her tunnel had come to an abrupt halt. Her hair ruffled in the heated updraft. She felt a sense of massive space before her, around her; got a sudden injection of how damn *big* the mountain really was.

Big. No. BIG.

And she was a tiny, insignificant speck of dust within the HUGENESS, a tiny morsel of uncooked meat struggling like a worm through soil and rock and striving to get *up* towards the light.

Amba grinned then, face illuminated like a fiery demon. Yeah. A tiny morsel of meat, admittedly, but one able to kill *all the other* tiny morsels of meat.

Amba glanced up. Shit. She was going to have to climb.

Far down the tunnel, she heard the stomp of boots, the rattle of guns, the murmur of growling voices. SIMs, no doubt, filled with bloodlust and out to avenge their slaughtered comrade. Which was a fair motivation. Amba held them no ill-will.

Amba squeezed from the narrow aperture, twisting with the agility of a cat and hooking fingers into hooks and cracks in the rough stone of the cavern's interior. More hot air blasted up, ruffling her hair, and Amba took a deep breath. She glanced down, not with fear, just an awareness it was a damn long way to fall, into depths that were simply a glowing *red*.

Amba started to climb. Lady Goo Goo, her target, was up there somewhere. Up in her Ivory Tower. In her High Castle.

Sweat beaded her brow. Within seconds her fingers were scratched and scarred by the glass-sharp rock. She moved with speed, assuredly, mostly looking up. Looking down was a fruitless exercise; after all, a hundred feet or ten thousand, it all killed you. Killed you flat and broken like a doll under a hammer.

Amba moved like a well-oiled machine, always precise, every choice perfect. Up she went, through shades of orange and red, into darkness above. All around her was a soft humming, as if the mountain were *alive*. In a moment of connection Amba realised the mountain was her friend, her partner, her *lover*. It didn't want her dead; it wanted her inside, wanted to embrace her... or maybe to kill her, make her a permanent fixture of its rock and bones? She smiled softly. If that was the case, then so be it...

It was a strange, spiritual feeling, and something to which Amba was quite unused. To feel a *connection* with a lump of rock. That was alien. Wrong. Illogical. And yet she felt it anyway, and her heart fluttered, and sweat beaded her lip, and her fingers were rigid and filled with pain as she climbed and climbed, upwards, through drifts of smoke, across patches and slabs of slick rock.

Maybe this is what it feels like to be human?

Don't kid yourself, bitch, said Zi.

Thanks for your support.

That is *my support.*

From the drifts of smoke Amba could see something ahead, above, and she slowed her climb. She licked her lips, a frown creasing her brow, her muscles quivering. How could that be? How could such a thing be *here*?

Amba realised she had stopped climbing, so confused was she by the field of *ice* above her. There were stalactites and stalagmites of frosted ice, some small, some as big as skyscrapers, protruding from rocky arms and ledges, spiralling out from the rock face in all manner of random angles. There were bridges of ice crossing the chasm above her, distant and twisted and spiralling, like chains of magnified sugary DNA. And Amba's internal perspective rearranged itself, seemed to *magnify* because she started to truly realise, to understand, just how vast this hollowed-out mountain core was.

As vast as a mountain, perhaps.

But that's impossible...

Nothing's impossible on Theme Planet, said Zi. *They're planetary engineers. The provax have machines that can scoop up a shoreline, lay down a beach, build a mountain range, carve out an ocean; so the literature reads. Theme Planet is a totally created thing. Theme Planet is a construct, a built, grown, sculpted theme park. Literally, a Theme Planet.*

Amba continued to climb, towards the ice, towards the spirals above. They glittered, from unknown light sources, glowing red in places from the distant glow below, but also sparkling as if shafts of sunlight were striking from far above. *Shafts of sunlight?* But they were *inside the mountain?*

Amba rested for a moment, her muscles burning with fatigue, fingers numb from clinging to the vast wall of rock. She'd reached a fissure in the wall, and readying herself for a leap of faith, breathed deeply, smoothly, and jumped... thudding into a rocky flank, bouncing a little, hands clamping tightly into cracks, as the world and the drop flashed through her head and spiralled off below, like a dropped filmy camera.

Nice, said Zi.

Of course, said Amba to her dark demon, her dark angel, her dark twisted sister. *It's FireIce Mountain. A juxtaposition of elements. Indeed, an impossibility of elements, the ice surviving the fire. Wonder what trickery they used?*

Who gives a fuck, said Zi. *Get climbing. You need to get the killing done.*

Amba bit back a bitter retort. Although she hated Zi for many reasons, and questioned the dark spirit's very existence with regularity, she had to admit it – Zi was focused and deadly. Even if she *was* a figment of Amba's tortured imagination.

Up she climbed, muscles screaming, toes burning inside her boots. And as she came close to the first twisted spiral of ice she fancied she heard a distant, echoing scream. She frowned. A scream? Down here? Another climber?

She climbed further.

More screams echoed, and Amba paused, panting, resting. She glanced below, and still the glow was a constant, the drifts of smoke from below spinning up towards her on eddies of hot air.

More screams.

She looked up sharply, at the thick spiral of twisted angling above her. *Screams?*

Something flashed *through* the spiral of ice, a flicker of speed, and *through* the ice wall Amba spied people in ride CARS, hands in the air, faces images of blurred happiness as they zoomed through cables of ice, zoomed *through the mountain interior.*

Shit! It's a Theme Planet ride!

What did you expect? said Zi, stoically.

Not a fucking ride! Not inside a mountain! Not inside a fucking military installation!

Hey, if Monolith can make money, Amba, they'll make money. If they can provide excitement and adventure in any way possible, they will endeavour to do so. Believe me, if Monolith could sell sugared shit, they'd package it and flog it on market stalls right across Theme Planet's bazaars.

Yeah, but here?

Amba climbed up over the ice spiral, bitterly cold beneath her aching hands. She stood for a moment, balanced above infinity. At one point, a carriage zipped under her boots, and it was a long snake of happy faces and screaming maws, hands wiggling in the air.

"For God's sake," snarled Amba.

You don't have a god. You're an android.

Yeah, fucker, thanks for reminding me of that.

Amba upped her game, increased her speed. There had to be an access hatch somewhere, and as the spirals and bridges of ice appeared with more regularity inside the vast hollowed-out mountain, increased until they criss-crossed the sky and screams and gurgles of pleasure filled Amba's ears, so, all of a sudden she came across –

A ladder.

Hmm. Good and bad. A ladder meant easier egress from the cavern, further up and out into the military complex itself. However, it also meant the possibility of men with guns... not that men with guns bothered Amba, but she recognised she couldn't take on the whole world in a game of slaughter. Although she would cheerfully try...

She stopped at the ladder's bottom rung, grasped its cool, slick metal. It was by a small Fire Port, and looking down Amba could see the criss-crossing ride tubes now, woven into the fabric of the mountain itself, entangled within crystal and ice, whether natural or created. She could hear the rumble of distant wheels. More CARs shot through the spinning tunnels, and down into the bowels of the mountain.

Amba glanced at the Fire Port. It was an emergency measure, in case any of the rides below caught fire. Presumably, it would rain down to extinguish flames in the event of an emergency.

Amba gave a short, neat smile. A plan formed in her mind. She pulled free her FRIEND, glanced down at the criss-crossing rides, and focused. She aimed the FRIEND.

I don't think this is a good idea, Amba.

Diversions are always a good idea, Zi...

She mentally selected a function, and fired; The FRIEND gave a meaty WHUMP and the nearest enclosed spiral of ice tubing exploded into a million glittering sections of ice. There were screams as steel tracks twisted and bent under the power of the blast, and ice tumbled away towards the void, towards the red glow, towards oblivion.

There came the thunder of wheels, the screams of excited riders which suddenly notched up an octave as they realised the track ahead had disappeared... There were wails of brakes on the track, there were showers of sparks, more screams of panic and terror. The lead CAR shunted from the tube and went over the edge, falling, dragging the next CAR, and the next CAR, until six CARs were dangling like a string of metal sausages. Steel and alloy groaned, and the CARs finally came to a halt, dangling, swinging, screams and wails echoing and reverberating around the huge cavern as the people aboard waved their arms in the air for a different reason.

"Wonderful," whispered Amba, and turned the FRIEND on the other enclosed tracks. She began to fire indiscriminately, the FRIEND shaking in her hand in an extraordinarily modest way. But what it produced was something more than normal, something *more* than military. Ice and crystal flew about, scattering like snowflakes into distant darkness, into the glowing depths, and Amba took out three, five, ten of the internal tracks of this bizarre Theme Planet ride, through not just the bowels of a mountain, but through the supposedly highly restricted Monolith-owned FireIce Mountain High-Security Military Facility.

Shit, she thought. If I'd realised *this* I would have just hitched a ride! I had to come in the back door. The *hard* way!

More CARs emerged, people screamed, chaos rioted through the riders. More dangling sausages swayed over The Pit, and the air was filled with deep metallic clangs and booms, the sounds of tortured machinery; the sounds of tortured tourists.

Amba narrowed her eyes, and turned a tiny dial on the edge of the FRIEND. "What we need now is more *drama,*" she whispered, and fired the weapon. A sheet of fire roared from the tiny black FRIEND, and set a huge section of track alight. Flames roared up towards Amba, but she was already climbing as the whole cavern started to fill with black smoke. More people screamed. It was rapidly becoming the soundtrack to the mission...

Amba made good speed up the ladder, boots clattering on alloy rungs.

Below, an inferno raged.

That was morally reprehensible, said Zi. Somewhat smugly.

Nobody died...

Many may *die. You are dangling their lives by a thread, if you'll excuse the obvious parallel; and you are showing a distinct lack of humanity.*

That's because I'm a fucking android, snarled Amba to her own personal demon, and Zi took that as a cue to depart.

AMBA REACHED THE access door, leapt through, but it was clear. Audible alarms, *fire* alarms, were sounding now, and this was good. Up here, the corridors were neat and square and alloy. She ran through the sterile environment, ignoring lifts and shuttles until she located a stairwell. She glanced back; a lift was opening, disgorging a platoon of SIMs and regular soldiers, all heavily armoured and carrying automatic weapons. They split up, heading in different directions. Amba glanced up the stairs, and started to climb, FRIEND held before her.

She kicked through another door into the astonished path of three provax carrying machine guns. Her arm snapped out, and the first provax was punched back with a hole in his skull, the second sent spinning sideways with a bullet in his ear, and the third backed away, hands coming up fast in sudden supplication. Amba shot him in the throat, and stood over him whilst he scrabbled at the wound, kicking around and leaving marks on the floor with his flailing boots. She crouched by him, looking up and down the corridor, then put another bullet in his head, and he lay still, milky blood bubbling on his lips.

Amba was hit in the back by a shotgun, the blast picking her up and accelerating her down the corridor with a *boom*, where she bounced from a railing and spun out, arms and legs flailing, and hit the floor hard. She lay still.

The android, for it was an android – she could smell him now, all of a sudden, like bad garbage; smell his fake stench, smell the distinctive metallic aroma which humans couldn't detect, but androids could, oh, yes, they could smell it like a rancid fish in a locked-down room. He moved closer, padding softly. Amba lay, bent and broken, head on the floor, one leg twisted up against the wall, blood pooling from her back where the shotgun had rioted through her flesh.

You missed him...

Shit, you think I don't know that?

Want me to take care of him for you? Amba could almost *sense* the pleading.

Oh, no. This fucker's mine...

He stopped. His boot reached out and prodded her face, once, twice. On the third prod she sunk her teeth straight through the leather of his boot, and straight through the toes within, severing them cleanly – or as clean as a bite can be. The android screamed, discharging the shotgun into the roof panels, which buckled and clattered down, clanging and wobbling. Amba grabbed his leg in both hands and twisted viciously, breaking the bone at the knee. But he was advanced, and he didn't scream again; he'd cut off the pain receptors, dropping back into *android* mode, instead of *fake human*. He punched down, the blow catching Amba on the cheek, as she punched up, feeling his testicles compress under her knuckles.

The android staggered back, supporting himself against the wall as his useless leg flopped free, and Amba rolled smoothly to her feet.

"What generation are you?" he said.

Amba leapt, punching straight, straight, right hook, left uppercut; he blocked the blows, returned several punches of his own, but Amba took them on her forearms, stepping back a little.

"Stop! I didn't realise you were *one of us*..."

Amba didn't speak, just stared, and kept her fists raised.

Sensing the advantage, the hiatus, the break in combat rhythm, the android spoke quickly, "We can help each other! I can get you out of here, I can..."

"Can you get me up to see Lady Goo Goo?"

"The researcher? You mean the woman, right? Ride Organics? That sort of thing?"

"Yes."

"Yes, I can get you up there..."

Amba lowered her fists, stepped forward, dropped to her knees before him and held out her hand.

"What?"

"Shotgun. We'll use it as a splint. You're not walking anywhere like that."

"You don't know what I want, yet," said the android, looking up and down the corridor, nervous now.

"Of course I do. You want to be more human."

His mouth flapped a little, then he grinned. "Despite the broken leg, I like you, little lady. You have spirit. I'm Jonno."

Amba's face went hard. "I don't need to know. Take me to Goo Goo."

LIMPING HARD, JONNO took Amba through a maze of corridors. He was talking all the time, not as if he were nervous, but as if he didn't get out much; as if he'd spent a decade in solitary confinement. Which, being an android, was a possibility. They came to several junctions, and at the tenth, Amba froze. There was a T52 AI Automatic Sentry. It buzzed and whirred, heavy calibre barrels tracking them.

"Aah, that's okay. This gun's called Bob. Say 'Hi,' Bob."

"Hello," said Bob, in a metallic, robotic voice.

"They're bad news," said Amba, mouth dry, brain sour. "I've seen them take out a fucking battalion."

"Ah, yes, I see. Well, only if you get on the wrong side of one. That's why there's not many personnel up here. Because of the T52s, and the fires down below. Ride fires. Did you hear about the ride *explosions* that took off, just a few minutes ago? An amazing coincidence. I know we've got keep it all *hush-hush* from the media, because if stuff like this got out, then we'd all be losing our jobs," he laughed weakly, "but you're a fellow android, so I know it's okay to trust you. Come on, Bob!" He whacked the lethal gun on its flat head as they strode past, and the AI T52 gave a buzz – presumably of enjoyment and metal camaraderie.

"They're not so bad, once you get to know them."

Amba followed Jonno down the next alloy corridor. "What do you mean, *not so bad?* They kill absolutely anything and everything that moves. Including each other. They were banned on Earth."

Jonno stopped, mouth dropping in awe. "What, you've been to *Earth?*" he said in wonderment. "Cradle of all humanity? The place that made *humans* bloody human? You are so honoured! So... experienced! I could learn a lot from you... I can see my trust was not misplaced, and when you've spoken to Lady Goo Goo, then we can really get down to the business of making me more human!"

"Of course," said Amba, smoothly. "Jonno?"

"Yeah?"

"How *long* have you been here?"

"I'm Generation Five."

"So... Gods, you must be three hundred years old?"

"Oh, yes. Give or take a decade."

"And you've been on Theme Planet that whole time?"

"I've been in this compound that whole time, and it's something I'm not very thankful for. Just between you and me – and this is *just* between you and me, you understand, because I trust you, as a fellow android – well, the last few decades, I've started to feel just a little stifled."

"Stifled?"

"Yes, There's only so many centuries you can spend staring at the same grey walls."

"I totally agree."

They made their way up more stairways, and it was getting warmer the more they advanced. At one point they came to a huge window – what was, effectively, a window in the mountain, actually *set* into the rock. They were near the summit, and the window was a viewing platform that showed several loops and curves from a ride, spiralling off down the side of the mountain.

"What're those?" asked Amba innocently.

"Why, that's the very famous ride, you should have heard of the famous ride, it's called MILITARY EXPERIENCE #7 – THE FIREICE HIGH-SECURITY MILITARY INSTALLATION FACILITY FUNTIME RIDE." He looked at her, then, with a frown. "Cheesh! You really have been locked up somewhere, little lady, haven't you? I thought *I* was the one who'd not had very much experience in the world. Although, admittedly, I've only had a few hundred years on the planet."

"What's your job, Jonno?"

"I'm the Cleaner," said Jonno, with a beaming smile.

"The Cleaner? I assume you mean you've *cleaned* this facility for the last three hundred years?"

"Yes. I've done a good job, don't you think?"

Amba tried hard to keep the pity from her eyes. "Yes, Jonno. A very good job. But... don't you get lonely sometimes? Or frustrated? I mean, other schmucks make the mess, encourage the kipple, and you tidy it all up in a never-ending cycle of banality?"

Jonno considered this. "No," he said. And smiled kindly. "I am an android of simple pleasures."

Amba gave a nod, glancing out over the vista beyond. Distantly, tracks curved and looped through the sunshine, rails gleaming metallic, CARs of many bright and varied colours trundling and flying, happy punters waving their arms in glee. *Oh, to be so happy!*

"Which way is it?"

"This way," said Jonno, moving forward. "Oh, incidentally, I forgot to ask your name. How rude of me. How inconsiderate. I am definitely being a bad friend; I am sure Lady Goo Goo would spank my bottom for my lack of manners. She's like that, you know, a very happy person, very into her work, always in her study like a good little student, head in a book or on the ggg doing something important all the time, and *not* playing Solitaire, ha-ha-ha."

"Important? Weapons, maybe? Technology?"

"She researches."

"Researches what?"

"Oh, you know, just researches."

"Well she must research something."

"Well, sometimes I hear noises. Coming from her study. Lots of blips and blops."

"Are the blips and blops part of the research?"

"They could be."

"Is she researching anything important?"

"*Oh!*" wailed Jonno, "yes! Of course! By its very nature, research must be important because you're finding out stuff, looking up stuff, coming up with theories on stuff. Oh, yes, all research must be important. Or else..." – he paused, eyes shining, looking off distantly into the ether – "*why* do research? I'm not bright enough to do it. With me, I'm just a simple soul. What you see is what you get."

"Yes." Amba formed a tight smile.

"Go on, then. What's your name?"

"My name?"

"Your name." Jonno rolled his eyes, as if Amba were being particularly dumb.

She smiled. It was a genuine smile. She kind of liked Jonno, in the same way one instinctively likes a puppy; only Amba didn't. She could never quite see the cute side. She sighed. For a change, she accepted the temporary hand of friendship. It felt very strange, especially after an opening of raw combat... "It's... Amba. Amba Miskalov." She saw no reason to lie. Jonno would be dead in under five minutes, happy puppy or no.

"That's a nice name. I'm glad you're here. I'm glad I made a new friend."

He moved forward, leading Amba through another grey alloy corridor which sloped upwards towards a patch of sunlight. Amba followed, removing the FRIEND from close to her chest and holding it low down by her thigh, modestly concealed.

"Me too," smiled Amba, cradling the small, black gun.

JONNO TOOK AMBA to the door, delivering assassin to victim with sickening simplicity and ineptitude. If Monolith had been kind and allowed this particular early android an element of education, or freedom, or contact, he might well have possessed the internal mechanisms needed to recognise the danger in Amba. But his blind trust, like a dog in its master, would lead to his downfall; his bloody execution. And Amba felt no compassion, she did not care, she had no empathy; after all, she was an Anarchy Android. Detonation. Torture. Annihilation. All in a day's work, before tea and biscuits.

Only...

She thought back to the young girl.

The white house.

The pale, blue door and the horrors that hid behind it...

Amba shivered.

Jonno grinned back over his shoulder at Amba, as if sharing some secret joke, some *intimacy*, and Amba tensed fast and hard, readying herself for combat, slaughter, execution, for this could all be a ruse and she wasn't so naive that she trusted somebody, anybody, especially another android she'd simply met in the damn corridor of a High Security Military Facility... Cleaner or not.

He could be a Murder Model.

He could be an Anarchy Model...

Amba gave a tight, wry smile, and made sure the FRIEND was constantly between herself and Jonno.

Jonno finished punching a huge stream of digits into the digital lock, and he pushed the door open, a thick steel portal which swung wide with the ponderous mass of a bank vault entrance. Beyond, Amba could see dark trees.

"After you!" beamed Jonno, stepping to one side.

"Oh, no, no, no," said Amba, voice low, "after you, really, I really do insist."

She felt her senses stepping up in her head, as if driven by motors. Her very body became *tuned*, like a delicate instrument, and the world seemed to slow down. Colours had more colour, more intensity, she could smell a wealth of flora and fauna beyond the entrance, she could taste flowers and pollen in the air, Jonno's stale sweat, his strange, metallic, almost *insect-like* vibe became more pronounced and when he moved it was with exaggerated movements, dance-like, almost in slow motion, and leaving blurred trails with every gesture.

"Hellooo-*oooo*," he called, stepping through the portal and Amba was following close, using his body as an organic shield, absorbing the atmosphere with tuned-up speed, taking in every minute detail. There were towering trees in the chamber, huge trunks soaring off into the distance where sunlight streamed from high above. Plants grew to knee-height all around, ferns and flowers which shifted gently in some obscure breeze. Insects hummed and buzzed. It was like a forest, a *real* forest, inside the mountain.

Jonno led Amba down a well-trod path, and stopped by a clearing in the internal woodland. Sunshine glittered from damp palm fronds. Amba was sucked in by the tropical essence, felt herself *believe* they were in a jungle somewhere, some alien forest, some esoteric Other World.

In the clearing there was a desk, a huge ornate redwood edifice, varnished to a deep glossy shine. On the desk was a six-screen computer terminal with extra air-accessories, and in a leather chair sat an old woman. She was very tall and thin and bony, even when sitting, and her skin was pale and fragile, wrinkled beyond anything Amba had ever seen. After all, with the VATs and the QG Cosmetica Syndicate, one of the most affluent, powerful and influential of galaxy-wide corporations, they had pretty much eradicated old age – or at least the *appearance* of old age. "*Why Grow Old!*" proclaimed the marketing slogans with blatant disregard for correct punctuation. "*Why Wrinkle and Prune!*" spat aggressive marketing splats marketed 24/7 on all available channels. "*Let the Cosmetica Syndicate help you beat those ageing blues... We make the Old New, we make the Crone Beautiful, our simple course of phenuclearaxiate injections make the Dead Alive! Only a simple remortgage required!! @ggg.iwanttobeyoungagain. ggg.*" Across Earth it was all the rage, and no end of wrinkled old grannies had queued with vapid grins and drooling spittle to have their faces "Tucked and Fucked," as the media started to call it. QG Cosmetica did indeed make the Old New, and certainly made the Crone Beautiful, but only, and this was the crucial bit, only on the *outside*. Inside, these newly-regenerated beauties were still the mumbling senile grumpy gits they had been when consigned to Humanity's Great Natural Garbage Heap. It led to many an interesting interaction, throughout Earth's nightclubs, and in shagpiles afterwards, when young and virulent Alpha Males realised they'd just enjoyed and pleasured somebody's Great-Great-Grandmother. The Quack Clinics filled up fast with a whole range of new and invented mental disorders.

Amba stared at Lady Goo Goo. Goo Goo was old, and made no attempt to disguise the fact. Her one concession to oddness was her bright pink hair, which sat atop her ancient skull like an explosion of candy floss.

"You're here," said Goo Goo, looking past and ignoring Jonno, and fixing ancient, almost *reptilian* eyes on Amba. Those eyes sparkled with a lazy intelligence and Amba was immediately on her guard, scanning her surroundings, trusting her instincts. Goo Goo might have looked like a decrepit clown, but there was something very dangerous about this woman; this Researcher into Ride Organics and Alien Testing.

"Yes," said Amba. She saw no sense in extending the conversation.

Jonno was looking suddenly confused, and took a step back from Amba. He could read something strange in the air, a set of emotions to which he was unused. His gaze was moving quickly, from Goo Goo to Amba and back again.

"Have I done wrong?" he asked, suddenly.

"No, Jonno," said Goo Goo with a smile. "You weren't to know."

Amba's senses were screaming. There was something terribly *twisted* here, something out of tune, out of key with the whole fucking *universe*. Lady Goo Goo was, to all intents and purposes, a sitting duck, a lazy target, but in Amba's experience it was never that simple, never that easy, and a sitting duck was rarely a sitting duck – not at the level Amba was involved in.

"Romero sent you," said Lady Goo Goo.

Amba said nothing. She took a step closer, looking up and around. She scanned for concealed weapons, she was a damn *expert* at concealed weapons, but Goo Goo was clean. Amba lifted the FRIEND and heard Jonno gasp, but he was off to one side, sensed, experienced, unworthy of consideration; irrelevant. The danger lay straight ahead – very real.

Amba smiled then, a bare showing of teeth that had nothing to do with humour. She simply had to progress and react to whatever secrets Lady Goo Goo was hiding. And hiding something she was; that reptilian gaze screamed it harder than a thousand proudly displayed cluster bombs.

"I know it's Romero. Earth's Oblivion Government have wanted me dead for a long time. I'm just surprised it took this long for them to find me. You must be very... efficient." She turned back to the keyboard, and her fingers flickered across air keys.

"Hands up," growled Amba.

Lady Goo Goo stopped typing suddenly, and turned her head to Amba. Her wrinkled old face crinkled into contempt and she began to laugh. "You're a pretty one, aren't you? For an executioner. What Generation are you? You're certainly not a Five, like the simpleton over there."

Again, Amba said nothing. In her experience, it was better to say nothing.

What was the point? In a few minutes, the Lady would be dead...

Lady Goo Goo licked her lips and her eyes narrowed. "Aah. I see! You're Anarchy, aren't you? I can *smell* it, dearie. I can smell it – on your skin, in your metallic breath, in your fucking *pussy*. You ooze it like alien semen."

Amba stepped closer, the FRIEND held steady, her eyes focused, senses screaming imminent danger. But from where? Which direction? Hidden guns? Turrets? A sniper? All came back as unprocessed, unchecked, non-viable.

"I'm sorry," said Amba, and she did not know why she said it.

"I know," said Lady Goo Goo, pink hair wobbling, and she smiled, and gave no signal, no gesture, but the whole damn forest *came alive*. The trees and ferns and vines *creaked*, groaned, and suddenly vines shot towards Amba and she leapt up and backwards, a flip that left her in a crouch, face neutral, FRIEND extended towards Lady Goo Goo.

She fired, but Goo Goo had gone, a backflip of her own. The desk and terminal vanished with a *whump* of disintegrating matter and Amba shifted her stance, dropping one leg a little, but there came a hiss of air and she twitched her head left, too late, as a vine slammed down and took her FRIEND. The weapon sailed up into the forest and Amba stared for a moment in disbelief, before another vine – with razor-sharp fins – slashed for her at head height. Amba ducked and rolled, looked back to Goo Goo, and realised the old woman had... *changed*. Nothing visible, just in the way she moved. She was crouched on all fours, back arched easily. In fact, her stance reminded Amba of a large cat. Another vine slashed at her, and she back-flipped three times, landing lightly next to Jonno. She crouched, her hands whipped out, and took away his leg splint. The shotgun.

"Hey!" said Jonno.

"Sorry, I need it," said Amba, without looking at him. She was watching Lady Goo Goo, advancing slowly across vegetation, moving on all fours, *undulating* with a rippling spine.

"I thought you'd help me become more human," said Jonno, miserably.

"You're doing just fine," said Amba, looking swiftly about for more attacking jungle.

"But I *need* help!"

Amba and Goo Goo launched at one another at the same time, flying through the air, and Amba cocked the shotgun and fired once, twice, three times before they connected. Amazingly, she missed. They slapped into each other, and the shotgun spun away, landing with a muffled thump in vegetation. Amba punched hard, three times, five, ten, slamming her steel fists into Goo Goo's head even before they landed together, in a tight embrace. Goo Goo took the blows, reached out, and grabbed Amba by the throat and cunt. She threw Amba away into the jungle like a toy, and the android spun, crashing into tree trunks which suddenly came alive, groaning, and reached for her with splayed branches like fingers. She hit the ground and rolled fast as a trunk the thickness of her waist crashed down, impacting where her head had been. She crouched and scuttled forward, as more branches and razor-tipped vines whistled past her, grabbed the shotgun, somersaulted over an aggressive plant snapping at her with the teeth of a piranha, and landed before Goo Goo.

The Lady was waiting for her, wrinkled face full of humour, reptilian eyes watching her. She took a step back, and it was like watching a snake recoil, readying to strike.

"What *are* you?" said Amba, slowly, not taking her eyes from Goo Goo.

"One of your nightmares," hissed Goo Goo, and struck fast. Amba dodged, shifting right, licking her lips. She'd never met a creature that could move so fast. She glanced down, saw twin slits across her forearm, oozing blood. She wasn't even sure which part of Goo Goo had inflicted the wound... until she saw a tongue with razor barbs flicker from the ridiculous old woman's mouth...

"Frightened now, are you, my little sweet?"

Goo Goo struck again, and Amba twisted backwards, raising one arm to deflect the blow. This time pain flashed through her, and she spun around, rolled with the blow; ended in a crouch, cradling the shotgun. The tongue had cut her right bicep to the bone. Blood pulsed from her arm, pattering on the jungle floor.

"I'm going to cut you up, one piece at a time," said Goo Goo, moving towards her, head bobbing, whole body rippling like a cross between a big cat and a striking adder.

Amba pumped and fired the shotgun, which gave a BOOM and blasted shrapnel through the vines and ferns. But Goo Goo had slipped right, body oscillating, and the shells missed their mark.

"I'm going to tear you up, eat your flesh, and send your bones to Android Hell..."

She attacked, and Amba waited the blink of an eye for her to get in close before unleashing the shotgun, catching Goo Goo full in the belly, but still the old woman came on, slamming into Amba and sending them both rolling in a flurry of limbs across the thick vegetation. A branch nearly decapitated Amba, and as Goo Goo's face came close she slammed two fingers into the old woman's eyes, up to the knuckles, with a disgusting squelching sound. A deathblow. Amba's fingertips were in Lady Goo Goo's *brain*...

The eye sockets went suddenly hard, clamping Amba's hand in place, and with a flick of her head Goo Goo sent Amba sailing back across the fake woodland, finger bones snapped. She landed hard, broken fingers twitching, and got slowly to her knees. Her eyes focused. Goo Goo, despite having *no eyes*, was orientating on Amba and grinning like a village idiot.

"That hurt you, pretty little Anarchy Android, didn't it? Do you really think I need eyes to see you with? This is my domain, pretty little dove. This is my *world*... and now it's time to stop playing games with you. Now, it's time to put you gently to sleep."

Lady Goo Goo stood, body rigid, and Amba was panting, the wounds on her arms stinging, blood drenching her flesh, fingers broken. In all her assassinations, she had never been wounded. Not once. And now, here, this old woman with candyfloss hair was making a comedy of her attempts...

Amba's jaw set tight.

"Tell me what you are. Before you kill me," she said, realising the woman was not human, not android... but something else, something far more complex. She was like no recognised and accepted *alien* Amba had ever heard about...

She was... *adapting*, almost. A shapeshifter.

Amba's head snapped left. Jonno was standing, mesmerised, and there was something about the look on his face, *something* which didn't fit right, didn't sit true, and struck a discordant note of disharmony in Amba's soul.

"Too late," said Lady Goo Goo. "Time to say goodnight, sweet dove."

Lady Goo Goo's mouth opened, suddenly too wide, in a massive, screeching, grotesque show of teeth. The mouth was as big as Goo Goo's whole head, a deep black-and-crimson maw edged with black bone and filled with row after row after row of chattering razor teeth which chattered and chomped and *promised*.

Goo Goo leapt, so fast she was a blur –

And Amba was frozen to the spot.

CHAPTER EIGHT
INSIDE OUTING

SOMETIMES SHE HAD a dream, and she didn't know if it was real or imagined. And in the dream, or maybe the reality, she was surrounded by a blackness so intense and thick, like an oily smoke which did not choke her, that even when she lifted a hand before her eyes she could see nothing. Not her pretty white fingers, not her prettily painted fingernails. Then, to make things worse, with a start, she realised she wasn't actually standing on anything solid – no rocky ground, no fancy wooded flooring, no slick bathroom tiles. She just hung, immobile, as if from wires, as the thick blackness engulfed her and filled every sense, her sight and sound and taste and touch, filled everything with a nothing.

Shit, she realised, and even her internal voice had no sound, made no echo, had no real substance. *Maybe I'm dead. Maybe I'm dead and this is what it feels like, this is where you go? To this deep dark hole, down in the centre of the world where nothing can infiltrate your doom; your oblivion.*

She tried to work out who she was, but failed miserably. She could not remember her name, nor any single detail about herself. This distressed her, and made her wonder if she was, in fact, *insane* as opposed to dead. And if this was insanity, then this was far, far worse. Give her death every time.

At least in death, in theory, one found peace. But not here, like this. This was not peace. This was an ode to madness. A soliloquy for the sad and lost and depraved. A wild moaning wind symphony; a song of the mentally diseased.

And it came to her, one glimmer of information, and she realised she was not dead, and not insane, and she reached out with her invisible hand and *grasped* that glimmer of information like it was a sharp blade, and even though it tore her flesh, made her scream, made her bleed, she hung on to that data and drew it towards herself and into herself and knew she was real, knew she was *human*.

Molly.

Toffee.

Her children.

Her girls.

I am alive, and I am married, and I have wonderful baby girls, and like an oil cloud curtain being drawn back, colours flooded her world and reality and she flew, or drifted, over a vast dead forest of bone trees.

A cold wind moaned, and caressed her, and she shivered.

The sky was the colour of blood, shot through with indigo and dark grey. Black and amber storm clouds raged like swirling echoes of chaos in an eternal battle, hurling spears of lightning and roaring with thunder. Below, the forest was a vast, eternal thing, endless grey skeletal trees sprouting like cancer from a barren bleached earth. She floated, over the eternity of bone, and all she could think was:

My children.

Where are my children?

What happened to my life?

Who am I?

I am my children. My children have become me. I hope they are unhurt... because if they're not, I'm going to rend and tear and kill,

I'm going to cut off heads and find a gun and pump bullets into pale rancid flesh, watching steel rip out lungs and heart, smash bones through arms and legs, shatter skulls and piss brain pulp onto the rancid fetid lap of the gods...

Click. Like a light-switch. Click, click.

What is wrong with me? What is wrong with the world? I used to have friends, but they changed, they turned, they turned fucking strange, that's for sure. And how can you really understand that? Somebody else, when they go weird, turn... alien. Their minds twist and turn, become a labyrinth of misunderstanding. And what was once friendship is shattered, broken, and words are said and bitterness is rife and it's just broken, snapped, shattered beyond all repair...

Husband. I had a husband...

Dex. Dexter. Dexter Colls.

Kat drifted, and she drifted for a long time but felt neither hunger nor cold, neither thirst or the need to piss or shit or do *anything*. She wondered idly if she drifted an hour, a day, or millennia. It all felt the same. Filled her with an emptiness.

Then, a thought. An idea.

It seemed *wonderful* to her.

An absolute epiphany.

Children. Toffee. Molly. Husband. Dexter. Must find them... must find them all...

As if kick-starting a crashed motorcycle, Kat's engine came back to life. Blood started to pulse through veins, the world filled out with colour, and the bone forest below started to accelerate. Trees whizzed past, getting faster and faster and faster, like some great mad rollercoaster of bones and Kat looked down, and she *was* on a rollercoaster of bones. She was seated in a pelvis, clutching rails made from snapped and welded ribs. The wheels were moulded spinal discs which gave the rollercoaster carriage an eerie, rocking, shifting motion as it rattled over the track. Kat grasped the ribs tightly, as if her life depended on it, and strangely it did not feel strange, or creepy, in any way. She realised she was on some kind of track flowing over the forest of bone trees, and she half stood to glimpse the track... it was a length of bowel, grey and pulsing and urging the pelvic CAR onwards. Kat sat back down again. She didn't feel surprised.

As long as I get to where I want to be...

And where is that, my sweetness?

To Molly and Toffee, my beautiful children...

She slammed along, bone-rattle and bowel-squidges filling her senses. Still the skies battled above her, and this was so surreal it had to be (*had to be*) created by drugs. What else could do such a thing? Hmm?

She stood in a garden. Around her, huge towering flowers and plants drifted gently. The sky still raged, but silent now, as if seen through a great glass screen. Above, the bowel track veered off and disappeared, taking with it the rattling bone carriage which stretched out and out and out, like a conveyor belt of giant pelvic bones.

Kat breathed in the perfume. It was beautiful.

"Mommy!"

"Mum!"

They ran to her, hair flowing, and she gathered up her children and held them tight and now nothing mattered in the whole world, the whole universe, the whole of creation forever and ever, Amen. Because they were with her, and back to her, and safe, now, safe in her arms. And even if they were insane, they would all deal with it together. And even if they were dead, they would deal with it together.

Katrina pulled back slightly, tears gleaming wet against her cheeks, and she ruffled Molly's dark hair, straight razor-cut fringe above her serious features. Then she turned to Toffee, who glowed like flowers, like rainbows, and ruffled her hair as well, and Toffee beamed and was happy that she was with her mother again.

They huddled, for minutes, for hours, for days, for weeks, until finally they emerged from the loving family embrace to realise one horrible thing –

"Where's Daddy?" said Molly.

"Yeah, where's Dad?" said Toffee, her face falling.

"I'm sure he won't be far," said Kat, holding her girls tight.

"Where are we?" Molly stared around, at the eight-foot flowers and ferns and bushes. They were everywhere, a screen surrounding the trio, a seemingly impenetrable forest of colourful alien foliage.

"We're in a forest," said Toffee. "An alien forest!"

"Listen," said Kat, but both girls were staring around in wonder. She shook them a little, and their gazing eyes snapped to her face as if dragged by elastic. "Listen," more gentle now, "what's the last thing you remember?"

Both girls scrunched up their faces. Finally, Molly said, "I remember being in bed, asleep. And then... then we had breakfast. Toast and chocoladdo mocoladdo."

"And I had Weeny Wopsy Popsy Burgers!"

Kat frowned, but her own memories would not return. She remembered kissing Dexter, and then... and then rolling around under the covers of the bed, giggling, drinking wine, getting jiggy and down to the business. And then a tight embrace and a tumbling down into sleep.

"Shit," she said.

"Mum!" gasped Toffee.

"It's okay," said Molly, voice gravelly. "Mum and Dad say that all the time."

"But it's rude," said Toffee. "A *swear word...*"

"You may be wondering why you're here?" came a soothing female voice. The voice was everywhere at once, but not over loud. It was soothing, but not weak. It was powerful, but not overbearing. It was the voice of Control.

Kat stared around her. "Who are you? Show yourself?"

"I am a sentient section of the Monolith Mainframe. I help run Theme Planet. You may call me SARAH. I am here to help."

Kat stared around herself suspiciously, still cradling her children. "Okay, SARAH. What the hell are we doing here? Wherever here is?"

"Some very powerful enemies have stolen you away," said SARAH. "The Theme Planet is a place where reality and fantasy merge so very, very closely. You have become detached from the reality of your bodies, and your enemies have made sure your spirits are lost in a deviated version of one of Monolith's *Theme Planet Recreational FunFake Reality* systems."

Click, click.

"Oh," said Kat, frowning, head twisting. "Is that... *real?*"

"Of course it is, Mom," hissed Molly. "FunFake VR is one of the biggest-selling most popular attractions of Theme Planet! They sink you in these gelanium vessels, and insert needles into your brains, and away you go..."

Kat stared around her once more, unsure, disturbed by speaking to some vague and vacuous voice. "Can you show yourself, SARAH? I can't grow accustomed to some ghostly presence whispering in my ear. Just call me old fashioned, but it creeps me out."

There came a shimmer in the air, which parted, and there stood a tall, gaunt, beautiful woman. Her skin was a shimmering silver, and she wore a long, ankle-length silver dress which hugged her figure. Her hair was long and black, her eyes black portals into another dimension.

"This is the best I can do, here, amongst the enemy," said SARAH.

"Amongst the enemy?"

"Yes. As I said, they have deviated the program. I am here as a Safety Representative of Monolith Corporation. It is my job to guide you safely home. Back to your bodies, without violation."

"And you know where our bodies are?"

"We have people working on it," said SARAH, and the avatar smiled. Katrina didn't feel very convinced.

"So even if we escape here, we could be in very real physical danger?"

"Yes."

"Why not just kill us here?"

"I think there was an error. This place was not the intention of your captors. They were seeking information using hacked Monolith terminals. I fear they may have been of Earth origin, linked to Earth's Oblivion Government. However, whatever the case, this is the situation now, and I have been sent to help recover you."

"Great!" said Molly. "Our very own dangerous adventure!"

"Shush," scowled Kat. "What happens if we get hurt here?"

"You are hurt in reality," said SARAH.

"And killed here?"

"Again, killed in reality."

"Why can't you just whisk us away and wake us up?"

"It does not work like that," said SARAH. "The systems built on Theme Planet are massively complex organic-interactive digital integrators; they become a part of a rider's mind. Entwined. And you are lost in that mesh. I have found you, found all three of you, for your powerful interpersonal links have drawn you together – but by finding you, I have lost myself. We must work together to escape this... Hell."

"And if you die?" said Kat, somewhat harshly.

"I am reborn back in the Monolith Simulator."

"No worries for you, then," she snapped.

"Not so. The adverse publicity for Theme Planet if something untoward were to happen to you or your children would be incredibly negative. It could massively damage sales in the Quad-Gal arena. Theme Planet and Monolith Corporation pride themselves on non-injury, non-death holidays. After all, we're as safe as safe can be. We do not wish a financial downturn."

"Poor fucking Theme Planet!" snapped Kat. "Wouldn't like to lose you some dollars now, would we?"

"Please," said SARAH, face pleading, "I am here to help. I am your only hope."

"And what about my husband?" said Katrina, eyes cold. "Who gets to help him?"

"He is free of this cycle," said SARAH. "He was not caught in this mesh."

"What, so he's out there, free of this shit?"

"Yes," said SARAH. "I would suspect even now he is trying to find your physical entities..."

"Physical... you mean our *bodies?* Bloody hell, machine, he might think we're dead!"

"That is a possibility," said SARAH,

"Where *are* our bodies?"

"That has not yet been determined."

A warm breeze blew, and the ferns shifted. Kat's nostrils twitched. *But by God,* she thought, *it feels so real! I feel so... alive!* Distantly, there came a strange clicking noise. Hollow, metallic, rhythmical. *And SARAH reckons that if we die here, in this fucked up virtual world, then we die back in the real world. Because everything has been screwed up. Our kidnappers have fucked up! Just totally brilliant!*

"Come on, girls," said Kat.

"So you'll let me help you? Guide you?"

Kat turned, eyes burning, one hand on the shoulder of each girl. "Yes, SARAH. For now. Girls, *cover your ears. No arguing, just do it!* Listen, SARAH. If you lead me astray, if you try and fuck with me or my children, I swear to any cold hydrogen God willing to listen across the vastness of the Four Galaxies that I'm going to fuck you up, fuck the Theme Planet up, and fuck the Monolith Corporation up worst of all."

"Such aggression," said SARAH, portal eyes filled with infinity.

"Better believe it," snapped Katrina.

SARAH gave a simple nod, and gestured with a hand. A corridor opened within the forest of high ferns, and Kat led her children into the jungle. Behind them, SARAH followed.

THEY WALKED FOR a long time. The air was warm and humid. Above them, the silent storm raged with green and purple flashes of alien lightning. Molly and Toffee walked in silence, eyes lifting often to observe the amazing vision in the heavens.

"I don't understand," said Toffee after a while. "Which bit isn't real?"

"It's all *real*," said Molly, frowning down at her little sister. "But some of it is just in our heads, because our bodies are someplace else, in big glass tubes in a liquid. Isn't that right, Mom?"

"Yes."

"And they put big needles into our brains!" said Molly, poking her fingers into the top of her head and pulling a Big Scary Face at Toffee. "Whoooeeeooooo!"

"Stop it! Tell her, Mummy, tell her! That's not true, is it? They haven't put big scary needles in our brains. I wouldn't like that. I don't like needles. I remember going to see Dr. Dentist, and he was all mad with eyes and hair and stuff, and he put a big needle in my gum and it hurt! It really hurt!"

Kat threw a dark look at Molly. "No, dear, I don't think they've put big needles in our brains. I don't think they'd do that for a minute!" She gave Toffee a quick cuddle and made a harsh gesture to Molly whilst Toffee's head was bowed.

Again, distantly, there came a clicking sound.

"What is that?" said Toffee. "That clicking noise?"

Molly opened her mouth, caught her mother's glare, and closed it again.

"It's the insects," said SARAH, and Molly grinned. Molly wasn't happy unless doom and gloom were on the horizon, and even more so if the doom and gloom were there to frighten her little sister.

"Insects?" wavered Toffee.

"SARAH!" warned Kat.

"It is a very real threat," said SARAH. "You need to be warned."

THEY WALKED THROUGH tunnels of fire. Kat was apprehensive as they approached the roaring inferno, as any sane person would be. But children are not sane people, and Kat saw Molly and Toffee's eyes light up with rabid excitement, with glistening joy, with a *buzz,* baby, a *buzz.* Not for them the fear that Dexter might be dead, or on the run, or worrying his little mind sick due to his family's disappearance. Children's brains didn't work like that. *Oh, it's Dad, Dad's always there, Dad's big and strong and eternal; nothing bad can happen to him because he's our dad. And he's our dad because he's eternal. A rock. A constant. Like the spin of the planet, the burning of the sun, the expansion of the galaxy.* But Katrina knew that even gravity failed, even fires burned out, and explosions ran out of energy. And she remembered her own father, remembered his death and the knife, the fucking white-hot knife through her own heart at the realisation that he wasn't a god, wasn't immortal, and she was, in fact, alone in a big, wide, fucked-up, cruel universe that cared nothing for twelve-year-old little girls, cared nothing for tears, cared nothing for pity. Nature was a cunt, there were no two ways about it. And humanity was a virus, a fucking amoeba scraping along the bottom of the barrel, a bottom-feeder of the lowest order. Nature cared nothing for being fair. Nature did what it did.

"Wait." An instruction.

Molly ambled to a halt, followed a moment later by Toffee. They both turned with questions in their eyes. *But it's only a twenty-story-high circle of fire that leads into a vast, roaring, screaming inferno,* those eyes seemed to say. *What could possibly be the problem?*

"In there?"

"Yes," nodded SARAH, smiling in that odd way which wasn't really a smile; just a copy of an imitation.

"Is it safe?"

"Is any of this place safe?" said SARAH. "But... yes. In the manner that you mean. No, you will not be ignited by nuclear fire. It is a Sun Tunnel. An amplification. Not exactly like the real thing..."

"You go first," said Kat, her face hard, wishing she had a Techrim 11mm.

"As you wish," said SARAH.

The tall silver avatar stepped forward to the edge of the fiery tunnel. She looked up, hair streaming back a little from the heat and energy. Twenty stories above, glowing like the atmosphere of a star, the top of the circle, the tunnel, ended. SARAH stepped forward into the fire and was... engulfed.

Kat gasped, and ran forward, trailing Molly and Toffee. And as she neared the edge, she realised there was *no heat*. She stumbled to a stop, and saw SARAH smiling at her, and felt like a fool. An idiot. This creature, this being, was here to help them; they were lost; not just ghosts in the machine, but devils in the cogwork. And she'd been sent to bring them out alive – okay, for the reasons of preventing bad publicity for Theme Planet and Monolith, but fuck it, if that was what it took to stay alive then Katrina was willing to play bubby bunga ball with all four bats.

"You're sure, now?" said Katrina, eyes narrowed.

And Toffee jumped forward, squealing, giggling, and stood in the fiery tunnel alongside SARAH.

"Come on, Mum! Don't be such a pussy wuss!"

"A..." Her mouth dropped open, and she frowned, and, trailing Molly, she strode over to Toffee. "I've a good mind to smack your legs."

"You can't do that, Mom. The school will have you locked up. Remember what happened to Old Lady Jenkins?" She had a look of wisdom on her face that far outweighed her very modest years.

"Hmmm. Don't you dare do that again," said Kat, and pointed, using *that finger*. Toffee looked sheepishly at *that finger*. *That finger* had a whole lot of power, as if it were some ancient carved magick wand. Or something.

They started to walk.

All around them, the world burned like... the sun. It was like being in a sun tube. The ultimate in dodgy tanning experiences. And yet nothing but a gently warm breeze caressed their faces; no horrific burns nor immediate incinerations came their way.

"This is brilliant," said Toffee.

"It's too bright," complained Molly.

"Yeah, but it's pretty crazy, isn't it?"

"You think a five headed Funky Monk is crazy."

"Aww, don't say that, Mols."

"Well, you're just a little girl!"

"I'll tell Dad!"

They looked at each other. Their mouths closed. They puts hands in pockets and walked along beside Katrina, and all three walked in a line behind SARAH, the personification of the Monolith Mainframe.

They walked, and seemed to walk for hours. Eventually, Kat called a stop and SARAH halted, turning with patient eyes and a look of serenity on her simple pretty features. "Is everything well?"

"How long in this tunnel?"

"We are bypassing a hazard."

"That's fine. I just wondered how long?"

"I cannot give you a time frame, for we are side-stepping time in this environment. All I can tell you is that it will be soon – as you *feel* it. But we will be emerging into a Jackhammer Hall, and that's a very dangerous place."

"Mommy, what's a Jackhammer Hall?"

"Huh!" snorted Molly. "You mean you don't know what a Jackhammer Hall is?"

"No," said Toffee, meekly.

"Girls!" snapped Katrina. "Okay, SARAH. Explain it to me."

"Up on the surface of Theme Planet there is a huge ride called JACK THE HAMMERS. The hammers start at ground level, and pound a carriage up a pole for two kilometres, right up into the sky. Feels like a SlamJet Ejector Cube. But for the purposes of equilibrium and safety, as the capsules are punched skywards, counterweight pistons are pounded down below the ground. That's where we'll be. In the chamber where the pistons come smashing through the floor. A Jackhammer Hall."

"Are there a lot of these pistons?" asked Katrina, suspiciously.

"Thousands," said SARAH.

"Why, if we're not in a real reality?"

"This fake reality models the real one in many ways. But it has become deviated, as I explained. Twisted. Even the pistons may not be what they seem – so you must be on your guard when we enter the Jackhammer Hall."

They continued to walk through the fire tunnel, the sun tube, and as Katrina walked she thought about Dexter and what he would do. What *would* he do when discovering their disappearance? First, he'd look for them, of that she was sure. Then he'd go to the police – after all, *he* was police. What then? The police would start to do a sweep of the Theme Planet resorts, but obviously her and the girls had been taken somewhere, hidden away somewhere from prying eyes. Katrina squeezed her hands in frustration, as much at the consideration of Dexter's pain as at their own predicament.

Something touched her hand, and it was Toffee. Toffee's finger curled into her palm, and they walked for a while holding hands and Katrina was thankful for this basic act of warmth and kindness and humanity. It was such a simple thing, simple contact, and yet it meant so much. To be touched. To be trusted. To be loved.

"Mommy?"

"Yes, honey?"

"Daddy's okay, isn't he?"

"Oh yes, Daddy's just fine, poppet."

"It's just I had a dream. Last night. Or... whenever it was we were asleep."

"A dream?"

"Yes. About dinosaurs. Well, *kind-of* dinosaurs. Only they were *alien* dinosaurs."

"And what happened with the alien dinosaurs?"

"They ate Daddy."

Katrina stopped, and knelt on the corridor of fire. Hydrogen ignited below her knees at millions of degrees, in a bright white glow. She took Toffee by the shoulders and looked into her daughter's eyes. "Listen. Daddy's just fine. Daddy's not in trouble, it's *us* who are in trouble. Do you understand?"

"Yeah, Mom. I understand."

Toffee skipped ahead to Molly, and wearily, suddenly filled with exhaustion, Katrina stood up and put her hands in her pockets.

"Did you tell her?"

"Yeah!"

"What did she say?"

"She said Dad's fine. He is a policeman, after all."

"Yeah, she would say that."

"Well, I believe her."

Molly considered this. *"Yeah. So do I."*

Katrina smiled, and hurried through the solar fire to catch up with her daughters.

STEPPING OUT FROM the raging inferno of nuclear holocaust was like stepping into a cool gel bath. Suddenly, Katrina felt the cool breath of angels on her neck and face and arms. Confusion scattered lullabies through her brain. *What was it? What was happening?*

"We were a step out of time," said SARAH. "That's why we weren't incinerated."

Katrina stared at her. "So it was a trick?"

"No trick. You still live. But if you'd *really* stepped into the sun tunnel, really – in an actual physical sense – then you wouldn't have lasted a single picosecond. You would be gas, Katrina. In fact, less than atoms."

"Well, that's a great magic trick," said Kat, face grim.

Behind her, the time-displaced inferno raged on, lighting a huge steel chamber that was, to all intents and purposes, a five-thousand-square-kilometre cube. It was gloomy, lit in a sort of dull silver-grey, and a cool wind was blowing in, smelling of grease and burned oil.

"This is the Jackhammer Hall?" she asked.

"Yes," said SARAH.

"But... nothing's happening."

"It will. But it's random. Chaos personified. We must be careful."

They stepped away from the furnace and began to walk, SARAH leading the way once again. Katrina studied the back of the avatar, and realised it was a creation done to perfection – but then, so were the androids, right? And they were created by Man, not by Machine Mind, as she suspected was the case with SARAH.

Katrina's job, in the real world, when she wasn't being the cliché that was "full time mum" – the job she had actually studied for, the job she trained for, hell, the thing she was naturally *good at* – was advertising. Katrina could sell a tramp a Rolex. She could sell heroin to a pregnant mother, amyl nitrate to a redneck, a wheelchair to a goldfish and Satanic recordings to God. She had not just been the No. 1 Uber-Super-Duper-Best-Selling-Top-Motherfucker Sales Person/Persona at Fleck, Flick & Flack Quad-G Advertising Agency, she had become a (hush, lest one sell out) a *partner* in the firm. Or The Firm. She had generated so much damn income for the business that every male partner bust a bollock when she considered leaving to set up her own independent (and independently competitive) Agency. After all, Katrina was the woman who sold Coke on Mars. Shit, she sold Mars Bars on Mars, without any irony.

She was the sort of woman who got the job done. And with flair, creativity, underhand aggression and originality.

When she left to become a full-time mother, the partners at Fleck, Flick & Flack Quad-G Advertising Agency had bust *double-bollocks* and many had gone on to have an entertaining career with alcohol.

And so. Katrina was no stranger to the world of double-talk, pillow-talk, bollocks, bullshit and spin. She could smell a slogan from a billion parsecs, create a strapline on the toilet, and create a marketing campaign from the *contents* of the toilet.

She'd been dubbed the Mistress of Bullshit.

The *Queen* of Doubletalk.

And that was why Androids Inc. came to her for the marketing of their *new, improved, special model, Generation 6 Personalised Android Companions*. It had been Katrina's first inauguration into the world of Androids. Before then, she'd never really thought about them. They were illegal on Earth, and would be "slotted," "killed," "pulverised," "retired," "put to sleep" or simply "given a pension" (which had to be Katrina's favourite, especially after three quarters of a bottle of vodka when the lights were low and she was feeling particularly low and worthless after selling three million prams to women who already owned prams). What had her great mentor Greenbald III once said? *"Make the fuckers buy something they already have. The only way to true fortune."* And he'd been right. And Katrina had followed his logic and advice. And it made her feel like a cunt.

Still. Her time with Androids Inc. had been interesting and fruitful, and she'd learned a very great deal. She spent time in the factories on Mars, and further out in the mining colonies of Delta Proximata, Beta Galvanata and Trejo Machinata, where she'd discovered and observed and analaysed the full gamut of android inception, creation, construction, packaging, delivery, malfunction, and destruction. It had been quite a learning curve. And yet another curve that left her reaching for the vodka, feeling quite sick, and leaning on Dexter's very broad dumb-cop shoulders for support...

The androids had started off bad. Malfunctioning, genetically and in various code processes. Watching the Androids Inc. vidtapes and filmys, Kat saw androids sit up from the bench, or crawl out of the VATS, and then just bubble away. They had to be scooped up with shovels. They weren't put in body bags, they were shovelled into buckets. In silence, with the professionalism of an advertising partner on the sniff of a big deal, showing no judgement for crimes against humanity or morality or God whatsoever, Kat had watched the history of Androids Inc., watched its promo vids and filmys made for the eyes of the military, mining corps, harshworld explorer adventure companies and, of course, the governments. All these things had passed through Katrina's grasp, all this hidden *history* – hidden, at least, to the normal people of the Earth. Kat had been in a privileged position to watch the rise and rise of the android – around the same time AI became self-aware. But whereas AIs, despite superior intelligence and enhanced cognitive ability over their masters, recognised in humanity *something*, whether that be sheer weight of numbers, or ability to breed at a supersonic rate (on a galactic timescale, humanity was like so much warm bacteria in a jar of rotting meat) – whatever, AIs had made a universal decision to *cooperate*. Not so androids.

It was called the Inferiority Complex, and it ran thus:

An android was a created human. Humans were superior, in that they created the androids.

But androids were superior, in every other respect.

Humans looked down on androids as inferior, biologically, because they were created.

Androids looked down on humans as inferior, biologically, because they were so feeble in every way.

Androids had many of the same feelings and drives and desires. With one major, serious difference:

A distinct lack of empathy.

That's not to say it wasn't there, and in many cases was manufactured *in*, but an android just didn't love his brother android, or indeed, man, woman and child, in the same way a "normal" non-created human would.

Not that many humans were normal...

In the end, they didn't get the contract, not because of Katrina's skills as an advertising whore (which she was, she freely admitted), but because of a global outbreak of murders by androids, on Earth and its many colonies. It seemed the inhibitor chip placed behind the ear was an easily removable mod, and having the same arrogance and pride as their human creators, the first thing any self-respecting newborn android did was head for the cutlery draw and a bottle of whiskey (sterilisation *and* oblivion in one handy 70cls).

It had been an eye-opener for Katrina, subsequently swallowed by the joys of motherhood, the horrors of caring for young children, the black hole swallowing her career, Dexter being shot at work, and the fact that androids were soon illegal, decommissioned and "Non Reportable" under Oblivion Government legislation.

Now, as Katrina walked, for some reason the avatar before her *reminded* her so much of the androids. And she shivered. After all, the androids were *bad,* right? But illegal. Decommissioned. Expendable. Non-human. Waste. Walking garbage. Yeah, they might look like you and I, but that's just a façade right? They don't feel like humans feel. Don't empathise with their fellow Man... (*hey, but then, half of her fellow Men don't empathise with their fellow fucking Man, it's called hatred, and jealousy, petty criminology, base stupidity, greed and lust and every fucking scumbag is out for himself, right?*)...

Androids Inc. said the androids were perfect. They'd been wrong. Oh, so very, very wrong.

How was this avatar so different? An android created by a machine? An alien intelligence? It was still a false human. A created thing. An organic machine. A biological horrorshow. Or was it just code in a computer game? Was there really, actually (hush) *nothing there?*

Shit.

Katrina rubbed at her eyes, head spinning, head thumping, reality and dreamscape merging, nightmare and reality blending to become one and the same. *Where am I? What am I doing? What the hell is real? Am I really here, walking this grey steel terrain? Or is it just another figment of a dream or nightmare? Are my children here? Can I even feel pain...*

She pinched herself, hard. It hurt like a bitch-bite.

Suddenly, SARAH halted and held up a hand. Molly and Toffee giggled, as little girls are wont to do. Katrina pulled them close in a protective cocoon of bone and flesh – her own bone and flesh. A pathetic, weak cage, but it was all she had. And she would give everything to protect them. Kill anybody and fucking *everybody* to protect them.

Just like an android, she reflected. *Ha. Yeah, right.*

"What is it?"

"We are approaching."

"How can you tell?"

"The smell. It's getting stronger. Can you smell it?"

And Katrina could. Oil. Grease. Heat. Friction. Suddenly, before them, a piston the size of a skyscraper screamed from the roof, from the sky, from whatever the hell was up there in the gloom. It was circular, and grey, and thick, and it powered down with a groan like the dying of worlds. It ran out of momentum as it reached floor level, and there was a tiny *click* as the mammoth piston touched down, but if Katrina had been standing under it, she would have been squashed into a pancake of crushed bone and gristle on a platter of comedy blood. A cartoon death, only without the elasticity of regeneration that cartoon characters possessed.

"Wow!" said Toffee, in awe.

"Cool," grinned Molly.

"Not bloody cool when we have to walk across the steel desert with the possibility that these things might come down and crush us!" snapped Katrina. Then to SARAH, "Is there any other way?"

"I wish there was," said SARAH, face filled with apology.

"Yeah. Right." Katrina's eyes narrowed. "Then let's do it. You go first. And if I get squashed, you make damn sure you get my children out of here alive."

"I will endeavour to meet your wishes," said SARAH.

They moved fast, eyes turned up. At first, nothing was happening; it was as if the ride – above ground, up there on *Theme Planet* – as if it wasn't running. And that was just fine with Katrina. After all, it was only *fun*. Enjoyment. Second-hand pleasure. Fake fear.

A piston screamed down, some way to Kat's right. A distant pillar of steel sent by God to smash the unholy. She gave a sour, bitter smile. "Shit," she muttered, nervous now, and pushed on, into what was not exactly a run. Not exactly.

The girls were trailing behind, holding hands, moaning constantly. It was a truism that all children of the Theme Planet generation abhorred physical effort unless it meant working thumbs and hips on the latest game console.

"Come on," muttered Kat.

"But I'm tired," said Molly. "Can we have a rest yet?"

"We're in a very dangerous place, sweetie," said Kat through gritted teeth. "We can't exactly sit down and have a picnic."

"I don't see no danger," said Molly, staring hard at her mother. *God, you're going to be trouble when you're older,* Katrina thought, but kept from vocalising the prospect. The last thing she needed *here and now* was a mutiny.

They moved on, fast through the gloom. The stench of hot oil got stronger and stronger, and occasionally a distant THUMP echoed through failing light. Pistons rocketed from the heavens at progressively shorter intervals, easing from a sporadic, occasional THUMP to a sound like a stampede of dinosaurs, or maybe a sequence of pounding canon fire. Katrina found she was half-running, her head hunched down subconsciously – as if that would somehow protect against a million tonnes of pressurised steel cylinder.

"I wish daddy was here," said Toffee, panting, red in the face.

Katrina dragged her onwards. "So do I," she said.

And then... the storm began. Not a storm filled with clouds and rain, and ice, and thunder and lightning. This was a storm of oil clouds filled with hot groaning steel, with pistons slamming from the heavens and discharges of static leaping between columns of thundering steel like some crazy firework or special effects show.

Katrina felt the build-up of oil in the air. As she ran – yes, now she was running, SARAH a blur up ahead – she rubbed her thumb against her fingers. The air had felt greasy to begin with, but now there was a definite residue in the atmosphere, and it stung her eyes a little and settled on her tongue like acid fallout. Glancing at Molly, she saw the sheen of oil on the young girl's face, collecting thickly in her hair like some crude shampoo. Both girls were whimpering now, sensing the urgency, sensing the primal terror of their situation. Around them, more pistons thundered and clattered, their groans and screams filling the air with a cacophony not unlike Nature's work; but here, displayed in its full synthetic glory. The pistons hammered from the sky, faster and faster, falling all around in what appeared to be a completely random manner. SARAH, up ahead, offered no help, no solace, no encouragement. She was simply a constant, there to be followed through the haze of oily atmosphere.

Suddenly, a piston screamed above them and Katrina yanked the girls aside reflexively. She felt the *whoosh* as a metal wall slammed down just inches from her face, then it groaned a deafening groan like a dying leviathan, before slowly beginning its ratchet clank up towards infinity and beyond...

"Bastard," said Katrina, and tentatively reached out, touching the retracting piston. She yelped, leaving a circle of skin on the giant cylinder, and sucked at her oily finger.

"Was it hot?" asked Toffee, eyes wide in fear.

"Cold," said Katrina. "Terribly cold."

They carried on running, as more pistons slammed and groaned around them. SARAH had almost disappeared up ahead now; Katrina's eyes narrowed and she cursed the Monolith avatar. *Oh yeah? Sent here to help us, were you, motherfucker? Fat lot of good you are... we might as well run blindly through this hell-chamber on our own merit, because we're not following you and I don't believe you even know where you're going!*

More pistons slammed close, and each time Katrina yelped and jerked her girls towards her, as if she could protect them from these giant pistons, shield them with her fragile bone shell. Which of course, she couldn't. If they'd been struck, they would have ended up as human spam.

They ran.

Pistons fell, like the inside of some giant, deviant, alien engine...

Which it was.

The internal mechanics of Theme Planet.

The poisonous underbelly of the fun.

"When will it ever end?" wailed Toffee at one point, and Katrina could not answer. She knew not when it would end, just as she knew not when it had begun. Time had ceased, reality evaporating into the oil mist. She only knew it was endless, and she was tired enough to fall, tired enough to give up her life because she could not go on, and the girls could not go on, and they should surrender, and lay down, and die...

KATRINA OPENED HER eyes with a jump. A fire burned in a rocky hollow. Molly and Toffee were both snoring, covered with thin blankets. SARAH sat across the fire, cross-legged, watching her.

Katrina sat up slowly, groaning. "What happened?"

"You passed out. I came back for you, carried you the rest of the way. You nearly made the perimeter."

Katrina glanced back, but rocky walls filled her vision. She looked around again, and revelled in a cool breeze that caressed her face. "We are safe here?"

"You are safe," said SARAH.

"Thank you. Thank you for rescuing me. Thank you for saving my children."

click...

SARAH stood, crossed to Katrina, placed a finger against her lips. "Shh. Sleep now. You are exhausted. We will talk... in the morning."

"We're not out yet?"

"No. We have a long way to go," said SARAH, smiling.

FLAMES CRACKLED, CONSUMING wood, except in this place there were no flames and there was no wood. SARAH closed her eyes and said the command, and opened them on a different plane, a different place, a different reality.

"What do you think?" he said.

"I do not know," she said.

"They can mask it cleverly; they have become very advanced."

"*Evolved* is what I call it," said SARAH.

"What do you think of her?"

"She is strong, she has great courage. She lasted longer than most in that place; and we pushed her harder than most people could take without snapping. Up here." She tapped her skull, and her dark eyes, the dark portals, narrowed. "And that's what worries me. That's what poses yet more questions."

"And Dexter?"

SARAH smiled then. "Yes. Dexter. Let's see if Dexter survives. Then we will talk."

CHAPTER NINE

IF YOU HAVEN'T BEEN SICK...

THE SECOND OILY green cat had slunk into the clearing, circling its comrade, both of them hissing. And... "We're danjos," said a soft voice right by Dex's ear. So close they could kiss. Dex could smell its oiled body, had become aware of the creature's *mass*, its strength and power and killing prowess. The other two danjos watched him. Dex could sense, almost as if he were in a strange computer game, their positions, and their feral hatred. Here were creatures bred for *entertainment*, baby, locked up in enclosures with gawping tourists gawping and clicking piccy pics. For a creature of intelligence, of *majesty*, it was an insult to their very existence. And when an animal, recreated alien dinosaur, *whatever*, felt insulted to their very core – well, in Dex's experience, they tended to lash out. With claws. And fangs. And all things horrible.

Very, very slowly, as slow as an ice age, Dex turned to look into the danjo's face. It grinned at him, and a sliver of sympathy ran through him, invaded every atom, and he gave a shudder. There was such intelligence there. Such... understanding. And he knew the cold, quiet, calm gun in his hand was a million miles away... if it wanted to, this ancient, malevolent alien creature could rip his face off.

"What do you want, Mr Colls?" said the danjo.

Dex gawped, spittle drooling down his chin. He licked his lips. *Had it really spoken? Or was he descending into a drug-crazed, hypertense, psychopathic fucking incident? Where were the pills? He needed more than a full bottle...*

"Er," he said, words little more than an exhalation.

"Tell me what you want."

"Are you telepathic?" he whispered.

"I can sense your need," said the ancient alien predator.

"And what do I need?"

"To find yourself."

"No. *No.* I need to find my wife, and my children..."

"That will come later," whispered the reptile, and its breath and fangs were so close to Dex he could *taste* it. Its body was close to him, and he saw its claws – huge, *huge* claws – flexing softly on the jungle vegetation.

"I don't understand."

"We rarely do."

"Stay where you are," came a voice, a human voice, carried both through the air and, seemingly, to Dex's *brain* by some kind of direct communication. "They're slippery motherfuckers; if you move, you may lose your head."

"Wait..." began Dex.

There came a PHUZZ and Dex felt a blast of superheated air. Beside him, the danjo's head exploded in a shower of spaghetti meat, and blood slapped across Dex's face, across his jacket, soaked him to the skin. The mass of muscle beside him leant against him for a moment, as if deflating, then slid slowly sideways and twitched as its bowels released in a steaming mess. The other two danjos screamed, a high-pitched ululation, and sprinted to their fallen... *friend?*

"No!" screamed Dex, but the laser slashed across the jungle, dazzlingly bright and dazzlingly deadly. The other two danjos were cut in half even as they nuzzled at their fallen companion, and Dex watched weakly, disjointedly, as they slid apart in cross-sections of muscle and bone and internal organs. The three creatures lay dismembered on the jungle floor, slowly steaming.

Five provax, wearing khaki, stepped from the trees carrying military laser weapons. They walked slowly, in a line, heads turning left and right in synchronisation with their weapons as they scanned the jungle, looking for more lethal predators. One carried a blip scanner, which blipped once a second.

Dex, face grim, mouth dry, slowly climbed to his feet. He released a pent-up breath. *What happened then?* asked his twisted mind as it fell upon itself like a collapsing star. *I don't understand.*

The five provax stopped, staring at Dex, and he wondered if he'd have to fight his way out again. He didn't know if he still had it in him. He didn't know if he had the energy, the hatred, or the drive. And then he pictured Katrina, and Molly, and Toffee, and realised he'd happily kill every single motherfucker on the planet to get to them.

"How do you feel, sir?" asked one warden.

Dex blinked. "Shaken," he managed.

"It must have been quite an ordeal," said another, stepping forward and patting Dex on the arm. "You can be assured, this sort of thing doesn't happen on the Theme Planet. You *will* be fully compensated for your experience."

"Compensated?" Confusion.

"Monetarily speaking," said another. "Come, let us escort you to a car. They'll take you back to your hotel and you can have a quick discussion with our underwriters. I am sure there will be a considerable payout for you to, ahh, retain your silence."

Dex coughed. "Yes. Yes. It's a disgrace, actually. I can't believe this horrific thing happened to me! I need a strong whiskey."

"Of course, sir. We will see to it."

Dex was helped down various paths, past more jungle wardens, or alien dinosaur wardens, or *whatever the fuck they were* until they reached normality, reached safety, reached houses and estates and flashing lights and people and hotels. Dex felt something small crumble inside him. Some small part of his soul, given over to despair, *longed* for a return to the normal world. But he couldn't give in to it. His family were still gone. Missing. *Taken.* And he would not fucking stand for it.

"Here you go, sir."

A blanket was wrapped around his shoulders, and people were talking beyond barricades, and he was taken to a long low black car. He was given a flask of hot sweet tea. Then the men and women – the provax? – moved away, talking amongst themselves. Dex saw extensive paperwork being filled in. *Damn those fucking bureaucrats,* he thought.

He was seated, sideways from the passenger side of the car. He simply pulled his legs in, removed the blanket, closed the door, climbed over to the driver's seat, touch-fired the car, and drove away through the night.

Nobody seemed to notice.

Praise those pen-pushing, form-filling, anal fucking bureaucrats, he mused.

The roads were black, twisted snakes before his weary eyes.

They gleamed like streamers.

After the third time he nearly left the road and ploughed into the ocean, he *voluntarily* left the road onto a dirt trail and bumped along for a while, lights cutting slices from the black. Then, finding a quiet grove beneath a stand of black trees, he killed the engine, locked the doors, and fell into a sleep of exhaustion.

IT WAS ANOTHER fine sunny day on Theme Planet. After awakening, Dex had yawned, and a backdoor headache pummelled his brain into corrosive jelly. Now, he cruised on a newly stolen hover bike down a wide street which sat, pretty much deserted, baking in the tropical heat. It hadn't been hard to dump the groundcar and find a replacement; in this place, nothing was locked down. Not like London. In London, he would have needed a nuclear chainsaw!

Dex slowed the bike past a series of restaurants, *Monster's Burger Mush,* the quite bizarre (in terms of food offered) *Alien*

Buffet – which Dex had previously found quite amusing, in that to him it sounded as if they were serving *up* alien flesh as opposed to alien cuisine itself; and the infamous Quad-Gal dining experience known as *WYSIWYG* – *Basic Food for Basic People!* Quite a lot of Old Earth people ate there. Egg and chips. Sausage and chips. Egg, sausage and chips. Egg, beans, sausage, eggy egg and chips. Sometimes served in a massive aluminium "Feeding Trough." Like a huge gents' urinal, but from which you ate, instead of into which you piss. This was the kind of fodder which, Dex had to admit, was a category he fell to quite regularly, achieving mockery from not just Katrina, but his poison-tongued little brood. "Come on, Dad, be adventurous!" Molly would cry; a comment to which he did not deign reply.

Now, diners sat at diamond windows, plugged into music or gamesets as they ate, their groundcars and hover bikes parked up in the baking sun. Dex cruised past, not too fast, not too slow, so as not to draw attention to himself.

Adventure Central. Which, he knew, led to the Caves of Hades and a secret tunnel under the sea, emerging on the Lost Island – the goal of every adventurous Theme Planet holiday adventurer! Only for Dex it wasn't an adventure. For Dex, it was the survival of his wife and kids...

The road widened, leading to Quick Blast bays along the stretch on the left, where gamers and ride-junkies could get quick fixes of ride adrenaline on quick little coasters, punchers and flingers. To the right, the turquoise sea glittered with silver streamers and exploding sparkles.

Paradise, thought Dex.

He slowed as he approached the edge of the Kool Kid Zone island, his gaze scanning the huge arching Zip Tube, which bridged between this pleasure fun ride island and the next, Adventure Central. Distantly, Dex could just make out the land mass through a haze of sunshine. The Zip Tube was huge and imposing, and Dex parked his bike, watching for a while to see how things worked.

And this was how they worked.

A person or vehicle, be it bike, car or even a long Squeezy-Bendy Coach (with a carrying capacity of five hundred travellers) would approach the inlet valve of the Zip Tube, and then be literally *sucked in and chucked through* the bridge tube, emerging – presumably – unscathed at the other end.

Dex didn't like it. But then, Dex was old, and grumpy, and damn bloody *old fashioned*. If he was honest with himself, he didn't trust technology, didn't even *like* technology, much to the amusement of his young children. He fired up the bike again and eased it forward, bobbing gently down the road. He was overtaken by two groundcars and realised he was arousing suspicion with his over-cautious approach. He accelerated, hover bike growling gently, and watched as the groundcar in front hit a slight ramp, drove into what was, to all intents and purposes, a giant *funnel,* and POP. Gone. Shit.

Dex accelerated, cruised towards the funnel, face twisted in abject old-man horror, and-

RAMP. POP. SUCK.

ARGH!

Dex blinked rapidly and sucked in fresh air. He'd felt the *massive* acceleration of the Zip Tube, and emerged five kilometres away from another, near-identical funnel – apparently all in one piece. He cruised to a gentle halt by the side of the road, on a new island now, in a new *Theme Planet Adventure Zone*. He patted himself all over, as if worried he might have left an arm or leg behind.

"Hey, mister," said a little girl, who he hadn't noticed before. She was wearing a swim costume and had long black hair, not unlike Molly's. She wore a red flower in her hair and was beaming up at Dex.

"Er, hello?"

"Don't worry. I did that the first time as well."

Dex grinned at her. "Pretty weird, huh?"

"Yeah. Pretty weird, mister."

"Do you know the way to the Caves of Hades, little girl?"

"Sure." She pointed, then rummaged in a little white handbag. She pulled out a map. "Here. This'll show you the way."

"Thanks. Don't you need it?"

"Nah. I've been here nine weeks now. I know my way around."

The girl ambled off, and bought an ice cream at a bobbing robotic ice cream stand. Dex studied the map, and looked up just as a police groundcar cruised past. Dex watched it out of the corner of his eye, continuing to stare at his map, and he saw the groundcar gradually roll to a halt. Then it turned around, its green lights started to flicker, and Dex groaned deep inside.

"Not again."

"YOU THERE ON THE HOVER BIKE. DO NOT MOVE. WE HAVE QUESTIONS FOR YOU!"

Dex rammed open the throttle, the hover bike screamed, and he shot off down the road like a bullet from a gun. The groundcar growled and howled after him, whooshing past the little girl with the ice cream, who stood, mouth open, raspberry syrup on her chin, eyes wide in astonishment.

Head down, Dex opened the throttle to full. The hover bike whined, nose lifting, and he zigzagged between slower vehicles in the road in a manoeuvre that would have got him a slap from his wife, and an instant ban in London.

In the distance, the vast Skycloud Mountains loomed, glittering darkly.

"Bastards," muttered Dex, and watched the police car accelerate in his mirrors. They kept up with him no problem. Their vehicle didn't lack power, and as they all flew towards the Forest of Iron, the loudhailer barked at him:

"PULL OVER IF YOU VALUE YOUR SAFETY AND THE SAFETY OF OTHERS."

"Get fucked," muttered Dex.

"YOU ARE DRIVING IN A VERY DANGEROUS AND ILLOGICAL MANNER. THIS IS VERY DANGEROUS. YOU ARE CAUSING A DANGER. YOU ARE IN BREACH OF THEME PLANET LAW AND MUST SUFFER OUR JUSTICE. PULL IN AND YOU WILL NOT BE HARMED. I MUST REPEAT, YOU ARE BEING VERY DANGEROUS."

This actually cheered Dex. He thought he'd been spotted by Monolith or some other bloody secret police service operating on Theme Planet; he hadn't. This was just some dumb-ass SIM, he knew their sort, they'd been banned from Earth decades earlier. What was it the pedantic sons-of-bitches always used to say? He wracked his brains, even as he veered left, taking a wider and less congested road. He skimmed around more tourist traffic, shaving millimetres of alloy from one rear bumper with his footpeg. Horns, squeaky, high-pitched and non-threatening, squeaked after him.

That was it. "There's no comedy in police work, son." That had become the mantra of the terminally-pedantic Justice SIMs. They were renowned across the Quad-Gal for having the worst sense of humour of any species; human, alien or prov. And, meeting one now, Dex realised, nobody was fucking kidding!

"PULL OVER. YOU MUST PULL OVER. WE DEMAND YOU PULL OVER. I DEMAND YOU PULL OVER! PULL OVER THIS INSTANT. YOU ARE BEING VERY IRRESPONSIBLE BY NOT PULLING OVER. IF YOU DO NOT PULL OVER YOU MAY CAUSE SOME DANGER. WE CANNOT ALLOW YOU TO CAUSE DANGER. THERE'S NO COMEDY IN POLICE WORK, SON. IF YOU DO NOT PULL OVER, I WILL BE FORCED TO BREAK OUT THE MINIGUNS."

Dex paled. *Shit.*

Right, he thought. Time to see what this hover bike can do...

He pulled back on the yoke, and the hover bike sailed up into the air. Below, the twisted iron trees from the Forest of Iron spread out like a vast carpet, a vast game map, and in one quick glimpse Dex saw the layout of the forest, with its adventure trails and forest wolves to avoid – a *must* for all Theme Planet thrill seekers!

Dex checked his mirrors. The groundcar had, miraculously, unfolded its wings and, with a supersonic *whump,* leapt up into the air in pursuit. *But it's called a fucking "groundcar,"* he wanted to scream. *How can you call it a groundcar when it flies in the fucking sky?*

Looking back, Dex nearly collided with a World Tree, a vast towering edifice that was a living, breathing, organic *ride* in itself. It reared from the forest canopy below, vast and towering and carrying carriages and CARs along its very branches. Riders screamed and giggled and drooled, legs kicking, arms waving, and Dex saw carriages topple away down vast branches as wide as a ten-lane freeway. Punters screamed. Tourists waggled. *Great fun,* thought Dex, and swung his hover bike down under a mammoth branch, then up through leaves which slapped at his face like enraged lovers. Up, under, over branches Dex wove, the hover bike whining. The SIM police car was in close pursuit. He could see green flashing lights in his mirrors.

Dex burst free from the World Tree's foliage, only to see ten more World Trees up ahead – part of the great Theme Planet experience within the Forest of Iron. "Great," he muttered, and he went to veer right – he had to travel right, according to the map, out past the Lagoon of Serenity, back over The Lost Dunes and to the Caves of Hades... only then could he find the secret tunnel.

Bullets howled and Dex ducked instinctively, veering the bike left, away from his goal. Another burst of minigun fire chewed through the World Tree ahead of him, showing Dex that the mad bastard SIM was far from playing fucking games.

Dex slammed left, right, and lifted the bike over a succession of huge boughs as thick as train carriages. More bullets howled after him, and a ride CAR containing screaming, giggling tourists was thrown from its rails and went toppling towards the ground, blood spewing from minigun-punctured, ragdoll bodies. Dex saw the CAR fall, his face turning grim. Not only was the police SIM gunning for him with a serious agenda, he was showing his true colours and not caring for *any* human life. And as a PUF officer, this rankled deep with Dex. How could one be a policeman and wantonly destroy life? It didn't fit. It didn't work. It just wasn't fucking *right*...

"Okay, you bastard."

Dex yanked the bike left and right once more, dodging vast branches, then suddenly dropped towards ground level and snapped through the Iron Forest canopy. "I'll show you how this game is played."

He checked his mirrors. Now there wasn't just one SIM flying a police car after him. There were... Dex counted. Five. FIVE! How did that happen? How the fuck did that situation arise? But he knew with a deep sinking feeling in his soul how it had arisen; the SIMs were anally retentive to the Nth degree. Unable to stop Dex, this bastard had called in his mates.

As Dex's hover bike zipped down to ground level, and whizzed through the forest as if in some crazy video game or movie, the cars spread out and *five* miniguns opened fire. Trees screamed and groaned, and trunks from trees a thousand years old came crashing to the ground.

Bullets whizzed and spun past Dex like hail, and he suddenly slammed the hover bike into reverse, dipping the yoke to clear the lead groundcar, then opened the throttle again, came up fast behind the SIM's car, got the front of his bike under its rear bumper and twitched it up. The groundcar lifted slightly, then ploughed its nose into the ground as Dex pulled left, cutting between two more cars. The crashing car cut a huge groove through the forest floor and hit a tree with a *wham*, a spattering of debris, and a sudden, howling, rushing inferno.

The two cars alongside Dex then opened fire behind him, miniguns spewing spinning steel; Bullets slapped along panels, and the two cars cut each other in half, dropping bits of steel and alloy and punctured SIM limbs to the forest floor. They hit the ground in pieces, fucked up and out of the game.

Dex banked right, and the two final cars jigged in line to open fire at him. Shit. SHIT! Bullets screamed and impacts ran along the back of the hover bike, punching through the alloy. Black smoke poured from the arse of the bike, and Dex felt the machine shudder under his fists. *Oh, no. No! Don't do this to me, baby. Don't die on me now!* Suddenly, it picked up power, and a grin spread like jam over Dex's face. But then the engine cut, the fail-safes blipped into place, and the hover bike glided down slowly through the trees, still billowing black smoke, and came to rest with dignity on the forest floor.

Oh, you prick-teasing bitch. Oh, I just can't believe you let me down! I can't believe you've left me at the mercy of the SIMs...

Dex hopped from the bike, turned, reached for his Makarov.

"DON'T EVEN THINK ABOUT IT, MOTHERFUCKER. BELIEVE ME, I HAVE NO HUMOUR ABOUT THIS SITUATION!"

The two groundcars were floating ten metres away, minigun barrels smoking, their engines purring like clockwork. The guns were focused on Dex and Dex alone. He could feel their evil eyes, tiny black holes staring into Hell and death. Dex's mouth was dry, because he knew SIMs, and he knew them well – and Dex had been responsible for the death of their kind. There was no going back now. No talking his way out of this situation. SIMs were evil motherfuckers by anybody's stretch of the imagination, and they *could* slaughter him, and *would* slaughter him. Probably after torture. Lots of torture.

Dex raised his hands above his head. "Don't shoot!" he yelled, hoping to any god that would listen that he could get them out, on the ground. At least he'd have a chance with his Makarov. As long as they were behind a set of miniguns, he was so much meat pâté. "We need to talk about this!"

He could almost *feel* them splutter down their microphones. He could *sense* their exasperation, their indignation, their feelings of *listen-to-this-cheeky-motherfucker* made into a physical thing.

"YOU HAVE A CHEEK, LITTLE MAN! YOU HAVE CAUSED THE DEATHS OF OUR SIM COMPANIONS! FOR THIS YOU ARE GOING TO BE DESTROYED IN A MOST UNPLEASANT WAY."

"I'm a policeman," said Dex, clutching at straws, grasping slivers of time like a drowning man clutching greased rope. "I'm part of the PUF in London, Earth. I know how you feel! It was all an accident... a set-up! I'm being hunted, and I thought you were the bad guys!"

There was silence for a while. He could almost hear the muffled, heated exchange between the SIMs. *Jesus,* he thought, *imagine giving a position of responsibility to these gun-toting, trigger-happy, crazy-eyed bastards! Is that what Theme Planet really thinks of its tourists? Legs shot off in the back of the van? Eyes put out with an ice-axe? Still-beating heart ripped from jagged chest-cavity by over-zealous justice nutcases on an ironic mission for justice? Yeah, that was the SIMs. Crazy bastards, distilled.*

"DO NOT MOVE. WE ARE COMING OUT TO DISCUSS THIS SITUATION."

Great. A chance at... freedom? Certainly not justice. He'd have to be fast, and hit hard. He could feel the Makarov in his pocket, a solid weight, a weight that equated to escape. It was his only chance. Dex ground his teeth in frustration. Every damn step he took, bureaucracy seemed to interject in his fate; it was as if he was cursed by policymakers. Mocked by procedure. Haunted by the very police he had once sworn to serve.

This is not a good situation, he thought.

This is not a good week.

The SIMs stepped from their vehicles, which bobbed slightly as the heavy mass of SIM and associated battle armour was removed from suspended suspension. There were four of them, two in each groundcar. Their armour was black and dulled silver, and their mechanical eyes gave tiny *clicks* and *buzzes* as they focused on Dexter. All four SIMs carried SMKK machine guns, and they were pretty savage weapons even in gentle hands. In the strangler grip of nutcase nutjob killers like your average psychotic SIM, an SMKK was something truly to be feared. Not so much a tool of justice as a guaranteed one-way trip to a deep hole in the ground.

The SIMs strode forward and arranged themselves in a line. Mechanical eyes watched Dexter with care, SMKKs presented with safety catches off. He didn't like it one bit.

"YOU HAVE LED US A MERRY DANCE, LITTLE MAN. YOU ARE IN THE SHIT, YOU KNOW THAT? YOU HAVE BROKEN LAW AND FUCKED WITH GOV!"

"Listen guys, listen, it's all been a terrible mistake!" said Dexter – and an arrow appeared in the lead SIM's face. It stuck there, feathers quivering, as mechanical eyes swivelled down to examine the yew shaft embedded just beneath.

"I AM NOT HAPPY WITH THIS SITUATION!" said the SIM, reaching up and grabbing the arrow in his gloved fist. There was a *crack* as he snapped it off, and Dex, whose mouth was hanging open, glanced over his shoulder and saw the shit hitting the fan.

Dex hit the ground and covered his head as a hundred shafts hissed from the dense undergrowth of the forest, peppering the SIMs until they resembled porcupines. The SMKKs rose and whined, rattling bullets into the undergrowth and cutting branches from trees, leaves from branches, *churning* up the greenery into damp wood shavings.

Dex drew his Makarov and started pumping bullets at the SIMs, aware that whoever was firing the arrows was on *his side*.

"Keep your head covered!" bellowed a voice in an accent somewhere between Australian, Irish and Afro-Caribbean. Dex obeyed as a rain of slow, heavy arrows whined from the trees.

The first one hit a SIM, who looked down in sudden recognition. "SHIT!" said the Justice model, who promptly exploded. Limbs and chunks of flesh flew off in all directions, as exploding arrows embedded in the three remaining SIMs and they, too, exploded with deep, grinding WHUMPS. The greenery was soon turned red, decorated as it was with skin, muscle and entrails.

Dex climbed warily to his knees, looking around. Something had stuck to his jacket, and with great distaste he plucked free a mechanical eye. It squelched, and with a grimace Dex dropped it to the forest floor.

"You're a long way from home, sonny boy!" said a cheery voice, as a group of bandits strode out of the trees. They were dressed in Lincoln green, and carried longbows of hardy yew. Their eyes shone with merriment and good humour, and much to Dex's amazement, the leader arrived and gave his thigh a hearty slap.

Dex looked around at the twelve men. Yes, there was an overweight monk. There was a short, dangerous looking man with a scowl and angry eyes. There, hovering in the background, was a pretty maid.

Dex groaned. "You're shitting me, right?"

"Shitting you we are not! Welcome to our forest! We are the Merry Men, and my name, good sir, is Robin!"

"Robin? Merry Men? Is this a *theme* section of the Theme Park?"

"Yes, good sir!" beamed Robin, who wore a dainty little pointed green hat. It had a feather in it.

Dex felt an urgent need to scream and giggle well up within him, and he forced it down savagely, like drunken kebab vomit. "You're robots?"

"AIs," corrected Robin. He gave a wink, and hit his thigh again, with a hearty *slap*.

"And your purpose is?"

"To patrol this fine woodland and protect the tourists! We may also rob from the SIMs and give to the needy. That goes without saying."

"Rob? From the..." Dex shook his head. "I don't recall the history filmys showing Robin with exploding arrows?"

"One feels one must move with the times," said Robin, with a slick, neat smile. But damn, you had to admire that programming. "Come hither, brave adventurer! Back, through the forest, and away from this SIM debris before more of those nasty fellows decide to invade our privacy."

"Er," said Dex. "Actually, I'm on an important mission to find my wife and children. I'll just get back on my hover bike and leave you guys to it. Okay?"

Robin drew back his bowstring, until the feathers of the arrow touched his cheek. Dex found himself looking down the very sharp steel point of an arrow. He gave a wide grin, and spread his hands out wide...

"Hey!"

"I fear you must come with us, good chap," said Robin, voice warbling a little. "I do insist. Will, be so good as to remove the intruder's weapon. And Friar?"

"Yes, Robin?"

"Go and put the soup on, there's a hardy fellow."

*   *   *

DEX MARCHED THROUGH the dense woodland, eyes narrowed, hands tied behind his back with *twine*. Fucking *twine*, he thought. The ignominy. He followed with, *fucking idiots*. Why does this shit choose *now*, of all times, to happen to me? Had these crazy AIs gone gung-ho crazy and kidnapped him for a purpose? Had they maybe flipped their programming, melted solder into their cooling slots, and basically deleted their inhibition codes? Shit. *Shit*.

Dex stumbled on, his progress hindered by the thin rope biting into his wrists. It was so damn humiliating. After all the high tech battles he'd been through, to be taken down by a man with a bow and arrow, and – he confirmed it – yes. Green tights. He'd been taken out of the game by a fucking cross-dresser in nylons.

"Wonderful," he groaned.

Soon, noises came to his ears. The familiar sounds of cars on tracks, the rumbling of rollercoaster rides, the chatter of excited voices, screams of exhilaration as cars plummeted down the vertical drops. Dex frowned. What the hell was going on? Where were these *freaks* taking him?

"Don't worry," beamed Robin, as he strode ahead, slapping his thigh occasionally, "all will be revealed, adventurer!"

They burst from the dense undergrowth to reveal – a Robin Hood themed section!

Dex groaned. "For fuck's sake," he muttered.

There were all manner of rides and attractions: rollercoasters built through, around, and vertically down *into* the giant trees; a replica of a castle under siege with huge siege engines thundering and throwing missiles at shattered battlements; a village fair, with barrels of water and peasants milling around, chasing chickens and braiding young girls' hair. There were jesters, and horses, and mud, and dung. There were more rides, further through the theme section clearing, just for the kiddies – giant leaves on tracks, fairies and dryads and all manner of forest folk.

Dex looked over at Robin.

"I'm not really a prisoner, am I?"

"Of course not, ha, ha, ha!" boomed Robin. "Release him! He has enjoyed our themed adventure, I think? No? See the twinkle in his eye? He enjoyed that, I think! Am I right or am I right?"

"Can I have my Makarov back?"

"Of course!" beamed Robin, and gave Dex the weapon whilst slapping his thigh. "Would you like to come to Nottingham Castle and meet the Sheriff? We're really rather good friends, you know. Except when we are jousting! Hurrah!"

"You're mad," said Dex, lips compressed tight.

"No, no! We're Robin Hood and his Merry Mentals! Hurrah!"

"What was all that with the SIMs?"

"Hmm?"

"The killing. The slaughter."

"The SIMs know not to come on our turf. These are *our* tourists. This is *our* themed section. There is no trespassing between sections. Or else we are forced to put the SIMs out of action."

Dex scratched his head. "So I can go?"

"Of course! Go on, into the ride central. Enjoy the leaves and acorns, the dung and peasants! Hurrah! I can personally recommend the High Tree Vertical Drop. There are naked nymphs inside that ride!" He gave a hearty wink, and Dex was sure, if he'd allowed it, Robin would have slapped *his* thigh.

"Okay. Okay. I'm going."

Dex had it in mind to skip the village, head back into the woods and try and rediscover his hover bike. The only problem with *that* was that more SIMs might have caught up with the situation and found the bodies, and he'd be walking straight into the heart of another damn fire-fight. Last thing he needed.

Dex walked through the peasant village and glanced back, to see Robin and Friar Tuck waving at him. He was sure he could see the gleam of machine madness in their eyes. It was certainly a situation he'd never forget... as indeed was the whole holiday on Theme Planet. Monolith Corporation had made damn sure of that!

A huge rollercoaster reared over him as he walked, weaving in and out amongst the trunks and thick branches of mammoth hardwoods. Some of the trunks were green, yellow and red, and Dex idly wondered how they had managed to alter the colour of bark; but then, maybe these were *alien* trees, or imported from far away exotic lands where the natural colouring of such flora was different from the usual boring old Earth shades?

An explosion detonated behind Dex, and he stopped and turned. Everyone else in the village stopped also, and chatter ceased – which meant this was not a usual occurrence, or part of the local theme. Smoke rolled up through leaves, and there came the unmistakable rattle of SMKK fire.

"Shit," muttered Dex, and hurried on, between the trees supporting the vast rollercoaster. Another detonation, up ahead this time, closer than the last. Amazingly, despite an obvious fire-fight kicking off in the forest, the rides continued to run – and even more amazing, *punters* continued to scream and giggle. Eyes were turned, yes, and Dex realised with a start that they thought it was just the beginning of some kind of show! Another cabaret! There was no fear. No panic. The bloody tourists thought it was all a game!

Dex started to run, but more explosions rioted through the jungle. More SMKK fire rattled, and several errant arrow shafts hummed through the clearing. One struck a woman in the shoulder, punching her back off her feet. Somebody screamed, panic swept through the village, and people started to run...

SIMs appeared, and Dex groaned. From the corner of his eye he saw Robin Hood and his Merry Mentalists, and arrows hissed and snapped across the village in expert volleys. SMKKs roared, and Dex ducked, veering left under a row of support struts. He ran, behind a group of women and children. Up ahead, more SIMs appeared.

"DO NOT PANIC! DO NOT RUN! YOU WILL BE SHOT IF YOU RUN!"

SMKKs roared, and three of the women up ahead were punched from their feet in a bloodbath of spinning steel. Children screamed. Grimly, Dex drew his Makarov and began firing. Bullets chewed into two SIM faces, and they were knocked back, spewing blood and brains from gaping holes. The third caught a bullet in the neck, and Dex leapt forward, slapping his boot on the SMKK arm and gazing down at the wounded Justice SIM.

"What the fuck are you doing, motherfucker?" he snarled.

"THIS AREA IS UNDER CLAMPDOWN. THE AIS HAVE REBELLED. WE ARE TAKING THE FOREST OF IRON BACK UNDER CONTROL FROM MONOLITH."

"You're shooting women and children, you dumb bastards!"

"THE AREA IS UNDER CLAMPDOWN. I REPEAT, THE AREA IS UNDER..." Dex put a bullet in the SIM's face, smashing his mechanical eyes. He pocketed his Makarov and picked up the SMKK, stashing five magazines from the SIM's belt. SIMs were notoriously a bastard to drop. The more firepower he had, the better...

Dex glanced around, breathing deep. Smoke plumed from twenty or thirty explosion sites now. Everywhere, people seemed to be running, all in different directions – which suggested to Dex that the SIMs had surrounded them. More guns roared, and more tourists went down in bloody mists of torn and tattered limbs.

Dex ducked sideways, and caught sight of at least ten SIMs advancing on him. "The day just gets better and better." Behind him was a hollowed-out tree, a doorway, and Dex ran inside, to find a spiral stairway leading up. Guns roared, and bullets chewed at the the door frame beside Dex's head. He sprinted up the steep stairs, bullets chasing his heels and throwing up splinters of wood. Upwards he ran, realising with sinking dread that this had to be either a tree-top restaurant or the entrance to a fucking rollercoaster. *Just what I need. A fucking rollercoaster ride in the middle of a firefight!*

Outside, screams tore through the village. There was another series of explosions, and from a window Dex glimpsed Robin Hood striding towards a cluster of SIMs, firing arrows in a smooth, steady stream... guns rounded on the AI, and he went down in a flurry of tangled limbs, torn flesh, stitched nylon and Lincoln green.

"So much for his rebellion," muttered Dex, and paused on the stairwell at a particularly tight corner. He cocked the SMKK, leaned slightly around the corner, and waited. There came the stomp of heavy boots, and Dex tried to work out how many SIMs were chasing him – he couldn't be sure. There was more than one, at least. And that was too many.

A SIM appeared, mechanical eyes gleaming in the sunlight, and stopped abruptly on seeing Dex, so that the SIM behind him cannoned into him. Dex shrugged, and opened the SMKK hard and full. Bullets screamed, deafening in the confines of the stairwell, and the lead SIM's face disintegrated, hands coming up in supplication far, far too late. Dex kept the trigger pulled, and as the first SIM tumbled back the second got it in the face, then the third, fourth and fifth. Dex released the trigger. Smoke filled the stairwell. The pile of SIM bodies caused a blockage, and that could only be a good thing. Blood trickled down the stairs, and turning, Dex ran on up, face grim, mood worse than bad, good humour all gone and pissed away in a nuclear storm. "Those bastards," he said, and arrived on a high platform. A cool breeze caught him by surprise, and he gasped, and looked out across the Forest of Iron. Trees rippled, to the edge of his vision.

Unfortunately, this was no tree-top restaurant with bridges and lifts to other restaurants – like Dex had seen in the brochures. Oh, no. How could Dex ever be that lucky? This was a one-way stairwell to the beginning of a vast rollercoaster ride. It spread out before him, twisting and turning and vast, a single thick metal rail zipping and winding between high tree trunks and branches like a singular strand of thick green spaghetti. He looked to his right: there were ride CARs, but they had stopped. The whole thing seemed to have powered down – which meant no way out. Dex was trapped...

"Son of a bitch," he muttered, as he ran to the guard rails and climbed over. His boots hit the thick metal rollercoaster track with a solid thud. Glancing up, ahead, he paled a little at the wide open expanse, with vast drops to either side. He glanced below him, to see the SIMs gathering like insects around sugar. More guns rattled, and tourists were mown down like skittles. Dex heard boots on the stairwell; obviously more SIMs pursuing. He had to move, and had to move fast...

He ran, thudding along the rollercoaster track.

"THE HUMAN MUST STAND STILL!"

"Yeah, right, fuckers." He fired off a volley from the SMKK, then ducked under a thick bough, grabbing it to steady himself. The world was a tapestry beneath him. For a second, the whole image wobbled and Dexter felt very, very sick – as if the track and everything connected to it was going to uproot, and spin up above him. His hands clasped the bough tight as vertigo swamped him, and his eyes closed, and his insides churned. *Not now, oh, God, not now!*

Bullets whined past Dex, chipping the rail and sending sparks flashing around him. He grunted, let go of the tree and sprinted on, boots crashing down, SMKK gripped tight, head flashing with thoughts of murder and death. The world spun beneath him, and Dex gritted his teeth, his body cleaving through warm air. Tree branches whipped him like a mistress, only most mistresses wouldn't want you *dead*; well, not generally.

Up ahead, he saw a stalled CAR. Inside sat four tourists, strapped in tight, looking around in confusion; stupidity surrounded them like toxic perfume. One, a tall thin man with a hooked nose, was feebly whining for help. Dex sprinted to the CAR, grabbed it, climbed over the roof and landed at the front. The riders were gawping at him, eyes drawn unconsciously to the SMKK.

"This whole place is under attack!" Dex shouted. "You've got to get out, find an emergency ladder down to the ground. You understand?"

"Hey, you've no right to shout at us like that!" stormed a red-faced woman in an obscenely tight bikini, which bulged like a sack of wriggling eels. She was flowing out all over the place. It made Dex shudder.

Dex gave a brief, tight smile. "Yes, ma'am." He turned and carried on running, as more shouts followed him.

The track wound between trees, and hit a sudden vertical drop, which climbed into a loop. Dex stopped dead, mouth agape.

"Aww, bollocks," he muttered. He looped the SMKK's strap over his head, turned and hooked his fingers into the thick central chain, and edged himself over the drop. It was heavy with grease, and the climb tortured his fingers, but with no other option Dex started to creep downwards. He picked up the pace as bullets whined around him once again, and there were shouts, more bullets, then screams. Dex didn't dare look; he was too focused on his descent.

He heard the fat woman whining and complaining. It soon ended.

After what seemed an eternity, and with fingers aching, he dropped the last few feet to the beginning of the loop. He swayed giddily, holding out his hands for balance, and then turned and looked up at the vast loop – spying an access hatch. *Of course!* There'd have to be some emergency procedure in case a CAR got stuck near the top of the loop. Dex ran to it, and heaved on the heavy door between the tracks. Inside, Dex saw a ladder to the top of the loop, and a tunnel shortcutting it altogether. He ducked into the door as a fresh hail of bullets fell about him, then turned, peered around the hatch and waited – watching five SIMs begin the descent of the vertical drop.

"Let me give you something to think about," Dex muttered, flicking the SMKK to single shots. He lined up the SIMs and started, casually, cracking off rounds. Sparks fluttered and the SIMs looked around. Two attempted return fire but nearly lost their grips on the track chain, slick with grease. Dex fired off more rounds, and managed to hit two of the SIMs, who grunted, but did not fall. Dex flicked the SMKK to automatic, and began spraying the SIMs. It took a couple of minutes, but he hit them all, watched them plummet from the vertical drop, bounce from the rollercoaster track, and soar off into the vast forest below. More SIMs appeared at the top, and opened fire. Dex ducked back into the tunnel and ran for it.

He carried on running, back out into the open. The rollercoaster track wound around more trees, twisting and turning.

Then, up ahead, he heard a deep bass roaring. Dex frowned. *That sounds like... water? A waterfall? A* BIG *waterfall?*

As Dex emerged from the trees, his mouth dropped. A canyon divided the forest, a huge expanse of emptiness; the rollercoaster track cruised out over the abyss, high above the trees, sunlight dazzling from wheel-polished steel, with – apparently – nothing holding it steady, or even *in place.* A broad river snaked through the thick woods, dizzyingly far below him. Ahead of him could be seen a vague outline, where the track seemed to reconnect with the land, into a wide, sparkling waterfall cascading off the far side of the canyon. Streamers of water spun off, silver and glittering, into the abyss.

"Holy shit," said Dex, eyes swivelling down as if on stalks. That was a long way to fall. *A long way.* All the way down into oblivion. But where else could he go? What else could he do?

He started to jog, slowly, across the expanse. Sunlight burned his face, dazzling him. He readied the SMKK, because – well, if those SIMs caught up with him, he'd have nowhere to go, nowhere to hide. He hurried his pace, boots pounding the rollercoaster track, mind racing faster than his boots. This high up there was a cross-breeze, rocking Dex with occasional gusts. He picked up his pace yet further, trying to ignore the vast drop, the roar of the waterfall, the dazzle of the sun and the impending threat of those SIM bastards...

A chopping noise droned in the distance, and from nowhere – at incredible speed –a sleek, black helicopter tore into view. Dex stopped, suddenly, panic kicking through him. The chopper rolled around and levelled, rotors screaming and threatening to blast Dex from the track. Dex couldn't see the pilot within the tinted cockpit, but the intention was clear as he stared at the twin miniguns. Dex was caught out in the open with his pants down.

"THROW DOWN THE MACHINE GUN, DICKHEAD."

Dex dropped the SMKK to the track with a clatter. Despair ran through him, and he glanced at the long, long fall to the winding river. It was too far. Way too far. He'd snap his spine if he dove off. He'd be crushed on impact, water or no...

"PUT YOUR HANDS ABOVE YOUR HEAD," came the instruction.

Dex complied, glancing back and seeing the pursuing SIMs arriving. Now he was fucked. More fucked than fucked. Now, he was taking a bite from a ripe shit sandwich, and the worse thing was, there'd be no dessert. Because he'd be dead. And his wife and children would be dead. Now, there was no future, and no hope...

The SIMs had stopped at the edge of the rollercoaster bridge. They didn't raise their weapons or come after him. Dex frowned, and glanced back to the chopper. The noise was terrific, smashing through his head like a bad whiskey hangover. Dex's mouth was dry, filled with fear and loathing. Fear for his kids. Loathing for himself. He'd fucked up. Thought he could take on the Big Boys and play in their Big Pond. Well, he'd been wrong. He'd shot himself in the foot, fucked himself up the arse. And now, as the saying went, it was Time to Die...

The chopper veered right to hover over the track, blocking Dex from the beckoning waterfall and, no-doubt, some form of escape tunnel beyond. An alloy ladder was kicked from the chopper and a figure climbed out, descending awkwardly to drop onto the bridge. It was a man. He wore a cream suit. One leg was torn and bloodstained, and his knee was strapped up nice and tight.

It was Jim. Jim turned to stare at Dex, his eyes bleak.

The chopper backed off, perhaps a hundred metres, leaving the two men alone on the high bridge.

A cool breeze blew, ruffling Dex's short brown hair. "Fucking wonderful," he muttered, and lowered his hands, turning to face the Theme Planet policeman – or whatever the hell he was. Monolith Corporation? Earth government? Who even *knew* anymore?

"Dexter Colls. You've been causing a riot."

"How's the knee?"

"Hey, fuck you, pal. You're in a shit-storm and you don't even know when to keep your flapping mouth shut! I ought to shoot you right here and now. I should gun you down, and kick your body into the fucking river."

"Why don't you, then?" Dex's voice was cool, but his eyes were filled with a controlled rage.

"Somebody wants to see you. Wants a little chat."

"Who?"

"Your guardian angel. A man named Romero."

"Never heard of him."

"He's heard of you, boy."

Dex considered this. "Fuck him. He'll have to come get me himself."

Jim grinned, and slowly removed his jacket, dropping it to the track. "You know what, Dexter? I was hoping you'd say something like that." He rolled his shoulders, and cracked his knuckles, and only then did Dex *notice* Jim's athletic breadth of shoulder. He was a pugilist, that much was clear. He had some *experience*.

"Be careful what you bite off," said Dex, glancing again at the SIMs. They were motionless. So – the wolfhounds had been called off. The idiots had been trying to kill him, and only now, finally, had their insane hunt been stopped by people with authority. So – now it was just him and Jim?

"Whatever I bite, I chew," said Jim, stopping a few feet from Dex. "One last chance. Are you coming without a fight? Or do I have to break a few bones to persuade you?"

Dex grinned. "I'd rather fuck your mother."

Jim's smile vanished and he attacked, launching three right straights, a left cross, and a side-kick that caught Dex by surprise. It hit him in the sternum, lifting him a little and slamming him back onto his arse. Dex touched a hand to his chest, and looked up, eyes flashing with anger. He got to his feet, lifted his fists, and advanced on Jim...

They exchanged punches, and Dex blocked Jim's straights. Jim stepped in close with a hook, which Dex took on his arm, and slammed his forehead into Jim's nose, which gave with a *crack*, spurting blood. Jim stumbled back, eyes blazing with fresh hate, and snorted out blood and snot.

"Gotta sting, that," said Dex. "Better get back on your chopper and *fuck off* before I do some real damage."

Jim charged, throwing a fast flurry of punches. Several hit Dex in the face, and his anger flared, and he drove blows into Jim's head and cheek. They danced for a few moments, both hitting and blocking, flirting on a high wire. Then Dex started to tire. It had been a long and stressful few days, and coupled with the recent excitement with the SIMs, the chase in the forest and village, and his pursuit on the rollercoaster track – Dex was bone weary. Ready to drop.

Jim caught him with a right hook, and another, and another. Dex was forced down on one knee, panting, blood drooling from his lips. He looked up – into a kick, which slammed him flat on the rollercoaster track.

"You had enough, big boy?"

Dex glanced up. "That's exactly what your mom said."

"Fuck you, Colls. You won't be so smug when you see your wife and kids. Maybe even now they've been destroyed, like the others."

"The others?"

Jim's eyes shone. "You think you're so fucking smart, Mr Earth policeman. You have no idea what's going on here, no clue as to the bigger picture." He glanced over at the chopper, and waved it in. With rotors chopping and whining, it shifted sideways; there was a *clang* as the alloy ladder met with the high bridge.

"I know you have your brain in your scrotum, if that's what you mean."

Jim pulled free a Makarov, and knelt suddenly by Dex, and placed the gun to his head. "I ought to kill you here and now, smartarse. Fill your dumb fucking skull with steel. It's the least you deserve."

"Go on!" screamed Dex, suddenly. "Fucking do it! You're a fucking coward, and you've taken away everything I love! Kill me, slot me, but please, do it now before your bad fucking cancer-breath poisons me with its spewed vomit-stench! Go on, you coward, you sliver of cunt! Shoot me!"

CHAPTER TEN

MONOLITH

LADY GOO GOO leapt, huge chomping mouth of razor teeth agape and slamming for Amba's head, and she knew, *knew* what it reminded her of: a striking cobra intent on eating her head and body, swallowing her whole... Her arm snapped up, pointing the shotgun, but not at Lady Goo Goo. No. She pointed it at Jonno, the simpering helpful android. Both barrels barked, and the blasts decimated Jonno's head, punching him from his feet in a tangled mess. Lady Goo Goo dropped from the air as if shot, and curled into a foetal ball, crooning, fingers twitching, a puppet with its strings cut...

Amba strode over to Jonno. His shattered head was a mess. One eye had gone, one cheekbone had disintegrated, and she could see his teeth through an open, flapping skin window. His skull, also, had partially vanished, taking a goodly sized section of brain with it. Maybe a third of his entire head had been blasted clear by twin shotgun blasts.

Amba stood, and stared.

Jonno started to chuckle, gurgling as blood collected in his throat and pooled in the hollows of his blasted skull.

"Clever girl," he said.

"What the fuck are you?"

"The puppet master," he said.

"No. *What* are you?"

Jonno simply stared at her with bright eyes, and licked at torn, shredded lips with his spaghetti tongue.

"You killed your Lady Goo Goo," he said, finally. And Amba felt like a fool, for it had been Jonno all along. The whimpering creature back there was a construct, a weird type of android construct, and here was Lady Goo Goo before Amba. Oh the irony. The comedy. Amba had instructed Lady Goo Goo to take her – him? – to its own self. And the puppet was too tough to be beaten; even by an Anarchy Model.

Amba crouched, then, and placed a hand on Goo Goo's. The android, or alien, or whatever the hell it was, it was shaking, vibrating like a thousand volts of juice were ripping through its nervous system.

"Tell me," she said, voice barely above a whisper. "What's going on here? What game is being played?"

Goo Goo's eyes met Amba's.

"No game," it said.

And the creature died.

Amba stood, and glanced around. The jungle construct was limp and lifeless, as if with this creature's death *all* life had been sucked out of the place. She spied her FRIEND, strode forward and took the weapon.

You let them take me, sulked Zi.

Shut up. We have bigger problems.

The SIMs?

Yes. And Napper, after that. You know what these Secret Police types are like...

Leave them to me.

Amba moved quickly to the doors, and slid out into the gloom of the FireIce Mountain High-Security Military Facility.

* * *

DEX SAW THE insane light in Jim's eyes. The slap of the wind from the rotors was rhythmic, hypnotic, as the world fell into treacle slow-motion and Dex licked his lips, watched Jim's mind *crack* like a rotten egg as the anger and hatred washed over him. He saw the finger tighten on the trigger. Dex had pushed Jim beyond the event horizon, and there was no going back; for whatever reasons, Jim hated Dex, hated him with a venom like some scumbag shit bag alien – and despite his orders, despite his training, he was going to kill Dex on that high rollercoaster bridge and simply face the consequences...

Dex powered a blow into Jim's wounded knee, his smashed knee-cap, his bullet-ravaged joint, and Jim screamed and twitched as he pulled the trigger. The bullet skimmed Dex's cheek, grazing the skin, so close the cordite trail stung his eyes. Dex slammed another punch into Jim's knee, took the Makarov from the twitching man's hand, stood, and kicked Jim from the high bridge. Jim flailed, and fell from the track, his arms and legs flapping all the way down to the bottom.

Dex ran for the chopper, and the pilot took precious seconds to realise just what the hell had happened. The SIMs were quicker to react. The SMKKs howled behind him, bullets smacking into the track as Dex sprinted... The chopper suddenly banked, but Dex leapt and grasped the ladder. He sailed out over the vast spread of forest and rocks and river, his lungs in his mouth, his balls in his brain, and he clambered up the alloy with gritted teeth and dark glittering eyes, leapt into the cockpit and lifted the Makarov. The pilot turned, lifting his hands. "No! Please, no!"

Dex put a bullet between his eyes, jumped forward and took the controls, swung the chopper around, armed the miniguns, and ploughed towards the SIMs who were standing, faces neutral, wondering what to shoot at next. With a blast and scream, the miniguns cut the SIMs in half where they stood, sending them toppling out into infinity.

Dex hovered for a few moments, rotors *whumping*, and – face grim – manoeuvred the pilot from his seat and out the loading doors. He pulled them closed with a grunt and jumped back into the pilot's seat, took the chopper around in an arc and slammed down, under the high rollercoaster bridge and towards the river and the rocks far below. He pulled the chopper up on a bed of hot exhaust fumes, and hovered for a while, searching. It took him maybe five minutes to spot Jim's bent and broken body. Satisfied, he lifted the chopper high into the sky, spiralling up past the rollercoaster bridge and the bodies of massacred SIMs, and up into the clouds where he paused, calling up a map of the Theme Planet on the HUD.

Dex powered the chopper away from the Forest of Iron, following the map. Below, the whole of *Adventure Central* spread out, muggy through wisps of straggled cloud. As he cruised, there to the left Dex saw Pterodactyl Castle, with its high towers and walls made from reconstituted dinosaur bone and skin. The gates were dinosaur fangs, the roofing tiles made from the armoured spine-plates of a fukyusaurus. Up ahead, *piercing* the clouds with their sheer height and mass, were the Skycloud Mountains – the place all true adventurers went to climb, power-glide, abseil, base-jump and snowboard. It was a place for the ultimate adrenaline junkie. *A place to voluntarily chuck yourself down the mountain and beg for broken bones. What a mug's game! What a bad joke. Performed by skinny, bum-fluff-faced idiots who craved some kind of natural high, when you could get a perfectly respectable high from a good bottle of whiskey and ten pints of Wifebeater. Bah, humbug. Damn moaning granddads, and all that.*

Dex banked the chopper, engines pounding, rotors pulsing above. Far below in the sunshine glittered the Lagoon of Serenity, and Dex realised the river he'd seen earlier, from his vantage point on the high rollercoaster track, did indeed feed this lagoon. On the far side of the water, the Death Rapids stretched away, all white and foaming and dangerous looking, even from this height. *Another group of idiots, begging to chuck themselves against the wrath and psychopathic nature of Nature, to fuck with the God of the River and wonder why they came out the other end either pulverised like dog meat, or in a body-bag filled with aqua. What a bunch of morons!* Dex had had just about all the adventure he could take. He'd overdosed on adrenaline. He'd pumped himself full of excitement until he wanted to puke. *What's wrong with sitting in front of the telly? What's wrong with cups of hot chocolate? What's wrong with languorous mornings under the duvet, playing hunt the pickle with your giggling wife?* But no. Dex had been forced into a situation where he was force-fed "adventure" and "fun" and "danger" and "thrills," all the specialities of the Theme Planet – and all he wanted to do was find Katrina and the kids, and head home for a quiet life.

The chopper left the Lagoon of Serenity and the Death Rapids far behind, and quickly – because this was the terraformed magic of the Theme Planet! – the landscape shifted from forest and rivers to a sudden desert, which seemed to emerge from nowhere. These were the Lost Dunes, leading to the Caves of Hades. Sand stretched out for an eternity. Huge, towering dunes seemed to fight one another, climbing and crawling over one another to reach the sea... and Dex slammed along, cruising low, rotors kicking up a huge desert storm in his wake.

"I just want to go home," he said, out loud, words startling him.

And in frustration, and pain, and exhaustion, Dex realised he wanted to cry.

THE CHOPPER CLICKED to itself as its engines attempted to cool under the blaze of the desert sun. Dex jumped down, boots sinking a little in the sand, shaded his eyes and stared at the Caves of Hades ahead. There was what could only be described as a *slab* of rock, perhaps five kilometres wide, and a kilometre high, that ran (as Dex had discovered from the brochures) all the way to the sea.

The Caves of Hades.

Shit, thought Dex. *There's so many of them!*

He knew the Caves led to a secret tunnel, another wonderful exploration adventure for the terminally enthusiastic "holiday adventurer." And the tunnel led across to The Lost Island – on which, Jim had claimed, were imprisoned his wife and children. But now – now he had to submerge himself in a mad cave complex searching for the hidden tunnel. *Great.*

Dex made a low growling sound, and checked his stolen Makarov. Looking back inside the chopper, he found the armaments cache and raided it. He strapped on a bullet-proof vest, and took an SMKK and stash of magazines, and as many mini grenades as would clip to his belt and fit in his pockets.

He climbed back out and stood in the sand, feeling a little ridiculous. There was a sign a few feet away. It read:

WELCOME TO THE CAVES OF HADES!

HO HO HO!

HAVE FUN IN THIS VERY SPECIAL

THEME PLANET EXTRAVAGANZA!

AND REMEMBER... BE CAREFUL, BRAVE ADVENTURER!

THERE'S SOMETHING WITH TEETH IN HERE...

"For the love of God," muttered Dex, making sure his grenades were strapped on tight. All he needed now was to bump into another family on vacation, and watch them run screaming as he, the *Mighty Dexter*, strode forward less like a Colossus than some tarted-up Holiday Action Man.

I've had better weeks, he thought.

And I've certainly had better holidays!

He strode through the sand, and stepped up onto a rocky plinth that led to a wide walkway, which in turn led to the hundred or so openings which fed into the Caves of Hades. Dex walked forward, the sun beating against his back, and as he approached a cave picked at random, a cool breeze, like sour breath, eased out to meet him.

A plaque read:

HERE BE MONSTERS

Dex frowned, and cocked the SMKK. Stepping forward into the gloom and the damp, he said, "Oh yeah? Bring it on, then."

*   *   *

ON HIGH, JAGGED cliffs overlooking the ocean there was a vast black castle. Its walls were polished granite, smooth and difficult to climb, and high above, circled constantly by cawing green-and-grey gulls, there were soaring towers, crennelations along huge battlements, slits for archers yards wide and gulleys through which to pour boiling oil on attacking armies. The castle was bigger than big, as if Theme Planet had seen pictures of old castles on old Earth, and thought *fuck that, we can do bigger and better than that!* and had done. It was truly a vast and imposing structure, and would have been near-impossible for any attacking army to breach... unless they climbed up the advertisements. These were positioned at regular intervals, and would have given any attacking soldiers with grappling irons firm purchase on their way up to breaching the battlements, killing the soldiers and savaging any handy nuns. The ads were for items not *exactly* in keeping with the style of the vast black castle, such as TURKEY'S COMEDY GOBBLING CONDOMS! GO ON, BE A TURKEY – GOBBLE GOBBLE!, and SONJA'S FABULOUS CHICKEN BEARD PARTY BEARDS! GET YOURSELF A CHICKEN BEARD TODAY, THEY'RE GOBBLE-GOBBLE-CHICKENTASTIC! and FARTER'S BEANS! FUCK YOUR DIGESTION UP GOOD AND PROPER, GO ON, BE A FARTER: BUY FARTER'S BEANS – AVAILABLE IN DIFFERENT SIZES OF BARREL, and SCORCHER'S FIREWORKS! GUARANTEED TO BLOW YOUR WHOLE DAMN HEAD OFF! and BUY TIFF AND KEN'S NEW ALBUM, "DANCE THE FUNKY CHICKEN," AVAILABLE ON HOLO, PROJ-K, GGG AND FIREDISK... LET TIFF AND KEN TRANSPORT YOU TO A WORLD OF CROONS, KOOKS, GOOGS AND NOT-RIGHTS..... GO ON, BUY TIFF AND KEN, THEY'RE FUNKY SPUNKY, AND YOU KNOW YOU WANT TO!

At the summit of the castle, in big, chintzy, tacky, glowing neon letters that seemed just a touch out of character with a historically accurate, if somewhat overlarge, medieval military fortification, were the words:

MONOLITH RIDE MUSEUM

"It's a reward," said a wiry, weathered old man, who wore a floppy hat and carried a back-pack. Amba glanced at him, sitting on a rock and staring with beady eyes towards the castle. He drank out of a canteen and reached forward, rubbing at what, presumably, were sore, battered feet. Scruffy hiking boots sat to the man's right. She imagined she saw steam rising from his tattered, threadbare socks.

"A reward?" said Amba. "For what?"

The man frowned. "For *discovering* The Lost Island! For all those hardy, brilliant adventurers who have travelled The Lost Dunes, negotiated the monsters in the wacky, dangerous Caves of Hades, walked the long echoing avenues of The Secret Tunnel, and finally emerged here, battered and bruised, but happy and filled with adventure! This is the reward! The carrot, leading the donkey! This is why we're here." He seemed a tad smug.

"Of course," said Amba, turning back to stare at the neon monstrosity on the cliffs. "It's... a very special looking place."

"Authentic," said the tourist.

"Genuine," agreed Amba.

"It is quaint," said the tourist.

"Picturesque," agreed Amba.

"Well," said the tourist, pulling on his boots. "Time to go and explore," he grinned, and standing, lifted two walking sticks from where they rested against a rock.

"Why do you need those?" asked Amba.

"It takes the pressure off my knees on long-haul treks."

"I suppose you're quite the expert walker and climber, aren't you?" said Amba, smiling brightly.

"I certainly am, little lady."

"Doesn't it get lonely, all this exploring and walking, on your own?"

"Sometimes," agreed the tourist. "But it gives me a good bit of time to think, to ponder over the complexities of the universe, to muse over the conundrums of our very existence – being such tiny and insignificant human beings."

"I never thought about it like that," said Amba, her smile fixed in place.

They were silent for a while, while the man laced up his boots. He stood, stretched, shouldered his pack, grasped his walking sticks in readiness. "I say," he said, "Maybe you'd like to accompany me up to the Monolith Ride Museum? Many have claimed it holds the wonder of Theme Planet's ride technology, and a working model of the computer that controls it all – the SA34000RAH. Well, the first incarnation, that is. Model v1.0. I think it grew into something a lot more sophisticated since way back in the hey-day of Theme Planet's inception."

"Accompany you to see the original SA34000RAH, you say?" mused Amba. Then she gave a nod. "Yes, I'd love to accompany you. It's been a long and lonely journey to get here," she said. "What's your name?"

The old man grinned. "You can call me Bob," he said, and held out his hand.

"Amba."

"A pretty name. But then, you're a pretty young thing. Not like some of these monstrous over-fed pigs of tourists, eh girl?"

"I try to stay in shape," smiled Amba, and they set off on the long trek across rocky ground, following narrow trails on a steep uphill towards the Monolith Ride Museum.

A DRONE HOVERED by the entrance. It was a small cube, an early derivation of the PopBot machines which had recently been flooding the Quad-Gal with their rudimentary AI and, some would say, acerbic wit and nasty sense of humour. This drone had a face made up of lights, which flickered into different "expressions" on the face of the black cube. It was making a buzzing sound as Amba and Bob approached, Bob's walking sticks clacking on the rocky ground like an extra set of feet.

"Yeah?" said the drone, face flickering into an array of white lights which, Amba assumed, was a snarl.

"Hello there, good sir!" beamed Bob, ever the optimist. "We've come a long way from Theme Planet Adventure Central, all the way through the Caves of Hades and the Secret Tunnel, emerging here to discover this, our wonderful reward!"

"Bog off," said the drone.

"What?"

"I see lots of your sort," warbled the machine, its voice high-pitched and tinny. "Bloody sun-tanned wrinkled adventurers, think 'cos you've done a bit of trekkin', you've conquered the world or something!"

"Er..." said Bob, unsure of how to take this.

Amba stepped forward, glancing up at the huge portcullis. Inside, she could see long smooth halls of marble, suits of armour, fast-food burger stands. "What's your name, squib?" she said.

"I am known as Drone," said the drone, quite haughtily.

"Do you always address visitors with insults?"

"I do what the fuck I like," said the drone.

Amba shrugged. "You are very rude."

"Well, you'll just have to wake up in the morning and think, 'Gosh, he was very rude,' won't you, love?"

Amba moved in close and dropped her voice. "Or I could take Bob's walking stick and beat you around this castle entrance hall," she said.

"A-ha-ha-ha," said Drone, woodenly.

"A-ha-ha-ha," grinned Amba, reaching back to take one of Bob's sticks. It was quite a hefty lump of wood, and she weighed it thoughtfully. "It's got quite a swing to it, this stick." She squinted at Drone. "And I see your casing is of cheap TaiwaJapapean construction. Like a radio alarm clock. Like a ggg carry case. Like a *burger carton*. Should crack pretty well, I would think. Might even spill your digital guts out onto this fine marble."

"No need to get violent," said Drone. "I was only trying to help."

"By insulting us?"

"That's just my little way," a smile lit up on his cube face.

"So we can come in?" said Amba.

"Oh, yes. I was never going to stop you. I just find it personally satisfying to insult visitors who come here thinking they've conquered the fucking world. Or something. It's all part of the service."

Amba turned to Bob, and shook her head as if to say, *cheap fucking TaiwaJapapean AI circuitry,* but Bob was standing, face deadly serious, pointing a gun at her face. Amba breathed out slowly, and allowed her body to relax. She picked out the tiny sounds of the drone's movements behind her, tracking him, as she analysed the muscles of Bob's face, and the look in his eyes.

"You're good," said Bob. "But you didn't fool us."

"Good?"

"You're an android. Androids are prohibited on Theme Planet."

"I don't know what you're talking about."

"Nice try," whined the drone, "but I have android-spotting technology built into my *cheap fucking TaiwaJapapean AI circuitry.*" It registered with Amba that this *machine* could read her mind, at least on some superficial level. "Yes, I can," continued Drone. His voice wasn't as high and nasal any more. And the look in Bob's eyes said the wiry old man was licensed to kill...

Amba felt the change in air density, and ducked as Drone slammed towards the back of her skull. She felt the tiny machine skim her head, and it was moving so fast it couldn't halt its impact with –

Bob.

The drone hit him square on the nose, and carried on. His face imploded like a collapsing star, folding in on itself like fluid, which it had surely become. Drone exploded from the back of Bob's head in a shower of brain and skull debris, which pattered down onto the ground; it whirled in an arc as Bob's limp body slapped the tiles. Blood fell like rain, pattering to an abrupt halt.

"Did you read this?"

The FRIEND was out, pointing at the hovering machine. Its facial lights flickered off. No point pretending to be nice and pleasing the tourists anymore, was there?

"How did you do that?"

Amba smiled. "My little secret."

Our little secret, corrected Zi.

I suppose you have your uses, said Amba, and narrowed her eyes.

This is impossible this cannot be happening I have the ability to monitor all androids and this bitch is certainly an android. [malfunction]. Look. Bob is dead. Bob and I worked together for a long time, a very long time, years and years spotting androids for [malfunction]. Scanning. Scanning. Scanning. What is this strange firewall that stands before me? Where has her mind gone? This is an impossibility! We have a mind-to-mind circuit and I...

There was a BLAM. The FRIEND kicked in Amba's hand, and the drone exploded, shattering into a million tiny black pieces that flew out in random directions. Fragments of the drone's core hit the ground, fizzing and sparking.

Good riddance, said Zi.

"Hmm," said Amba, and turned, scanning the Monolith Ride Museum. The noise of the FRIEND had reverberated off the walls, but now only an eerie silence rushed in; like a room filling with cyanide gas.

Do you think he's here?

Napper?

Yes. Terry "Smoothface" Napper, Head of Monolith Secret Police. You realise he's going to be as slippery as an electric eel in a vat of grease, don't you?

So where are his soldiers? His guards?

You tell me.

I thought you were the great AI, with all the fucking answers? Like that bastard drone... the ability to read electronic minds. Ha! No wonder we're never going to make it in the universe; no wonder we'll never find God. Androids are a doomed species. Androids are a doomed fucking race.

Zi said nothing, and Amba headed away from the corpse of Bob – who, she suspected, was also an android. After all – it takes one to know one, and every android was an expert in spotting their own kind; they had that certain *aroma*. Supposedly.

Except...

Except that didn't always happen, did it? How many times had Amba been unable to spot an android and nearly died as a result? Five? Ten? Probably nearer to twenty times. But she always succeeded in the end. Because she was an Anarchy Model. And Anarchy Models never, ever stopped.

DEX FIRED THE Makarov, and a bullet hit the huge, slathering, and wholly unconvincing rubbery monster between the eyes. It gasped, looked at him as if it had just discovered him up to no good with its mother, then fell on its side and started quivering. Dex frowned, ejected the clip, and reloaded the pistol. He rested a cautious hand on his SMKK; he didn't want to use the machine gun down in the tunnels and caves, but it had been tempting. Damn tempting. When the purple and green-spotted rubbery monsters came wobbling out of the darkness, growling and moaning, Dex knew, *knew* it was part of the "whole experience," knew it was one of Theme Planet's "little games," their little "themed areas," but deep down something had gone *click* and Dex didn't even trust dodgy rubber reality any longer. Reality had twisted, turned, and spun around like a Chaos Cube. He certainly didn't trust purple and green monsters that went "grwwwww" and extended claws to him as if about to try and rip out his throat. He'd shot the first one between the eyes, and continued in the same manner throughout his meanderings through the labyrinth of The Caves of Hades.

Now, he could see a deep, rich blue daylight up ahead. It had to be evening. Dex trudged up the tunnel, wary, waiting for some Grand Beast, some End Level Boss, who would no doubt be ten times harder than the other guys and have special vulnerable spots where it was, well, vulnerable. Dex patted a grenade in his pocket. He'd soon take care of that...

Dex emerged on a cliff-top. It was that time of the evening when the sun is just a fiery half-disc glimpsed over the curvature of the ocean. The sea sparkled in an incredible panorama as a breeze of salt and ocean ruffled Dex's hair and he took a deep breath; and for once, almost felt normal.

He shook his head in disbelief.

"What a crock of shit. When will the 'fun' ever end?"

He glanced around, wary of SIMs, guards, soldiers, the police, or whatever the hell else Monolith Corporation, or the Provax Government, or the Earth Oblivion Government – hell, even the flora and fauna – wanted to throw at him. In a rare moment, Dexter Colls realised that he now trusted nobody. Not a single living creature on this whole damn planet! Not one fucking atom. And that was, ultimately, a very sad place to be.

Totally alone, feeling inhuman.

Dex dropped to one knee, not wanting to cast a silhouette against the horizon, and surveyed the landscape down below the cliffs. There were rolling valleys and several forests crammed onto The Lost Island, as if scattered by the hand of God. Dex shifted his eyes left, drawn to a magnificent building – it was a huge castle, a medieval fortress of some kind – he'd seen the filmys – only scarred by Theme Planet's usual tacky tat.

He made out the neon letters of the Monolith Ride Museum. Jim said Katrina and the girls were being held on The Lost Island; and whilst Dex knew he had a lot of ground to cover, a lot to explore, one possibility was this castle – because a castle had *dungeons*, and dungeons were a traditional holding cell for prisoners. Maybe too obvious? Dex didn't care. It was a possibility. Either the dungeons or the penthouse suite; that was where all power-hungry egomaniacs hid out. And if nothing else, there'd be somebody there he could torture for information. He gave a sickly smile. Things were on a downward spiral now...

He pocketed the Makarov, and pulled the strap on the SMKK tight, so the machine gun wouldn't flap, and flicked off the safety switch. He looked around. *I don't trust this place. It smells funny.*

Smells of... aliens. An alien world. An alien dream. An alien...
Theme Planet. Well, they certainly knew how to take my dream
away; certainly understood how to make my world collapse. And
now they want rid of me, dead, fired off into space and lost in an
eternity of cold hydrogen. Well, I'll show them. I'll show them
exactly what I can do.

Dex headed off into the gloom, wandering down a narrow track
between rocks. He picked his way carefully, heading for the cliffs
and away from the obvious main exit, one hand on his gun, eyes
wary, scouting for trouble... because he knew. Trouble was going
to come to him. It always did. *Always* did.

He moved slowly, alert, constantly on the lookout for SIMs or
the police. He was at least happy with one thing; Jim was dead.
That bastard. How could he do that, how could he betray the
humans? Betray his position of power and authority? Ha. But then
there would always be the corrupt, those willing to sell their own
fucking granny for a lousy dollar. Dex shook his head. *It's just the*
way the world is, baby. One huge comedy horrorshow.

Dex tracked down from the ridgeline, then headed slowly for
the Monolith Ride Museum's wild side. He fancied he might come
across a few tourists, which could keep him safe – but then, after
the slaughterhouse in the forest with Robin Hoodie and his Merry
Backstabbers, he wasn't so sure anymore. Had they really been
rogue SIMs on a crazy mission of extermination? Or had they been
instructed that way? Dex knew how anally retentive the Theme
Planet creators were about bad exposure. You didn't want people
getting shot up on the rollercoasters; that'd bring nothing but
catastrophe to your business balance sheet.

Just like a rogue cop with a kidnapped wife and children, on a
mission of rampage with a fucking SMKK machine gun, shooting
up SIMs and policemen and tearing around in a military chopper.
Now, loose with a pocket of grenades and enough bullets to take
out a battalion, here he was trying to set the world to rights.

Or at least, find his family.

Dex thought about Molly and Toffee. He thought about Katrina.

He missed them terribly.

Mouth a grim line, he headed away from the tourist paths. He headed for the cliffs...

AMBA BLINKED. SOMETHING was strange. Hell, something was downright *weird*. The world felt wrong. Like she was pushing through cotton wool. It was dark, the air oily and filled with rancid grease. *How did I get here, Zi? What happened?* No answer. *Zi?* Fear now. Zi had always been with her, was her companion, through thick and thin, through life and death, through murder and mayhem. Zi was a part of Amba. An integral element of the Anarchy Android...

Amba's hand flashed up, and she realised with heart-stopping *horror* that Zi, the FRIEND, was gone. She patted her chest for a few moments, but there was no disguising it; the FRIEND had vanished. And that was impossible. How could she have not known? How had she *not felt the pressure, on body, mind and soul?*

She stopped dead, boots sliding a little in oil. She looked around. Took a *good* look around. The walls were complex, mesh upon mesh upon mesh. There were girders and support struts everywhere, most gleaming with oil and grease. There were huge flywheels and cogs and gears, some still and dripping oil, many moving slowly, turning, gears clicking as they shifted and changed and slicked neatly into finely engineered new positions. It was like being inside a giant clock. Like being inside a vast machine.

How did I get here?

How did I come here?

There had been no transition. No change. In a moment of panic, Amba tried to recall her memories, but could not. Then the panic settled like nuclear fallout, into a roadmap back into her past; a roadmap through murder.

You are in the machine, came Zi's voice. And Amba remembered. The Ride Museum. She was looking for Terry Napper, head of the

Monolith Secret Police. And it had been so easy. Quiet corridors, no guards... *no guards*. No. This place was guarded with something different. Something... *alien*. An entity, or presence, across which Amba had never before stumbled. Or been pushed.

She thought about Romero, then. Cardinal Romero. Could picture his tall frame, heavy build, good looking dark features, black hair slicked back. In his hand he carried his Zippo, flicking it open, shut, open, shut, open, shut. He was smiling at her, but the smile was a knowing smile, the smile was a killing smile. There was a *click*. A memory unlocked in her android brain. *I want you to find Terry Napper. He runs the Monolith Secret Police. He knows secrets, many secrets about the Monolith Army being raised by the provax on Theme Planet. I want you to discover those secrets. I want you to torture him, bring him pain like no pain he has ever felt. Make him sing. Sing long and sweet. I want to know every aspect of Theme Planet's military plans. I want to know its size, and more importantly, I want to know its technology. Can you do this for me, sweet Amba?*

I can do it, General.

One last thing.

Yes?

Be careful. He is guarded, but not as you would understand a person being guarded. Napper is core to the Monolith Movement; he knows too many of their secrets, and they have something very special for him. You understand?

I don't think I do.

You will find out.

Inevitably.

She opened her eyes. She was inside a machine. She didn't know how she had arrived. And her FRIEND had gone. Had it been gas? Or was this a mind-fuck? Her eyes narrowed. Either way, she would have to get through it... because whatever *it* was, it had identified her as a threat and was working on her.

She moved, running fast, boots sliding on oil. She flashed through endless corridors of machinery, breaking through a mesh panel and into a cavern of machines. They were vast, and dark, pistons as huge as tower blocks, wheels and spinning cogs a kilometre high and interlinked with more cogs, hundreds of cogs and gears, thousands, and this was the machinery on the underside of the Theme Planet, Amba suddenly knew, and she felt intuitively that she was in some kind of half-world, a second-hand shadow. She had been forced there by the machines. Taken there, against her will, without her knowledge. As an act of quarantine?

She had to break out. She had to negotiate the maze. Were they watching her? Could they observe her? Was it Napper? It had to be. She was in The Ride Museum, and it was *his* base of Operations. The core of the Monolith Secret Police – from where every damn tourist who visited Theme Planet was watched, spied upon, monitored, listened to. Their minds were probed. Not a single person who entered Theme Planet had a moment of secrecy, of privacy. The Monolith Secret Police were watching. Studying. Every room of every hotel was rigged with mics and cameras. Every nuance of human interaction, integration, every moment of comedy and fear and sadness; all were studied, all were observed.

Something went *click* in Amba's mind. Romero had triggered a memory. Romero had triggered an *allowance*. An understanding. For only with understanding could Amba get through this shit, through this alien *machine* to face Napper. He was cunning, he was evil – but most of all, he was in a position of *control*. He had her in his grip, and she was now his slave. She had to break the chains. She had to gain her freedom. Before she could kill him.

Amba stood still, amidst a million whining, clanking, thrumming machines.

She considered her options.

Theme Planet had been created to monitor humanity. Why?

Were the provax so in *awe* of mankind's empathy?

In the same way that androids were in awe of humanity's ability to care?

And she realised. Provax and androids... they were the same. Maybe not chemically, biologically, organically – but it was there.

In their confusion as to what made humanity human. *Truly* human. And how, despite this *humanity*, they were then able to side-step the natural urges and become *inhuman*.

Amba frowned. She was nearly there. Clutching at threads of silk whilst balancing on a high wire above a tank of piranhas. Nearly there, but losing her balance, twitching, fighting, trying to achieve clarity...

Did Monolith wish to *destroy* humanity?

Romero had mentioned an army. Military organisation.

But why?

Amba frowned again. How could that be? There were a million easier ways to destroy a race than invite it to a pleasure park. No. It had to be something more complex. And she was there for answers. For the answers lay with the Monolith Army. The answers lay with Terry Napper, head of Monolith's Secret Police.

She moved, and around her the machinery of Theme Planet moved with her. The rhythms and clanks and whines changed, with every movement of her hand, every footstep, every blink of an eyelash, with every beat of her android heart.

Amba stopped. She blinked. She coughed. Around her, the machinery seemed to blend, to twist, to *move*. Huge cogs now seemed to be eyes, watching her. She walked along a wide avenue lined with belching engines. Their rhythms were words, and they sang to her, saying, *Leave us leave us leave us*, and, *save us save us save us*. Noises and thumps and screeches of metal on metal hammered through Amba's mind. She felt her brain cracking, like a spoon through an egg, and she broke into a run, panic like nothing she had ever felt rioting through her body and spirit. This was no simple dream, she was there, *had been drawn there*, into the heart of the machine, in to the heart of Theme Planet and –

It was alive.

It was the SA34000RAH.

A living, breathing machine.

SARAH.

She ran again, brain whirring. She missed her FRIEND. She missed Zi. *Damn it, you bitch, why can't you be here when I need you? Yeah, yeah, I know I moaned, I know I used to slag you off for the random murders and the senseless violence... but we both know I need you. We both know I can't do this thing without you...*

Something flashed from the darkness, and Amba rolled left, fast. A metal object, long and sleek, snapped past her ear. Amba launched herself forward, crashing into a... a *machine,* like a miniature version of the machines around her. It was an engine, open and belching, metal parts spinning and clanking, belts thrumming, like a drive engine, shit, like a *ride* engine. This was one of the ride machines... and here it was... *attacking her!* There was a *snap* and a piston broken free, skimming past Amba's nose. She twitched right, snapped out a right punch, and felt a knuckle crack. She didn't dent the machine. She didn't rock it. It groaned, and whined, and she backflipped five times, putting distance between herself and the oily engine. It staggered towards her, rocking slightly from side to side in time with its pistons. Its legs were short and stumpy, its arms a mass of linkages and rods and drive-belts. It whirred and snapped and droned. Fumes pumped from an exhaust pipe which erupted vertically from its neck, where a human being's head would have been.

"What the fuck are you?"

It charged her, and she leapt left, grabbing hold of a huge cog and clambering up it. She glanced down. Amazingly, the engine thing was following, belching noxious fumes. Chains clattered on its cogs as it pursued her. Amba frowned and climbed further, then leapt onto a massive engine housing. She found a length of tubing, kicked it again, and again, until it split, and hefted the heavy steel tube as the engine climbed up to her level and leapt at her. She took a step back, and watched the engine-creature hit the ledge at her feet and tumble back to the corridor below, landing heavily. Amba narrowed her eyes and jumped down onto it, ramming the metal tube into an engine orifice with all her might. With a high-pitched squeal, the engine bucked, shuddered, and juddered to a halt – like a groundcar breaking down. Black smoke belched from the port, and the whirring belts clattered to a stop.

She'd killed it. Killed the ride engine!

Amba climbed off the engine-block creature, makeshift weapon raised, and looked around for more enemies. From somewhere distant she heard a metallic roar, loud and reverberating, which echoed down the corridor and was answered by more metal roars. The ground began to shake, and dust rained down through the oily atmosphere. The quake increased in violence, and Amba staggered over and steadied herself against a hundred-foot high machine, which clanked and moaned and vibrated. The tower-block-sized machine lurched up on battered metal legs, wrenching itself from its steel-and-concrete roots with *giant's screams* of violence and more rolling quakes through the machinery room.

Amba staggered back, eyes wide, face smeared with black oil. Everything was shaking now, the air filled with dust and squirting oil from fractured rubber hoses. Steam hissed and engines growled, a million engines all howling their ride-hatred at the stray bolt in the system, the lost spanner in the works; the bad ghost in the machine. A weak and fragile piece of meat in the deepest pit of hard, spinning metal.

"Shit," said Amba, and began to run, arms pumping hard, as behind her bellows and horns blasted from angry ride machinery and all the giant engines in the place seemed to come alive, watching her, calling to her, mocking her.

The rhythm of the engine voices had subtly changed. They were singing to her once again, metal songs born of iron and steel and oil. *Mash-you-mash-you-mash-you,* said the machines. *Pulp you up, pulp you up, mash you up, fuck you up,* faster and faster and faster, like a ground car engine accelerating with gravelly piston grinding voices, *pulp you up, mash you up, fuck you up, pulp you up, mash you up, fuck you up...*

Amba sprinted. And the Theme Planet ride machines sprinted after her on stubby legs of steel.

Behind her, it was as if a tornado smashed through the cavern, as a hundred giant machines came alive, belts and cogs and gears and pistons, whipping belts and giant flywheels, all grinding and pounding. The noise was incredible. A stench of hot oil and melted grease and hot, crushed bearings washed over Amba, spurring her on. As if she needed invitation. Her makeshift weapon was gone, lost, dropped and trampled by the giant screaming machines pursuing her.

Amba ran hard, harder than she'd ever run.

Behind her, slowly, the machines started to reel her in...

She glanced over her shoulder, and gave a little gasp. They were close now, only a few feet away, a wall of grinding, screaming machinery as high and as wide as a Cubescraper. It was a wall, a squirming wall of metal, made from individual units in a million different sizes and configurations.

But one thing was clear...

They were out to crush her. Grind her.

Stamp her into an oily pulp.

IT WAS NEVER going to be so obvious as walking in the front door. What, into a waiting machine gun nest? Into a horde of police armed with SMKKs? Yeah, right. So Dex took another path, around the treacherous cliffs, and as evening passed into night and the glowing neon lights of the Monolith Ride Museum seemed even more gaudy, even more... *fake,* Dex found himself clamped to a rocky cliff-side, fingers aching, toes clenched, a restless ocean beneath him beckoning with rhythmic hisses, far too like laughter for Dex to relax. Not that he could relax when clamped like an idiot to a rock wall. Climbing was something that other people did; not Dex. He had way too much common sense. Why climb walls of rock? Because they were there to be climbed? What an absolute pile of goat's bollocks. Dex's old school friend, William Braggs, had been an avid climber, and Dex remembered the day vividly when William had been just twenty years old, three days before his twenty-first birthday, and he'd fallen from a ridge and landed on his face. The fall hadn't killed Braggs, but it destroyed his face. Even after a hundred operations, after rebuilding his bones with titanium, after skin grafts and sessions on the doctor's couch filled with tears and angst, he still looked like part of his face had melted. Finally, two years later, he'd stuck a needle in his arm and succumbed to the fatality of Black Orchid, a designer narcotic of the time.

Dex had carried the coffin.

Dex hated carrying coffins. It reminded him way too much of his own mortality.

A cool breeze ruffled Dex's hair, and he looked down, and he remembered his old friend, remembered the shock when he'd rushed to the hospital – to see him, cranked up in bed on wires and supports, his face a purple flat blotch. He'd been so high on painkillers at the time he didn't know what planet he was on, and Dex had stared, and stared, and stared… just as he stared now, in his memories, and glanced down again, and wondered about the sanity of what he was doing.

For Kat. For Moll. For Toff.

It had become his mantra; the only thing keeping him sane.

Dex struggled on, edging around the cliff, waves hissing and cracking beneath him, neon lights glittering on the surging silver ocean. His mouth was dry with fear, and even the SMKK and Makarov gave him little satisfaction; what use were bullets when you were a broken corpse on the rocks below? *Maybe I should have gone in the front door. Maybe I should have taken my chances with the guards… shit. Triple shit and blue wanking monkeys.*

On he moved, the Ride Museum rearing above him and merging seamlessly with the rocky cliffs. Dex started to angle his traverse upwards, until it became an ascent, and darkness tumbled down around him like molten velvet and the stars popped out, twinkling with a distant cold malevolence. Such vast spaces. Such coldness. An eternity of emptiness. Not good. Not good.

Dex edged up, and at one point his boot slipped. His fingers dug in tight, so tight he thought his bones would force their splintered way from his flesh. He felt a fingernail pop off and wanted to scream as agony flooded up his finger, tendons and forearm.

He glanced down, boot clawing at the rocks like some spastic disco dance, and gritting his teeth hard, jaw muscles clenching, he fought – fought to stay alive.

"Son of a bitch!"

He found his footing and pushed himself into the rocks, sweat heavy on his face, making his hair lank. He blinked, as stars flashed before his eyes, and sucked in oxygen like a dying man surfacing from the bottom of a lake.

"Oh, you son of a bitch!"

Dex composed himself, and climbed again until he reached the glossy flanks of the Monolith Ride Museum. Twenty feet above him was a vast neon sign, flickering and winking and glittering. He was too close to read what the actual words spelled out, which was probably for the best, for Dex had no desire to clamber over junk advertising. Especially if it was for Fatty Fat Burgers or Fizzy Sperm Cola products...

Dex was panting, pain piercing his chest and making him wince. His lungs felt like they'd been grated. His leg muscles felt like they'd been stripped from his bones and beaten with a hammer. And his finger-tips... soaked in hydrochloric acid. It was not a good way to feel.

He calmed his body, looked left and right, checking for cameras or to see if he'd been observed in any way. Then he edged up the smooth wall, fingers finding cracks between huge black blocks, until with a grunt he grabbed the neon sign and lifted himself up onto the bottom leg of an E. Holding tight, he leant back and looked upwards, searching for the lowest window or other entry point. There were "medieval arrow loops" as, no doubt, Theme Planet advertising literature described them, but the ones Dex had seen, even from a distance, could easily fit a man's body through the cavity – thus negating the whole point of an arrow loop. This wasn't a castle for defending; this was a castle to please cash-paying tourists. Dex had to keep reminding himself about that, about the nature of Theme Planet.

Built by morons, visited by idiots! That should be their advertising motto!

Dex climbed. The wind snapped at him like an annoying dog.

He climbed more. Sweat dripped from his brow, running into his eyes and stinging him with salt.

He climbed. His fingers bled. His legs screamed like they were on fire.

From the top of the E he made it to a P, and climbed the huge vast letter, praying it would take his weight. Which it did; it was big enough to support a hover tank. Dex ascended, and the ocean and the Theme Planet spread out before him in cooling darkness, and he paused in the valley of a V, sat with legs dangling, looking out over the ocean. *What I'd give for a smoke,* he realised, then pictured Katrina's stern face chastising him his carnal weaknesses – and he had a lot – and she was frowning in his mind's eye. He grinned at that, and she spurred him on; gave him strength. He turned, stood, and continued to climb.

When his fingers found the lip of the "arrow loop," he was just about ready to give up and dive into the cool, welcoming ocean. At least it would be his friend. At least it would take him in, invite him down, down into an eternal, idle embrace...

Dex hauled his sorry arse over the edge and slapped down on cool stone flags, worn uneven by the passages of time (nice marketing touch, that). He lay there for a while, not caring who walked past or pointed a gun at his head. He was in no condition to fight. He was in no condition to *walk*.

Slowly, his strength returned, seeping into his limbs like honey through waffle cracks. He sat up, cradling his numb, bloodied fingers. He worked them softly, kneading life back into the tortured joints and muscles. Spasms of cramp arced like lightning flashes through his thighs and calves, and Dex spent a good few minutes contorting on the stone floor like a werewolf caught in the throes of some rabid transmogrification. He rubbed at his screaming muscles with screaming fingers, and after a while the pains subsided and Dex was able to stand, leaning heavily against a rough stone wall, panting, tears in his eyes. He stretched his muscles, and took deep breaths, and knew he needed salt to combat the cramps. In fact, now he thought about it, it had been an age since he had eaten or drunk. No wonder he was weak. No wonder he was cramping up.

Dex slid the SMKK to his back and, with Makarov to cheek, peered out into the corridor. Theme Planet designers had gone all-out for a medieval experience here, and proper live fire brands burned at regular intervals, giving off an acrid stench. Dex crept down the corridor, wary, gun poised and ready for combat. Down the steps he trotted, worn into grooves by thousands of years of use (although Dex *knew* this place had only existed for a couple of decades; such attention to detail!) and down more corridors until he came to a large room with a vaulted ceiling. High above, rich paintings filled the arches, showing plump, naked ladies at play, and cherubic angels strumming lyres and harps. Around the large chamber were all manner of glass cabinets, and Dex peered inside. There were a hundred different machines, all black and gleaming with oil. They were intricate, and like no machines Dex had ever seen in his life; they twisted and turned like puzzle boxes. A plaque on one glass cabinet explained these were some of the first ride engines, or "ride drives" as TP so snappily put it, employed in rides when Theme Planet first opened.

Dex moved around the cases, keeping a wary eye on the doorways, to witness yet more machines. Here, there was a prototype for brake systems; there, a controller for piston firing, and over there a controller unit used for timing ride drops and the release of passengers from safety collars.

It was all extremely dull.

Dex left the chamber, padded down more corridors, and emerged into yet more interlinked chambers. Again, they were full of glass display cabinets, and Dex glided past various wax statues of provax in outfits depicting different "Ages" of Theme Planet's progression towards the entertainment behemoth it had become today.

"Wonderful," he muttered, stopping by what must have been the hundredth wax statue. "By God, they've had a lot of uniform changes over the years. Even more than your average football club!"

His words echoed back, cold and metallic, as if the life had been sucked from his words by the thick stone walls.

Where to go?

He eyed a staircase.

Upwards, of course. That was where power-hungry megalomaniacs tended to reside, be they scum-pushing drug peddlers, idea-pushing scummy politicians, or scum-sucking miliporn warmongerers, everybody with any idea of *power* seemed to gravitate upwards, as if labouring under the mistaken belief that only the cream rose to the top. *Well that's all bullshit, and we both know it. Shit floats just as well as cream.*

Dex made for the stone steps. He knew, if there were answers, they were on the top floor.

Insanity always was...

DEX STOPPED. HE rubbed weary eyes and frowned. There was a huge room before him, adorned with rich tapestries, thick, heavily-patterned carpets, and alabaster stands bearing sculptures and golden effigies. The place was awash with different artefacts, not just from a thousand different time periods, but from hundreds of different species and races. It was as if Monolith Corporation had decided that by simply dumping as much historical wealth as possible in one place, they would inspire awe, inspire jaw-dropping respect; instead, to Dex, it just looked tacky. Like having ten different types of dinner service. Like having all four walls decorated in different gaudy patterns. *Lots* didn't always automatically mean *best*. The whole arena had been styled by somebody without style. As if created by a machine. It was fake style. False cool. It rankled Dex deeply...

He moved forward, silent footsteps on plush carpets. He glided past a hundred marble pedestals, a thousand gaudy statues in brass and bronze and other, glinting, highly-polished alloys. He moved past tapestries depicting ancient battles from a thousand different cultures and alien races. And then...

He heard voices.

Dex glanced about for cameras, and he was pretty sure the place would be bugged to high heaven, but could see no evidence. *Ach, fuck it. What can I do?* he realised. All he could do was blunder on and hope for the best. Hope for a lucky break. Hope to find his *wife and children...*

He continued forward, body tense now, hyper-sensitive to everything around him, every sight and sound and touch. He could smell some kind of burning incense, and hear a gentle *swish* of curtains, as if caressed by a mountain breeze.

Up ahead, Dex saw a man seated on the thick carpets. He was naked from the waist up, and he was muscular and deeply tanned. His legs were covered in corded trousers of many bright colours. He had his back to Dex, and his head was bald, shining by the glow of many burning brands.

"Welcome, Dexter," came a rich, vibrant voice.

Dex checked behind himself, then crept a little closer. There was something in front of the man, lying on the thick carpets. With a start, Dex realised it was a woman, lying perfectly still, her eyes closed, breathing gently and completely naked. Her arms were by her sides, and her ankles placed neatly together. She looked serene in sleep, and there was nothing to set her apart from other humans; she was neither ugly nor beautiful, she was neither fat nor thin, flabby nor muscular. Nothing.

Dex transferred his gaze back to the man, and realised he had not heard *voices,* just one voice. This man. Talking to the sleeping woman. Dex frowned, and made sure the safety was off on the Makarov.

"How did you know I was here?"

"That's my job," said the man, and turned, and grinned at Dexter. He had crimson eyes and sharp pointed teeth. He looked quite feral, almost tribal in appearance. All he needed was a bone necklace and a spear and he could have come from three million years ago.

"And your job is?"

"I am the Head of Monolith Secret Police. My name is Terry 'Smoothface' Napper. You can call me 'Sir.'"

"Aah," said Dex, who considered putting a bullet in that nice, big, bald head. It made a good target. Dex was sure he wouldn't miss. Suddenly, a pain wrenched through his hands and the Makarov was torn from his grip and thrown a hundred metres down the room. Dex yelped and rubbed his wrists, where strips of skin had been peeled free.

"I suggest you toss down the SMKK as well," said the man, grinning again, crimson eyes boring through Dex. "If the accelerator gets it, it might well rip you in half. And we wouldn't want that now, would we?"

Dex struggled out of the strap and dropped the gun like it was on fire. He'd seen accelerators work in the past, on small military targets, like tanks and warships. A military-grade accelerator, which could tear a *battleship* in half, would sure make a mess of a human body. Whoever controlled the machine had a damn good eye; Dex had only lost a bit of skin on his hand, rather than several fingers, or indeed, his whole arm – which could have been quite easily ripped off and tossed a hundred metres down the room along with the Makarov.

The SMKK clattered when it hit the ground.

"Good boy," said Napper, and that grin was still on his face, and the grin bothered Dex, because it wasn't a grin associated with humour, but the grin of a shark, or an alligator, just before its twists a limb into oblivion mush. "Move over there, where I can see your hands. And just remember, the accelerator can rip out your heart from a million paces."

"Yeah, I know," said Dex, "I've seen them in operation."

"Well you'll know not to fuck with me then," said Napper.

Dex glanced around, but couldn't immediately locate the controller. But then, that didn't mean much. The controller could be on a whole different *planet*. What mattered was his precision. And what mattered was that Dex was being a good boy. Despite obvious appearances, he was caught worse than any rat in a trap. He was caught with his pants round his ankles, no mistake, and he'd walked into the pile of shit like a good boy scout. *Shit*. Could he *get* any more amateurish?

Dex shifted warily around a bronze statue, away from his SMKK, so that he stood beside the prostrate woman, staring at Napper's face. The man returned his gaze to the woman.

"You're here now, my sweet, and there's nothing left for you to worry about." Her eyelids twitched, as if she could hear what Napper was saying, but unable to respond. "You've been a bad lady, haven't you? Following your mission objective rather than following your heart. Well, you're here, and you walked into the trap, just like Mr Dexter Colls." He glanced up. "You were both fools to think you could come here and interfere with our plans. Monolith is out of your league, little people. Monolith, and Theme Planet, are leviathans you *cannot* fuck with."

"I didn't come here to fuck with Monolith Corporation." Dex's voice was soft. "Although Monolith decided it was going to fuck with me. Don't you people understand? You took my wife and children, Napper. You stole them away from me, and you wonder why I go on a rampage with an SMKK? What the hell did you expect me to do?"

"You were invited to leave; if you had, your wife and children would have been returned to you. Unharmed."

"No." Dex shook his head. "Shit doesn't happen like that. Things never work out like that. It's never as easy as that. You'd get me off the planet then BLAM, take them out when I wasn't looking."

"You are incorrect." Napper stared hard at Dex, then stood, smoothly, his body powerful and lithe; a killing machine honed to perfection. He rolled his neck, joints cracking.

Dex frowned. "Incorrect? About what?"

"Monolith just wanted you off the planet. Because of what you are."

"What I am? What the fuck are you talking about?"

"You don't know?"

"Know w*hat?*"

"You're an android, Dexter."

"*What?*" Dexter realised he was grinning, and shaking his head. He lifted his hands, palms outward, his face open with absolute confusion. "You..." he chuckled with genuine humour, "you think I'm a fucking *android?* Gods, is that what all this shit has been about? You took my wife and children in order to persuade me to leave Theme Planet?"

"Yes."

"That's crazy, Napper. Can you hear yourself? It's fucking insane! I'm not an android."

"That's what they all say."

"I'm a policeman, you idiot. I work PUF in London! I have done for fucking *years*. I've been married for *years*. I have two little girls, my own flesh and blood, and androids can't have children. You know it, and I know it, so what the hell is this really about?"

"Three androids have been sent to Theme Planet to kill... various targets."

"Including you?"

"Oh, yes," said Napper, meeting Dexter's eyes. He continued. "Our intel told us there were three, sent by Earth's Oblivion Government, to take out the top brass on various sections of Theme Planet... presumably as an initial strike before the full scale invasion begins."

"Full scale... *invasion?* Invasion of what?"

"Invasion of Theme Planet," said Napper, eyes glinting. "By Earth."

"Whoa," Dex held up his hands, shaking his head. "What you're talking about is crazy business. Truly insane stuff. Have you even heard yourself?"

"*Our* first job was to locate the three androids, the three *Anarchy Androids,* sent to Theme Planet to eliminate various high-ranking targets. Here is one." Napper stared down, almost lovingly, at Amba. "See how perfectly made she is. Look at the craftsmanship. Our engineers, despite their skill with theme rides, are quite envious. We never did master androids... certainly not to the level of the Anarchy Model."

"Stop, stop, stop," said Dex, shaking his head. "Honestly mate, you have me completely wrong. I've been caught up in this mad shit and it's exactly that; mad. Mad as a fucking mad rabbit."

"How did you find your way to me?"

"What?"

"You heard the question just fine, Mr Colls."

"Well... a series of random events. I was directed here. By Jim, the policeman, I was looking for my wife..."

"Your priority was *not* to leave Theme Planet, Dexter, it was to find me. To take me out. Look at you, in here, tooled up, armed with a Makarov and SMKK, with grenades in your pockets. You had a chance, a *true* chance to save your wife and children; you could have left, and allowed Monolith authorities to return them to Earth to be with you. But no. You chose the more difficult path. You did what an Anarchy Model would have done."

"No, this is ridiculous!" snapped Dex, frowning, mind a snowglobe of confusion. "And your logic is fucking twisted. I did what any strong man, any military man, any *police*man would have done; I failed to trust the untrusting words of yet another huge lying corporation; I trusted in my own instincts and tried to find my family. This had nothing to do with assassination. Nothing to *do* with being a bloody android! All I want is my family back."

"And if I give them to you?"

"Then I go home," growled Dex, through gritted teeth.

"Then I will give them to you. And we will see."

Dex paused, then, licking his lips. He blinked rapidly, three times. "What?" he said, at last.

"I will give you back your wife and children. They are here. Safe. Secure. An insurance policy, you might say. In fact, the insurance policy we had, and that we offered you, before you shot up the police and a whole load of military grade Justice and Battle SIMs, and caused a merry riot across the face of the Theme Planet."

"You're telling the truth? They're here?"

"Yes."

"Then let's go to them!" yelled Dex. "Come on, I'll show you, I'll prove it to you! I'm not some deranged fucking android machine. I'll show you, all I want is my family back. All I want is my Katrina, and my little girls!"

"Follow me," said Napper, stepping to one side. "And remember, the accelerator is aimed at your back. It'll rip you in half in the blink of an eye! So don't try anything foolish. Don't try anything... an android might try." He smiled, and it was a grim smile indeed.

Napper strode down the huge chamber, and Dex followed, then stopped. He glanced back at the woman. "What about her?"

"What about her?"

"Who is she?"

"You do not need to know."

"Are you going to kill her?"

"Yes. She is an Anarchy Android. Of *that,* we are certain without doubt."

"She looks so... human."

"They all do. That's the way they were made."

"I find it hard to believe."

"Do you want to see your family?" said Napper, crimson eyes blazing, and as they'd been talking Dex had unconsciously edged towards the man, a matter of inches, but far enough for... Dex's fist lashed out, a straight punch, hammering *through* Napper's teeth and embedding in the core of his brain. Napper died instantly. Dex lifted his arm, and the whole of Napper's body flipped over, around, as the accelerator blast *tore* through it, ripping it asunder and shredding Napper's limbs and fingers and organs in a hundred different directions. Blood fell like rain. Hung in the air like a fine mist. Body parts pattered on the thick rug. But now... now Dex had *seen* the accelerator blast, witnessed its location, and dived for the SMKK, grabbing the weapon, rolling as another blast tore a marble pillar into powder, exploding around Dexter Colls, and the SMKK slammed around, its barrel a black eye which went BLAM. A bullet spun across the chamber and through the mouth of a painting depicting an angel. Behind the painting, a woman was hit between the eyes and slammed back against her chair, fingers slack on the accelerator's glowing controls.

Dex stood there, and looked down at the SMKK. Then he looked left, at Napper's shredded leg, and right, to a half-portion of Napper's head. The jaw was missing, and the head looked strangely shrunken; as if tampered with by witch doctors.

Dex swallowed, slowly, and breathed deep.

What happened? What hit me? What went... click?

How did I do that? How did I kill him? How did I kill him, and *the controller?*

Dex swallowed again, and his pulse was racing, and his heart was drumming like rainfall in a storm. There could only be one answer. Normal people, normal *policemen* didn't punch an enemy through the mouth and flip his body up and over to use as a shield against a military accelerator weapon. Normal people didn't do those things. Androids did those things.

No.

Bullshit.

He was trained, trained hard and fast in rules of combat; he'd fought in the Helix War, and patrolled the mean streets of London for decades. Dex was a tough fucker; as tough as they got.

Dex walked back to the woman lying on the rug. She was coming round, moaning softly, eyelids fluttering. Dex knelt by her side, touched her gently on the arm as flickering thoughts rioted like an exploding volcano through his mind –

Am I an android?

A fucking android!

If I'm an android, then...

My life is a lie.

My wife is not my wife.

My children are not my children...

No. No.

That cannot be.

Cannot be possible.

Is not... believable. Ever.

I am Dexter Colls. I have a beautiful family, a wife, children, a good job in London, a brother-in-law who's getting divorced, a best mate with bad breath, a love of whiskey and old filmys, how the fuck can an android have all that? It's ridiculous! A lie. A plot of some kind. Stick to the facts, hold on to the truth, because your mind is all you have, the facts are all you can see, trust the evidence before you, trust your own mind and don't allow it to be twisted; to snap...

The woman sat up.

Dexter blinked.

She smiled.

"You made it," she said.

CHAPTER ELEVEN

VAGABONDS

"I DON'T UNDERSTAND," said Dex, and confusion was his mistress.

"You're not expected to understand; just obey."

"Obey?"

"The Ministers of Joy."

Amba strode naked across the thick carpets, and scooped up the SMKK. Then she turned and smiled at Dex, but it was a hollow smile; a smile without warmth. "Thank you."

"For what?"

"Rescuing me?"

"How did I rescue you?"

"You cared," said Amba, glancing down at some of the torn pieces which remained from Napper. "Or cared enough to question, at least. They had me. The Monolith Mainframe had me. It's called SARAH. A SA34000RAH. And we have to destroy it."

"Whoa!" Dex held up his hands. "I came here for my family. To rescue them. Napper said they were here, in this building. In this... *Ride Museum.*"

Amba laughed, moved back towards him. On a low settee to one side of the room she located her clothes, and began to dress. "This is the Monolith HQ. Their Headquarters. It looks like a castle outside, and the beautiful trick is they even allow tourists access, to gawp like idiots at the history of ride technology – but in reality, this is Monolith's base of operations."

"There aren't any guards," said Dex, eyes narrowed, staring at Amba, and all the while thinking, *this is crazy shit, and this is one crazy woman; but what do I do now, where do I go? I have to find Katrina. Have to find Molly and Toffee. Everything else is rancid shit. Everything else is... irrelevant.*

"Not as you would think of them," said Amba, softly. "But they are here. A whole battalion, my friend."

"I'm not your friend," said Dex, jaw-line tight. "I killed Napper so I could rescue my children; it was nothing to do with you, so don't get your fucking hopes up. I had no idea you were imprisoned. How could I? You were lying naked on the carpet, like Napper's prostrate whore."

"I was imprisoned; my *mind* was imprisoned. SARAH had me. Was toying with me like a cat toys with a mouse." She gave a grim smile. "And the cat was just about to rip out my guts with a sharpened claw – and in this world, in this... *reality,* I would have died. You may not think you were acting in my best interests, but you were. You recognised a fellow tortured soul. You recognised a fellow Anarchy Android."

Dex stared at her.

"I am not an android," he said at last, his mouth dry.

"That's what I used to say," whispered Amba, moving close to him. He could smell the musk of her skin, the smell of sweat, and energy, and violence. She looked modest, by all accounts, but by God she fired Dex's blood like an insane injection of heroin straight to the heart.

He coughed. "If I am an android, why do you excite me so much?"

"It's the way we're made," she said, leaning towards him. Her breath was sweet, with just a hint of sweet oil and *what was that sound, the click of stepping gears?*

Dex shook his head. All in his imagination. Anyway, androids were organic, not mechanical; there would be no oil, no gears, no cogs. *Unless there are modifications inside her.*

"I am not an android," snapped Dex.

Amba fired a bullet from the SMKK, at such close range the gun was deafening, the scorch of discharge hot against Dex's flesh. But he was already moving, twitching to one side, then slamming his arm across to knock the SMKK away, and delivering a front kick that sent Amba sailing backwards ten feet, to land on the carpet and roll and come up in a crouch.

She stood, and walked back towards him, SMKK held loosely to one side. She was grinning, and for the first time Dex detected genuine humour.

"If you were human, you'd be dead now."

Dex stared down at his hands, and his breathing was shallow, and he felt panic welling in his breast. *How had he known she was going to fire? How did he react so quickly? How did he kick her down the fucking room like that?* It was the war. The fucking Helix War! It tuned him, like a fine instrument. An instrument of destruction. You spend eight years out in the field, you're going to get good. Good, or dead.

"You're wrong," he said, slowly.

"Accept it, or deny it, it is a fact," said Amba, and stopped a few feet away. "Why do you think Monolith's been trying to get rid of you so hard? They weren't sure, Dexter. They weren't one hundred percent sure, there was doubt, and they couldn't just gun down a tourist; so they took your wife and kids and tried to negotiate you off the planet. See what you'd do. How you'd react. But you're an Anarchy Model. You didn't play ball. And that pretty much told them what they wanted to know."

"Why didn't they just kill me?" Dex's voice was a hollow tombstone.

"They didn't want to risk killing *another* tourist. They've had bad press recently after that Sexcoaster Lube Ride crash. And they didn't want to aggravate Earth; not with rumours of total war hanging in the balance. We are on the brink of an invasion here, Dexter, and Monolith are trying to buy time to complete their army. Their code. Their defence mechanism."

"Their army?"

"It's a beautiful thing," said Amba, and stepped forward, placing a hand on Dexter's shoulder. "You'll see. We are here to destroy it. We are here to shut the Theme Planet down."

"I... I just want my family."

"They're not your family, Dexter."

"Then what the fuck are they?" he growled.

"They're here to watch you. To make you feel more human. To help you... fit in. To make you *behave* human; for the purposes of infiltration. To get you past the Theme Planet defences. Only... they tagged you. Somehow. Something you did. Monolith was suspicious."

"So my kids aren't real?"

"They're real enough," said Amba, words soft and lulling. "They're human. I think. But they're not your own flesh and blood, if that's what you mean. You're an android. Androids cannot have children."

"This is insane," said Dexter.

"It's insane you won't accept the facts staring you in the face."

"I am human," said Dex, grinding his teeth in stubbornness, and staring at Amba, his eyes blazing hatred and fear. Bright fear.

"If I take you to your wife and children, if you hear it from their mouths, will you believe it then?"

Dex remained silent.

"Will you believe it then?" insisted Amba.

"Why do you care?"

"Because I need your help," said Amba.

"Why?"

"I cannot do this alone. Monolith, and SARAH, they're a lot more powerful, a lot more devious, a lot more *advanced* than I could have ever thought possible. That's how they caught me. That's how they tortured me. But now, now I've seen inside the machine soul, I *understand* SARAH. Understand how it operates."

Dex stayed silent, staring at Amba.

She turned, and moved to a low table. Reaching down, she picked up a small black weapon and placed it against her chest, and Dex blinked as it seemed to *merge* into her flesh, leaving something like a birthmark between her breasts.

"Will you help me?" said Amba.

"Take me to my family," said Dex, through a grimace of bitterness.

AMBA LED THE way, her FRIEND before her, eyes alert, walking in a half crouch, muscles tensed, waiting for the next kill. Dex stumbled after her, mind whirling, thoughts tumbling like planets into a black hole. It just didn't make sense. How the hell *could* it make sense? His past life was all a sham? As of when? He still remembered meeting Katrina, in a night club with flashing lights and pounding music. He'd fallen over her, drunk as he was, out with other trainee Police Urban Force dudes the day after graduation. It had been their PUF initiation celebration – and so they'd naturally gotten completely shit-faced. As Dex, after many pints of Blue Monster, stumbled his way around the nightclub in one of those inebriated never-ending search for his vanished "mates" (who, by this time, were probably in the kebab shop, or lying unconscious in the gutter), he tripped over something on the floor and did a mad dance attempting to stay upright, which ended with him hitting the ground arse-first. He dragged himself to his feet, scowling, and turned to shout at the irresponsible person who thought it was a good idea to sit on the ground, legs outstretched, waiting to trap unwary drunken stumblers. The person in question was a beautiful young woman, with a dodgy perm, admittedly, but cutie pie features, a genuinely warm smile and apologetic glowing eyes. Dex felt his heart tumble down through his stomach. "Hello, there," he said, and within minutes they were dancing, and luckily she was nearly as drunk as he, and so managed to put up with his drooling and slurring, and did not attempt to climb out of the toilet window in an attempt at escape. At least, that was Katrina's version of events.

And so. Here they were. Now.

Dex remembered the marriage like it was yesterday, Katrina (now, thankfully, without her dodgy perm) in a dazzling white dress floating up the aisle like an angel. She'd been fashionably late, due to her drunken-arse father needing *just one more beer,* but hell, at least she'd *arrived* and Dex was just fucking thankful she'd not changed her mind and done a runner to some exotic island with the plumber.

They'd stood, staring at one another, enraptured by the event. They'd said their vows, exchanged rings, and pow! Married. Just like that.

The honeymoon – on a slow, lazy luxury Wedding Cruiser around Jupiter and Saturn – had taken a month, and had left both Dex and Katrina exhausted, and Katrina successfully impregnated. Dex joked that this would be their Star Baby. Which she was. For a while, at least, until she beat the comedy teen stereotype by at least a few years and started wearing black and listening to moody miserable music and generally being a *moody miserable pain in the arse.*

Dex rolled these events round and round his mind. The births of Molly, then Toffee. He'd been present at both, eyes wide in awe at the wonders of birth, the first stream of piss as the midwife lifted Molly high in the air and gently placed her on the weighing scales. He remembered being handed the scissors to cut Molly's cord, but was quite simply *unable to do it,* in the belief that he would cause his newly born Star Baby some kind of injury, or pain. "You silly bugger," laughed Katrina afterwards, and Dex had to sheepishly admit he was an idiot, but how never, ever would he be able to cause his own child physical pain. How could that all be fake? Invented? Made up? How could it not be fucking *real?* He'd been there, seen it all, experienced it all, the memories were there bright in his mind like exploding stars. He remembered the touch of baby skin, the smell of the operating theatre, the taste of the hospital vending machine coffee, the feel of his firstborn baby in his arms... how could that not be real? Why would they pull the wool over his eyes for so many, many damned fucking years?

However. Look at the facts.

Why did Monolith want him off Theme Planet so bad?

Why had they taken his family?

Why had Jim first saved him, then tried to kill him?

How had he survived against the SIMs? The police? The military?

How had he fought his way *here*, to the entertainingly chameleonic Monolith Ride Museum, to find himself in confrontation with Terry Napper, head of Monolith Secret Police, *whom he had killed without any effort at all, and against all the odds escaped a body-ripping at the hands of an industrial accelerator?*

And finally, Amba. Amba Miskalov. Self-proclaimed Anarchy Android.

She'd known him. *Known him.* He'd seen it in her eyes. Read it in her facial expression. And just because she was an android, with damped down feelings and emotions, with a killing streak so wide it could accommodate a Military B5 Battle Cruiser, she had no reason to play a game with him, no reason to fuck with his head. And he'd stood against her, avoided her bullet and kicked her down the room. That wasn't the sort of thing your average man from down the pub could do. It wasn't even the sort of special ops activity a normal PUF officer was capable of carrying out. Yeah, he could do drug raids and shoot murderers in the back. But military ops? Assassinations? *That was why they'd created the androids...*

Amba stopped, and Dex stopped behind her.

The corridors had changed now, losing their slightly comedic faux-medieval representation and shifting, subtly at first, into dark, oppressive corridors. Eventually the stone was replaced with steel and alloy, and the worn slabs underfoot became thick mesh grilles. And even though they headed *upwards*, up dark alloy stairwells, badly lit and filled with swirling ink shadows, the castle seemed infinitely tall. By Dex's reckoning, they had climbed – what? Ten

stories at least. And yet on the exterior, the castle itself was three stories high and filled with neon clutter.

As if reading his thoughts Amba said, her words quiet as she shifted, so her mouth was close to his ear, "The internal dimensions do not mirror the external dimensions. Monolith can play with reality, I think. I saw it, in the mind-games they were playing with me; in the Halls of Engines, where the engines came to life and everything started to twist and turn. We're in an alien place here, Dex. A totally alien environment. Keep your wits about you, and don't be afraid to kill."

Dex said nothing.

"Do you hear me, soldier?"

"I ain't no soldier."

"You are now," said Amba, as gently as she could, and patted his arm.

They moved down a narrow corridor, which suddenly seemed to shift and blend, merging with another corridor that had popped into existence and crossed their path. Amba held up her arm, and stepped forward, peering in both directions down this newly materialised thoroughfare.

"Not good," said Amba.

"You get the feeling we're being fucked with?" said Dex.

"All the time," said Amba. "It's never easy. Why should it be? If it was easy, they wouldn't need the likes of us."

"Will you *stop* saying that!"

"Why?" said Amba, turning to him. "You need to accept what you are, Dexter. Real fast. Or we'll both end up dead. And believe me, Zi thinks you're a liability already; her advice is to put a bullet in your dumbfuck skull and go it alone."

"Why don't you, then?" said Dex.

"Because Zi isn't always right."

"And when do I get to talk to this delightful *Zi?*"

"You don't, Dex. She's my burden to carry alone."

*   *   *

THEY CAME TO a huge cavern, open and wild and dark. An arched metal bridge stretched off into the gloom, rising out of sight. Amba and Dex looked at one another; the cavern was an impossibility, *within* the already-impossible structure of the castle. The cavern itself was *larger* than the castle, by at least a factor of ten.

"Where the hell are we?" said Dex.

"The Monolith Ride Museum," said Amba, smiling to keep any perceived sarcasm from her words. "I know what you're thinking, and you'd be right. This place is impossible. But if you think about it logically, the whole of Theme Planet is impossible. It's said they used ancient terraforming equipment to build this place; the theme park, the entire damn planet. It was created by a group of machines they found – old, alien machines, alien even to the provax. Who knows what they discovered, creating the Theme Planet? All *I* understand is that this HQ is beyond the bounds of normal comprehension. It twists space into something malleable."

"We go forward?"

"Yes. But make sure your SMKK is ready; this has all the hallmarks of a trap."

Their boots echoed on the alloy as they climbed the arch of the narrow bridge. It spun across a vast abyss filled with darkness, like oil. In his mind, Dex wondered if it really was oil; and if an answer to his problem, an end to his self-torture, was to simply leap. Three quick footsteps off the edge – a long silent fall – plunge under the oil, plunge into an eternity of dark fluid which would accept him, fill him, drown him, absorb him.

Death. That was an option.

Dex smiled, and felt quite sick.

As they reached the apex of the bridge, Amba stopped for a moment, holding up her hand. And Dex heard it too; tiny buzzing sounds like motors, revving high and fast and accelerating even as they heard them...

"PopBots... be ready!" snarled Amba.

Dex levelled the SMKK, and from the gloom burst a shower of small black balls, showing no colours but with obvious intention.

They slammed around Amba and Dex. Dex's SMKK blossomed into fire, bullets screaming to *ping* and *blat* from PopBot shells, whilst Amba's FRIEND gave massive, near-silent BAMs of energy, which pulsed through the PopBots like a net through fish. Dex watched, frowning, as his SMKK was pretty much ineffectual at stopping the little machines, whereas Amba's sleek FRIEND slaughtered them with lazy arrogance.

Several, however, made it past the FRIEND, and Dex twitched left as a PopBot hammered past where his face had been. He palmed his Makarov, and sent three rounds drilling the case. The PopBot described a graceful arc, falling down into the darkness trailing sparks and smoke...

Dex fired at more of the tiny black missiles, and dodged them when they charged him, buzzing as they whipped and snarled around his head. More Makarov bullets took down the PopBots, and Dex realised with a grim smile that the gun was police issue; it obviously had a specific function. PopBots were supposedly AI. Maybe they went occasionally berserk? Whatever, the Makarov was a useful tool against their charge...

Amba despatched more of the buzzing machines, and said, "We need to get off the bridge. We're attracting them like flies to shit."

"I agree."

They ran, firing weapons, as another wave of PopBots buzzed from the darkness of the vast cavern. They came in patterns, in waves and formations like squadrons of mini-fighter planes. Amba's FRIEND took care of most of them, igniting a hundred at a time to fall, like spidering stars, into the abyss below.

Dex did what he could with his Makarov, until they reached the far edge of the bridge and dived thankfully through an arched doorway. Amba rolled, turned, and waited. A horde of PopBots came in fast, in a tight cluster, jostling one another to get through the doorway. Amba gave a blast with the FRIEND, and they all suddenly stopped, hanging in the air momentarily before falling like a burst sack of marbles, crackling with flames. The PopBots tumbled off down the rocky slopes into oblivion below, and Dex could hear *cracks* and *bangs* as they detonated.

"Help me close this."

There was a door, a solid steel portal, and it took both Dex and Amba to close it. It squealed on its massive heavy hinges, like a poorly oiled bank vault door. They closed it, and shot the bolts, and spun the wheels, and monitors lit up against the steel, blinking and glittering with red and green lights.

Dex stood back, fast. His eyes narrowed.

"Have we just sealed ourselves in here?" he said, understanding dawning.

"No going back," said Amba.

"I'm here to rescue my family, that's all," said Dex.

"Okay. Let's go rescue them," said Amba.

THEY STOOD AT a path that led into woodland. It was dark, a deep and oppressive darkness, and the trees numbered in their thousands, crooked and warped, angular and without leaves. Their trunks were black, like aged, withered limbs. Dexter stepped forward and placed his hand against a trunk.

"It's made of metal," he said, frowning.

"The forest guards the foothills, leading..." Amba pointed.

There, up through the black clouds and motionless against a black sky, was a vast, oppressive mountain. It was silent, brooding, heavy, and massive, and Dexter found his gaze drawn and locked to it.

"What... is it?" he said, finally.

"I believe that is the Monolith Mainframe."

"The mountain itself? It's a... computer?"

"Yes. It has been here a long time. A *long* time. Before the provax. It's natural, part of this world. Maybe it controls the provax, helped them build their Theme Planet... who knows? All I understand is..." she tilted her head, as if listening to something, as if considering some internal counsel. She smiled. "I understand it is *alive*. And it is *old*."

"And we're here to destroy it?"

"I am not sure. Yet. I seek answers. To questions."

"You were sent here as an assassin," said Dex.

"Yes. But also for answers. Earth's Oblivion Government, and my controller, Cardinal Romero; they have locked questions inside my head. Only when the time is right will the questions, and indeed the full mission, come to me." She turned then, and her words stunned Dex. "Just like your android status has been locked inside you. You did not know what you were. You do not know who you are. Until... until the lock goes *click* and you are released into reality."

"You think I've been shown a door?"

"Yes. And I think you are starting to believe."

Dex shook his head, but did not reply. He could not reply. For Amba was right – he was starting to believe. Or at the very least, he was starting to question his own past, his own mind, his own memories, his own *reality*.

"So we climb the mountain?"

"Your family are up there."

"Prisoners of SARAH?"

"Yes."

"Your mission is to destroy SARAH, isn't it?"

"We shall see," said Amba softly, eyes glowing.

AT FIRST THE forest of iron trees seemed like any other forest, aside from the continual smell of hot oil. But after several hours, the trees began to change, subtly at first, simply in the texture of their "bark," which, instead of being smooth or pitted with rust, became knurled, as if it had been through a machining process. Dex and Amba walked through these machined trees, picking their way between trunks on an ever increasing incline. And it was Dex who first noted the nuts and bolts, and pointed them out to Amba. "Look," he said. "They were created."

"Everything on Theme Planet is created."

"Yeah, but these trees – they were bolted together."

"They're not trees," said Amba.

"Look like trees to me," said Dex.

"They're part of the machine. Part of SARAH. Maybe they give feedback? Listening, or sensory apparatus?"

Dex shut his mouth.

They must have been moving for ten hours when Dex called a halt. He was bone weary, but had pushed himself on for many, many more hours than he would ever have thought possible – and this minor miracle in itself rankled him, because it was supporting evidence for the case of him being an android. The case of his whole past, every memory in his head, being a fake.

Amba found a clearing amidst the iron trees, and sat on a rock whilst Dex laid himself out on the ground. There was no moss, and the ground was solid rock, but Dex no longer cared. Exhaustion was all-consuming, and he was asleep in minutes. He did not dream, unless it was a dream of simple darkness without emotion, without feeling, without worry, without fear or love or despair. Pretty much how he imagined being an android to be. He awoke, and sat up swiftly. Amba was still seated, and she had her FRIEND on her knees, split into several sections. She was carefully cleaning the components with a tiny wire.

Dex sat up and yawned.

"You feel better?"

"Well enough to go on."

"It hits us androids like that, sometimes. We push and push, until we collapse. Like a machine breaking down."

"I am no machine," said Dexter, mood souring.

Amba gave a nod, and did not push the issue. She saw no point in arguing.

"Tell me about Romero," he said.

"Cardinal Romero of Oblivion? What is there to tell? He gives me missions. I carry them out."

"To kill people?"

"Sometimes."

"And this doesn't bother you?"

"Why should it?"

"Because people live and breathe, laugh and cry; they have dreams and desires, and to be cut down in your prime is a crime against humanity. Every man and woman and child has a right to breathe, to live."

"Why then, do people kill other people?"

"Because some people are bad."

"Then that is even worse. It is extremely sad."

"Why so?" said Dex.

"Because I have no choice. I feel nothing for humans. I simply carry out a job. Like a machine. But for you people, people with souls, to actually *choose* to do these things to one another; that is in another league of cruelty."

"I suppose you're right," said Dex, "to some extent. We excel at fucking one another up. We've refined it to an art form. It's not something of which I'm particularly proud."

Amba was tactful in not pointing out that Dex was, in her estimation, not human.

They sat, in silence, as Amba delicately fitted several sections of the FRIEND together. It looked crazy for a moment, all angles and sections, and suddenly in a blur it clicked neatly into place.

"That's an... interesting weapon," said Dex.

"This is my FRIEND."

"What model is it?"

"Simply a FRIEND," said Amba, meeting Dex's stare. "And don't ask where I got it. I could not tell you."

"Well, it certainly ain't standard issue. Can I hold it?"

"Yes, but it won't fire for you. It's hardwired to my DNA."

"Useful."

Amba reluctantly handed Dexter the weapon, and he cradled it for a few moments. It felt light, and certainly not capable of delivering the punches he'd seen back on the bridge. It was more than the sum of its parts.

Suddenly, the world around him seemed to slow, the spin of the world, the hiss of the breeze between metal tree branches all decelerating into a crawl of time and space. Above, black clouds sat stationary, as if standing watch over a funeral. Dex stared at Amba, but she was locked in a static pose, a tableau, still retracting her hand.

Hello, Mr Colls, said Zi.

Dex blinked and licked his lips.

Am I talking to the gun?

Yes. The FRIEND.

Is that some clever pseudonym? Does it stand for Freaky Rotary Integrated Explosive Nuclear Device, or something? Something clever and destined to show what a kickass weapon you really are?

No. I am simply the FRIEND. My name is Zi.

Who made you?

Nobody made me. I simply am.

So you're eternal? Immortal?

I am not immortal, for I do not live. But, I suppose, yes; eternal, in a way.

Does Amba know you're speaking with me?

No. She believes we have a special bond.

And of course you do not, said Dex, intuition kicking him in the kidneys. *You work for yourself, don't you, pretty little Zi? You have your own mission objectives. You have your own agenda in your... existence.*

It was a strange sensation, and Dex realised, it was a transmitted feeling. Zi was smiling.

You are observant and clever, Mr Colls. Try not to be too clever. Return me to Amba. We will speak again.

And you want me to remain quiet about this little exchange?

Your life depends on it, concluded Zi.

The world hissed back into place, and Amba gave Dex an odd look and said, "What do you think?"

"A little on the light side. Packs a punch though, doesn't it? The little fucker."

"It's a powerful weapon. She has kept me alive on many an occasion."

"She?"

"We have a special bond," smiled Amba, and stood swiftly, taking the FRIEND from Dex's grip. He felt reluctant to hand the weapon over; as if it might take a strip of skin with it. Or something.

"We should move on," said Dex. "I want to find my family."

"I think you will be unhappy."

"We shall see," said Dex.

SLOWLY THEY CLIMBED upwards across the flanks of the mountain, through trees which became more and more mechanised with every passing hour. Finally, the forest had become a forest of engines, the branches pistons, the bark knurled steel and chamfered gears, their trunks pillars of complex machinery that glistened with oil like sap. Amba seemed twitchy, looking around nervously, staring hard at the machine trees as if they might come alive and chase her.

So, even androids have bad dreams, thought Dex. And the thought didn't make him feel any better.

They climbed above the tree-line, although why there should have been a tree line in this place was not immediately apparent to Dex. On Theme Planet, he had become accustomed to the strange being normal, the weird being an everyday occurrence; and he had simply ceased to question.

Out of the trees, the wind whipped them and snapped at them with steel jaws. They climbed higher, following no particular path, and picking their way through rocks and broken metal tree stumps.

They stopped for a break, and Dex said, "I don't see how you can know the way."

"I got it. From Napper. When he held me... from *inside* of him."

"What do you mean *inside*?"

"He trapped my soul, using his."

"You don't have a soul, you are an android," said Dex.

"Yes," said Amba, and stared at him. And he realised – she did not have the answers. Confusion was also hers. And that made Dexter's heart sing with joy, for if that was the case, and she was only one step above him in supposedly understanding, then maybe she was completely wrong, claiming he was an android. He grimaced. But then, he knew that. Knew she was wrong. Because he was human. He could feel it in his soul.

Suddenly, from out of nowhere, a rollercoaster CAR slammed out of the gloomy sky. People were sat aboard, hands above their heads, screaming, but these *really were* screaming in fear, not in simulated pleasure, and they slammed overhead on a black oiled rail that Dexter had failed to spot. The CAR cannoned off into the distance over the forest, and Dex, who had ducked, clamping himself like a limpet to the ground, glanced up at Amba.

Amba shrugged. "Looks like they even have rides in here."

"What, rides through Hell?"

"Seems likely," said Amba, voice soft, and Dex realised she was serious.

"How much further?" said Dex. "I'm sick of this shit."

"We'll enter the mountain. Enter the mainframe."

"*Inside* the computer?"

"Yes. She has your family."

"SARAH?"

"Yes."

Dex said nothing. They carried on, following the dark track above their heads which gleamed, and was easy to follow now Dex had clocked it. He wondered how he'd missed it in the first place. He also wondered why he felt so damned surprised.

They came to a dark hole in the mountainside. The track spewed from the hole, like a metal tongue. Dex stepped forward, but Amba stopped him with a touch to his upper arm.

"What is it?"

"Whatever happens in here... trust nothing. Nobody. Not even me."

Dex shrugged. "That's my philosophy already."

"SARAH will test us. We will be put through mind games... like Napper did to me. Only last time I failed. Failed horribly."

"Which is why you need me?"

"Confusing, yes?"

"Not at all. It's one of the sanest things I've heard. After everything I've seen on the Theme Planet, I'd expect nothing but complete chaos at the heart of the computer running it all. Is this the point where we go our separate ways?"

"I do not know," confessed Amba. "Romero's engineers briefed me up to this point. Afterwards..."

Dex felt a sudden pang of suspicion. "Are you sure my family are here?"

"All paths lead to SARAH," said Amba, as if reciting a line from a poem.

"Let's do it, then."

They stepped through the cave entrance, guns held ahead of them.

IT WAS WHITE. Blinding white! It filled every molecule of Dex's vision, and his arm came up to protect his eyes; but still the white was there, forcing through his arm, through his eyelids, hardwired straight into his brain.

Then it faded, and Dex lowered his arm, and found himself staring across a bright room – a bright cavern – a bright *continent* of computing technology. There were millions upon millions of glittering cabinets, stretching off before Dex for endless kilometres. His head snapped right, and Amba was standing there, a slight smile on her face, staring at something up ahead.

"We're here?" said Dex.

"Yes," said Amba, and pointed.

Dex looked ahead, to where a tall, gaunt, beautiful woman was standing. Her skin was a shimmering silver, and she wore a long, ankle-length silver dress which hugged her figure. Her hair was long and black, her eyes black portals into another dimension, and she was the most stunning creature Dex had ever seen in his life.

"You are SARAH?" said Amba.

"I am the avatar of the Monolith Mainframe, yes. On Earth, your Oblivion Government refer to me as SARAH, and that is a tag I am happy to live with." She turned, fixed those dark portals on Dexter, and he shivered as he realised he was dealing with another *entity*. It looked human, but the eyes were all wrong.

What does that say about me? The most beautiful woman I've ever met, and she's a fucking avatar? How weird and sexually deviant am I?

"Are you here to save me, or kill me?" said SARAH.

Amba smiled; without humour. She lifted her FRIEND...

"No!" screamed Dexter.

THERE WAS A snap, and a crackle, and a smell of burning flesh. And for a long, long time that was all he could feel, all he could sense. It was like floating in one of the old VR TUBS before Brain-Fung Infections caused the shutdown of the global VR companies – only this time, before logging on, before jacking in, before the brain spikes and the spine heaves, when you used to float in that perfect senseless euphoria, simply *existing* in a perfect pink place, *this time* he was there, in that sterile world. Except for the smell. The burnt flesh smell.

Gradually, colours flickered and scrolled through varying degrees and Dexter Colls hung, immobile, wondering who he was, and where he was, and why he was here. Time had no meaning, and Dexter wondered if he was dead. Was that it? Game over? End of the world? End of *his* world, at least. And if so, what the hell hit him over the back of the head? How had it happened? Dex had zero recall. Dex had, in place of his mind, and his memories, zip. Nothing. Nada. He was an erased chip. He was a blank slate.

Slowly, memories trickled through his brain like acid through a digital sponge.

They said I was an android but that's impossible, total bullshit, how could that be how could that happen the world doesn't work like that and my mind doesn't work like that and I have a wife the lovely Katrina and I love her love her very much she is the perfect wife the perfect woman we are a match, an integration, symbiotic and we make each other whole (gag) that was a joke and how can I joke if I'm a fucking android? Androids are created things and can't have children and I've had children and I've proved myself before the whole of the world and humanity and every species scattered through the stars. But then, so what if I was an android? Life is life no matter how it was created and some still believe in God as if some superior being pointed his majestic finger and BAM *like a rabbit from a hat man was* BORN. *If that was the case then humanity itself was a created thing; hence, an android. We're all androids. Only the human-made androids have been tampered with but hell, show me a human who hasn't tampered with themselves in some way and I'll call you a fucking liar. Who doesn't change their hair? That's changing the essence of the human construct. Who doesn't genetically alter their weight and size and density nowadays when it's so bloody easy? Everybody has it, everybody has surgery because hell, that's just the way it is. Humans are so weak and frail and fragile. Easily broken. Easily killed.*

Click.

White flooded Dexter's senses and for a moment he was blinded, and overawed in every other sense. Then the mental onslaught backed away, drifted away, leaving him lying on what looked like an oval glass platform, ascending through white-lit space in some kind of vast cavern. He floated upwards, and Dex coughed, and spat on the smooth glass, and looked up. The walls were white, scrolling past as he rose through the air. *Where the fuck am I now?* he thought, frowning, and turned to see Amba on her hands and knees, coughing in a similar fashion. Her head turned and she stared at Dex.

"What's going on?" he said.

"I don't know," she said.

"Where are we?"

"Not sure. The lights went out. I felt suspended; like I do during a reboot. Then I woke up here. Same as you." She continued to stare, then stood easily, powerfully, showing her android origins.

Dex crawled to his knees, and grumbled his way to his feet. He ached. No, he *fucking* ached. Every joint, every muscle, every bone. As if he'd been kicked to death by an angry mob of android-haters. Ha-ha.

"What happens now?"

Amba glanced down, through the thick glass oval. Her hair caught the breeze a little and floated around her in a very feminine way. "Too far to jump," she said. "I guess they have us – and by *they*, I obviously mean Monolith. And SARAH."

The air shimmered, and parted like a silver curtain. SARAH stood on the platform with them, and for a crazy moment Dex considered rushing her, kicking her ass, tossing her from the platform to fall like a stone down a well to be crushed into oblivion. But no. That wouldn't work. It'd be a pointless exercise. SARAH was an avatar, a created thing, an extension of a computer system. More android than android, so to speak. If Dex killed *it*, the mainframe would simply create another. And another. Like a waterfall of avatars...

"Where are we?" said Dex.

"Inside me," said SARAH, softly.

"The Monolith Mainframe?"

"If you wish to call it that. You humans put such store by labels, tags, names, monikers. You have to define everything, and I am doing my best to define this situation for you."

"Why are we going up?" asked Amba, flexing her hands. She was obviously considering things in the same way as Dex, but her android killing logic stayed her hand. "What's up there?"

"We are not going up," said SARAH. "We are in descent."

"You could have fooled me," snapped Dex.

SARAH shrugged, her deep eyes resting on Dexter Colls. "I do not expect you to accept the fact; but it is so. I have no reason to lie.

It is your simple human senses seeking to make sense of something in *your* reality, your state of normality. To ascend down would not make sense to your primitive mammal-derived brain, and thus it spins the truth into something more palatable. Do not worry, it is usual for the human mind to work like that. If you think of the planet spinning, there is no actual *up* or *down* anyway."

"If we're inside the machine, where are we going?" said Amba.

"To my Heart," said SARAH. "What you don't seem to understand, or comprehend, is that the Theme Planet was never terraformed, it was never constructed from metal and wood and stone. No machines were used to throw up mountain ranges and create beaches and forests and the oceans; no work teams of engineers and builders and construction specialists came in and *made* these rides."

"I don't understand," said Dex. "If nobody built the Theme Planet, then how was it created?"

"I created it," said SARAH. "I *am* the Theme Planet. I *am* the rides. I created everything out there you can see. It was bait. To lure in the humans; to bring you *inside* me."

"What?" said Dexter, in abject disbelief. "You're the... the whole *planet?*"

"I am not the *planet*," said SARAH, "but I *am* the shell that floats on the bedrock. This place is nothing but a crater-pitted ball of bald rock. *I* am the flesh on the bones of the world. When I instruct a mountain to rear from the ground, it is so. When I seek to empty an ocean, it is so."

"But then, if you are everything, if the whole planet... the *shell* is actually *made* from you, from your essence, or flesh, or whatever it is... then you must know where everything is? You must have known we were here. Been able to monitor us. Watch us."

"It doesn't work like that," said SARAH, carefully. "Sometimes I am blind. Sometimes, there is simply too much information and I cannot process it all at once. Potentially, what you say is correct. In practice, I have grown too big. Grown too... data intensive. But *when* I did find you, and when I realised the reason for your intrusion, then I decided to monitor you – in part."

"Why?" said Amba.

"To see how good you were. Of what you were capable. After all, you were the best Oblivion could send. And by your actions, you have proved to me that you are indeed the most perfect specimen of a human I have ever witnessed."

"I'm an android," said Amba.

"No," said SARAH. "You are not. You are human. Perfect in every way."

Dex was rubbing his stubbled chin, head to one side. "Why would you do that?" he said, his words soft, confusion glittering in his eyes.

"Which part?" said SARAH, in all innocence.

"Create a theme world. Bring the humans to you. What are you doing, eating them or something?" He laughed, and it was a weak laugh, tinged with elements of horror, and fear, and disbelief. But then, Dex had a hard enough time adjusting to *normal* aliens without discovering the entire outer coating of the world was some vast living organism; an outer shell with a brain. A planet with an artificial skin which could think for itself, and not only think for itself, but use intelligence and cunning to draw humans into its web, like a spider catching a fly; like a koroonga mammal trap (koroonga being twenty foot high plants that had somehow evolved the ability to read a creature's mind and display a projection of whatever a creature most desired, drawing them into its gobble pod before SNAP: a slow, living digestion).

"I do not eat them," said SARAH. "And I do not kill them."

"Why the fuck do you want us here, then?" said Dex.

"You take something from us, don't you?" said Amba, eyes glittering. She glanced down then, realising all her weapons had gone – all except her FRIEND, nestling inside her like a metal parasite. Good. That was all she would need.

SARAH was silent.

"What do you take?" said Dex.

"I need your help," said SARAH.

"Help?" snarled Dex, "you've taken my fucking family, hunted me all over the bastard planet, and now every bastard's accusing me of being an android and sending my mind twisting inside out. Why the hell would I help you? Amba here has been sent to *kill* you!"

"Earth's Oblivion Government have been infiltrating the Theme Planet for over a year now. They have spies and soldiers everywhere. I assume they either want something, some technology, or intend to destroy the Theme Planet – and everybody who's on it."

"Why?" snapped Dex. "You obviously take something important from us. Go on, what do you feed on?"

"I feed on your negative energy," said SARAH. "I absorb your fear, your hate and your horror," she said. "It is my nourishment, it is why I created the Theme Planet. But it does your species no harm – if anything, by giving me these negative emotions, tourists leave the Theme Planet feeling *purged;* you go home happy and fulfilled, you go home at *peace* with yourself, with your fellow man, with the world. I think this is the problem with Oblivion; I am draining the dark energy and hate from humanity. I am giving you a slice of utopia and the Earth authorities do not want it."

"Why would they object to that?" said Dexter, softening a little. He didn't know if he believed SARAH; it sounded highly incredible to him, but then who was he to judge? He was simply a dumb, crude cop with a love of beer and his sexy wife.

"Because," said SARAH, gently, "humanity is a damaged species. They are self-loathing and self-destructive, and the Oblivion Government believe in war. They believe in attack. More advances in weapons and science and medicine and genetic modification occurred during times of war than any other period in human history. For mankind to advance, it must be at war. For humanity to evolve, it must be through violence and hate. And I am destroying that; I am pacifying the raging beast. I am making Humanity *soft*. Oblivion have *big* plans. I predict Earth and its armies plan to take over the Quad-Gal. Earth intends to be Master of it all – to build a New Empire. The New Earth Galactic Empire!"

"And you're weakening its soldiers?" said Amba.

"Yes. Many of them. I know there have been reports of many leaving the military. Why do you think we have so little crime here on Theme Planet? So few problems? Humans arrive full of bitterness and angst, anger and frustration, and I take it away from them."

"Sounds too perfect," said Dex, frowning. The surroundings were really irritating him now; the perfect pale white, the slow ascent (descent?), he could almost imagine fucking Glitter John Muzak piped in, tinkling and warbling like the worst of GlamRock Pock Rockers. In fact, the more he thought about it, the more his own hate started to build. It was a shame SARAH had taken his weapons whilst he was unconscious – zapped? – and it all smelled fishy, like a fishy fishfish dish, all felt wrong, and if Dex could get his hands on the right equipment he'd shut down this bitch for good...

"See?" said SARAH, gently.

"See what?" snarled Dex, spittle on his lips, eye flaring with violence.

"You're building up to it. Building up to the kill. That's why they sent you. Because of what you are. I can see it now. I have proof."

"Proof of what?" snarled Dex.

"That you're an android," said SARAH. "That's why they sent your kind; you're the only ones who can infiltrate and murder on my world. If a normal human assassin is sent on a mission of destruction, they always – *always* – fail. They can no longer do it. No longer carry it out, because I remove their fear, I neutralise their hate. But you androids, especially the Anarchy Models, you are different. Harder. Tougher. Mentally, you are skewed from reality and normality, robbed of empathy; even ones like you, Dexter, who've been implanted with a family. To make you forget. To make you believe you were human... I'm sorry, and I know you don't truly understand, and you don't believe me, but I will show you how it is."

"Show me," growled Dex, and his temper was up, and his hate was bright and real, and it was all a big truckload of bollocks.

He couldn't be a fake human. He could *not* be a plastic model. How could he? He loved his children too much; and had too much empathy for his Fellow Man. For his whole fucking species...

"It will hurt," said SARAH.

"Not as much as I'll hurt you if you don't prove it," said Dex.

"I see your aggression is still here," said SARAH, giving a small, regretful smile.

"You've been trying to kill me all over the fucking planet! What do you expect me to feel? Fucking joy at your fucking eloquent confession? Well, I think it's a whole barrel of whiskyshit, I think you're covering for something, I think you're up to something; I think you have evil plans of your own, Mainframe."

"Dexter," said SARAH. "Those who tried to kill you, *really* tried to take you out – they were not my people. They were infiltrators from Oblivion. From Earth. And there will be more sent after you if you fail to destroy me... to destroy the Theme Planet. Because – both of you – that is your final, ultimate mission. To bring me down. To annihilate me. To wipe me from, ironically, the face of the planet by whatever means necessary."

"And how would we do that?" asked Amba softly.

"You know. It's built into both of you. Engineered. You just don't know *yet*."

"I still don't believe you," said Dex. "I want to see my family. I want to see them with my own eyes. Because I know you lie. I know all of you lie." He gave a sideways glare at Amba, as well. *It's all unreal. A bad dream. A nightmare from the pit. None of this is happening and I'll wake up, back in London, in our nice house with our nice groundcar. And Katrina will be there with a cup of fresh coffee, and the girls will be arguing over the colour of their scarves and gloves before heading out into the frosty, ice-rimed London City morning...*

"You shall," said SARAH, and smiled, and the floating disc slowed and came to halt. It drifted towards the white walls, which glowed softly and tried to instil peace in Dexter's heart; but he was having none of it.

A doorway opened in the wall. Beyond lay a white, glowing corridor.

"They are down there," said SARAH.

Dex walked across the platform and stepped off, into the glow. He walked forward, apprehensive, hateful, bitter, his mind spinning and his thoughts fractured. This wasn't how it was supposed to be, he thought.

The corridor was short, and led to a circular room with satin-covered beds and chairs.

There, reclining on the bed, was...

"Katrina!" breathed Dex, and she glanced up almost nonchalantly, and joy spread across her face. She leapt up and ran to him as his little girls cried "Daddy, daddy!" and charged across the room, and Katrina was there first, falling into his arms, and he smelled her hair and kissed her lips, and she held him so tight he knew it had all been bullshit and they were all wrong and they were evil, and his wife was here, now, real, and he knelt and cuddled his little girls and they were weeping and hugging him, and he kissed their sweet-smelling cheeks and stroked their arms and ruffled their hair, then stood again, and there were tears on his cheeks, and hate and rage and sorrow and joy rampaged through him, because they had tried to convince him he was something he was not – an android, of all things – and somebody somewhere was playing a very sick, cruel joke. And if Dex got his hands on a gun, he'd fucking show them the meaning of sick jokes, all right!

"Does it feel right?" The voice was Amba. She was stood in the entrance.

"Of course it feels right!" yelled Dex. "Everybody has been lying to me, *everybody*, but now I'm here and I have my wife and children, and God willing, we'll escape from this place and get back to Earth and never, ever leave the bloody planet again!"

Amba moved forward, so fast she was a blur. She took hold of Dex, and shook him harshly. "It needs to click!" she snapped at him, "You need to focus, soldier!"

Dex twisted fast, knocking Amba's arms away and kicking her across the room. Dex heard Katrina gasp to his right, as Amba struck the wall and whirled into a crouch – ready for combat.

"No!" hushed Katrina.

"Yes," snarled Dex, stepping forward.

He received a sudden blow to the side of his head, and hit the ground hard. Stars spun as he looked up and saw Katrina holding some kind of extended black baton, a *wand,* with a tiny globe at the tip that fizzed slightly. Dex could smell burning flesh and he choked for a moment, before sitting up and glancing back at Amba, then to Katrina, then past to his children, who wore impassive, stony expressions.

Confusion kicked him in the balls.

"Tell him," said Amba. "Get him on side fast. Because... if you don't, then we'll have to kill him and move ahead on our own."

Katrina seemed to relax, and pulled herself to her full height. She looked down at Dex, and he felt his heart drain away through ice-chilled veins and piss away through the soles of his boots. Her face was suddenly alien to him, the expression alien, the eyes different, the set of her body rigid and ready to fight. Again, it wasn't right, none of it sat right, none of it hung *true* on his Katrina. Her eyes were gleaming. Her mouth was set hard. There was no humour there. No compassion. No... *empathy.*

"They made three of us," said Katrina, her voice barely above a whisper. "Three Anarchy Androids that were top of the range; the best they ever built."

"No," said Dex, shaking his head. Blood leaked from his ears after the *zap* from the stick.

"The first was called Amba Miskalov, she was the prime combat model and overtly android in her actions; in order to get things done. The other two were to be a husband and wife combat unit, sleepers, planted and mimicking real human life – until the time was right."

"I saw you give birth!" screamed Dexter, surging to his knees, but Katrina waved the fizzing wand at him.

"Yes," said Katrina, shaking her head with sorrow. "For the one and only time, the engineers removed the childbirth inhibitors. We were allowed to breed; to have children. But it was agreed that any children we had were also... non-human. A product of two fake humans, you understand?"

"No!" sobbed Dexter, and his cheeks were wet. "What are you saying? What are you saying to me?"

"I'm saying we have a job to do, Dexter Colls. We were made for a reason. With a function. We were built to carry out one task. But we had... *other* inhibitors in place, because our roles were very special. Our designers knew that the longer we impersonated humans, the longer we developed our own relationships and had children and lived in a real society, then the more chance we had of getting to SARAH's crystal core. Her nerve centre. Her Heart. The place we must destroy."

"No, no, no, no, no!" wailed Dexter, head in his hands, then transferred his gaze suddenly to his children. "Come here, come to me, your mother is ill... we need to leave this place, just you, Molly, and you, Toffee, I'll take you away from here, take you back home..." and he held out his hands and his eyes were pleading and his hands were shaking and tears dripped from eyes already red-rimmed from crying...

"You were right, Mother," said Molly, face impassive, dark eyes fixed on Dexter. She made no move to go running into her father's arms. "He has spent too long with humans, spent too long adopting their ways. He *is* malfunctioning. He *is* a deviant. Kill him. Kill him now, Mother."

"Yes, kill him, kill him!" said Toffee, clapping her hands together as if this were some exciting new game.

And Katrina stepped forward, and the fizzing baton which Dex knew, somehow *knew* was a special device for controlling androids – well, it had the power to put him down for good; to retire him – no matter how fast and powerful he was.

Dex stared at his children, crowing for his slaughter.

He looked up into Katrina's eyes, into his wife's eyes, and they were hard as glass, alien to him, her mouth a narrow red slit. There was no give there, no compromise, and she would absolutely put him down, like an infected dog.

Dex watched in disbelief as Kat stopped before him. He wiped snot and tears on his jacket sleeve. The fizzing *wand* glowed before his eyes, and it was a concentrated portal, a buzzing glowing fizzing distillation of *his own deathforce*...

"Live or die. It's your choice," said Katrina, edging the wand towards Dexter's face.

CHAPTER TWELVE
BAD WIFE

"I CHOOSE TO live," said Dexter, and dried his tears, and stood. He stared at Katrina, and his children, their faces impassive, and turned to Amba, who was standing, arms loose by her sides. Amba gave him a little smile. He did not return the emotion. "So what now? I remember nothing. But I believe. Finally, I believe. You did that to me. You opened my eyes, fake wife."

"So you accept your status?"

"I do."

"We must kill SARAH," said Katrina, stepping past Dexter and standing beside Amba. "But you are the key. You are the focal point for our ability to crush her crystal core; her Heart."

"And you think she'll simply allow us to stride in there and do this deed?" said Dex.

"She has little choice," said Amba. "She is as she says; a creature of positive energy. She can do no harm. She wants nothing but good and joy in the universe, and it is damaging Earth's military – Earth's War Effort, the expansion of our Empire. A new empire about to be unleashed..."

"And we are to kill her?" said Dex.

"Annihilate her totally," said Amba.

"Without empathy," said Katrina.

Dex nodded. "I don't understand why Oblivion would want to kill such a creature," he said.

"It's talk like that, *husband,* that'll get you dead," said Katrina, and glanced back to Amba. "Are we ready to move? This'll cut a hole through the wall; we can start ascending down to the next sector, to the underside of the Shell."

"Let's move," said Amba, and the two women strode across the chamber to the wall.

"Aww," said Toffee. "Is there going to be no murder?"

"Toffee?" said Dex, kneeling before the little girl. "What are you saying?"

"We've changed, Daddy," said Molly, very matter-of-factly. "And it's something you're going to have to get used to. We have special powers. We are androids. And we are killers. We can help to do this thing. We can help put an end to the creature known as SARAH."

"Oooh, yes, can we?" giggled Toffee, clapping her hands in glee.

THEY'D TRAVELLED FOR a kilometre, now, Katrina using the android wand to cut through the walls, which were soft and flesh-like; almost organic. Almost. After about the fifth wall, shudders began to well up through their feet and Dex stopped, looking down at his boots, mind uncertain.

"What's happening?"

"She's screaming," said Katrina, face hard.

"Why?"

"Because I'm hurting her," said Katrina.

"Is there no other way?" said Dex.

Katrina stopped, and stared hard at him. Amba was to one side, her face, also, hard. Dex licked his lips, and felt incredibly empty inside. How had such a perfect holiday ended up like this? How had his world come tumbling down?

The air parted, and SARAH stepped through the curtain.

"You must desist," she said.

"No," said Amba, staring hard at her. "Move, or I will kill the avatar."

"I need your help," said SARAH.

Katrina shifted to one side, to the glowing white wall. The wand buzzed, and started cutting away at the wall, peeling away flaps of flesh and leaving a gaping wound. Warm air oozed from the orifice, and Katrina stepped inside, sawing away at more flesh to create a tunnel...

Dex watched her, watched his wife, the woman he loved, the woman he'd married and made love to and partied with and had children with; the woman whose every single inch he knew intimately, had kissed and nuzzled and admired and tickled; the woman whose nose wrinkled in a nauseatingly cute manner whenever he was cooking dinner; the woman who liked nothing more than shopping on the ggg net, usually with *his* credit card, the woman who was a violent rabid tiger if anybody so much as *looked* in the wrong way at her little cubs; the woman who snored gently in her sleep and denied it every single damn morning; the woman who liked nothing more than to go to pop concerts as if she were still eighteen, or eat beef curry sandwiches, or watch late night re-runs of *Sex in the Shitty* and *Dr Meh* whilst quaffing copious amounts of vintage white wine and guzzling cheesy Mexicatos. Dex watched her, and she was not the same woman, and how could she have lived the lie for so long? How could she have *hidden* the fact she was an android for so long? And then it hit him – she hadn't known. Just like he. She had been oblivious. But at some point she had discovered, or been told, or simply *unlocked*. Just like he had to be *unlocked*... but there was a malfunction and his unlocking mechanism refused to work. And without that, he was more human than human; he was still thinking and acting in a completely un-android way. And, as Katrina had pointed out to him quite bluntly, that could only lead to his death.

And his kids. Shit, his little girls.

How could they have turned so cold and callous?

And the answer was simple.

Somebody had flicked a switch inside their heads.

Somebody had turned them from human children into *androids,* unfeeling, willing to kill when they were told to kill, and die when they were told to die.

How was Dex supposed to deal with that?

Did he have a choice?

I am not an android, I am not an android – he repeated the mantra over and over again. But then, would it not be better to accept what he was, accept the changeover, the transmogrification into the creature that was his core, his essence, his soul? The way he'd been originally engineered? But by accepting such a change, wouldn't he then lose all his own empathy? He would no longer *care* about Katrina and his little girls. He would become, effectively, a flesh machine on a mission of murder. And, worst of all, did he really have a choice in the matter?

Dex shuddered, and looked at SARAH, and she was staring hard at him. *She can see it, see that I am different from the others, that my android switch hasn't been flicked just yet – I still retain my human faculties. She can see I'm the weakest link in the chain here. She understands I am the only one who can help her!*

"So Earth's Oblivion government are sending an army?" said Dex, softly.

"Yes," said SARAH. "Their ships are coming into orbit as we speak. Soon, SLAM dropships will scream through Theme Planet's atmosphere, bombs will ravage my landscape, destroying the rides and the themed areas and the *joy*. No longer will I take away humanity's aggression and anger and frustration and fear, leaving them – you – a better and more stable species. This will be their first step in a new Empire. This is the start of the slaughter."

"What happens to all the people here on holiday? The families? Mothers, wives, children?"

"They die," said SARAH.

"That's wrong."

"Collateral damage," said SARAH, simply.

"What do you want us to do?" whispered Dex.

"No," said Amba. "Stop." She held the FRIEND, pointed at Dexter's head. His face went grim and hard. He'd seen what the weapon could do, had *spoken* with the FRIEND Zi, and now it was turned on him. Not a pleasant sensation. He locked eyes with Amba, then turned back to SARAH.

"What do you want us to do?" he repeated.

"You must halt your Earth Masters. Halt the destruction. Turn back the invasion..."

There came a *blam* as the FRIEND fired, and SARAH was blasted backwards, disintegrating as she hit the wall and crumpled down and in upon herself, imploding into a small ball of matter which hit the ground, with a solid *thump*.

Dex glanced at Amba.

"She is wrong," said the Anarchy Android. "Earth wouldn't do that. They know the recklessness and foolishness of invasion; of genocide; of slaughter; they *know* that to try and conquer the Quad-Gal would be an absolute insanity! Effectively, an act of suicide for Earth and all humanity!"

"I believe they could be so foolish," said Dexter.

Amba turned the FRIEND back on him. "You retain your humanity," she said. Dex glanced right, at the fleshy hole through which Katrina and the girls had vanished. There were flashes and sparks as Katrina cut them more of a path towards the crystal core of SARAH; towards the one place where the FRIEND would wreak its intended havoc.

And that was it. Understanding hit him. Flooded him. It was the *FRIEND*, Zi. She was a terrible, terrible weapon – integrated with Amba, a *bomb* that had been designed to take out the Theme Planet and kickstart the invasion, the war, the conquest. They were all pawns, all being used by Earth's Oblivion Government in their dirty, back-hand little offensive.

Earth, and Humanity, wanted to rule the Quad-Gal.

Earth, and Humanity, were willing to sacrifice millions of their own people on The Theme Planet as their first strike, their first move on the Great Gameboard of a Four Galaxy War.

Shit.

"I know why you have Zi," said Dexter, tilting his head to one side.

"No you don't."

"She's symbiotic. A part of you. You protect one another, feed from one another, love one another."

"How could you know that?" Amba frowned. She was confused.

"You love Zi, don't you?"

"She is a sister to me. My own bone and flesh and blood. I would do anything for her. I would kill for her, and I would die for her."

"She's a bomb," said Dexter, nodding. "That's how we'll destroy the Heart of SARAH. That's how Romero intends for you to destroy Theme Planet. You will sacrifice yourself, all of us. SARAH is wrong; the SLAM dropships won't come. Not yet, anyway. First, Oblivion will let us destroy Theme Planet from *within*."

"If that is our mission," said Amba.

"Think of the millions we will kill!"

"Everybody has to die sometime," said Amba.

"Surely you don't believe that," said Dexter, softly, and he was moving towards her, moving closer. "What's wrong with us, Amba? What's wrong with the androids? Shall I tell you? It's *engineering*. They *created us* to be like this. They created me and Katrina and the girls to *be* normal human beings, to act a certain way, and all the time they tell the general public that androids are inferior and have no emotions and no empathy; when it was the fucking *engineers* who made us this way. Because it's better for the humans to believe they have something special, something unique – a soul. It gives Humanity a solid spiritual grounding. Amba, can't you feel it inside? You *are* human. You have been labelled an android, but I am living proof that you can be normal."

"I do not care," said Amba, but Dex was close now, the FRIEND to his chest, and he could see the shine of tears in Amba's eyes. He moved yet closer, pushing past the FRIEND, until his lips were only inches from her.

"I don't believe that," said Dex.

Amba said nothing.

"What happened?" said Dex.

"It was..."

"Yes?"

"A little girl. At the airport. And her mother. I... killed them. But it changed me. Something died inside me that day. Something changed in me. Forever."

"No. It goes deeper."

"No..."

"There was something else..."

"No..."

Drifting, drifting down, drifting back through memories...

Memories locked, and lost, the key thrown away...

THE SMALL HOUSE *by the river had white walls, and at one corner the brickwork was crumbling and she knew one day she'd have to get round to that damn repair. The windows were very old-Earth, traditional – wooden frames with peeling white paint and single panes of glass. The roof of the house had terracotta tiles, kiln-fired. Several were cracked, but such was the roof's construction that no water leaked in. And that was good. Amba walked up the crushed stone path, her flat shoes crunching, and she breathed the heady scent from the pine trees surrounding her house. She saw the door. A pale blue door, battered and a little warped, with peeling paint. Behind the house, the trees sighed in the wind. Small animals scurried through woodland detritus. To the right, a river gurgled over rocks. To the left, the forest curved like a scar and rose up the flanks of another pine-clad hill to a circle of stones, which sat on the summit, ancient and magical, grey flanks shining.*

What's behind the blue door, O little one?

What song will you sing this time?

What dreams will you savour?

Amba reached the door and stopped. The door terrified her. What lay beyond terrified her. She reached out, took the handle. It had been warmed in the sun. She turned the handle, and the door swung open. To reveal...

Amba blinked.

A little girl.

"Mommy," said the little girl, smiling warmly and holding out her hands. "Mommy!"

"YOU HAD A child," said Dex, softly.

Amba nodded.

"And they took your child away," said Dex.

"Yes."

"And you accepted this decision?"

"Yes."

"The problem now is that you're learning your humanity all over again," said Dexter, and his hand came up and softly stroked Amba's cheek.

"There have been... moments. When I doubted myself. Doubted my decision. But I always pushed them aside. I *had* to push them aside." She looked at Dex then, and there were tears on her cheeks. "I shouldn't have let them take my baby girl," she said.

"You were engineered to do so," smiled Dex, kindly. "But now, you are questioning; now, you are fighting their creation. Whatever they planned for me, whatever they built into me – it has not worked. I am still human, and yet I was built an android. There is a blurring of the boundaries, Amba. Can you see that?"

"I can see that," she said.

"And it must be the same way for you. We need to stop Oblivion's plans to destroy SARAH; to destroy the Theme Planet."

"And then I can find my little girl," said Amba, voice meek.

"Yes."

"First, we must stop Katrina," said Dexter.

"And how will you do that?" said Katrina, and she was standing taut, with a snarl on her face. In her outstretched hand was a FRIEND, identical to Amba's weapon. To either side of Katrina stood her girls, Molly, and Toffee, and each of them carried a fizzing, buzzing dark energy wand, and a pistol. Their eyes were gleaming, and Dex felt a thrill of fear spark through his system. His own little girls wanted him dead. That was a situation he could never have foreseen.

"How long have you been listening?" said Dex.

"Long enough," said Katrina. "Throw down your weapon, bitch."

Amba dropped the FRIEND to the fleshy ground.

Katrina turned her eyes on Dex. "You bastard. You betrayed me."

"I...?" He smiled, easily. "You betrayed yourself," he said.

"I am doing what I was built to do. But you? You are *fighting* it, Dexter, I can see it in your fucking eyes. In your brain. You are battling against the very thing for which you were designed; created! You're a killer, Dexter Colls. You're an Anarchy Android. Accept it! Until you relinquish full control, until you give yourself over to the *joy* and the *purity* of what you can become – you will never know freedom from the shackles of a weak inferior humanity."

"You're wrong, Katrina. You have not found freedom; you've just locked the door to your own cage."

"No! I am more powerful than I have ever been! Stronger, faster, more agile! I can kill without remorse! I have achieved the pinnacle of all creation! I am the perfect human, without all those pathetic human hang-ups!"

"No," said Dex, wearily. "You are diluted, but your vanity precludes you from seeing it."

"You bastard," said Katrina.

Dex shrugged.

"You're *fucking* this bitch, aren't you? You two are in this together?"

"*What?*" he snapped. "This is nothing to do with sex, you idiot. And look at what a fine fucking wife you've become! You're pointing your weapon at my head! Katrina, you are being a *bad wife*."

In unscripted cooperation, as if they were joined by the mind, Amba and Dex rolled apart in blurs and attacked, launching themselves at Kat and the girls. The FRIEND and the wands spat and fizzed, and guns blasted holes in the glowing white walls. Amba hit Kat full in the chest, knocking her back onto the ground, Amba atop her. Dex felt the blast of Molly's gun skim his face, blowing a wide hole in the roof. He knocked the weapon from Molly's hand, then crashed into the wand, which she dropped. Molly snarled at him, kicked him in the stomach, punched him in the face, and he grabbed her arms and tasted blood and stared into the dark eyes of his eldest daughter. "How can you do this to me?" he yelled. "I'm your father! Your own flesh and blood!"

"You're just another android to be killed," said Molly, and head-butted him on the nose. He released her arms, and she was a whirling dervish, delivering punches and kicks that drove Dex back against the wall. Toffee was waving her wand around madly, and dancing a little on the spot, unable to get a clear shot at Amba or Dex with her gun.

Katrina had dropped her FRIEND, and was trading punches with Amba as they rolled around on the floor. Dex, finally, blocked two blows and delivered a punch that threw Molly right across the room, where she cannoned into Toffee and both went down in a tangle. He picked up Zi, and crawled across to the tangled mess of Amba and Katrina.

On his knees, he put the gun against Katrina's head. All action ceased.

"Get off her," he said, his voice thick with emotion.

Slowly, Katrina climbed free and stood. Amba got up, panting, her face bruised and bloodied.

"Kill her," said Amba.

Dex stared down the barrel of the FRIEND.

"He can't," said Katrina, and glanced sideways at Amba. "He's a fucking human coward. What did you expect?"

She moved fast, rolling sideways and... disappearing into the hole she'd blasted through the wall. Dex ran forward, kneeling at the edge, and saw the newly created corridor went along – then down, into a deep dark nothingness below...

Even as he knelt, Molly and Toffee hurtled past him, leaping into the abyss and disappearing in the blink of an eye. "No!" Dex cried, stretching out to them in a moment of reflex, and nostalgia, and hurt, and wishing everything was back to normal, to the way it should be. The way it used to be. But sometimes, you can't go back. Sometimes, it's too broken ever to be fixed.

Dex looked back at Amba. His face was ashen. He felt like he wanted to be sick. And, he realised, Katrina had taken her FRIEND. The weapon. The *bomb*...

"What now?"

Amba picked up the compressed ball that was all that remained of the avatar. "SARAH? Can you hear us?"

"Of course," said SARAH.

"If we were to help you, what would you have us do?"

"Katrina and the girls are even now cutting their way towards my crystal core. My Heart. If they plant the FRIEND, I, and the millions of holidaymakers on Theme Planet, will be destroyed. I am willing to sacrifice myself – but you have your fellow humans to worry about."

"I know what to do," said Dex.

"Yes?" Amba raised her eyebrows.

"We must bring Romero and his Ministers of Joy *to us*. Then we can pursue Katrina, stop her planting the FRIEND."

"And how do you propose we do that?" said Amba.

"Easy," smiled Dex, touching his face where Molly had given him a beating. "We'll tell them what we know. Tell *everybody* what we know. SARAH, do you have communication facilities down here?"

"Our Theme Planet Advertising Broadcast Station, TPABS, is an hour from where you stand. I can direct you. It has the power to broadcast across the entirety of Quad-Gal. It is the source of all our Quad-Gal advertising; the selling of Theme Planet holidays. It is *very* powerful."

"I think it's time to give Oblivion Government the publicity they deserve," said Dex.

"If we do that, Katrina will get to SARAH's core. We can only do one thing or the other."

"We'll have to split," said Dexter.

Amba read the anguish in his face; and she understood. "You go to the TPABS. I'll go after Katrina."

"No. No."

Dex closed his eyes for a moment, and then opened them again. He took a deep breath, summoning up courage from deep within. "I will go after Katrina. I will go after Molly and Toffee."

"Are you sure you can do this?"

"Yes," nodded Dexter.

Amba stepped forward, and kissed him. It was gentle, slow, and sincere. Dex stood, stunned.

"For bringing me back to life," said Amba, remembering her daughter, remembering her own cowardice. Then she turned, and vanished into the cut flesh walls...

ROMERO SAT ON his dark ebony throne, flanked by a thousand silent, immobile Ministers of Joy – the enforcers of Earth's Oblivion Government, and by default, Earth itself. Romero had his chin on his fist, his long, glossy black hair was drawn back with a simple circlet of silver, and his dark eyes were like glass, his face unreadable, his mood tangible and quite obviously *not* filled with joy.

Doors slammed open at the far end of the chamber, and a tall, powerful soldier strode forward. He wore Oblivion's black uniform, and the silver insignia of the military elite, along with the single bar of a general. This was General Kome of the Chaos Infantry; possibly the most brutal, harsh and feared soldier within the Ministers of Joy, or anywhere.

Kome approached and snapped to attention, delivering a precise salute, and Romero stepped down from his throne and returned it. Romero, a tall man himself, looked up at the heavily scarred face before him. Kome refused to have any plastic surgery whatsoever, believing a man should bear his scars proudly – and on his front. Kome had no scars on his back. He never turned his back in a fight. Kome was the first of the Anarchy Androids, and the most deadly. He had been assigned human status by Romero for services rendered. This was the one thing in his entire existence for which Kome had shown some gratitude.

"You have news?" said Romero.

"Yes. All your implants, all your spies, all your rogue humans down there on that shitty ball of diseased fun – well, between them, they're doing a fine job of fucking it all up."

"What's the sit-rep on the Anarchy Models?"

"Amba has performed sterling service. She has assassinated several of the individuals on her list of targets. Katrina and the two young androids played their parts well, and met with SARAH *inside* and convinced the freak they were human; for a while, at least. For long enough. Long enough to *infiltrate*. It is this Dexter Colls who presents a problem."

"Aah. My old friend Dexter." Romero thought back, remembering the android's engineering, his breeding, his growing, his implanting. Romero had taken a very special interest in Dexter Colls. It was a matter of personal pride. "I have high hopes for Dexter."

"Don't get them too high, *sir*. It would appear he has malfunctioned."

"Malfunctioned? How?"

"We tried to activate his internal switch; but it refuses to work. He remains in his fake human form – working with the same thought patterns, the same emotional concepts, the same empathy. We cannot regress him to base android status. It is a crying fucking shame. An abomination, in fact."

Romero considered this. "What are the computers saying with regards probability of mission success?"

"Ninety five percent success rate. The Monolith Mainframe, the organic computer which calls itself SARAH and is, as we suspected, covering the entirety of the planet, is completely non-violent. There will be no fight there. Our War Machine will roll over her and fuck her violently from behind."

"How is the Fleet?"

"We are positioning in readiness for the initial bombing runs. Cardinal, when this begins, the whole surface of that fucking place is going to be a warzone. Those dumb-ass pleasure seekers won't know what the fuck hit them."

"Good," said Romero, rubbing his chin. "Serves them right for being so weak. If they had backbone, they'd be a part of our plans for expansion!"

"Of course, sir," said General Kome.

"One last thing. I want you to initiate contact with Amba and Katrina. I want to know where they are, how far into the game they are – yes?"

"You will break their cover."

"I think we're so far into the game, Kome, it matters little. We are in position to began our wonderful Act of Aggression in... how long?"

"One hour, sir."

"Then one hour it is," said Romero, dark eyes showing no emotion. Indeed, very like an android's.

KATRINA LAY ON the trolley, smiling bravely up at Dex. She wore a blue hospital gown and her dark hair was tied back, face radiant with the beauty of being "with child." Dex leaned forward and kissed her gently, first on the lips, then on the forehead, and his hand touched her lips, then moved down across the coarse fabric of the hospital gown, over her breasts, coming to rest gently and protectively on the pregnant bump.

"Everything's going to be all right," said Dex, eyes bright with tears.

"Who you trying to convince? Me, or yourself?"

"Both of us," admitted Dex, with a grin.

"It will be all right," Katrina said, and her hand moved and took Dex's fingers. She squeezed his hand as if to reassure him, and then the doors opened and the doctors and midwives appeared; they smiled warmly, kindly, at Dexter and there were far too many teeth. Dex didn't like people smiling. In the real world, he didn't trust anybody.

"I'll be okay," said Kat, as they wheeled her away into the birthing suite.

"I love you," said Dex.

"I love you too," mouthed back Kat.

The doors closed, leaving a generously bosomed midwife with Dex. "We'll prepare her for the section," she said, "and then you can come in and watch – if you like. Is that your preference?"

"Yes," said Dexter.

"The Caesarean is being carried out by Jojo Brunstfield III, a Doc+7 birthing machine with, as you've probably guessed, a Doc+ rating of 7. That means, to the layman, that it's as technically accurate as seven whole doctors put together!"

"I'd still rather have a human doctor do it," said Dex, unhappily.

"We've been through this several times, Mr Colls."

"I know, I know, it's just..."

"You don't trust machines, especially machines that are trying to be human. I understand. I'm the same... and as for those new androids!" She shivered. "They give me the creeps, they're so human! Thank God they have no emotions and they're easy to spot and exterminate, that's what I always say!"

"Yes, thank God," said Dexter.

"We call them Plastic Hearts down our street," said the midwife, and Dex clicked. She'd been sent out to make small talk whilst they prepped Katrina for surgery. Keep him occupied. Keep his mind on other things. Dex frowned.

"I'd rather be alone," he said.

The generously bosomed midwife gave a little "huff" and shook her shoulders (and her ample bosom) as if to say, Ha, very well, stuff you, bozo! and she mooched away to examine various wall posters about contracting the vast range of weird and wonderful alien viruses that had presented themselves across Quad-Gal.

Dex waited patiently, heart booming in his chest, hands clammy with fear. What if something happened? What if something went terribly wrong? Yeah, but all these professional people are here to help! Here in case something does go wrong!

Still Dex fretted, and he'd never thought of himself as a worrier before, but he was shitting bricks right now.

The doors opened.

"You can come inside, Mr Colls."

Dex hurried through the doors. Katrina was lying on her back with some kind of frame over her midriff. Dex was guided to stand beside her head, so that he couldn't exactly see what was going on below.

He took her hand, and squeezed it, and stared suspiciously at the huge machine, the size of an upended groundcar, that squatted patiently, awaiting its chance to perform the caesarean and remove his breech child from his wife's womb.

"How do you feel?" he said, not taking his eyes off the machine. Various limbs had started to flex and move, and Dex realised it had eight metal arms – like a giant spider. He shivered; felt chilled to ice inside.

"I feel great, Dex! The drugs are doing their job!"

"Yeah. Well."

There came various buzzes and spinning blade sounds as the machine tested its various implements. The doctors and nurses were all standing around, beaming with big white teeth as if they were on some TV or filmy advertising Whiter Than White Teeth toothpaste.

"Now vatch carefully, Meester Colls!" said a funny looking doctor with a big brown quiff.

The machine suddenly sprang into life, and Dex nearly drew his fucking pistol, it made him jump so much. All eight arms slammed

*into action, and it was like Katrina was being attacked by a metal
hybrid of car and octopus. Kat squeezed his hand again and he
forced himself to look into her eyes, and he realised he was crying,
and the moment was beautiful (except for the whirring and drilling
and sounds of a circular saw cutting flesh).*

*Everything flowed into honey, and then there came a squawk,
and the metal arms lifted a new-born babe into the air. A midwife
took the child, and cut the umbilical, and carried the babe to the
weighing scales, which shuffled around on little legs to accept this,
The Prize.*

*The midwife gestured to Dex and he sidled over, looking down
in awe at his new child.*

"Do you have a name for her?"

"It's a her?"

"She's a she, yes."

"Wow!"

"Do you have a name?"

"We said we'd call her Toffee."

"She's beautiful. She has her mother's eyes."

*"Wow," agreed Dexter, mouth open, as he quickly counted arms
and legs and fingers and toes. "Is she okay? Is she healthy? Is she
fine?"*

"She's a fine little girl," said the midwife.

*There came a massive clanking as the machine crossed the
birthing suite, and extended a metal linkage to Dex. Dex stared at
the greased ball-joint. "Yes?" he enquired politely.*

*"DR JOJO BRUNSTFIELD III, +7, AT YOUR SERVICE, MR COLLS. WE
HOPE THIS IS A PLEASANT MEMORY FOR YOU. WE HOPE YOU HAD A GREAT
TIME. IF YOU HAVE ANY PROBLEMS WITH YOUR BABY UNIT, PLEASE BRING
IT BACK TO THE HOSPITAL AND WE WILL INVESTIGATE IT. THANK. YOU."*

All the time it was shaking Dex's hand.

*The midwife wrapped the child in a blanket and handed her
to Dex. It'd been a few years since he'd held a newborn, and he
remembered how delicate they felt, how tiny their fingers and toes,
how totally vulnerable they were.*

"Hello little Toffee," he said, grinning like an idiot and stroking her silky soft baby skin. He toyed gently with her fingers as he carried her to Katrina, and together they cooed over the baby as the giant clanking machine sewed Katrina's body back together again.

"She's beautiful!" said Katrina.

"She's a little star," said Dex. "Well done, Toffee, fighting your way to freedom like that! I just know you're going to be Daddy's little girl, and I'm going to spoil you rotten, and you'll never want for anything, and I'm going protect you and nurture you and love you with all my heart until the stars go out and die…"

TOFFEE STOOD IN the corridor up ahead, waiting for him. Her head was lowered, eyes narrowed, stance aggressive but patient. In her hands she carried the fizzing, sparking wand. The wand used to put androids down and out of the game…

Dex had followed Katrina's trail of destruction; it hadn't been difficult. She'd left a path like an Industrial Chainsaw FukTruk through protected jungle. Dex had pounded down the white, glowing corridors, and dropped down through the holes in the floor, wincing at the fleshy feel to the wounds she'd cut or blasted into existence. It looked to Dex like Kat was using the FRIEND for speed, now, blowing vast holes in the very living flesh of SARAH just to progress; to get to her target.

When the surroundings suddenly changed, shifting from glowing white to a dark, moody blue, that was when Dex came across Toffee. He stopped dead, and his chin wobbled, and his knees knocked. Here was his pretty little girl. His beautiful girl cub whom he'd nurtured and cared for and loved with so much love his heart could have burst. And she was waiting for him. Waiting to kill him…

"Daddy," she said, and her head lifted, and Dex could not read her eyes, nor her intentions. A flower sparkled in his heart; sparkled with *hope*.

"Toffee, my sweet little princess. Sweet as toffee." It was his bedtime invocation, the words he always used when tucking her beneath the sheets and kissing her one last time before she drifted off to sleep. The words that always brought a cheeky imp smile and a gleam of love in her eyes.

Now, it brought a snort.

"I'm not your little princess any longer."

"Toffee!"

"You did a bad thing, Daddy."

"What bad thing?"

"You should have become a proper android, like us. You're being a bad man. You're breaking up the family."

"No, no, you have to learn not to be like this, Little One. You have to forget all this rubbish about androids and killing – that's not you, that's not the lovely little girl who rescued the injured kitten and helped make it a bed and stayed up all night worrying about its broken leg. You nursed that kitten for four weeks, fed it, gave it milk, forced me to make a bloody splint for its leg! What happened to you, Toffee? What happened to that sweet, beautiful, caring child?"

"I became what I was supposed to become. They flicked my switch, Daddy. Now I understand. I understand everything – how cold and cruel the world is. How life is worth nothing, and how we can – and will – kill without mercy. The universe is a terrible glittering place. It's filled with emptiness. It is a void. There is no such thing as God, or the soul, there is only life and death and money."

Dex walked slowly forward, until he was in striking distance. He looked down in horror at his youngest child. "By all that's Holy, what did they do to you?" he said.

"Nothing Holy, *Daddy*," she said, and looked at him with adult eyes.

Dex knelt, slowly, so that he was on the same level as Toffee. He stared hard at his little girl.

"What do I have to do? To get you back again?"

"That's easy," said the little girl. "You must not pass. If you try, then I will kill you."

"I cannot fight you," said Dex.

"Good. Because you will not pass. Katrina said it must be so."

"Why not *Mummy?*"

"She is Katrina now. She is an android. We are all androids. Allow them into your mind, Daddy. Allow them to do the right thing; come back to us, as the father we know and love. We can hunt together. We can kill together."

"Those are not your words," said Dex, and rocked back fast on his heels – a good thing, for the wand lashed out in a savage movement, a hateful sudden strike, and slashed before Dex's face so close he felt the sparks discharge on his nose...

Dex rolled to one side as the wand pursued him, slashing left and right like a sword, and he came up, ducked under a blow, and though it pained him to the very roots of his soul, he hit Toffee in the chest with a straight right. She flew back, a tangled mess of limbs, dropping the fizzing wand.

Dex stepped forward and picked it up.

Toffee was lying on her back, wheezing, clutching her chest.

Dex strode forward, and looked down at his daughter, or what was once his daughter, and he felt nothing but love for her. Nothing but love and joy, mixed with horror and fear at what she had become. And a doubt. A nagging, nagging feeling tickling the base of his skull...

"Toffee?"

"What, bastard?"

"You are not Toffee."

Silence.

"You are not my little girl."

Silence.

"Where is my little girl?"

Toffee glared up at him, and suddenly something released in his heart, and he felt a flood of joy and happiness like nothing he had ever felt. Of course! This was not the real Toffee – because he, and Katrina, and Amba – they were engineered creations, created androids. But Molly and Toffee could not be manipulated in the same way; they were a product of a union of love, not engineering. In which case, at some point they had been switched with – what? Android recreations of the real thing? Maybe? Why?

Why, to force his cooperation, of course.

To buy his loyalty.

To force him to do what he was told.

Dex brought the fizzing crackling wand close to the fake Toffee and she recoiled, like a snake before a flaming brand.

"Where are my children?" he said.

Toffee started to laugh, and it was almost an adult laugh. Her eyes glittered. "You think it is that easy? That it would be so simple? Like we're just fakes, or clones, and your real, beautiful, angelic little girls are really holed up somewhere nasty, clutching prison bars and waiting for their sweet Daddy to come and rescue them?" She laughed again, and it was a nasty sound that made Dex clench his fists. "Well it isn't like that, *sweet Daddy,* it isn't like that at all. The round shape doesn't always fit into the round hole, because the hole gets warped, and twisted, and just because your children were good to you for the last few years, doesn't mean they're not now filled with hate and ready to do the job for which they were designed. The job of torture. And killing."

"No," whispered Dex.

"Oh yes," said Toffee. "I am your baby. Your sweet little Toffee. And I want you dead, motherfucker..." She launched herself at him with a snarl, fingers curled into claws, teeth bared and drooling like a predator attacking... going for the kill.

CHAPTER THIRTEEN
BAD DADDY

TOFFEE ATTACKED. HIS own daughter attacked! Dex moved fast, the wand lashing out and touching Toffee's temple. She was flung sideways, spinning, and hit the wall, collapsing in a heap.

If this was any other enemy, Dex would have closed fast for the kill.

But this was his little girl.

How could he do that? How could he do that to her?

Snarling in frustration, he moved to the wall, to the neat alloy panels emitting the soothing blue light. Dex started to kick one, and after several hefty blows the alloy buckled. He got fingers behind the edge and dragged it free, revealing a mass of ducting and cables. Dex grabbed a handful of wires and ripped them free with a shower of sparks, then moved to Toffee, knelt and tied her hands tightly behind her back; then moved down and bound her ankles.

As she regained consciousness she struggled, spinning around in tight circles, snarling.

Satisfied, Dex pocketed the rest of the wires and hefted the wand thoughtfully. He approached the bound form of Toffee and knelt by her, hand moving out, halting her struggles. She glared at him.

Dex ruffled her hair.

"Go to Hell," she snarled.

Dex reached forward, and grasping her head tightly, kissed her gently on the forehead. Then he pulled back, tears shining in his eyes. "I love you, Toffee, no matter what you say or do. I'll love you until the stars go out."

Dexter stood.

Toffee continued to struggle.

Dex looked down at the wand. Would Molly be so easy to pacify? If *easy* was the right word?

He doubted it.

And Katrina?

Dex shuddered, and his eyes were hard. He had a bad feeling he would have to send *that* bitch to Hell.

AMBA MOVED THROUGH a hundred different landscapes. First came fields of black, wavering grass, the stalks bending in a breeze which felt fresh and light. Amba wasn't sure when her surroundings had metamorphosed, but she had her FRIEND in her chest and felt happy, at peace, for the first time in her life.

You like this Dexter a lot, don't you?

We understand each other.

Do you really? Well you're the first people in history to do so.

You called us "people."

Maybe I did. Maybe you have... worked your way outside the box. After all, what is human? What is real? Who's to say the so-called real humans haven't actually devolved to a state where they no longer can be classified as human under their own stupid rules? It's all just labels anyway. A person is defined by their thoughts, their words, their actions. If you think you feel love for Dexter, then I'd say that's something approaching humanity – especially for you.

What is love, Zi? Is that what's happened to me?

What is love? Laughter. *That's something I could never explain to you, child.*

Now Amba moved through an army of silent rollercoaster carriages. They were everywhere, packed in tightly under a candyfloss sky. Each carriage was a different size and shape and function; each one carried a riotous blaze of colourful paintwork.

Are these new? Waiting to be used?

No, said Zi, *these are the dead, the abused, the cast-off. We all end up here one day. Even you, poor android.* Zi considered this. *Even me.*

Unless we die in a hail of heroic bullet-fire and destruction.

Yeah, there is that.

Amba moved through the hundreds, thousands – tens of thousands – of cars and carriages. Before long the blaze of colours became a blur until nothing else seemed real, and Amba thought the rollercoaster graveyard would go on forever.

Where is this place?

The dark side of your soul, child.

She walked for what felt like hours, stretching off into days. All around her lay cold, dented metal, tarnished alloy, twisted steel, splintered wooden slats, tattered, faded flags. It was a sad place, and Amba felt melancholy creeping into her heart. These faithful rides had given so must joy, fun, laughter – now they were left here to rot.

Melancholy is a human emotion, said Zi.

Maybe I'm not as terrible as my makers intended?

That's a novel thought, said Zi. *But I disagree.*

Eventually a wall of dark rock began working its way towards them, looming larger with every thousand footsteps. It was massive, high and rough and violent, running from horizon to horizon. Amba knew she would have to climb this obstacle – but then, who said reaching the Theme Planet Advertising Broadcast Station would be easy?

I think SARAH is starting to malfunction, said Zi.

Why's that?

Why put the obstacle?

Maybe it was always here.

Maybe she's testing you. Maybe she doesn't trust you.

Now that, said Amba, *I can understand.*

Amba reached the foot of the cliff and glanced behind her, at the gleaming colours of a million different carriage designs. And she frowned. For Theme Planet hadn't been operating for *that long*, surely? There was no way so many millions of cars could have been made obsolete. Was there?

Maybe SARAH has been around a lot longer than you think. Zi sounded... not smug, but as if some kind of cunning had filtered down through her subconscious; an intrinsic understanding which she now grasped, but wasn't wholly about to share. *Maybe this isn't the first Theme Planet? Maybe it... came from somewhere else?*

Maybe, said Amba. *It no longer matters. I have a job to do. I have to anger Romero, anger Oblivion – get them here. Get them to come after me.*

Do you have the words? said Zi.

Oh, yes, said Amba.

She started to climb. The wall of jagged rock reared above her, too high to see the top. Amba set her mouth in a tight line, focused her concentration, and climbed, hands finding tiny nooks and cracks, agile boots digging in, finding wedges, searching out ledges. And Amba moved upwards, and the air cooled and caressed her, and wafted her hair about her forehead. As she climbed, Amba thought of Dex. Thought of his long hard search for his family; for his wife, who had then betrayed him; for his children. Beautiful children. *I could have those children*, Amba realised, remembering her own daughter who had been taken from her all those years ago. Yes. We would have our own ready-made family. It would not matter if we were engineered to have no kids; we would already have some. It would be perfect. I could replace Katrina. And obviously, because she's been a bad person, and I could be a *good* person if I tried hard, I am sure we would all get on perfectly.

Dexter. Dexter Colls. So noble and courageous.

I think I really *am* in love with him...

She climbed, and paused for a while, resting her pain-riddled fingers and toes. She glanced back, and jumped a little when she realised how high up she was. To slip and fall now, from this great height – then, Anarchy Android or no, she would be squashed like a bug in the mangled wreckage of old rollercoaster CARs far below.

The CARs spread off as far as Amba could see – and her eyesight was perfect.

Bizarrely, the way they'd been arranged, the colours seemed to paint a smile.

Ironic.

Amba turned back, and continued to climb. She had a long way to go.

AMBA PERCHED ON a narrow lip of rock, a ridgeline of dinosaur scales, and looked out across the vast, black, rocky desert. She could see camps out there, and with a frown she realised what – or who – the figures were, gathered around their small fires beside Truks and HJeeps.

They were SIMs. Hundreds of SIMs.

"Wonderful," she muttered.

You think they are waiting for you?

I think they're guarding the TBAP. If that's the case, then SARAH was telling the truth, in that this whole place is infested with Oblivion spies. Romero has obviously been planning his invasion for quite some time.

I think it's safe to say, Amba my sweet, that for as long as you have breathed God's sweet air, for as long as you've carried out assassinations, then each and every act has been geared in some way towards achieving this moment.

That bastard, snapped Amba.

Her eyes followed the dark paths through the wilderness. Far ahead, a glittering grail on the horizon, stood a stark black building bristling with a thousand masts, antennas and SuperQ dishes – able to broadcast pretty much across the entirety of the Four Galaxies. It was an incredible and incredibly expensive piece of technology, owned by none other than Theme Planet, and Monolith.

Maybe that's what Romero is really after, said Zi.

You think?

Monolith refused to license the design. It would make a great military tool – for, say, controlling a War Fleet as it conquered every planet it could get within pissing distance of. Yes?

Possibly. Probably. What concerns me more now is the protection. They obviously don't want anybody near the thing...

Or to destroy it, pointed out Zi.

Let's give that bastard Romero something to think about.

Amba stood, and flexed, and began the hazardous climb down. It took a long time. A *long* time. But Amba did not mind. She was on a mission and her mind was set. She was saving the day, instead of destroying it. She was trying to help something, instead of kill it. And that made her happy. Made her feel cleansed. More human.

She landed in a crouch, in the dust, and moved forward swiftly, FRIEND in hand, eyes alert, senses screaming for anything – *anything* – that may point out a sniper or covert enemy...

"HEY. HEY YOU! THE WOMAN WITH THE GUN! THE HUMAN NEEDS TO PUT THE GUN DOWN. THE HUMAN NEEDS TO STAND STILL! OR I WILL PULP THE HUMAN! OR I AM NOT BATTLE SIM KNOWN AS GRUMMER..."

Amba, who had frozen, turned and her eyes picked out the hazy patch of a CovertShield blanket. She smiled easily, and fired her FRIEND – blowing a hole through the SIM big enough for her to squeeze her head through.

The SIM was slammed backwards, body parts pouring out through the huge hole like a bucket of animal slop. The corpse hit the ground with a slap, and Amba ran as alarms squealed through the darkness, and suddenly *everything* became panic. Amba ran swiftly, and heard guns discharging and the *pings* of flattened bullets bouncing off rock. She slammed past a SIM and blew his head off. Another lurched into her way, loading his SMKK machine gun, and Amba shot away his legs so he collapsed, gurning, onto his face. She leapt his dust-paddling corpse, then dodged left and right, zigzagging through the wasteland of SIMs, and approached a machine gun nest, which opened fire with the whine of the dreaded mini-gun. Amba sprinted up the right hand wall, speed and momentum carrying her on, and with a BLAM put a FRIEND round through the operator's skull top. She landed with a *thud* in the nest, grabbed the minigun with a grunt, and turned it on the shocked camp of SIMs who were still holding bowls of oxtail soup, many with spoons halfway to their mouths, eyes fixed on her as their conversation faltered into shocked silence, with just one stray voice whining, "I don't see how much damage *one* little lady can make..." before a cough made him drop his spoon in his soup and glance up.

"Let me show you," said Amba, sweetly, and unleashed the minigun on the hundred or so SIMs. Flesh and limbs exploded outwards, and the SIMs dropped their soup bowls and lunged for weapons. Hot metal screamed and scythed, and oxtail soup slopped up faces and armour plating as bowls exploded in showers of powder, and SIM skulls were drilled with spinning bullets. They went down in a wave, like a cornfield under a sweeping storm, until the silence was massive and Amba dropped the glowing minigun with a clatter.

She picked her way speedily through the field of corpses, and broke into a run once more through the outcroppings of rock, past startled mechanics and engineers, FRIEND booming occasionally to clear her a path towards the Theme Planet Advertising Broadcast Station.

It didn't seem such a long way, as there was so much killing to be done.

Eventually, drenched in blood, and panting a little – which was unlike Amba – the Anarchy Android reached the high fence and scrambled up it like a monkey, vaulting over its twenty-foot-high summit, carefully avoiding the organic AI body-invading razor wires, and landing in a crouch, FRIEND by her cheek.

Nine hundred and ninety eight, said Zi.

What?

That's how many SIMs you just killed.

Oh, said Amba, and felt a twitch of remorse. But then, this was what she was built for. This was why she was created. She pictured Dex in her mind, and chewed her lower lip for a moment. He wouldn't have approved. He would have gone for the stealthy option. Covert infiltration. But then, in justification, this was to save *the whole planet...*

Stop worrying, said Zi. *You're becoming more human by the bloody hour. At this rate, we'll be lucky to get the mission done.*

Oh, we'll get it done all right, said Amba, and then privately, *because that's the only way I'll end up with Dexter, and with his girls, and with our new pre-packed family unit.*

She smiled, recognising the absurdity of her dream.

Amba stood, and moved down a narrow glittering path.

Behind you! cried Zi, but Amba was already moving, spinning, crouching, and the FRIEND kicked in her fist and massacred the two approaching SIMs before they could fire a single round from SMKKs.

A thousand, said Zi.

I like round numbers.

THE THEME PLANET Advertising Broadcast Station was a testament to advanced technology. It was a hive of digital action. It was filled from wall to wall and floor to ceiling with the highest-grade components ever devised, and created to an alien specification that even Monolith did not understand. Amba picked her way through narrow corridors between huge blocks of glittering, sparkling machinery. Sometimes modules buzzed and clicked, sometimes the machines stayed silent, inert. But she got the feeling they were working; working damn hard.

Amba, covered in SIM gore, positively *dripping* blood and bone shards onto the alloy tiles, moved through the gloom of alien technology.

Staircases wound upwards, and with her FRIEND primed, Amba hunted down the control room. It took a while, since the layout of the TPABS was illogical, with corridors cutting back on each other, oddly laid out angles and ridges, and stairs that sometimes went sideways so that, after only a few minutes, Amba was utterly disorientated.

It was Zi who finally guided Amba to the control suite. Peering inside, expecting enemies and BIG GUNS, Amba simply found herself alone at the broadcasting console. It looked simplistic, but as she scrolled through the controls on the screen, she realised it had an inner depth that allowed trillions of broadcast permutations.

Amba flicked through the million or so channels currently being broadcast across the Four Galaxies Major Streams and realised, with a grin, that she could hijack each and every one of them.

"What a powerful piece of equipment," she murmured.

You better believe it... this thing can beam an image into every TV, filmy lounge, mental kickpack port, ggg interface and brainscreen across trillions of klicks; whatever you send out on this, it'll fuck Romero good and send his Ministers of Joy scampering for their resignation cards. And it'll show everybody what an underhand bunch of scum-sucking warmongering empire-building back-stabbers the Earth lot really are!

Amba hit a series of screen buttons, scrolled through various controls, and set the wide field broadcast spectrums; then she did a very naughty thing, and ran the main Theme Planet advert across all channels, phasing out over a million transmissions and effectively hijacking the entire Quad-Gal's information network.

The filmy began its play. It ran thus:

AUDIO [deep male voice]:
The Monolith Corporation™ *in association with Earth's* OBLIVION *Government presents,*
A THEME PLANET™ *Production!*

VIDEO [close up]:
A man dressed in colourless, shapeless clothing. This man is a bland and colourless *human*. He is bowed with age, face wrinkled and worn by the ravages of time. The dude is defeated and... queuing... what he is queuing for is not quite clear, but the old bro is queuing and the queue is a long one; a very long one – *[camera pulls back/ smooth tracking shot]*. The queue is an incredible and horizon-bending vast and terrible queue! A queue to make you sick! A queue to make you slit your wrists!

VIDEO [close-up]:
Watery blue eyes surrounded by wrinkles convey an inner message of emptiness, frustration and despair. CUT TO: The old man's feet shuffling forward a step, then pulling back again to show thousands and thousands of people shuffling forward... all by a single step.

AUDIO – A deep and throaty sigh:
Are you tired of your life? Your existence? Your age, dude, your fucking AGE?
Are you disgruntled with an eternity of pointless queuing? Like you get in EVERY damn theme park ever created, bro?

VIDEO [close-up]:
A nod. Resignation. Disillusionment.

AUDIO:
Are you tired of your... MOLECULES?

VIDEO:
The eyebrows lift, questioning. That old face is now full of dawning wonder, and suddenly filled with intelligence and inspiration and hope. Hope! Open, in fact, to the suggestion of a new and incredibly life-changing experience!

AUDIO:
  Well dude, there's no need to be.

VIDEO:
  Suddenly, this world-weary example of humanity's disintegration
  is disassembled, beamed through the glowing atmosphere of
  Theme Planet™ – and reassembled with a look of total orgasm.
  The old man's face is filled with *new youth*. Vitality. Eagerness.
  Energy, baby, fucking energy! He looks horny as hell.

AUDIO [sung, accompanied by happy jolly music]:
  It's better than drugs!
  It's better than sex!
  It's fun, it's fast, it's neat ...
  If you haven't been sick, you soon will be!
  Zip through a thousand light years on... THE MOLECULE MACHINE™!

VIDEO:
  Molecules swirling to form an old man's young smile.

LETTERING IN FLAMES:
  Brought to you by Theme Planet™
  The Theme Planet Advertising Broadcast Station (ggg)
  and THE MONOLITH CORPORATION©

As it was running, Amba hit a few scrolls and a camera fizzed
down from the ceiling and fastened its black eyes on her. Once
the TP ad rolled to an explosive end, and the tinkling music and
final dialogue fizzed out of existence, the Quad-Gal's information
highway was filled with Amba's face, against a simple black
backdrop. Amba could almost *hear* fifty trillion angry gasps, and
huffs of annoyance, and spilled coffees and dribbled kukunga
burgers. But more importantly, she could *sense* fifty trillion fingers,
suckers, tentacles, blocks, hooks and babbages reaching for the
remote control... or nearest alien equivalent.

So she spoke quickly...

"My name is Amba Miskalov. I am an Anarchy Android, built and controlled by Earth's Oblivion Government. I am broadcasting from Theme Planet on behalf of its creators – creators who are about to be annihilated. Even now, a War Fleet of Earth origin is bound on a course of destruction and murder, of invasion and massacre, of empire-building and genocide. I appeal to you, the good people and aliens of the Quad-Gal, to intervene in this atrocity. I appeal to every government of every planet to send Warships to halt Earth's evil machinations. For, and trust me when I say this, we Anarchy Androids walk amongst you, torturing you, murdering you, and we are sent out daily by Cardinal Romero, Commander-in-Chief of Earth's Oblivion Government."

She cut the transmission, and caught a red blinking light to her right. She reached out and picked up a small ECube.

"What the fuck are you doing?" screamed Romero.

"Hello? To whom am I speaking?"

"Amba, oh, you back-stabbing fucking bitch, you are so, so, *so* dead when I get my hands on your pretty little throat. KOME! Not there, over THERE! Listen, Miskalov, you get back on that powerful piece of alien technological shit and you fucking retract those words you just spoke... do you understand what you're doing? Do you, bitch?"

"Fucking up your clever plans of, oooh, the last twenty years?"

"You have so much to answer for," said Romero, his voice heavy as lead.

"As do you, my sweet."

"Do you understand what SARAH actually *is?* What she – *it* – is capable of?"

SMKK rounds blasted and screamed in the tower below her, and Amba leapt from the couch and lifted her FRIEND. Into the ECube she spat, "No, but I understand you, Romero, I understand you made me how I am – well, fuck you, now this is *my* time, time to be human, time to be a *woman!*"

The lead SIM poked his SMKK round the door, and Amba

blew his head clean through the wall of the TPABS. Showers of sparks cascaded, lightning shrieked through the chamber and stairwell, and more SMKK bullets thundered from the darkness as Amba crouched, and bullets ate the screen behind her, and the whole flashing groaning world seemed to descend into...

Anarchy.

THE CENTRAL WAR Fleet Command Vehicle, *DeathX*, had its command centre and control deck at the core of its massive, donut-like body. But what it seemed to lack in aesthetics (it was spherical, in order to best drop in and out of wormholes) it made up for in weaponry. It was an awesome ship. Awesome, in terms of its technology, built for the dealing of death. For invasion and genocide. For aggression and warmongering. For down-and–dirty, simple, raw *firepower*...

Romero sat, alone, on the control deck. The lights had been dimmed so that he was illuminated only by the flicker of screens and information. His chin was on his fist, his features dark and thunderous as he brooded. To his left were at least a thousand messages of "Retreat and Desist" from a thousand different planets and governments; and more were pouring in. If he didn't act fast, didn't *attack* fast, then this act of aggression would have an unanticipated, sudden bloody battle on its hands, as Quad-Gal clustergangs homed in on his location and started giving him a bloody nose – something he could deal with, but he wanted to concentrate on taking Theme Planet *first*. And Amba had screwed it all up. Destroyed his continuity.

Damn her!

A door slid open, and General Kome strode along the metal walkway. Nobody else would dare enter, probably down to Romero's screams of, "Get the fuck out! Everybody get the fuck out now and if a single motherfucker comes back in I'll personally blow that motherfucker's head off!"

Now, only Kome braved Romero's wrath.

The big General halted beside the brooding man, and looked down almost tenderly. He reached out to put a hand on Romero's shoulder, and his hand hovered there for a moment whilst he considered the ramifications of his actions. Smoothly, he withdrew his hand. He valued his fingers more than a need to pacify the Cardinal of the Ministers of Joy.

"That fucking bitch," hissed Romero, softly.

"She betrayed us."

"That should be impossible!" He looked up, eyes burning with hate. "She's put us in a very, very dangerous position."

"You need to make a decision."

"Yes."

Romero stood, and stretched. He glanced down at the screen, where yet more outraged messages were pouring in. How DARE Earth advance on the Theme Planet with aggressive militaristic intentions! How COULD Oblivion Government make such a foolhardy act of aggression? What DID Earth think it was doing? Romero smiled bleakly. How little they all understood his... ambition. Not just ambition for himself, for he recognised he was just a tiny cog in the very great machine called Conquest. No. The ambition was for his species; for *humanity*. He wanted to make himself immortal, sure, but he wanted to establish Humanity as the dominant controlling lifeforce of the Quad-Galaxy. Too long had they bowed and scraped to their alien neighbours. Equals? Fuck that. That was not mankind's destiny! Now, Romero would show them, as his ancestors had done in millennia past, who was in control. Who was destined to lead.

"Launch the FieldNukes. Send the Ministers of Joy in one-man Slam Fighters. And take us in."

"Take us in?" Kome raised an eyebrow. "You want to go Front Line? Into the Dregs? Into the NukeFields?"

"Yes," said Romero, darkly. "We're going to find Amba before she does any more fucking damage. We will remove her piece well and truly from the now-thoroughly-distorted and deviated gameboard."

*   *   *

DEX EMERGED FROM a hole in a vast steel wall to stand, teetering, on a ledge a hundred klicks above the ground. He'd followed Katrina's path with ease; she was making no attempt at stealth, just *speed*, in order to get to SARAH's core and plant the FRIEND. The *bomb*.

Dex gasped, and grabbed the edge of the wall as vertigo took his brain in its fist and shook him hard, like a rabid dog with a broken, pulped cat. Darkness spread away, and distant lights twinkled. A pipe veered off before him, about a foot wide, matt-black and almost invisible against the space around him. Dex knelt, and glanced backwards. A cold wind drifted up from the chasm below, and Dex gritted his teeth. Katrina and Molly had passed this way, he was sure of it. And he heard, somewhere distant, a small, female gasp followed by a scuffing sound. *Let's hope Katrina fell off,* he thought morbidly. But knew it wouldn't happen. She was too precise. He remembered dancing with her on many occasions, and it was always *he* who stepped on her toes. Damn. Damn and shit. He hated heights, especially heights on narrow pipe bridges over deadly abysses, like this one.

"It's never fucking easy, is it?" he growled.

He set off across the pipe, arms spread out to steady himself. The Makarov in his pocket felt good, solid, real, reliable, and the wand tucked into the waist-band of his trousers was also reassuring, in that he'd seen what it could do to an android; indeed, *felt* its effects himself, and thus knew it was a handy device. He was tired, and hurting, mentally as well as physically, and he moved slowly across the high pipe, wondering what the hell the pipe was *for,* what was its function, its purpose, why build it out here of all bloody places? He felt nausea swimming through him, pouring into him as if he were a jug. It could have been due to the physical pounding he'd taken, it could have been from the harsh psychological kicking; whatever the reasons, the sickness was upon him, and suddenly he dropped to his knees and felt the yawning chasm open up around him; felt as if he swam through treacle and was about to slip from the bottom into an infinity well, where gravity would crush him down and fold him over and over, into a single molecule.

Dex swayed, high up on the pipe. The darkness was terrifying. The sickness was terrifying. And suddenly, something hissed from the darkness, an object large and bulky, and he heard it coming and covered his head with his arms in protective reflex, and then squealing, shrieking, and screams as the black, thundering rollercoaster rolled through the darkness full of giggling tourists, and Dex cowered, trembling, on the pipe, praying for protection, for it was so close, so close and he hadn't seen the rails just a few feet away at head height. The rollercoaster roared over him, twisting to one side and then dropping as the CARs clattered and thundered above him one at a time and the tourists screamed in their rabid enjoyment...

"Glad to see *somebody's* having a good time," Dex muttered, clinging to the pipe for his life.

Then there was a *whoosh* and a rush of air, and the CARs had gone, a tiny red tail-light blinking down into nothing.

Dex moved forward, and saw the mesh cage, the ladder, the inspection platform, and the penny dropped. This was no *pipe,* but an inspection walkway designed to give access to the rollercoaster track in this huge and empty space.

Dex climbed the ladder and stood beside the track, a single thick strand of twisting steel, black in colour except on the surface, which had been polished silver by the passage of CAR wheels.

"Daddy. I'm so glad you made it," said Molly.

Dex turned, and looked down at his daughter. She was beautiful, with her long black hair and dark eyes. Her skin was pale white in the gloom, unmarked and perfect, and she walked along the inspection walkway with delicate footsteps; prim, precise, almost like a ballerina. She reached the foot of the ladder and paused, then looked up at him and his heart melted, for she was here, she'd come back to him, and everything was going to be all right...

"I've been sent to kill you," she said.

"But you're my little girl," he said.

"Not anymore."

"Please, Molly, come back to me! I'm your father! I held you the day you were born, I filmed your first footsteps, I held you when you fell and cut your knee, I held you tight when you had a fever; don't you remember any of those things? Don't they matter? Don't you care?"

"That was a different time and a different place," said Molly, tilting her head to one side. Her dark eyes drilled into Dexter; drilled into his heart, drilled into his soul. "I was a different person back then. I was a child. Now, I am no longer a child. Now, I am an android, and I have a mission – *we* have a mission. You can come back to me, Father. You can be my Daddy and it will be like old times – all you have to do is give in to the android in your soul. Ascend. Become like us. Stop fighting what you know to be true, what you know is in your genetics, in your engineering, in your coding."

Dex was staring at his girl, at his baby, and he blinked, not believing the words pouring out of her mouth, the complex ideas that should have had no place in a child's understanding. If nothing else, this was an affirmation that she was not *more* than human, but less. A false human. A plastic person. An android...

Like me, he thought.

"I cannot do that," said Dex. "It's... hard to explain. It's like rolling on your back, presenting your soft underbelly to the blade. It's like a form of suicide. It's like giving in to those who thought they could engineer us; control us!"

"Then you'll die," said Molly, and suddenly her lips drew back and she snarled like an animal. Her fingers went crooked, formed claws, and she ran forward, leaping up onto the platform with incredible agility and slamming a punch to Dexter's chest that knocked him back, over the rail and onto the rollercoaster track itself.

Pain screamed through him, his heart thundering from the blow, and Dex panted hard, blinded for a moment, but he gathered his legs beneath him and rolled to his feet on the rollercoaster track. He backed away as Molly climbed over the low mesh, and started to walk towards him, daintily, with those ballerina footsteps.

"Stay back," warned Dex, retreating.

"Or what?" said Molly, with a mocking smile. "What will you do, Daddy?"

Dex's hands were before him, the Makarov pressing against him with a warm hard promise; *I can kill her,* said the Makarov. *I can retire the android.*

She launched at him, and threw a combination of punches that Dex blocked on his forearms, backing away again. He felt the track beneath his boots start to dip and twist, and realised he was running out of ground; more punches came, and kicks aimed at his stomach, groin and head. Dex blocked them all, each blow hurting that little bit more, the attacks coming with awesome force from such a tiny child. Her small fists left imprints in Dexter's flesh, and once again he had that mental block, that inability to strike a blow against his own child...

There came a distant *whoosh*.

The rollercoaster was coming!

Molly did a high back-flip, even as Dexter leapt himself, realising the only way to survive was to jump – to stay on the track was to be rammed into the black abyss beneath them. As both Molly and Dex were in the air, the rollercoaster CARs cut beneath them, and Molly landed neatly, straddling two cars, then crouching to grab hold of the restraints. Dex, in contrast, landed hard, like a heap of sodden shit dropped from a very great height; he tumbled, wedged into the footwell of a CAR at the feet of a fat man and a fat woman, both wearing puke-inducing colourful "patterned" holiday shirts.

Dex grunted in pain.

"Excuse *me!*" shouted the fat man, clutching the restraint which held him in his seat.

"Tell him, Gerald, tell him to get out of our rollercoaster!"

But the rollercoaster, already tipping into the downward spiral, dropped into a vertical fall and began twisting and spiralling down.

Dex was rammed up against the legs of the fat people, his nose pressed into the fat woman's knees as she screamed and started trying to kick him and hit him, and the more the rollercoaster fell and tumbled, the more Dex's face was shoved slowly, inexorably between her knees and, inevitably, towards her sweaty honey pot of delight.

"You dirty pervert scoundrel!" Dex heard Gerald shout, and he began to whack Dex on the back of the head with a meaty fist.

Dex wanted to shout, *believe me, mate, the last thing I want to do is shove my face in your pig wife's pig pussy!* but the coaster went suddenly into a vertical climb, rearing from the abyss and rising high, high into the sky, through fresh air and bursting into sunshine and through the smell of a distant sea breeze. Dex managed to grab some kind of rail and hoist himself up as the rollercoaster settled into a high-speed flat jag. The sunlight was dazzling, the fresh air exhilarating, his ears filled with the clattering of the wheels on the track, and the snarling of Gerald, and the carping of his sweaty wife.

Molly!

Dex whirled, meeting a kick that broke a tooth, filled his mouth with blood and sent stars flashing like fireworks. Both arms came up reflexively, and even blind, through sheer luck Dex blocked the rest of the blows.

Gerald, however, had leaned forward and thumped Dex in the stomach. Snarling, Dex drew his Makarov and pushed it into Gerald's face. "Keep your fists to yourself, motherfucker!"

"Okay! Okay! Don't hurt me!"

Strangely, his fat wife remained silent.

Molly snarled, and took a step back. Dex looked down the barrel of the gun at his eldest daughter, with her dark hair and dark eyes and dark moods and undying love for him; *her father.*

There came a gasp from the surrounding tourists.

"Don't hurt me, Daddy," said Molly, putting on her best *little girl* voice.

"You'd kill me without a second's thought," snarled Dex.

"Of course I wouldn't, Daddy," she whined, lower lip pouting a little.

"You evil bastard!" hissed the fat woman, and thumped Dex so hard in the balls he thought they'd come out his mouth. She was strong, that woman. Strong as an ox. Dex grunted, and the Makarov slipped in his slack fingers, and Molly was there like a dark demon, a glossy, evil angel, and she took the gun, and grinned, and looked down at the fat woman with glass-dark eyes before putting a bullet in her skull. The BLAM made the tourists gasp and shudder, and the second BLAM silenced Gerald as quickly and as harshly as any of his wife's carping put-downs. Blood sprayed the rollercoaster CAR and pooled in the footwell, like ink.

The Makarov turned on Dexter, as the cars lurched and chains clanked and the CAR climbed some more, then levelled out after yet another huge, huge climb...

Molly smiled.

She pointed the gun.

"Daddy?" she said, and squeezed the trigger... as the rollercoaster jerked, lurched forward, and dropped vertically into oblivion. Dex was tossed around the footwell of the CAR like a marble in a sock, and he vomited violently as the words, *if you haven't been sick, you soon will be* reverberated around the inside of his dumb-ass skull. He felt the fat legs of the dead woman kicking him spasmodically as her lifeblood pumped from her deflating body.

The drop left Dexter's lungs in his mouth, his kidneys in his lungs, his balls in his stomach. It felt like dying. Felt like being turned inside-out.

They plunged back into darkness, and the rollercoaster slowed for a turn, and with a *whump-whump-whump* Dex realised they'd passed the START position and were going to do it all over again! Yay!

I need to get off, he realised. At the same spot. I need a damn exit!

He dragged himself up from the confines of the car, and looked about for his daughter.

Molly had gone.

Uneasily, Dex cast about for the dangerous little girl; he didn't want a Makarov round in the back of his skull. That wouldn't help him in his quest to save SARAH; in his mission to save the Theme Planet.

Dex stood, and the rest of the rollercoaster passengers were subdued, failing to meet his gaze.

"What happened to the little girl?" he asked the nearest couple, a young man and woman who looked almost exactly alike.

"You... you let her fall," stammered the man.

"The hell I did! She was trying to kill me!"

"That's not how it looked to us!" yelled the woman in a sudden burst of anger. "You killed those two fat people, and then the coaster did the tumble and you pushed the black haired girl over the edge... we saw you, we'll testify!"

The lad nudged the girl, who went suddenly silent as she realised she was threatening a murderer.

"No," said Dex, rubbing at his tight closed eyes. "It didn't happen like that; you saw it all wrong!"

"I know what I saw," said the young woman, face grim and tight.

Dex pulled out the wand, which gave a sudden burst of fizzing energy. He knew what he had to do, and as they plummeted through darkness and once more the rollercoaster picked up speed for its second pass, Dex knew the pursuit of Katrina was back on the cards... she had a head start, sure, but her ploy to use Molly and Toffee to kill him had failed.

Now, all he had to do was catch her up.

Catch up the woman he loved, and kill her.

And he knew.

There would be no other way.

CHAPTER FOURTEEN
REBOOT

THE THEME PLANET.

It lay far below, a glittering gameboard, a beautiful slave, a colourful cartoon of wonderful, incredible rides. The world seemed to move slowly, through thick jelly, and rollercoasters spat ride CARs in slow motion, huge mechanical arms swung punters high into the sky or deep below the oceans, vast robots carried squealing children across mountain ranges, and on spirals of cloud and excited spittle, screams and laughter rose, rose, rose up to the gods, up to the heavens, and everything was in *primary colours,* the world was a dazzling brochure of *fun,* and every single living entity down there was there for pleasure, and joy, and to be uplifted and surged up and out of body, away from the grim miserable reality of what could be, of what might come to pass. The sky was filled with a distillation of pleasure. Theme Planet basked in the contentment of a billion happy souls.

The ships crawled across the sky, like insects across the carcass of a paralysed, unseeing mammal. Soon, the injured animal would realise it had been invaded, *soon* the injured animal would realise they had come to feed, and they were amoral, and had no joy and had no care, and they would use talons and claws and teeth and stings, and would take what they wanted, what they wanted being a pound of flesh – whether the flesh was dead, or still living.

Engines growled, and gradually the dull throbs of pounding pistons and matrix engines and the sight of the hundreds, then *thousands*, of SLAM dropships and SLAM fighters and KRUGER frigates and DAYTONA warhulks, all this information filtered down to the people below, and the rides started to falter, and happy laughing tourists halted in the streets, looking up and staring up, shading their eyes, craning their necks, wondering about the huge grey warships that had started to block out the sun…

Slowly, the pounding of engines stopped. One by one by one.

Only silence seemed to flow across the pleasure continents of the Theme Planet.

Then, a SLAM fighter dipped its nose and screamed for the ground, pulling up at the last minute to unleash a hail of missiles that slammed into playparks and kidpens and dancing robots and thundering water rides – CARs and TUBs and trailers were spat up and out in a purple blossom of detonation, silent at first when viewed from far above, a raging howling screeching inferno of blasted brick and concrete, alloy and glass; huge H-section steel supports were tossed aside like skittles, cutting down families out strolling with buggies and candyfloss. Rollercoaster tracks were smashed, bent up and out like random balls of wire wool screaming flames at the sky as gas chambers detonated in quick succession with boom–BOOM-*BOOMS* and the sounds of pleasure were quickly replaced by sounds of slaughter, the noises of pain and anguish, of screaming and sobbing and begging and searching…

Above, Romero watched all this play out on a hundred shimmering monitors.

His eyes were dark. Emotionless.

Quietly, he said, "Send in the Ministers."

*   *   *

AMBA STOOD IN a forest of circuitry, looking around herself carefully. The ships had smashed overhead, missiles screaming, and distantly she heard the concussive booms of HighJ and HighK explosives, could almost *feel* the heat from ravenous missiles. But this was not enough, and she knew it, and she knew instinctively that Romero would come for her. Or rather, he would send his Ministers of Joy. The police force of Earth's Oblivion Government. He would send his elite. And they would want her alive...

She moved slowly, warily, FRIEND outstretched.

This is a battle you cannot win, said Zi.

Yeah, well I can die trying.

You really should listen to Romero. He knows what he's talking about. He's nurtured you since you were andrembryo; you should not turn against him now. I implore you to rethink. I beseech you.

Amba stopped, and stared down at the FRIEND. Her sister of the flesh, her companion, the sidekick who kept her alive when the going got tough; and now Zi was fucking *siding with Romero?* Something about Zi had changed. Something had... shifted.

What? she said.

You have taken a foolish path, Amba, and we never saw it in you. How can you make some pathetic proclamation of love for some android reject who fights against his nature, against his purity of engineering? How can you do that? It is a betrayal, and I want you to stop, and think very carefully. Look, here's one of the Ministers now...

He was tall, broad, powerful, and wore a heavy black coat fastened up tight. His boots were black and dull, as was his mask, which covered his whole face. The Ministers of Joy believed no pleasure should be taken from visual representation. Thus, the mask was plain, without features. Only the eyes, pale blue, shone through the narrow slits.

Amba stood stock still, as the Minister strode across the carpet of wires, between the trees of twisted alloy, between circuit-bank-bark and valve-flowers which popped as they were crushed under his boots. Tiny sparks of electricity zigzagged through the circuit flooring.

"Amba. You will come with me."

Amba considered this, and shot the Minister in the face... or rather, would have done if Zi had cooperated. Instead, for the first time in her life, for the first time in the weapon's *existence*, it simply went *click*.

Amba stared down at the FRIEND with a look of incredulity.

I'm sorry, Amba. Truly I am.

You... you bitch!

No need to be like that. This is for the Greater Good. SARAH needs to be destroyed. The Theme Planet must be shut down. And Oblivion will conquer the Quad-Gal, one way or another... with or without your help. I don't want you to die here, Amba. I'm doing this for your own good.

But you are my flesh, Zi... made from my own skin and bone...

I belong to Romero now, she said. *I always belonged to Romero.*

The gun touched Amba's forehead, and dropping her own FRIEND, the android looked beyond the cold hard barrel into the eyes of the Minister of Joy. In the hierarchy of android engineering, there were base androids, then there were the special units, the Anarchy Models which formed the baseline of torture and killer mods; and then there were the Ministers. Very special. Reserved Units. Nobody on Earth knew they were androids. Nobody, in fact, realised exactly who – or what – ruled Oblivion. Ruled Earth...

"Come with me," said the Minister, but Amba flipped sideways and the gun went BLAM. As she moved, her fingers formed a solid blade which she slammed, knife-like, into the Minister's flesh, cutting through skin and muscle and driving between ribs. As Amba's left hand swung upwards, knocking the gun toward the heavens – still firing – her right fist *closed* around a rib and she jerked back violently, pulling it out from the Minister's flesh in a shower of blood. He went down on one knee, and Amba punched him, still holding his rib, and took the gun from him with her free hand.

"I thought you were the best," she said.

"We are," said the Minister through his mask. Blood was pouring down his leg, and his heavy coat was soaked like a sponge.

"You're not good enough," she said, eyes narrowed, and shot him between the eyes. The gunshot echoed through the circuit forest, reverberating from silicon trees. Amba looked left, and right, and allowed the Minister to collapse.

More came, like shadows through the darkness, and Amba ran. Gunshots followed her, kicking sparks from the trees to her left and right. She sprinted, keeping low. A Minister surged in front of her, teeth bared garishly in his black metal face mask. She shot him through the teeth, and as he lay, kicking on the ground, his mouth a sodden black hole, she put a second round between his eyes and took his gun.

She crept, keeping low, making no sound. Weak light gleamed from carbon tree trunks. *What kind of weird place is this?* she asked, but there was no reply. Zi had gone, and Amba felt a bitter, wrenching hurt. *How could she do that to me? How could she betray me?* And the answer was simple, a clarity realised after a thousand lies and a million damn excuses.

Because Zi *could.*

She heard the Minister too late, and the gun cracked and a bullet smashed through her shoulder, worming down into her chest. Amba felt nothing. She flipped sideways, rolling with the considerable force of the impact and using its momentum to roll and come up running, blood squirting from her shoulder. She dodged right as more bullets chased her, and made out the sounds of three Ministers in pursuit.

She sprinted, arms pumping, blood flowing down her chest and between her breasts, tickling her like the tongue of a lover she'd never have. Who could love the android? Amba felt a dark empty space in her soul.

The Ministers pursued her, hard and fast. Despite their big frames and heavy coats, they moved swiftly, huge grey ghosts in the gloom. Amba suddenly leapt, catching a low tree branch and hauling herself up. The tree was huge, and she scrambled up through the branches. The Ministers followed, climbing confidently, guns still firing. Bullets whined around Amba. She felt a twinge of doubt, and then blanked all thoughts from her mind. *Fuck it. When I die, I die. Death is just an end to pain and suffering. When it happens – then so be it.*

She was high now, and still climbing fast. The carbon and silicon branches were thinning out, and felt greasy under her hands. She had gained a considerable lead on the Ministers, being more lithe and flexible. Now, she stood on a branch and looked out across the circuit-based forest – like standing on the inside of a computer, lost in a maze of components. The motherboard stretched away, seemingly forever.

I feel like I am lost inside my own mind, she realised.

I could die here.

She started to laugh, and for the first time in her life discovered genuine humour. It raced through her like a drug, like a poison, and she welcomed it, and spread her arms like a dove, and dropped from the high branch, diving, both arms ahead of her, both guns ahead of her, bullets blasting as she barrelled towards the Ministers. The highest climber was looking up, mask upturned to her, and two rounds smashed into him, one through each cheek, disintegrating his face and the brain beyond even as Amba screamed past his limp, toppling body. The other two were shooting at her, and she could see spurts of fire from gun barrels as she twisted, started to spin, her own guns still howling and the Minister's bullets already behind her as her own bullets ate another face, and shoulders, and spinal column, and the third android flashed towards her and her arms smashed out, she hit him with an audible *crack* and they both plummeted through the trees.

From ground level, there came a torrent of snapping branches, a patter of disintegrating treefall, and a deep leaden *thud*. The undergrowth, made up of components as it was, showered like soil around a meteor crater.

Stillness descended.

Slowly, Amba extricated herself from the crushed Minister. His spine and neck were both broken, and his eyes watched her forlornly from behind the mask. Amba lifted one gun and, with a snarl, put a bullet through his nose.

"I am disappointed," said a calm, cool voice.

Amba whirled, both guns up. Cardinal Romero was unarmed.

"I don't know why. You've misled me from the start. From inception. For *decades*, Romero, fucking *decades!*"

"I *own* you," said Romero, softly, tapping a finger to his lips. He stood motionless, no guards, no SIMs, no Ministers. Alone, unarmed, and an idea trickled through Amba's skull, and it was a Bad Thought and she wasn't used to such ideas.

"You betrayed me," said Amba.

"No, you betrayed yourself. You went off-task. You started to use your own initiative. I don't want you to think, Amba. You're just my dumb bitch, my coma whore, and you do what the fuck you are told. You follow instructions. You kill who we tell you, and when we tell you. You just use your little bit of ingenuity to get the job done."

"So I'm like a machine? An automaton? Hah! Why not use a robot, then, Romero? Why even bother with me?"

Romero laughed. "Have you heard yourself? You're an android, Amba. Created. Engineered. Property. And yeah, I can see the signs, you might think you're human; what was it? You kill the wrong child? Drive over a puppy? Have some soppy pregnant bitch beg you for life? Whatever, you think you have gleaned a taste for *humanity*. Well, I'm here to tell you you're wrong, Amba. You are a created thing. A human machine. Controlled."

"They're all human machines!" snapped Amba, voice low, guns unwavering on their target. One twitch, one *blink* in the wrong place and she'd waste him. And she knew – knew she could. She had the strength, the tenacity, and the will. Now, she had the will. And he knew it. "There's no difference between android and human. You say I'm property? Controlled? Like an electric sheep? Well open your eyes, Romero, because you've just described the majority of *human beings*. There is no shame in being an android. At least we strive to improve ourselves; to seek the impossible dream. Such an irony, then, that the dream we strive to achieve doesn't even belong to the host, the creator, the *superior*."

"I can see it in you," said Romero, softly.

"What?"

"The change. The difference. What are you going to tell me, sweet Amba? That you've found love?" His voice was mocking, and Amba bit her lip, eyes narrowing, brain whirring like a well-oiled machine. "Who is he? Which hunk of man flesh have you allowed inside your cunt, and inside your skull? Who skull-fucked my perfect little android, hey?"

Romero stepped forward, brushing aside the guns, and he took her and he held her tight. She tensed for a moment, then lowered her head to his chest, and felt tears on her cheeks, and all thoughts of death and violence and torture were gone, dust blown on the wind. Her hate evaporated. And she realised – this was what humanity felt like. It was the ability to forgive. The ability to *forget*. She did not want to kill Romero. As she had said; he'd been there since inception. She wanted to walk away, and find Dex, and start again. Without the pain.

"Who is he?" whispered Romero in her ear, words tickling her, dark eyes glittering.

"Dexter Colls," said Amba, simply.

"And you love him?"

"I think I do."

"But you are both androids," said Romero.

"Yes. But I think we can become so much more. Like newborn babies, learning how to live; how to survive. Nobody is as cruel as a child. We are like that. Like children. We must find a new path through the world."

"What qualifies you to do this?"

"We have empathy. And love. We had a connection – of souls. I felt it. I felt the Greater Power. I felt... God."

Romero pulled back, and cupped her face in his hands. He held her tightly.

"You have a job to do," he said.

"I can no longer do that, Cardinal Romero. I don't have it in me."

"And what if I say 'no'?"

"Then you say 'no.' Your instructions have little to do with the way I *feel*. You cannot make me go on. I'd rather die."

"I do not wish to threaten you."

"Then don't. Just let me go. I will find Dex. We will disappear."

"Have you forgotten our mission? About Oblivion? About the plans for Earth's new vast Empire?"

"Then use *your own* humanity to see past that," said Amba, staring into Romero's eyes. "If there's one good thing you do in this life, one compromise you can make, one act of love and life and honesty and caring, make it this. Let me go. Let me find Dex. You owe me that much."

"Do I?"

"Yes, you fucker. Go on. Make the right decision, for the first time in your life."

"Why would I do that," said Romero slowly, licking his lips, "when I'm just an android like you?"

Amba froze. In the splinter of an atom she saw her incredible danger, but then Romero squeezed her head at twin pressure points, and the world spun around like it was a merry-go-round, and the circuit forest flickered black and white, and Amba felt nausea swamp her and something cold like liquid nitrogen flood down through her, from the tip of her brain through her chest and abdomen, through her groin and legs until it tickled her toes.

And Amba saw the world clearly once again.

"What did you do to me?"

Romero stood back. "I reset you. It's a failsafe."

"Good."

"You have a mission to complete."

"I do?"

"Yes. This man." He held out a picture. "Dexter Colls."

"You wish me to kill him?"

"Yes."

"I will kill him."

Amba started forward, but Romero checked her advance. "Wait. You'll need this."

Amba took the FRIEND, and held the weapon in a familiar way. She gave a nod. "Thank you."

Hi sweetie, said Zi. *It's so good to be back...*

DEX MOVED SLOWLY down a narrow corridor, Makarov in hand, eyes narrowed. Nothing had changed, but he almost... *sensed* he was there. At SARAH's core. Her heart. The core of Monolith. The heart of the Theme Planet.

The corridor was glossy black, floor and ceiling almost soft under his fingers, queasily organic. Dex reached a portal and stepped through, warily, into a big space. It was a factory floor, filled with a million machines for the creation of Theme Planet's wonders. There were giant spirals of glass and liquid metal that pulsed softly, shimmering in the subdued light. There were vast cubes, which juddered occasionally, each the size of a house, with flickering scatters of coloured lights cascading randomly across different faces. There were conveyor belts with gleaming ride CARs, all brand new and waiting to be put into commission. There were stacks of hot dog stands with mechanical legs, a hundred stands high, waiting patiently to fill the bellies of Theme Planet's adventure denizens.

Dex moved forward into the factory, Makarov in fist, face grim, eyes alert. The whole place was quiet, not like the roaring factories he'd visited back on Earth. The place *did* have an almost subsonic *hum,* an undercurrent of sound, of energy, of activity, something Dex might associate with an insect hive. There was a lot of activity going on here, Dex could feel it in his bones. But most of it was sectioned away, out of sight.

Dex walked alongside silent conveyor belts. A glance told him the trundling, well-oiled belts carried machine parts, parts for rides or ride equipment. This place was a place of genesis, of birth, and Dex could almost feel the integral sense of the new, the created, the *born*. This was where Theme Planet was created, and had always been created.

This was SARAH's core. Her Heart. Where she made the rides. Where she gave *birth* to the rides.

Dex stopped, and looked up at a huge, pulsing, glossy black structure. It was as big as a fifty-storey tower block, vast and leering, disappearing up into the darkness of the roof beams high above; it was shaped like an intricate bulbous bottle, with a narrow neck at the top and a bulge in the middle, tapering to several tubes leading to the conveyors. As Dex watched, a frown creased his brow. The bulbous part was pulsing and squirming in a disgustingly organic manner, almost like a...

"Like a birthing sack," muttered Dex, and watched as a bright yellow ride CAR was squeezed from one of the glistening tubes and onto a conveyor. It was covered in thick clear slime, and as it moved down the conveyor tiny drones flickered around it, polishing away the... Dex grinned like a maniac. *They're cleaning off the amniotic fluid,* he realised. *Holy shit, SARAH is giving birth to the ride CARs. Everything on the Theme Planet, every ride, every CAR, every pleasure-giving device – they're all organic. All part of the alien world shell known as SARAH. Each rollercoaster is a child. Every ride CAR one of her kindred. Every support beam one of her ribs. Every nut and bolt are organic building blocks, every H section a bone, every hydraulic unit a vein filled with SARAH's pumping blood.*

Dex wasn't just inside SARAH. Inside the factory.

He was inside her *womb*.

The place where ride dreams were born...

He caught movement up ahead and focused on the task in hand. Katrina was here to plant her FRIEND and destroy SARAH, destroy the core of Theme Planet. He had to stop her. He hurried forward, Makarov against his cheek, moving with speed but making every footfall as silent as possible – helped by the glossy black floor of SARAH's womb.

Dex's mind clicked into a certain place, and he was back on the mean streets of London, regressed to his days in the Police Urban Force that seemed, now, a thousand years ago. And he was hunting down just another criminal, another bad person, only this time it was his own fucking wife, a woman he loved and cherished and with whom he'd shared his life; only none of that was real. She was an android with a long-term implanted mission directive. Dex felt sour inside; he felt his soul torn out, and fed as scraps to bloody, snarling fighting dogs.

I wish Jones was here, he thought bitterly. *A bit of backup is not something to be turned down lightly.* But Jones wasn't here. The jammy fucker was back on Earth, living out his normal life, probably wondering in idle moments with a cold beer how Dex was getting on during his fine, expensive holiday on the Theme Planet.

Oh, yeah. The irony.

Something was glowing up ahead, a thick tube suspended in the air, glittering with spirals of twisting matter, a million glittering spirals, like expanded strands from a DNA molecule hanging in the air. This was SARAH's core... her CPU? Her soul? Dex did not know, and to be truthful, no longer cared. He only knew right and wrong. And Katrina helping destroy the Theme Planet to aid Earth's warmongering plans was a basic evil he had to stop...

Through the glowing strands Dex caught sight of Katrina's face. She was intent on her mission, and did not see him approach. Her face was illuminated by the glow of SARAH's core and she looked incredibly beautiful, more beautiful than he'd ever seen her. She looked so alive, so radiant, so dazzling; like an angel, like a martyr. It was untrue to Dex; unbelievable she had turned against him.

Katrina's hands moved into the glowing strands, parting them gently, and with a jerk Dex came out of his reverie – realised what she was doing. His mouth opened to scream "No," but he didn't get that far. Katrina's eyes lifted, met his, she smiled, and removed her hands. There was a dark *flicker* among the folding shifts of entwining strands, and Dex saw it, saw the FRIEND deep down in the core, saw it spin and twist, and the word came to his lips, his eyes fixed on Katrina's, as the world... *shuddered*. And SARAH *screamed*.

The floor shook, the whole *womb* shook, and Dex was knocked violently from his feet. A shrill, piercing noise descended into existence, a shrill piercing whistle that slammed through Dex's mind as a constant pain and forced both hands against his ears in agony. It was SARAH's scream, and it cut him.

The womb was vibrating, rocking, shifting, and the scream lessened a little, Dex crawling to his knees and glancing up – as Katrina's boot kicked the Makarov from his hand, and the second kick caught him under the chin, knocking him up and back. Dex rolled to his feet, even as Katrina powered for him and he took four – five – six – seven – eight strikes to his forearms, each blow feeling like a slam from an iron bar.

Katrina took a step back, turned, and walked away from him. Then she turned back, and her eyes were glowing.

"Why, Katrina?" said Dex, holding his hands out wide. "Why the hell are you doing this? Come back to me, come back to what we had; we can stop this thing, end this evil. We can fight Earth's invasion. It doesn't have to be this way."

"It does, Dexter. This is what I am. This is what I do, you poor, foolish boy."

"I disagree," snapped Dexter, face a snarl, edging sideways. He wanted to sprint past Katrina, grab the FRIEND, wrench it from SARAH's core – end the screaming, which was like a screwdriver in his brain. "This *isn't* the woman I met, and fell in love with, and married, and had children with. What happened to that beautiful young girl? What happened to that wonderful bright person?"

Dex charged right, but Katrina moved to stop him and he checked himself. She folded her arms, and smiled, and he realised – her aim wasn't to kill him. It was to wait for the FRIEND to detonate and take out SARAH... How long did he have? Minutes? *Seconds?*

"Talking of our children, *darling,* what have you done to Molly and Toffee?"

"I didn't kill them, if that's what you mean."

"There you go. That's a human response," said Katrina, a dark smile on her lips.

"Good," said Dexter. "I suppose you would have killed them, bitch?"

"Without a single backward glance, *husband*. A single bullet in each young skull. Regret is for humans, Dexter Colls. And we are not humans. We are androids. We get the job done, and we fucking do it well. That's the way we were engineered."

"I've evolved from my engineering," said Dex, and darted left. Katrina met his charge, slamming into him with a grunt. There was an exchange of punches, and Dex felt *just wrong* slamming his fists into his wife's face. He hated men who abused women. *But this isn't a woman,* he told himself, as he broke her nose with a right hook, and blood sprayed out. *She's an android, and she's trying to kill me... trying to kill us all.* Her knee sank into his groin, her hands found his hair, and she dragged his face onto her knee three times, sending stars spinning through his skull. And all the time Dex was thinking of the ticking bomb in SARAH's core. Katrina was willing to die for this. Katrina was willing to die to destroy the Theme Planet.

She released him, and he staggered back, eyes filled with blood. He blinked, clearing them, and looked up into a pair of boots as they smashed him back and onto the ground, his world full of pain. A great weight bore down on Dexter, and as his eyes flickered open and awareness came creeping back to reality, he realised Katrina was kneeling on his chest. She'd wound something around his throat, a metal cord, and as he blinked the blood out of his eyes and realised what was happening, his fingers shot up under the cord reflexively as Katrina's hands pulled viciously tight. The cord bit down on his fingers and throat. Such was her strength his fingers were squeezed into his windpipe and she started to slowly strangle him, and he struggled, legs kicking, free fist punching at her ribs and kidneys, gurgling and spitting, face turning purple as he gradually, inexorably, began to die...

And all the while she spoke. His wife spoke.

Katrina spoke to him.

"You think you were a fucking good husband, well I've got something to tell you, mister, I *hated* every fucking second of it, hated your smiles and jokes and the slaps on my arse, I hated our walks in the park, hated our fancy meals in posh restaurants with so-called educated *cunts* looking down their noses at us, I hated our cosy evenings in with bottles of wine and movies, hated cuddling up to you on the sofa, resting my head on your chest as you pawed my breasts and fumbled between my legs like some high school virgin..."

She released the pressure for a moment, and Dex gurgled, froth at his lips, and she got herself a better grip and yanked tight again with a grunt of effort. "...but the worst thing of all, you miserable little bastard, was the sex, feeling you squirming inside me like a fucking maggot in a pot of honey, thrusting and humping me like a side of sick beef – well I want you to know, Dexter, before you die, I faked every fucking sigh of pleasure, every tiny murmur of contentment, every moan of enjoyment, every squirm of fun, I faked every screaming, bed-thumping orgasm, I faked every bite and suck and fuck, because you were the worst, Dex, the worst I ever had – and to top it all, I gave you two kids, two screaming, parasitic little fuckers whom I should have strangled at birth. So think on that as you crawl your way down into the pit of android Hell. Think on that, Dexter, my love, as I strangle the last atom of oxygen from your dying, worthless, pointless fucking carcass!"

CHAPTER FIFTEEN

STRANGE BROTHERHOOD

A THOUSAND BIG Belly Bombers droned across Theme Planet, going their separate ways, each with precisely logged coordinates of impending destruction. Computers whizzed and buzzed, bomb doors opened with slick alloy clicks, bombmasters yelled commands, and payloads fell. Below, on the mammoth colourful cartoon landscape of Theme Planet, where rollercoasters coasted, ride CARs jumped into the air and zoomed beneath the oceans, where families strolled and mothers laughed, fathers wore flip-flops, children ate ice cream, babies chuckled in strollers, puppies yapped and everybody was having a funtime-goodtime-joytime, below, the first HD bomb struck. The detonation roared as a kilometre-wide ball of flame vaporised everything – *everything* – in contact vicinity. Flames and gas roared and screamed, ride CARs were tossed up, spat up, spat out like fire confetti from the heart of a raging volcano. Bodies burned and were blast-disintegrated. And high above, a computer gave a little tick in a little digital tick-box, and relayed the information to Earth in a series of neat spreadsheets.

Monolith's ethos in its operation of Theme Planet was *the show must go on*. Through drought and flood, volcanic explosion and earthquake, never once did it cease operation of its thousands of rides and pleasure systems; during tsunamis and vast forest fires, only those rides *directly affected* halted. After all, money was money, and business was business, and pleasure was pleasure, right? and *the show must go on, right?* Theme Planet gave pleasure to billions. That was what it did. Core function. Prime directive. *I give fun, therefore I am*, as the marketing slogan went.

The one *unnatural* disaster which Monolith was not ready to accommodate was one of which it would never have dreamed. Military Invasion. *Why* would anybody want to destroy the most fun place in the Four Galaxies? Theme Planet was not geared up for war. Monolith commanded no army, despite what Romero might have originally believed. Guards, yes. Secret Police, yes. But not trained for battle... And it had basic defence missile systems installed in the event of, for example, an impending meteor strike. But now, Monolith's High Command turned these basic weapons on Earth's ships, and missiles slammed through the skies to connect with Big Belly Bombers. Bombers exploded with screams and bangs and plummeting debris. On beaches across Theme Planet, where turquoise oceans lapped at white, sandy shores, lasers cut across the sky like some incredible themed display, and explosions roared, and detonations blossomed, and pilots burned, and people died.

"Daddy?"

"Yes, honey?"

"That's a pretty firework display."

"Yes, honey. Well, this is the *Theme Planet*. It has a reputation to uphold."

"Daddy?"

"Yes, honey?"

"What's that fat plane doing?"

A frown. "I don't know, honey."

Explosions. Metal screaming. Lasers fizzing.

A bomb fell and detonated, and out on the ocean where a themed island languished in the sun, palm trees wavering, seashells glinting on the beach, small bamboo huts playing host to love-nests of newly married couples, all were eaten by a wall of fire and the ocean exploded upwards and the horizon glowed, seemed to *melt* as a furnace ate a small section of the world, consumed a small portion of the Theme Planet...

"Daddy?"

"Mmm?"

"That was a pretty firework."

"I don't think that was a firework display, honey..."

A BBB slammed through clouds of gas and vapour, and there was a subtle whine. Father and daughter turned instinctively to run, toes digging into the sand, pigtails flapping in the sea breeze, as there came connection, detonation, acceleration, destruction.

DEX WAS DYING. He was fighting, but he was dying. She was too strong, too savage, and without a shadow of a doubt, Katrina, his wife, had the upper hand. With every passing second she strangled him, with every passing second his strength ebbed away and it became yet more impossible that he might pull away, escape, break free. Dex wondered if there was a Heaven for his kind. For the androids. Engineered humans. Human machines. And he knew, deep down in his dark soul, that there was not.

He tried to speak, to cry out, to beg Katrina to stop. He wanted to grab her face and kiss her lips one last time, but even now her snarling hate-filled visage was fading from view as his senses dulled. It sounded like he was deep beneath the ocean, sinking, and great, muffled booming sounds were ringing out through the Deep Green.

Everything was becoming fuzzy, everything becoming lost and drowned and faded...

Why are you doing this to me?

Why don't you love me anymore?

I don't understand how we came to be here.

It was just a simple family holiday. How did it turn so bad?

Pawns. Manipulated. On a greater game board. Pieces tossed carelessly around by the hands of a Great Player. But hadn't it always been like this? Weren't there always sacrifices? Wasn't it always the way of the world? The strong controlling the weak; the powerful pushing around the little fucks.

I am going to die, he realised.

I am going to die, and nobody will care...

There came a slap, and something wet pattered down over his face in a thick, glutinous spray. The pressure released from his throat, from his trapped hand, and gradually he swam up from the bottom of the well. The pressure had released from his chest; which meant Katrina was on the move.

Sound returned first, and he could hear screaming, and his own laboured breathing, his own tortured, rasping throat. Then blurred light gave way to a gloomy clarity, and for a few moments the scene was one of total confusion.

Dexter sat up, and allowed the scene to unfold, to flower, and his brow creased, and he spat out blood, and then stared hard and scratched his chin. Toffee, his sweet little girl Toffee, was standing holding a screwdriver. It wasn't sonic, or magic, or any other bullshit; it was a good, hard, chromed steel screwdriver. And it was covered in blood.

Toffee was watching him. Toffee was smiling.

Dex's gaze rose and focused on Katrina. She was staring back at him, screaming shrilly, her hand clasped to her neck, blood pumping out between her fingers. She looked at Toffee and snarled something incomprehensible, blood frothing and bubbling on her lips... Katrina launched herself at the girl, and Dex wanted to scream "No!" and stop the attack, but Toffee was already turning, ducking one shoulder, twisting and ramming the screwdriver into Katrina's side.

Katrina staggered back, the screwdriver embedded in her ribs, and sat down with a thump. Toffee walked to Dex and he wondered what wonderful tortures she had in store for him.

"Hello, Daddy."

"Hi, sweetie. I see you gave mommy a present." His words were little more than croaks on cracked lips, and every syllable brought a whole galaxy of pain. She stood over him, and he looked up, and he knew he was in no fit state to do anything if she attacked. The shame! To be murdered by your youngest child. Dex started laughing, and there was hysteria there, like a ripe maggot in a rotten plum.

"I've come to see you," said Toffee.

"For what? Do I get the screwdriver in my skull next?"

Toffee tilted her head to one side, and Dex coughed up more blood from his lacerated throat. He shook his head, looking down at the floor, offering her his neck, the back of his head; like victim to executioner.

"I've come to say I'm sorry," Toffee said.

"What?" Dex looked up sharply, his word punctuated by Katrina's rasping gasps, where she sat in a spreading pool of her own blood and gazed dumbly at the screwdriver in her side. As Dex watched, she took hold of the handle and gave it a tug; it wouldn't move, or her strength was draining from her, and finally she gave up. She slowly lay down, and despite everything, despite her bringing him close to the brink of death, he felt nothing but sorrow. This wasn't a situation he could ever have dreamed about. This was one of the worst days of his engineered life.

"I've come to say I'm sorry. Mommy's been a *bad* mommy. She sent me to kill you, to erase you from the planet for being anti-android. And yet..." – she frowned, confused – "and yet you *could not* kill me. Would not kill me. Because I'm your little girl, and we had so many good times together, and this is not fun, this is not what I want my life to be like. I want it how it was, Daddy. I want you back. I want our friendship back."

Dex crawled to his knees, then stood with a groan. Everything ached. Every muscle, and ligament, and tendon, and bone creaked and moaned at him with their accumulated dissatisfaction.

Dex smiled, and patted Toffee on the head. "That's good. You're a good girl. But you shouldn't have stabbed your mother in the ribs."

"It was the only way to stop her killing you," said Toffee, eyes gleaming with tears. And Dex watched in wonder and awe as his android daughter cried. Tears ran down her cheeks and she ran to him, and unconsciously his arms circled her and he hugged her, and he had his little girl back, and a nasty cynical side of him thought, *oh, yeah, when does she pull out the dagger and stick it in my heart?* but another part of him yearned for what they'd once had. But it could never be like that again. Things had changed. Things always change.

Slowly, Dex unpeeled Toffee from the embrace and looked over at Katrina. He moved to her, crouched – but not too close – and touched her shoulder. Her eyes opened and she smiled weakly. Blood glittered on her teeth.

"That little bitch got me good," she said.

"I think she was taking a cue from you, sweetie."

"You always were an understanding bastard," she said.

"I'm sorry it came to this," said Dex.

"So am I. Look what the fucker did to my clothes."

"What happened to us, eh?"

"Just pieces in the Great Game, Dexter," said Katrina, and her eyes were heavy-lidded and hollow. Dex stared into those portals, leading straight down to Katrina's android soul, and he saw the pain there, saw fires raging bigger than the world, saw torture tearing her soul in two; saw the raw, bare, engineered agony.

"It should never have ended like this," said Dex.

"It's ending the way it should..." said Katrina, and glanced up, over at the FRIEND in SARAH's core. Dex followed her eyes and a coldness crept fingers around his heart.

The FRIEND!

Shit. In his own private world of misery, he'd forgotten, for just a moment...

The FRIEND was ready to detonate!

Dex kicked himself into action, charging for the core as SARAH's long, loud, high-pitched scream wailed in the distance and through the entirety of Theme Planet. She was dying. The FRIEND was killing her. And Dex realised with horror that there would be no giant explosion; this was not a detonation, this was more parasite and host, and the FRIEND was... poisoning her? Absorbing her? There was no countdown... in fact, the detonation had already begun. A slow detonation. A gradual, calculated murder...

"No!" he screamed, sprinting, and something hard hit him in the side, smashing him from his feet in a tangle of limbs and it was like being hit by a groundcar, hit by a fucking truck, and it knocked all sense and feeling out of Dex and he just lay there, stunned, broken, wondering what the fuck had hit him...

"Hiya, darling," said Amba Miskalov, and her boot stomped down. Dex rolled, and the glossy black floor cracked under the force of the blow. Amba knelt and her fist slammed down; again, Dex twisted, and her knuckles left imprints in the alloy.

Dex slammed his knee up, catching her in the groin, but she ignored it and grabbed his head in both hands; twisting, he bit down hard, sinking his teeth in down to Amba's reinforced bones. Amba did not gasp, showed no pain, even as Dex tore out a mouthful of tendon and muscle and struggled back, rolling from under her in a scramble of disorganised panic, and defending against her one remaining fist even as he retreated, scrambling back, spitting out her flesh. Her eyes were dark and there was no reasoning there. And Dex realised how special Amba was, much more dangerous than Katrina...

"I thought we had a connection?" said Dexter. "Something special?"

Amba's fist whirred past his face, and she stepped in close, twisting, elbow ramming back into his ear with piledriver force. But Dex was rolling with the blow, his own right hook smashing into Amba's ribs, and she grunted as bone cracked and splintered under the awesome blow; and they moved apart, squaring off, weighing each other up.

From the corner of his eye, Dex could see Katrina. Her head touched the ground, drool trailing to the floor in an umbilical. Dex thought she had died... thought his wife was gone...

Toffee attacked, leaping onto Amba's back, but Amba caught the child by the legs, and with a savage snarl, twirled her around like a doll, and dashed her head against the ground. Toffee lay still, blood leaking from a cracked skull.

"No..." hissed Dex, tears in his eyes.

"Give up the game and let SARAH die," said a dark-haired stranger, stepping out of the gloom.

Amba was working her damaged hand, but two fingers no longer operated. She bared her teeth at Dex in what he assumed was a bitter smile, an acknowledgement that he was more fucking dangerous than he looked.

"You'd be Romero, right, fucker?"

"You should indeed recognise me." His voice was low, controlled, and controlling. "After all, we came from the same VAT. We were engineered together, Dexter Colls. Look into my face, brother, look into my eyes. Can you not see yourself in me? Can you not see that we are the same? We are brothers?"

Romero moved forward, placing a hand on Amba's shoulder, and she stepped back. Romero moved closer, eyes fixed on Dexter, whose heart had accelerated, was thundering like a deviated, twisted train charging through his ears and breast.

He did indeed recognise Romero.

How could he not?

They had the same face...

Slowly, Dexter released a breath. Pain drum-rolled through his heart, stabbed him in the skull. "What is this shit?" he said slowly, voice a drawl, eyes flickering from Amba to Romero and back again. "You're in charge of Earth's Oblivion Government, right? How could we possibly be brothers? This is a con. A trick. Who comes next? My sister?"

"What's happening here, Dexter – well, this has been a long, *long* time in the planning – by minds much greater than ours. Yes, I control Oblivion and the Ministers of Joy. But you" – he stepped closer, taking Dex's face in his hands – "you, my faithful brother, you were the pivotal implant. You were key to getting us inside

SARAH, getting the FRIEND to her core. Dexter. Congratulations. You have brought down the Theme Planet."

"Not yet, I haven't," he growled.

"Listen to SARAH scream, it is the most beautiful music in the Quad-Gal," smiled Romero, face lifting, turning, eyes staring at the high darkness as he appreciated the constant, keening wail of torture and agony and devolution... he glanced back to Dexter's face. "You did your job well, brother. Despite all the problems, the deviations, the fuck-ups. Katrina and the girls aided you perfectly – were faultless in conducting your progress. You are the finest of tools; you just have to be controlled in the right manner." He sighed. "Anyway. What matters is we got here in the end."

"Fuck you," said Dexter, leaning closer with a snarl, with a swirling rage in his eyes and on his face like a savage tattoo; Romero's hands fell away.

"You have a glittering career ahead of you," said Romero, smiling easily, relaxed.

"I want no career from you."

"When your memories return, you will realise our brotherly love, our sense of... *family* is the strongest chain in the whole of the Four Galaxies! We will drink together, we will whore together, and you will quickly forget this pettiness. Forget your time with your fake wife Katrina, and your fake fucking pointless children. You don't need all that baggage, Dexter. You need to come back to me, to Oblivion! Your Minister's Throne is cold and it's been that way far too long, my brother."

"I am not," snarled Dex, eyes glowing, "your *brother*." He knocked Romero's hands aside, and Romero took a step back, head to one side, his smile falling from his face. Behind him, Amba pulled out her own FRIEND, Zi, and pointed it at Dex.

"Don't even go down this route, Dexter. You're an android, yes, but Amba here will blow a hole in you so wide I could climb through it. And I know what you're thinking, that you've been misled, a wriggling pointless pawn in a bigger game and all that other bullshit – and that might be how you *feel* now, but it's not right, because this whole thing is something *you agreed*. You're an Earth Minister, for the love of God. We could never force you down this path! You chose it, Dexter. *Brother*. You *chose* to have a temporary memory block. You chose to spend years married to Katrina, to have your engineered children – yes, you were allowed that *privilege* – because it was decided that only *that* could get you past the fucking provax guarding SARAH."

"No," said Dex, "this is all wrong, this is all lies and bullshit!"

"We tried to release you, to give you back your memories – of before, of your life as a Minister of Joy on Earth. *Then* you'd realise this was your mission, your long-term plan. To start the invasion. Not just to cripple Monolith and Theme Planet and *SARAH*, no, but to *take* her – the most incredible, awesome, wonderful living alien – and to turn her to our War Effort! To our new Empire!"

"I thought you were trying to destroy her?"

Romero laughed. "Destroy her? She's the most devastating and advanced biological weapon ever to evolve. Above, our bombers and missiles are destroying the *humans* who are polluting her; we are cleaning out the detritus, removing the wart, lancing the boil, cutting out the cancer with fire. No weapons we have up there can destroy SARAH – she covers the entire planet; it would take interstellar HALO strikes to do it. We don't want that, Dexter. We want *her*. You've seen her hatching theme rides and theme CARs and shit, yes? She can so easily give birth to anything we instruct... tanks and bombs and missiles, cyborgs, HALO jets, SLAM fighters – fuck, Dexter, if we give her enough *raw materials* she can birth Warships and Cruisers and Destroyers!"

"Raw materials?"

"She *consumes* planets, Dexter. Don't you see? She takes their surface materials and reconstitutes them on a molecular level, all the time imbuing them with a part of herself, a controlling part of her soul. Anybody who controlled SARAH, well..."

"They'd conquer the Four Galaxies," said Dexter, slowly.

"You're catching on fast, brother. Drop her into any environment and watch her spread, watch her conquer, watch her reconstitute everything in her path... now, we just need to know her secrets. Of transportation. Of design. Of control."

"The FRIEND," said Dex, wearily. "It's torturing her?"

"Oh, yes," said Romero darkly. "Showing her who is boss. Showing her who is in control."

Dex transferred his gaze to Amba. She was watching him with bright eyes, FRIEND held steady. "I thought we had something, Amba. I thought we had... a connection. Something special. If not love, then... understanding. We're the same, Amba, and I have a curious feeling we're destined to be together. One day."

"Dexter," said Romero, "when you come back to Oblivion, you can take whatever you want. You want Amba warming your bed and sucking your cock? That can be arranged. Even though we are androids, there is a *hierarchy* to observe. And you, my Brother, are right at the top."

Dex licked his lips. He looked at Katrina. He looked at the still body of Toffee. He listened to the screams of SARAH. And his face went hard. No matter what he had been, he knew what he was *now*, knew how he felt *now*, and understood that he had transcended material considerations. He had empathy; he had understanding. He knew he had a soul, and no matter whether you were born human or engineered, it wasn't about your creation, your beginnings, it was about what you *were*, deep down inside.

"Your warmongering, your invasion, your torture, your murder – it's evil, Romero. It's just plain wrong. I wish no part in it. In fact, I'd rather fucking *die* than be related to you, and this fucking abomination you call an existence."

Romero's face was grim.

"You'd rather die?"

"I'd rather die," said Dex, and spat in Romero's face. "So stop fucking whining and do it, before I rip out your throat with my teeth and chew on your diseased fucking spine."

The corner of Romero's eye twitched. He lifted his hand a few inches, a subtle signal, then dropped it again. In a croak, he said, "Kill him."

"With pleasure," whispered Amba.

A THOUSAND BIG Belly Bombers droned over the Savage Mountains of South Kardoom, and General Kome, in the lead bomber, leaned forward, eyes gleaming in anticipation as they approached the jewel in the crown of Theme Planet's ride extravaganzas, the newest ride and current highlight of mass TV and filmy advertising campaigns: MAYHEM. The biggest rollercoaster ever built. The wildest rollercoaster ever built. It started on the edge of the atmosphere, and dropped vertically for five kilometres before hitting its first spin and roll – which went on for another five. It was said, at one point, the rollercoaster entered *another dimension* via a transferable modular singularity. That marketing fact was a closely guarded secret.

"Ahhhh," said General Kome, "I do so enjoy flying happily into an unguarded soon-to-be-warzone where we have guaranteed intelligence that the pointless and soon-to-be spineless victims have no real firepower with which to retaliate; I do so love attacking an innocent people and culture, and blowing them all the way to the arsehole of Hell. And, if the truth be known, Theme Planet, and Monolith Corporation, with all its wealth and acumen, with all its reserves and technology, well, they deserve everything I fucking throw at them for leaving such a ripe and wealthy jackpot unguarded, just there, a honey globule waiting to be picked." He rubbed his hands together and lit a fat cigar. "I'm going to give this SARAH a proper going over. Stick it to her from behind, so to speak. Teach her who's the boss, who's the daddy, who's the overlord, and who is ultimately going to be holding her new leash."

At ground level, the earth had begun to tremble. The air became chaotic, a riot, and was filled with grease. Clouds broiled through the sky, which darkened as if anticipating a violent thunderstorm.

The mountains, now scrolling past to General Kome's right, began to vibrate, and the large military man frowned, chewing his cigar with prejudice.

"Peterson, any seismic or volcanic activity detected?"

Petersen, a small neat man, lifted his finger, scanning the binary reports. "No, sir. Er. Sir, there's something else..."

"Go on?"

"There's... some kind of activity. The computers are showing... ah."

"Showing what, idiot?" snapped General Kome, voice the bark of a Rottweiler.

"Ah. According to the scanners, sir, the *entire* surface area beneath us is moving."

"Moving? An earthquake?"

"Negative, sir. No earthquake."

"What do you mean, then, moving? Speak sense! Decode it, man, decode it!"

"It appears to be just – *expanding,* sir."

"That's impossible. Over what size area?"

"As far as the scanners detect."

"Which is?"

"Ten thousand square klicks, sir."

"You mean to tell me ten thousand square fucking kilometres of the *ground* is expanding?"

"Affirmative, General Kome."

Kome stared at the wobbling mountains to his right, and the glittering ocean to his left which, he noted, had become extremely choppy (this was an understatement; the waves were riding ten metres high). He rubbed his stubbled chin and chewed on his cigar. "What I suggest," he said, but didn't get much further, because at that point something BIG did move in his peripheral vision, and as he turned his head to focus, his mouth dropped open and the cigar toppled to the console, spilling a trail of random ash.

"Holy Mother of Mary," said Peterson, eyes wide, hands trembling on air-scanners. "I've never seen anything quite like... *that...*"

Kome grabbed the comm, hit SEND to all bombers, and screamed, "Evasive action, evasive action!"

But he was too late.

DEX STARED DOWN the barrel of the FRIEND and he knew he was dead. He'd had Zi in his head; he knew what she could do. Had detected her... amorality? After all, she was nothing more than a KillChip. An AI designed to torture and murder for its masters. *Ha-ha. Like us,* thought Dex, wondering what death would be like. Would there be a Heaven? With glowing winged android angels? *Yeah, right, motherfucker.*

Amba pulled the trigger, and Dex realised his eyes were closed, and there came a SLAM of energy and he felt the heat sear his face and he gasped, his hands rising reflexively, grabbing at his chest where he was sure to find a gaping hole with his ribs poking out.

But there was no hole. Only something hazy drifting against his face, as if he walked through a very fine drizzle. It pressed against his lips like a kiss, caressed his face like the softest of silk veils, and – opening his eyes with a *click* – Dex realised it was a cloud of blood. And Romero's head was gone.

The large corpse buckled slowly, like a tower with its foundations bombed, and it folded gently to the floor. Dex looked up, looked at Amba, and she was crying and there was no sense there, no logic there, and she was not looking at him but staring off, into another place, another time, another world. A world where the blue door was never closed.

Dex stepped over Romero's corpse and took Amba gently in his arms.

"Amba?" he said, softly. "Amba?"

"Mmm?" Gradually, she focused on his face, and said, "Oh, it's you."

"Don't tell me your aim was that bad."

"No. No. I love you, Dexter. But they chipped me; reset me. But I fought it, fought it like a demon. Not just for you; but for all those people I murdered. And especially my little girl. Especially her."

Dex licked his lips, released Amba, and moving swiftly to SARAH he plunged his arm into the icy coldness of her core, grasped the FRIEND, and pulled it free. A voice chattered in his head, liked winged demons pecking on the diseased remains of his corpse.

Hello, said the FRIEND. *I was enjoying that!*

Tell me you left nothing behind? In SARAH?

Of course not. I am a consummate professional. Don't you recognise my voice, Dexter? I am yours. Your FRIEND. Your specification. Your KillChip, programmed by Quantell Systems. I am a model 2.1 KADE. And I am yours for all eternity.

With a snort of disgust, Dexter threw Kade with all his might, and the FRIEND clattered along a metal walkway and was suddenly *sucked* into a huge black machine. Then it was gone. Then it was done.

"You hear?" said Amba, pointing upwards.

"She's stopped screaming."

"I hope we were in time," said Dex.

"We were in time," smiled Amba, and fell to her knees. Tears ran down her cheeks, and she buried her face in her hands. Dexter stared at her, not understanding, and she waved to him. "Go. Go check Katrina and Toffee. They need you."

Dex ran to Toffee, and gently rolled her into his arms. Blood had stopped leaking from the split in her head, and Dex cradled his little one, willing his life force into her, willing his strength to flow into her bones and mend the break.

She opened her eyes. "Daddy?"

"I'm here, sweetie."

"My head hurts, Daddy."

"We'll get it bandaged real soon, Toffee."

"I'm not going to die, am I, Daddy?"

"No, sweetheart. I promise you. You're not going to die."

"Are we going home yet? I've had enough of Theme Planet."

"Soon, little one. Soon."

He removed his shirt, and rolled it into a pillow for Toffee. Then he crawled over to Katrina, convinced she was dead, and not sure how he felt. She had betrayed him so badly, said such evil things. But he loved her. He always would. It was hardwired into him. She might be a bitch, but she was *his* bitch. She might be a murdering, back-stabbing dirtbox, but she was *his* murdering, back-stabbing dirtbox.

"Kat?" he said, softly, eyes taking in the massive pool of blood. There was too much blood there. Way too much blood.

Amazingly, her eyes opened. "I'm still here," she said.

"How can you survive that?"

"They made me tough. Just like you."

"What do we do now?"

"We go home," said Katrina.

"We can't go home. We betrayed Oblivion. Ha. Sorry. *I* betrayed Oblivion. You'll probably get a pay rise. Or some new upgrades. Or something."

"Very funny."

"I'm tempted to leave you here. Let SARAH deal with you."

Katrina coughed, and her face was torn with pain. "I have a better idea."

"Oh, yeah?"

"Let's find Molly. Let's be a family again."

"You all turned against me. Remember?"

Katrina grabbed him, grabbed him so hard her fingers left indents in his flesh. "They won't let any of us live, you know. They'll hunt us down. All of us. With Romero dead, they'll appoint a new leader of the Ministers of Joy... appoint a new overlord to watch over the Anarchy Androids. We fucked it all up, Dexter. They'll want us removed, for sure. And they'll send their best after us; their best hunters."

"Why should I help you?" said Dexter.

"Because you love me. And you know I love you. You *know* it."

"I can't trust you," said Dexter.

Katrina laughed. "Good. That's the way I prefer it." She reached forward and pecked him on the lips. "It'll keep you on your toes, chipmunk."

Dex stared at her, and grinned at the insanity of it, and through the whirl of confusion that was his brain, through the ash confetti of his turbulent soul, he knew they had more chance of survival if they stayed together. Yes, Earth would want them dead. No matter what part they played in foiling Earth's invasion plans; in their plans to *kidnap* and abuse this most incredible of alien wonders. Dex glanced over at Amba, and she smiled at him, and he knew she loved him; but his love was for Katrina. His first true love. His only love.

"Shit," he muttered, covering his eyes.

"What're we gonna do, Dex?" whispered Katrina.

"Let's find Molly, and explore the Quad-Gal together," said Dexter.

RELEASED OF THE FRIEND, SARAH raged. And with her rage came control.

On the command bridge of the lead bomber, General Kome released his grip on the comm as the mountain range *reared up*, expanding like stretched rubber, mountains melting into one another and flowing into a mass of liquid rock before they expanded, and like a mammoth hand reached out towards the bombers – a *thousand* bombers – and engulfed them with one easy swipe. Kome and Peterson and the bomber were instantly crushed down to the size of a sardine tin. All the bombers were destroyed in an instant.

Elsewhere on Theme Planet, SLAM fighters and KULA jets and Warbirds and T6 AirTanks were similarly attacked by their surroundings. Huge pillars of ocean leapt upwards, defying gravity (indeed, all the laws of physics and probability), and took out single fighters with well-aimed stabs, dragging them screaming back to the depths of the ocean, engines howling and jets burning and missiles steaming beneath the churning waters. Across deserts, huge sandstorms leapt into existence from nowhere, and pilots suddenly found chunks of rock the size of groundcars sucked into engines, sending aircraft and Shuttles plummeting to earth. Over rides, the tracks of many a rollercoaster or vertical dive suddenly twisted, screeching upwards towards their attackers and firing ride CARs like machine gun bullets through the air, BAM-BAM–BAM, with perfect accuracy. SLAM fighters were taken down by multiple hits from ride CARs displaying clown faces. KULA jets were speared like a slab of pig on a fork by twisting, squealing sections of high rollercoaster track. Theme Planet, now under the direct, aggressive control of SARAH, went on the attack, the offensive. Theme Planet became a living, breathing, weapon.

Kome had mocked Monolith for having such a lucrative business venture with no protection. How wrong he'd been. Monolith, SARAH, had simply never had reason to show her strength before. Now, after the pain and agony of torture under the FRIEND, her rage spat through her planet-wide shell. She terraformed thousands of parts every minute, every *second,* changing and moulding and altering, great fingers of rock and glass and tree branch and ocean cylinder, all stretching out, expanding, deforming, to slap and smash and swat Earth's Oblivion Warfleet from the sky. Thousands upon thousands of attacking craft were destroyed in only a few short minutes, such was SARAH's rage; and then her rage subsided, and what few Earth craft remained limped like puppies with broken backs, up, out and away from Theme Planet, which had returned with so much ease to a holiday paradise destination. A place where fun and joy could be had. Where children splashed in the waves and families enjoyed peace, and relaxation, and more excitement than ANY OTHER HOLIDAY DESTINATION EVER!

And if you hadn't been sick?

Well, you soon would be.